BROKEN VEIL

BROKEN VEIL

the HARBINGER SERIES

JEFF WHEELER

47NORTH

Published by 47North, Seattle

www.apub.com

Amazon, the Amazon logo, and 47North are trademarks of Amazon.com, Inc., or its affiliates.

ISBN-13: 9781542092449
ISBN-10: 1542092442

Cover design by Mike Heath | Magnus Creative

Printed in the United States of America

To Tyler

The people who live in the Fells often have no other options. The streets are crowded with urchins, laborers, and those rejected by society. Different parts of the city are run by street gangs, which outnumber the officers of Law twenty to one. Everything that can be sold is sold. But much is taken.

I don't fear for my life or my wallet as I walk these streets. There is an unspoken truce between the Fells and me. The street gangs steer clear of me because they know of my hospital. The one Empress Sera endowed to me. Killingworth used to be an estate, but the owner fell into debt and lost it to a speculation. I've spent the last year transforming it into an institution for healing and research. We are the only hospital that treats gang members and gentry alike. Need is the criteria we use for treating patients, not wealth.

But as I walk these desolate streets, I see the fleeting image of a twelve-year-old girl. One with holes in her shoes and a threadbare dress. I see her face in the hungry faces of the urchins. I see her wince each time a child is slapped or beaten. Her haunting eyes watch me as I set a broken arm or stitch a wound closed. She's the ghost of the Fells. My own personal ghost.

Every child of the streets knows they can get a bun or a bowl of soup from Killingworth. They come in droves. Every day. And so I keep seeing her face. My ghost. My Cettie.

—Adam Creigh, Killingworth Hospital

CETTIE

CHAPTER ONE

KISHION BOND

The knife lunged toward Cettie's ribs. She twisted her waist, her reflexes honed by practice. The weapons master would cut her if he could. And he had before. In such moments, there was instinct only. She grabbed his wrist with one hand, elbowed him in the face with the other arm, and then wrestled him for control of the dagger. He outweighed her. But that didn't matter. She managed to get a grip on his littlest finger and quickly wrenched it so hard that the bone snapped. The dagger clattered to the floor, and the weapons master grunted in pain.

She had learned all the vulnerabilities in a human body. The ones at the throat, the eyes, the rib cage, the internal organs. And not all that knowledge had been taught to her at the poisoner school in Genevar. She had access to memories that were not her own, memories that sometimes sickened her but provided useful knowledge in times of need.

Cettie retrieved the dagger from the floor, holding it in an overhand grip, partially crouched and ready to repel another attack should the master attempt to fight on with a broken finger. Sometimes he did. Her heart beat fast in her chest, reminding her of the robin in the nest hidden in the eaves of the poisoner school.

"Well done," said her father, the kishion, from the doorway.

She hadn't heard him arrive or even noticed he was there. His announcement meant that the fight was over. The approval in his face did not move her, though she knew her abilities had improved. She'd seen all the seasons come and go, although Genevar was notoriously short on winter. Her old life seemed impossibly far away, as if it had happened to a different person.

Cettie straightened, watching the grim-faced weapons master rise, his brow contorted with pain. Now it was his turn to use the healing powers of Everoot. Everyone who trained at the poisoner school could use it, removing an injury almost instantaneously. The master didn't speak but nodded to her before leaving, a sign of respect.

Cettie returned the dagger to the weapons wall, which held various implements of death. Fighting wasn't her favorite part of the training she received, but she was good at it. She much preferred working with herbs and poisons. She was very sensitive to them and could detect even the smallest traces of winnow herb in a tea or crushed pondace seeds hidden in a crust of bread.

After relieving herself of the weapon, she turned and faced her father. "I haven't seen you in a few weeks. When did you return?" Theirs was not a caring relationship. She no longer hated him, but the kishion were not known for their tenderness. Especially her father.

"Last night."

"And where were you all this time?"

He gave her a small smile. "Killing Admiral Hatch. His loyalties became . . . conflicted."

She blinked at him, caught off guard, still, by the carefree way he talked about murder. But then, he'd been doing it for a long time.

"Why are you here now?" she asked, dreading his answer. He never did anything without a purpose.

"There's a new assignment for you," he said. "One that will be best suited for your skills."

Cettie frowned, her dread increasing. She didn't want to seduce or murder anyone. So far, although she'd received training in both, neither task had been asked of her. But she feared it was only a matter of time. The people at the school didn't care for her sensibilities. If she feared something or found it distasteful, she was usually expected to face it.

"Don't you want to know?" he asked, noticing her silence.

"I suppose you will tell me anyway," she answered, guarding her expression.

"You are going to hijack a tempest," he replied.

Actually, that sounded intriguing. "Really? Where is this tempest?"

"It's called the *Rage*, and it runs supplies from Brythonica to the battlefields over La Marche."

Her heart beat faster. "What is its mission?" she asked, keeping her tone flat.

"Never you mind," he said with a dark chuckle. "Seize it and bring it to Pree to prepare for its mission. A kishion has been assigned to work with you and dispose of the crew."

Cettie suppressed an inner groan. "I can do this on my own." If she did it alone, the imperial soldiers would survive.

Unless the Myriad Ones compelled her to do otherwise. Though the kystrel had improved her ability to control the dark spirits, it had not chased them out. They still lived inside her. They still whispered to her in voices that sounded like hers but weren't.

"I've no doubt of that, Daughter. But it's high time that you bonded with your own kishion. The connection will deepen your power. Your mother has been preparing this one to serve alongside you."

Cettie wanted to resist, but she was wise enough not to. In her time at the poisoner school, she'd discovered that the Myriad Ones asserted themselves more powerfully when she resisted the will of her captors, sometimes to the point where she'd black out. If she was agreeable, she had more control of her personal thoughts and actions.

Bonding to a kishion would mean giving him her kystrel, but doing so would not strip her of its magic. If anything, it would make her more powerful. She would have control of him, and he would be able to use her magic. The bond forced an intimacy that would allow the man to catch glimpses of her thoughts. And vice versa. She didn't want that, not at all.

If her father and mother knew how much she detested her new life, how much she ached for her old, they wouldn't let her anywhere near a sky ship. Yet maybe they *did* know . . . maybe it was the very reason they'd insisted on such an arrangement.

"Who is he?" Cettie asked, feigning unconcern.

Her father gave her a knowing smile. "Time will tell. This operation has been underway for a long time. There can be no failure, Daughter."

"And you won't tell me what it is beforehand?"

He shook his head. "You only need to understand your part. You'll earn our trust by fulfilling your duties. Don't fail us."

She bowed her head to him, but inwardly she was still rebelling. He left, and she decided to go to the gardens to see Jevin, the gardener of the various poisons growing at the school. Of all the people she'd met at the poisoner school, he was the only one who felt like a friend. He would talk to her whenever she was lonely, sensing her need somehow.

Some of the other girls who'd been there when she first started had already left, replaced by new ones. Each time a new girl arrived, Cettie's heart ached. The other girls had tragic backgrounds. For them, coming to the school had been a vast improvement. Cettie was different. In her old life, she'd been the keeper of the cloud estate Fog Willows, engaged to a handsome doctor.

Regret had started creeping up on her as soon as she regained some control by accepting the kystrel. She would have given anything to go back, to reclaim the person she'd been. Jevin understood that, empathized with it even. But he'd tried to help her understand that leaving was impossible. Her parents would never let her out of their web. She knew too much, and the students at the poisoner school all knew the price of treachery. It had happened once in the past year. The girl who'd attempted to escape had been executed in front of all the rest.

As Cettie emerged from the building to the inner courtyard of the beautiful estate, she saw some of the other girls tending their plots in the garden. Cettie enjoyed the feel of the dirt on her hands and the smells from the various herbs. There were no weeds, and the little shrubs and bushes each had familiar names and purposes. Valerianum for making people fall asleep. Wickshot as a quick-acting poison that paralyzed someone. Monkshood—a very deadly poison that brought an excruciating death. All of the little flowers, stems, and sometimes the oils produced from them were highly toxic. Some herbs were so deadly they could only be handled with masks and gloves. Even so, the act of caring for them appealed to her. It even made her think of Adam, the man she had almost married, although the plants he relied on for his trade healed rather than hurt.

Jevin rose before the sun every day and played his hautboie before the massive gong announced the meal. This morning, she found him sitting on the stone wall, guiding one of the younger students—a girl about twelve years old.

As Cettie walked the grounds, which were so familiar to her now, she felt anew the squeezing sensation of being restrained in this elaborate and fancy prison. At first, the school had appealed to her in a strange way. But with time, she'd realized the people who cooked the meals, who sewed the dresses, who healed the wounds were all slaves of a sort. No one there had the freedom to leave when they wanted, not even the poisoners themselves. And though Cettie and the other girls had access to the finest gowns, the sturdiest weapons, and the most elegant jewelry, none of it belonged to them. They were props, disguises. As long as the girls complied, they would have access to the spoils of vast wealth—but none of it was theirs.

Jevin had already noticed her, and she saw him give some final direction to the student before standing, brushing off his hands, and approaching her.

"Good afternoon," he greeted with a smile. His black cassock looked drab compared to the colorful jerkins available to him. But his modesty appealed to her. He had a trimmed beard and ash-blond hair and a wiry frame. His unassuming appearance was deceiving, however—she'd seen him conquer the hardest challenge the school had to offer, climbing a nearly sheer wall dotted with Water Leerings, without any perceivable effort.

"I didn't mean to interrupt your lesson," Cettie said.

"I could tell you needed to talk."

"Do you know about my mission?" she asked him. "I just found out I'll be leaving soon."

He raised his eyebrows and arched them quizzically. "Only a little. Something about a tempest?"

She nodded. "Do you know who they've assigned to be my kishion?"

He gave her a serious look. "I do."

"What can you tell me about him?" she asked nervously.

"I was asked for my counsel, naturally," he said. "Of the options presented, I thought one in particular would be suited for you. It's no surprise, in hindsight, that this particular kishion was also your mother's intended choice for you."

"I don't know if I should be comforted by that or not," Cettie complained, sitting next to him on the stone rim of the garden bed.

"Well, I suppose it's a matter of trust. This is an important assignment. If you succeed, it will lead to a much larger one. One we've been preparing you for."

"I know. You've hinted at it for some time," she said, not without a bit of pique.

"Secrets must be guarded, Cettie. Part of me thinks you are still a little reluctant to be here. Is that true?"

"What gives you that idea?" Cettie said with a small smirk. She decided to change the subject, not wishing to give too much away. "Was it the same for my mother? Was she assigned my father, or did she choose him?"

"That was over twenty years ago, Cettie. I wouldn't know the story firsthand. I'm not that old!"

"Of course not. But is it common for a hetaera and her kishion to form such an . . . attachment?" Obviously something had happened between her parents that had led to her birth.

"When two people work closely together under circumstances of stress and challenge . . . when they come to *trust* and depend on each other . . . well, as you've learned in your training, those are opportunities for attachments to form. Danger, or the threat of it, can often knit two hearts together. Look into your own past and tell me if you haven't seen this pattern?"

She blinked in surprise. Yes, they had discussed this in training, how a hostage might fall in love with her abductor. But she'd never tried to make the connection to her own life. Were her past feelings for Adam contributable to this effect? He'd been present for so many of the turbulent moments in her life. Had the fear she'd experienced in those moments biased her feelings for him?

"I hadn't thought of it that way before. In my own life."

"Well, I'm glad to have enlightened you. But that's all I shall say on the matter," Jevin said apologetically. "I cannot reveal who was assigned to you. But I will say that I think it's for the best. You tell me, later, if I'm wrong."

Cettie nodded in gratitude and retreated to the manor, where she intended to bathe and change into a new dress. Fighting for her life tended to work up a sweat. She made her way to the room where all the garments were stored. There were dresses from every country and every fashion. If she showed interest in something that did not fit her, then the seamstresses who worked for the school would make her something new. Cettie, who had never before cared for fashion, now knew all the different styles of clothing, hairstyles, and degrees of embellishments preferred. She could disguise herself so she would be unrecognizable to people who knew her best. Memories of Fog Willows threatened to surface, causing pangs of regret, which she immediately banished with her kystrel. Her feelings began to soothe again.

Opening the door, she walked in and saw a young woman in a shift, holding a dress in front of her while standing in front of the mirror. The sight of the face in the mirror made Cettie stop short and gasp.

"Becka?"

The girl turned in startled surprise. Cettie watched as her face quickly transformed back to that of Shantelle, a younger student.

"No, Cettie. It's me," the girl said, smiling awkwardly. "I'm sorry. I didn't know that you knew her."

Cettie did know Becka Monstrum, who was Sera's personal maid. Sera, who was now the Empress of Comoros.

Cettie approached her, noticing the dress in the girl's hands was in the court style of Lockhaven.

"What are you doing?" Cettie questioned.

The girl looked even more embarrassed. "I cannot say," Shantelle replied. "It's part of my assignment. I was just practicing in front of the mirror."

"You're leaving the poisoner school?"

"I am. Very soon. I'm nervous, Cettie."

Cettie swallowed. If Shantelle was practicing being the empress's maid, what did they plan to do with poor Becka? Worse, what would Shantelle be asked to do to Sera? She knew it would suit their purposes if Sera were toppled from her throne.

If only she could get a message to her friend . . .

It would be dangerous to let any of her thoughts or feelings show, even to Shantelle, so Cettie simply told the girl, "You should be more careful. You need to always be on your guard." The words were accompanied by a little frown.

The girl's cheeks flamed with mortification. "I understand. It was a mistake. I shouldn't have let myself be caught unawares."

"I won't tell anyone," Cettie promised, and the girl looked relieved. The poisoner school was not a place where the girls backstabbed each other. They genuinely tried to help one another, when possible.

After Shantelle left, Cettie chose a new gown and then went to the baths and quickly cleaned herself. The whole time, she could think of little else but the mission ahead and the kishion who would be assigned to her. By the time she finished, she had decided to seek out her father again to try to wrest more information from him.

She went to his room and knocked gently on the door before twisting the handle open. There were no locks on the doors, but it was still considered rude to invade someone's privacy without some forewarning. His was one of the upper rooms at the compound, a tower that overlooked the courtyard. Though the room was empty, she noticed the window was open and heard the creak of timbers overhead. She imagined he was on the roof. She'd been up there with him before.

Had he heard her little knock? Probably not if he was outside. As she cautiously entered, she glanced at the table where he had a haphazard assortment of weapons—including pistols and knives. A sudden sharp pang struck her heart. Was this the weapon that had been used to shoot Fitzroy? The unnerving thought made her clench her fists, but she cast it away to prevent her emotions from reacting. There was a woman's brooch as well. She fingered it, impressed by the decorative detail. Whom did it belong to? The noblewoman who'd sent him to his death? Biting her lip, she quickly began to search the room, looking for any clues about her assignment. The small details of a person's life could reveal much about their patterns and habits.

There was a small trunk stowed beneath the cot where he slept. A strong urge to look inside it swelled in her heart. She cocked her head, listening for more creaks on the roof. He had a very light step. But timbers were unforgiving to someone who wished to remain quiet, and these timbers were ancient. She hesitated only a moment longer before kneeling by the edge of the cot and sliding the trunk toward her. She undid the latch—quietly—and opened it. The room was still dark, so it wasn't easy to see the contents. There was a uniform there, a shirt with a bloodstain on it. And a book tucked underneath.

Cettie's lips pursed as she drew the book out of the trunk. Her father wasn't one for reading. She'd never seen a book in his hand, and there were none out on the table. She heard the ominous creak of the boards overhead. He was returning.

She looked at the cover of the small book—a notebook really—and her eyes widened with shock when she realized she recognized it. Her hands began to tremble. It was the notebook that Adam had given her, the one she had lost. Adam had entrusted it to her after receiving his commission to join the Ministry of War as a ship's doctor. She'd always suspected that her almost-sister Anna had stolen it . . . out of jealousy or some other motive.

What was it doing in her father's trunk?

CHAPTER TWO

THE MISSION

A shadow spread across the window, blocking the light. Her father had landed on cat's feet, not making a sound. It was everything Cettie could do not to display any signs of panic. When someone was nervous, there were little signals that they displayed for all to see. Cettie had been trained to counteract these impulses. She had almost decided to roll under the bed and hide, but her father's instincts were honed to a knife's edge. He'd probably heard her in his room and had come to investigate.

"What are you doing here?" he asked gruffly, eyeing her with suspicion as he climbed down from the windowsill.

She picked up one of the pistols on his table, examining the length of the barrel. "When is he coming?" She set it down. "The kishion I've been assigned to." Next, she chose a dagger from the table, weighing it in her hand before setting it down again.

"Soon. Why do you care?"

She turned and leaned back against the table. From her vantage point, she could see the little trunk stowed under the bed, just as she'd found it. She'd stashed the book in the pocket of her gown. She folded her arms and looked her father in the eye.

"I want to prepare myself. I wasn't expecting to be assigned already."

"Already?" he said with a chuckle. "Your mother was seventeen when she was assigned to her first kishion."

"Her first?" Cettie asked quizzically.

He walked deeper into the room. "I'm not the first she bonded with, but I *am* the one who has lasted the longest. It's dangerous working for her. Let me answer your question bluntly. He comes by zephyr. Tonight."

That was soon. Too soon. She didn't feel ready. She set the dagger back down. "Thank you," Cettie replied. She started for the door but paused, looking over her shoulder. "Did you know her beforehand?" She wanted to keep him talking, to reduce his suspicions that she had invaded his things.

"You mean your mother?"

Cettie nodded.

"Only by reputation," he answered.

"Do you know where she came from? Who she was before the poisoner school?"

His lips pressed together. He didn't answer her. She hadn't really expected him to reveal anything. Cettie's mother was Lady Corinne of Pavenham Sky. Somehow her mother, a poisoner, had infiltrated the upper echelons of the empire, becoming one of the wealthiest, if not *the* wealthiest woman in the empire of Comoros. And she had transformed both worlds—in Comoros, she'd killed the former emperor, Richard Fitzempress, and in Kingfountain, she'd helped foment a rebellion that had given power to General Montpensier. The war between the worlds, which had subsided for a time, had begun again, with renewed rage and fire. It had been underway for more than a year, with battles being fought all over Ceredigion, Occitania, Leoneyis, and Brythonica. But not in Genevar. The ones controlling the conflict were reaping the rewards of the violence. The Genevese were in the shadows, using their fleets and influence to protect Montpensier's crown.

Seeing that her father was no longer willing to speak, Cettie left his room and retreated to hers. Would he search his things to see if she had stolen anything? She had been meticulous about replacing the trunk, but sometimes the littlest things were what gave you away.

As she walked, she wondered if her assignment would lead her back to Comoros. Though that was what she wanted, more than anything, it would be a dangerous thing. One of the girls that Cettie knew had already been captured and killed by Sera's empire. Killed because she bore the hetaera brand on her shoulder. The same brand that Cettie had on her flesh.

The hetaera brand was bestowed by a Leering, though it was a different one than had been used in the past. The old Leering had rendered a hetaera's lips poison and made her a vessel for the Myriad Ones. Cettie had been told the new Leering was different, that it gave those who took the vow the ability to *control* the Myriad Ones. And so she'd taken the vow, only to realize the promises she'd been made were exaggerated. The dark creatures had not left. Would not leave.

The symbol imparted by the new Leering was a fountain lily, branded into the shoulder as if by fire and left to scar. It was the size of a coin and easily overlooked unless one knew it was there. The empire was hunting those with the brand. It was treated as grounds for the bearer to be put to death immediately. Yet the mark itself might be Cettie's only chance to escape her prison. Poisoners with the brand were allowed to travel outside the school; the rest were not.

She entered her room and shut the door, sitting on the ground with her back against it so she could hear any sounds of approach. While seated, she removed the small book from her pocket and began glancing through the pages. The little drawings of the various plants and birds had Adam's notes about each scrawled in the margins. Seeing his handwriting made her tremble. How many times had she perused this book? She turned from page to page, her heart swelling with longing and regret, an ache that grew and grew. He would never want her back. They could never be together again. The decisions she'd made had ensured that. She'd become anathema to his beliefs. Tears pricked her eyes. If she only could undo what had happened to her. If only she had not trusted Lady Corinne. There was no easy way to even get back to her world. The mirror gates were all heavily guarded, many of them destroyed, and although Sera had opened an enormous rift in the sky, connecting the worlds, only Comoros's air ships could make the journey. Was that her mother's plan? Steal a tempest and use it to cross through the rift?

And what about the girl who was preparing to pose as Becka? Would Sera's spies manage to catch her? Though she didn't want any harm to come to poor Shantelle, she wished to protect Sera and Becka above all.

Cettie dabbed her tears on the back of her hand and then invoked the kystrel to banish her feelings again. Longing for Adam would do her no good. Neither would worrying. The feelings ebbed, but not as quickly as they once had. She found herself using the kystrel more and more often to douse her feelings, because the feelings just kept returning. The kystrel numbed her, but whenever she thought about her old life, the sadness and longing rushed back with a vengeance.

She stared at the little book in her hands, turning it over and over. How had it ended up in her father's trunk? The last place she'd seen it was—

A little jolt shot through her, followed by an irrational throb of anger. What did it even matter? She should just toss the book into a fire and burn it. Adam must hate her now. There was nothing she could do to atone for her bad choices.

A frown creased her mouth, and she nearly hurled the book across the room.

She blinked, caught off guard by the strength of the emotion, and then rose from the floor in front of the door and slid the book beneath the mattress of her bed. She'd deal with it later. Again she felt the swelling feeling inside to destroy the book. But she walked away and left the room, her feelings muddled and dark. She would watch for the sky ship.

A sickening feeling inside her insisted everything was about to change.

⌐⌐

The zephyr came at dusk. Cettie was in the middle of playing a hautboie when she noticed the sky ship descending over the wall. She missed flying, the thrill of acceleration and the force of the wind through her hair. Pulling the instrument from her lips, she gazed at the sky ship longingly, nervously, feeling agitation churn inside her.

"Ah, he's arrived," said Jevin, who had been seated by her, enjoying her music and giving her advice on her technique.

Cettie put the instrument down on the table and stood, trying not to wring her hands but to project an aura of calm, despite her nerves.

"Remember," Jevin said, also rising. "It is a privilege to serve a hetaera. We all feel that way. He serves *you*. You are the one who will lead this mission." Cettie's throat was thickening with worry as she saw the pilot bound off the edge with a practiced air. There was something familiar . . .

"I know him," Cettie said in baffled surprise. The kishion she'd imagined was a grimacing, rough man who wouldn't hesitate to strangle a baby. Never in a lifetime had she expected to see Rand Patchett climb off that zephyr. Rand!

"I know you do," Jevin said smugly. "He's one of us now."

"But . . . but how?" Cettie said, watching as her old acquaintance strode up to them.

"I'll let him tell you," Jevin replied. He retrieved the hautboie and nodded to Rand. "Welcome to Genevar."

"Cettie," Rand said, ignoring the other man. His eyes brightened. "You hardly look the same anymore. By the blazes, just look at you!" As he reached her, he shook his head in amazement and put his hands on his hips. He wore his dragoon's jacket, the one she remembered, and had a pistol jammed into his belt. Seeing a familiar face, at long last, felt wonderful, even if it was the man she had rejected.

"What are you doing here, Rand?" she asked, half laughing, her voice trembling.

"I've been training to be a kishion," he said, arching his eyebrows. "It's much harder than dragoon training, if you can imagine. But if we're ever going to end this accursed war, we'll need more of us. When I was told I'd be working with you, I couldn't believe my luck." He gazed around the courtyard. "So this is the poisoner school?"

"One of them," Cettie replied. She wanted to burst inside. The relief was overpowering. "Where have you been?"

"I travel constantly," he answered. "I've never liked being in one place for very long. I tried making a go at parliament, as I told you I would, but I couldn't find anyone to back me. Until now, that is. There are many of us in the government, advancing in the ranks."

Jevin interrupted. "Now that you are here, Mr. Patchett, it's time to prepare for your mission. You both leave before midnight."

"Ah, yes," Rand said. "Formalities. I've been looking forward to this all day. Cettie is quite a pilot. We can take over a tempest. No problem."

"Come this way, then," Jevin said, steering them both to the inner domain. It was surreal to be walking alongside Rand. She kept glancing at him, unnerved by his presence. His demeanor and mannerisms were so familiar to her. He'd always had the inner energy of a predator cat, constantly pacing and stalking. He was also very impulsive, which she did not think was a good quality for a kishion. It didn't matter—she couldn't be happier to see him.

"This room," Jevin said, stopping in front of one of the smaller rooms. He twisted the handle and opened it, revealing a small table surrounded by some chairs.

Rand gestured for her to sit first, and he began pacing along the perimeter of the room. Jevin sat down at the head of the table and set the instrument down beside him. "This mission has been underway for several months," he said. "I won't explain the larger aims at this point, but let me describe once again the near-term goal."

"Steal a tempest. Dispatch the crew," Rand said with a shrug.

"Yes, to put it bluntly. The tempest you seek, *Rage*, should be arriving at midnight, according to our intelligence. Its destination is the Arsine warehouse here in Genevar. It must be commandeered upon arrival and flown to the Hotel Vecchio in Pree. There, you will pose as brother and sister. One of the rooms on the top floor has been arranged."

"What about my zephyr?" Rand asked.

"Your zephyr stays here until you finish your mission," Jevin said. "You will take a carriage together to the warehouse. Once you get to the hotel, you will wait there until further instructions arrive. It may be several days, depending on how other parts of the mission go. Do not leave the hotel until ordered or unless you are compromised."

Jevin leaned forward and looked at Cettie. He reached into his pocket and withdrew a gold ring. "This will help you impersonate Miss Patchett. She does not know her brother has joined our efforts. Since you have met her, you have knowledge of her looks and manners. The ring will aid in your disguise, although I recommend choosing a dress that will facilitate the transformation. Here, try it on."

She took the gold ring from him and stared at it. Then she slid it onto her finger.

"There is a word of power that activates the ring: *metamorphoune*. All you must do is *think* the word." He pursed his lips. "Try it. The magic will draw Miss Patchett's appearance from your memories."

Cettie gazed at the ring on her hand and thought the word. *Metamorphoune.*

A rippling sensation went through her. It felt strange, as if her ears were plugged from a quick ascent to a higher altitude. She heard the chords of magic, faint music, but soon it blended in with the noise of the room, and she heard nothing. Looking down at her hands, she saw that they were different. The shape was different, the nails longer and covered in polish. The ring was gone.

Cettie touched her finger with her other hand, feeling the ridge on her finger. The ring had vanished upon activation of the spell, but it was still there.

"Yes, it's still there," said Jevin. "And it worked wonderfully. Is this what your sister looks like, Mr. Patchett?"

"Indeed, it is," Rand said, sitting back. He chuckled to himself. "Her hair is a little longer now, but that's hardly—"

"It matters," Jevin said. "Now, Cettie. Give Mr. Patchett your kystrel. It will be able to access his latest memories of his sister, which will improve your disguise. It will help make the transformation more real. More convincing. Your voice will be the same to you. But others will hear the one they are familiar with. You will be able to speak in any language necessary for the situation."

"I will?" Cettie asked, intrigued. She tugged at the chain around her neck, loosening the kystrel from her bodice. In the past, whenever she'd thought about taking it off, she'd felt uneasy, wary, and protective of it. Though its magic had not freed her as she'd hoped, it was still a powerful protection. But knowing Rand was to be her kishion changed things—she was eager to share her power with him. She hoped that by doing so, she would feel a little more connection to the girl he'd known her to be. She hesitated for only a brief moment before pulling it off and handing it to him.

Rand took it, cupping it in his palm. She saw him swallow as he stared at the magical emblem with curiosity. Then he slipped the chain over his own neck.

A jolt went through Cettie's heart, and gooseflesh tingled down her arms.

"When do we leave for the warehouse?" Rand asked. "How far is it?"

"The carriage was summoned an hour ago. You'll be leaving after dark. Pack the clothes you need. Occitanian coins will be provided for expenses." He looked at Cettie and put his hand on top of hers, the one with the ring. "These are powerful rings," Jevin said. "If you do well, you will be permitted to keep this one."

"How will we find the hotel?" Cettie asked.

Jevin smiled pleasantly. "There is a hurricane hovering over it. It is one of our enemy's bases in Occitania."

CHAPTER THREE

THE STREETS OF GENEVAR

The carriage wheels rattled down the cobblestone streets. The carriage itself was a handsome gold-and-blue contraption, outfitted with plush padded walls inside and springs underneath to make the ride more comfortable. The rear wheels were larger than the front ones, and a team of four horses pulled it at a dramatic pace. The driver box was in the front, at the top, providing the passengers with an unobstructed view of Genevar when the horses lurched down the inclines.

Cettie wondered if the city-state ever slept. Light posts spread at even intervals along the path revealed the burgeoning crowds. They had passed multiple manors nestled behind iron bars or stone walls before reaching the inner rings of the city, where both the streets and the buildings were jammed tightly together. Although each home was different in style and decor, they blended into a harmonious whole that indicated the vast wealth of the trading nation.

"So unlike the City," Rand said, gazing outside the window on his side of the carriage. There were several other carriages out and about, although there were also pedestrians and some men and women on horseback. The tick-tocking noise of the carriage's wheels became difficult to hear as the traffic increased.

"It's very different," Cettie agreed, still giddy from the revelation that Rand was to be her kishion and the joy of being outside the walls of the school. Rand's hand was so near hers on the comfortable bench she thought they might touch if the carriage jostled more. A part of her wanted that to happen. She swallowed, gazing the other way. Despite her separation from Adam, it didn't feel right.

"I'm surprised you haven't asked me yet," he said, drawing her eyes back to him. The hint of a smile flashed on his mouth.

"Asked you what?"

"About Fog Willows. How everyone is getting on."

Cettie had been wanting to ask. Her heart had been begging it of her. And yet, she knew it was dangerous to appear too interested in home. She guarded her expression and shrugged. "If you want to tell me. I'm still surprised you're here."

"Why should you be?" he asked. "You know I hate nearly everything the empire stands for. The meanness. The hypocrisy. The small minds. I seek to change things, just as I have always wanted to. I tried to work through the system." He shook his head. "But without backers, you can't get anywhere in politics, and you won't get backers unless you commit to do what *they* want. It's so corrupt. No, when I was offered this chance, I leapt at it." He gave her a quizzical look. "How did you end up here?"

There was something suspicious about his question. Shouldn't he already know? It struck her that perhaps Rand's sudden appearance at the school was too good to be true. The first few times she had been allowed to leave the poisoner school—after she had donned her kystrel and accepted the brand—she had been followed. Then they'd allowed her to travel alone. She'd thought about escaping, but logic had intervened. They could have followed her through the kystrel, and she likely wouldn't have made it outside of Genevar without being captured . . . *killed*. Her mother and father were always watching her, judging her, testing her. Was Rand's presence yet another test to see if she was loyal?

"I was tricked into coming," Cettie said in an offhanded manner. "Lady Corinne brought me here."

His look altered, just slightly. She felt a connection to him through the kystrel—one that allowed her to read his emotions, but not his thoughts. She understood that the longer he wore her kystrel, the stronger that bond would become. To the point, eventually, that their minds would be open to each other. Right now, she felt suspicion in him— suspicion about *her* motives. It was strange how clearly she understood his feelings without relying on expressions or other clues.

"So . . . if you could leave, you would?" he asked in a low voice. He leaned closer. "I could take you back to Fog Willows."

Part of her wanted to leap at the opportunity. But his direct approach only made her more certain this was a test. She'd have to be very careful with what she said or felt.

"No," Cettie said, shaking her head. "As much as I'd like to see it again, I don't belong there anymore. Tell me about your sister. How is Joanna? How have you managed to keep her in the dark?"

"You *have* changed," he said, and she felt a little throb of relief inside him. "Joanna is . . . well, *Joanna*. She's quite popular these days. Fashionable too. She and Stephen Fitzroy have been . . . well, they've become close. Joanna could have any man in the empire, if she chose, but I think she's got her eye on Stephen. He's been very successful. He runs the mines and the family business. Selling secrets to the ministries, as you used to." He winked at her. "They've set up some of those storm glass contraptions here in this world. In Brythonica, I think, though it won't be long before all of the empire's allies have them. Occitania and Legault have each been vying to get them too. And since you won't ask, Lady Maren is also doing well. She's taken a lover, but that doesn't surprise anyone. An old flame of hers."

The words sent a jolt of pain through Cettie's heart. She squelched it, but not quite quickly enough, judging by the way Rand suddenly turned to look at her. He might not know how to interpret her emotions, but he could feel them. It was such a strange sensation, this union of hearts.

"You disapprove?" Rand asked.

Cettie looked out the window again. "She can do whatever she wishes. What of Anna?"

"She's engaged. To that doctor in the Fells." He said the words casually, acting as if he hadn't known that Adam and Cettie had planned to marry. "She goes to the hospital every week to volunteer, read to patients, that sort of thing. They're a handsome couple."

Jealousy. Envy. She felt their poisons work through her blood.

Well, at least Anna got what she has always wished for.

"You still care," Rand said softly, matter-of-factly.

Cettie invoked the power of the kystrel. She saw her eyes begin to glow in her reflection in the glass. The feelings melted away.

"Not really," she said with indifference.

Rand put his hand on top of hers. It was a gesture of familiarity. A sense of numbness overtook her, and she released the magic and turned to him. She'd expected him to be looking at her, but his eyes were trained out the other window. The carriage turned onto a less populous street, heading to a different part of town.

"I'm glad they chose you for me," she said, and meant it. Even if he, too, was manipulating her, at least he was a part of the life she missed.

He nodded, his eyes still distant. The carriage jostled and began to pick up speed again, and they butted shoulders. Sometimes she could feel the burn of the brand on her shoulder, remembered pain shooting through her from the mark with which they'd claimed her.

Like a slave.

She bit her lip and cast out the thought. The carriage's speed surged again, and her stomach lurched as the carriage bounced up and down.

Rand scowled and grabbed his arquebus and then tapped the roof. "Slow down, man!" he called.

That was when Cettie noticed that the reins were trailing behind the horses in the street.

"The driver's gone," Cettie said, realizing it instantly.

Rand's frown deepened. "Another test," he said.

They hit a bump in the road that nearly threw them into the ceiling. Cettie's heart fired with fear, but she'd long since learned to master it.

Rand lurched forward, smashing the butt of his arquebus through the window in front of them. Glass shattered and sprayed the street, and he used the gunstock to clear the remaining shards from the edges of the window. Cettie noticed they'd turned down a side alley.

"The reins are on the street," he said. Leaving the arquebus on the forward seat, he climbed through the window. The wind whipped through his hair as he looked back at her. "You climb up to the driver's seat."

Cettie nodded and opened the door of the carriage. The alley was very narrow, and she had to watch closely to be sure she didn't smash into anything. She reached up to the cargo storage above, and gripping it, pulled herself up the side. Her shoes weren't appropriate for the feat, but she'd climbed the waterfall wall many times by now, and this task was so much easier in comparison. The horses were panicking, running faster and faster as the reins slapped against the road. She had a moment to notice a crater filled with murky water in the middle of the street before the carriage struck it, jarring her bones and causing a curse to spill from Rand up ahead. Cettie finished the climb and hastily occupied the empty driver's seat.

Rand was walking on the tongue of the carriage, which connected to the traces, which in turn attached to the galloping horses. He poised himself, arms spread wide for balance, and inched his way forward. If he fell, he was a dead man. Cettie used the kystrel to boost his courage, but she sensed he wasn't afraid. In fact, he was excited by the challenge.

"Watch out, there's another pothole up ahead!" Cettie called out.

In a fluid movement, Rand ducked low and snagged one of the reins. His legs absorbed the shock of the impact without falling. Cettie then used the kystrel to reach out to the terrified horses. She felt their quivering fear, their panic, their mindless need to escape, and she drew away those emotions to steady them.

Still balancing on the narrow bit of wood, Rand dipped again and retrieved the other animal's rein. He stepped back and handed both leather straps up to her.

Cettie wrapped them around her hands and pulled, applying the perfect amount of pressure—enough to slow the beasts but not enough to cause them to rear up. The horses were already calming, as was her own heart, and they slowed to canter. Rand started to climb up to the driver's seat next to her, pausing midway. She heard his hiss and felt a gush of surprise and pain through their bond.

"What happened?" she asked as he finished the climb and sat down next to her.

"Cut my hand on the window just now," he said, squeezing his hand into a fist. It was a vicious cut, the blood dribbling from his hand. "Thought I'd cleared it all."

"I can cure it," Cettie said. She eased the horses to a stop. They were in a side street, empty of traffic. The fishy odor of the wharves and docks hung in the air, heavier now, as if the horses had brought them closer to the water. Handing the reins to Rand, she reached into a secret pocket in the upper vest portion of her gown. She withdrew the waterproof pouch, loosed the drawstrings, and pulled out a small clump of Everoot.

"You carry it with you?" Rand asked, looking at it.

"Every poisoner does," she replied. Did they also use it in the kishion training? That surprised her. "Let me see your hand."

His nose wrinkled, the only sign of his discomfort, but she felt the throbbing pain pulsing from his mind. The cut was a deep slice through the middle of his palm. She knew all the muscles and nerves of the hand. It wasn't fatal, of course, but it was painful. She gently pressed the Everoot into the wound and watched it close before her eyes, the blood absorbing into the mosslike plant.

"Ah," Rand said with a sigh. The sensations of being cured by Everoot were so extraordinary, she almost envied him his cut. She dabbed the root against his palm and, after it shriveled slightly, returned it to the waterproof pouch. After stowing it again, she examined his hand, making sure the injury had completely healed. He didn't attempt to pull back. And that was when she felt the shape of the invisible ring on his finger.

He jerked his hand away, flexing his fingers. "I'm fine now. Thank you."

Before he could quell it, she felt his alarm. He'd not meant for her to know about the ring he wore.

~

The Arsine warehouse appeared to be abandoned. Or perhaps it had only been made to look that way. Neither of them thought it a good idea to make a direct approach, and so they'd bribed another carriage driver to bring their carriage to the gate of the warehouse. They'd instructed the driver to ask if it was the Arsine warehouse and to inform the guards that a young couple would be coming later to talk to the manager about picking up supplies.

They both knelt on the street, concealed behind the carriage of the man they'd hired, their clothes spattered with muck. They watched as the driver arrived at the gate and called out to the guards. Cettie began to tremble, from anticipation and from cold, and Rand pulled her close.

As they huddled together, Cettie heard the sound of boots approaching the gate from inside. Four night guards emerged. She wasn't close enough to hear what was said, but after the driver addressed the guards, one of them raised a pistol and shot him in the chest.

She flinched. The others yanked open the doors of the carriage, pistols drawn, and there was a moment of confusion as they realized there were no passengers.

"They killed him," Cettie whispered.

"They knew we were coming," Rand answered darkly.

"But how?"

He shook his head and then breathed out. "My guess is it's another test. They know we're coming for the tempest. They're not going to just let us take it."

"But why would they do this?" Cettie said. "I thought the mission was important."

He turned her to face him. "What's more important is knowing if we can be trusted." He pursed his lips, and she felt him throb with excitement, trepidation, and . . . attraction? The danger they were in thrilled him. But he was also feeling something for her at this moment, being so near her, so close he could smell her hair.

The horses were spooked from the pistol shot, neighing and rearing up, so one of the guards took the reins and began dragging both horses and the carriage inside. A second guard hefted the dead driver, who had fallen off the seat, over his shoulder as if he were no more than a sack of grain. She felt a little pinch of guilt, which she immediately tamped down, something she'd learned to do often at the school. Life, she'd come to learn, could end abruptly.

There were still two at the gate, and they made no sign of leaving.

"What do we do now?" Cettie wondered.

Rand lifted his arquebus. "We do what we were sent to do. We're taking that tempest when it arrives. They weren't going to make it easy."

He slid the tip of his arquebus through the spokes of the wagon wheel. "Only four at the gate. That's foolish."

"Won't they hear the report?" Cettie asked.

"Not from this distance. This isn't one of their rifles, Cettie. It's one of ours."

She heard the familiar zip as a bullet flew from the shaft. No explosion, no flash of fire. One of the guards crumpled. Rand pulled a lever, loading another ball into the chamber, and a second guard went down an instant later.

"The gate is still open," Rand said. He gave her a little smile. "Go. I will cover you. Between the two of us, you are the more dangerous. I can feel their fear already. Can't you?"

His eyes were starting to glow. And he was right. She could.

CHAPTER FOUR

THE RAGE

Cettie crossed the threshold of the gate, her eyes fixed on the darkness. The carriage and horses had been led over to the wall, and the mounts were becoming even more skittish. Even though the kystrel now hung around Rand's neck, it allowed her to feel the presence of those left to defend the warehouse. Her senses were heightened in a way that she'd not experienced before. She could feel each quivering heart, each swallow of apprehension. Invoking the kystrel's power, she amplified the guards' fear, summoning her memories of the Fear Liath in the streets of the Fells.

One of the men broke cover from behind the carriage and fled. She sensed him abandon his weapon, his mind so frantic he didn't think. She heard the familiar zip of the arquebus—not through her ears, but through Rand's. The guard crumpled. She experienced a little thrill— Was it hers?—as she watched it happen. The interior of the courtyard was a mess of barrels and crates, which appeared to be empty. A tall wooden door barred the path to the warehouse, and a smaller door to the left seemed to lead to an office of sorts. She walked across the inner courtyard, sensing the huddled bodies hidden throughout. The guards could hear her footsteps, and they were terrified. Good. It would keep them from attacking her.

She sensed Rand leaving the shadow of the wagon as he began to trail her. Through their connection, he knew where she was, just as she knew where he was. She couldn't hear him, but there was an invisible line between them, a taut bowstring that quivered. He loaded three more balls into the arquebus. She passed the dead body of the driver whom they'd paid to approach the gate. Stooping, she fetched the small bag of coins from his belt and stuffed it into her own pocket. It would not serve him now.

One of the guards was gathering his courage for an attack. Cettie remained in her crouching position, her eyes fixed on the hollow crate he was using as a hiding place. The instant his courage had built enough, she knew it. He rose, swinging an arquebus up, and Rand dispatched him with a single shot. The man slumped onto the crate, the weapon still firm in his grip.

Cettie straightened and then continued to walk toward the main door of the warehouse. A light emanated from beneath the solid wood door. When she reached it, she rested her hand on the knob, trying to sense what lay beyond. The people inside radiated a sickly worry. The sound of the bodies collapsing had been loud enough that they'd probably heard it and were waiting on a report.

She twisted the knob and pushed her way into the room.

It was a messy office, full of ledgers and broken crates. A single lamp sat on an overcrowded desk, and a man cowered behind it. There were two guards next to the doorway, and both turned to see her enter.

"Who in the—" one said before Cettie's hand chopped his throat, cutting his question short. She struck him twice more, catching him so off guard he couldn't react, then shoved him into the other guard, who'd been trying to bring up an arquebus. Both were knocked off balance. Cettie increased their sense of dread, their fear of imminent death.

The man at the desk pushed his chair back as far as he could, the legs screeching on the floor. Cettie caught the second guard as he disentangled himself from the first, and she did a series of Bhikhu techniques, flipping him onto his back and knocking the wind out of him. She kicked the weapons away and strode over to the desk. The man there cowered in abject fear, his hands up, his face contorting.

Cettie shoved him up against the wall, attacking him with a blast of mind-numbing panic from the kystrel.

"P-please! Please, don't!" he wailed.

"When are you expecting the *Rage*?"

"How did you—?"

She jammed her forearm into his throat. "Answer me." She smelled the stink of urine and realized he'd wet himself. Reducing the pressure so he could speak, she said, "When are you expecting the sky ship?"

"It sh-should be here any moment. Don't kill me."

She had the sudden urge to break his neck, the sensation pressing at her. She knew how to. What would make this any different from when she'd shot at her father, the kishion, back in the Fear Liath's cave? She had tried to kill him then. The compulsion raged inside her.

It wasn't *hers*, but that knowledge didn't lessen its power. "How many are guarding the warehouse?"

"Th-thirty men. Four dragoons."

"That many?" Rand said, closing the door behind him. She hadn't heard him enter, although she'd felt it. "I'll go after the rest."

The quivering man's eyes bulged. "P-please. I have a wife . . . children!"

Cettie twisted a ring on her finger, exposing a poisoned needle, and quickly jammed it into the man's neck.

When she pulled the needle away, he groaned, touching the wetness at his neck. The poison worked quickly, though, and he slid against the wall and lay at her feet. A surge of confidence filled her heart. She felt powerful and cunning. They'd already defeated great odds.

Rand walked over to the two prostrate guards, both of whom were still alive, and cracked their skills with the butt of his weapon. It sickened her; it thrilled her.

"I'll go to the rooftop. See if you can find the manifest for the *Rage*. What cargo is it expecting, I wonder?"

Cettie nodded and quickly began to scan the desk as Rand exited through a rear door. She looked through the strewn papers, trying to find some sense of order. This unkempt desk was a sharp contrast to Lord Fitzroy's, always kept so tidy. She could almost see the meticulous notes he'd kept while testing the invention that would become the first storm glass. The memory, so intense it might have happened yesterday, made her stop short. A slow ache began to build, but a surge of anger slammed against it, quelling it instantly. Thinking of the past only made things painful. The mission should be her sole focus now.

After spending several minutes searching, she discovered the manifest. It was written in the curving, fancy script of the Genevese. She'd developed a passing knowledge of the language on her own, in case she should ever find herself without her kystrel, but the kystrel allowed her to decipher and speak all languages. Her finger traced along the document. The manifest contained information about jackets and boots of various sizes. Provisions for the military. Tens of thousands of men, young and old, had been conscripted for the war effort, in both worlds. There were enough uniforms in the order to outfit a new regiment. According to the manifest, the uniforms were intended for Comoros's allies in Brythonica.

The uniforms would never reach their destination, but whichever side used them, they'd soon be bloodied. They'd be shot through with holes. She could almost hear the groans from the battles yet unfought, smell the acrid stench of black ash.

A feeling of urgency struck her heart. It was Rand communicating to her. There was a thrill of excitement. The tempest was coming. He could see it.

Cettie joined Rand on the rooftop of the warehouse. The guards who hadn't fled for their lives had been dispatched, their bodies brought below to avoid the notice of anyone in the sky ship.

"I'm going to stay," Rand whispered to her. "I'll get a better view from up here. You just keep the sky ship from fleeing. I know you can overwhelm the pilot. I'll join you on board when you bring it low enough."

She nodded. "I'll wait down below."

She was about to leave, but he caught her arm. "You did well, Cettie." She felt his approval, his respect, and it made her cheeks warm. Rand wasn't the man whose good opinion she most desired, but there was something intoxicating about his admiration.

Are you sure he's truly Rand?

As she walked back down the stairs, she wondered at the ring she'd felt on his finger. She hadn't seen it, only felt it, which meant it was a ring that could alter his appearance. Did that mean this man was someone else, pretending to be the Rand she knew? But he was so exactly who she remembered him to be . . .

Were there other kinds of magic rings in this world?

The situation unnerved her, yet she tried to banish her feelings, lest he sense them too.

Back in the lower room, she checked the pulse of the man she'd drugged. He was still alive. Breathing a sigh of relief, which she quickly cut short, remembering Rand could feel her feelings too, she exited the room back to the courtyard. She sat behind a large crate, her back to it, and felt the night wind caress her hot face.

Sitting in the shadows, she waited and waited, and then she heard it. Faintly, just a whisper, almost as gentle as the breeze. It grew louder. Not the rush of wind, not the distant echo of voices, but a clear and simple blend of harmonies that carried on the air. Leering magic. The sounds came from the tempest descending to the warehouse's interior courtyard. As it lowered toward the ground, she heard the voices of the men on board. They spoke the language of the empire. Just hearing her own language again made her giddy inside.

Suddenly, the Leerings on the underbelly of the tempest were activated, and the courtyard was bathed in light. It was strong and made her wince. If she hadn't been hiding behind a crate, too near a wall and too far from the tempest to be seen from its vantage point, she'd have been exposed.

The tempest hovered over the courtyard. She could sense its magic, along with the confusion and fatigue of the tired crew.

"I don't see anyone waiting for us," someone said, his voice rebounding off the cobblestones. "Is this the right warehouse?"

"It's the Arsine. I've been here before," said another man. "They should be expecting us."

"I don't like it," said another man.

"Captain, want me to go down and knock on the door?"

Cettie frowned. If he did, he'd see the bodies strewn there. Where was Rand? Why hadn't he acted yet?

"Go down and see," said another voice. She could sense the changing mood of the crew—dread and worry creeping up on them the longer their welcome was delayed.

Cettie heard the noise of a rope ladder being unfurled and dropped over the edge of the sky ship. The stretching noises the rope made indicated a member of the crew was on the way down. She bit her lip, straining to hear the sound of Rand's arquebus.

The man's boots hit the ground and started across the courtyard. Peering around the edge of the crate, Cettie saw him reach the doors. She held her breath as he tried the handle, then pushed the door open.

That was when Rand struck.

In three quick bursts, three members of the crew were shot down.

"Up! Up!" screamed someone, and Cettie felt the Leerings thrum to life. She reached out to the ship's Control Leering with her mind and ordered it to drop the tempest lower and swing it around. It obeyed her at once, and she heard the cries and shouts of crew members as they were thrown down by the sudden spin. Some of them tottered over the side and crashed onto the cobblestones.

She felt the pilot struggling to wrench control of the tempest away from her, but her will, backed by the power of the kystrel, outmatched his. Keeping the tempest in a spin, she rose from behind the crate and walked toward the dangling rope ladder. Rand continued to fire down on the crew from above, killing those who'd fallen overboard with brutal efficiency.

As soon as she grabbed the scratchy rope of the ladder, she felt another will join the pilot's. There were at least two mastons on board, then—the pilot, and someone else. As the weight of their combined will pressed against hers, the tempest began to rise again. She quickly dug her boots into the rungs and started up, quelling their command with her own. The tempest trembled in the air, like a leaf caught in a gale.

She gritted her teeth, climbing up the ropes quickly, efficiently, as the tempest suddenly began to rise faster. She felt the wind whip through her hair. Cettie scowled, impressed with the strength united against her. Were there three of them? Was the captain one of them, perhaps? She felt a surge of anger from Rand as he united his will with hers. The tempest began to list toward the warehouse itself, its movement uncontrolled. If she were still on the rope ladder when it struck, it would crush her.

Cettie had climbed the waterfall wall dozens of times, and a rope ladder, even in these conditions, was easy in comparison. She grasped the top edge of the tempest just as a man looked overboard. She caught a glimpse of graying hair and enormous sideburns, before she grabbed him by the jacket and yanked him down. He landed in the courtyard with a thud.

Cettie cleared the edge of the tempest and saw two men standing tall at the helm. She blasted them both with feelings of terror, weakening their strength. Then someone grabbed her from behind. How she hadn't sensed him, she didn't know. She heard a zip from the arquebus and felt the ball whir over her head.

It missed.

Rand never missed!

There was no time to focus on why the man was still standing—she needed to ensure he did not do so for long. Cettie shoved her arms forward, then struck her elbow back into the man's ribs. He groaned but did not go down, so she found one of his fingers and torqued it hard. The man gasped with pain as she gripped his arm and swung him around. He spun and landed face-first on the deck.

The tempest lurched, and she was flung against the sidewall, barely managing to stop herself from going over. She pushed again at the combined will of the mastons, but despite their terror, their minds held firm. She respected that. Unfortunately, it meant they both had to die. She felt an irrational surge of anger toward these mastons who were defying her.

The noise of boots struck the deck of the tempest, and Rand rolled forward. The tempest had risen enough that he'd been able to jump on board from the top of the warehouse. In a low crouch, he aimed his weapon at the two men at the helm and fired twice. Both of his balls struck them, but they did not pierce their clothes. She heard the bullets drop harmlessly to the deck, then roll down the angled wood. She remembered that the arquebuses from the Ministry of War could not harm mastons. The Leerings embedded in the bullets were designed that way.

Rand frowned, undaunted, then threw down the arquebus and drew two pistols from his belt as he marched toward the helm. Cettie turned and saw the third man, the one who had grabbed her from behind, coming at her again.

And she recognized him.

They recognized each other.

Both of them blinked in surprise. It was Caulton Forshee.

Twin gunshots exploded, loud and deafening in comparison to the whir of arquebus bullets. The pilot and the captain were killed instantly, and Cettie felt their resistance vanish. The Control Leering obeyed *her* now.

Cettie stared at Caulton in shock. She'd not seen him in years. The last time their paths had crossed, he'd warned her, and Rand, of the dangers of the hetaera. She'd given him a kystrel. Oh, how things had changed. There was surprise on his face, a shocked look of recognition—and fear. Yes, he was afraid of her. He knew what she had become, despite his warnings. He could undoubtedly sense the power of her kystrel.

"Cettie," he breathed out in dread. His hands were poised, defensive. He was ready to wrestle her again, even with an injured hand. She could see the lines of pain around his eyes.

Rand's feelings came to her in a wash of malevolence from the pilot helm. He was smug, vindicated, even pleased by the mastons' deaths. He had studied under Caulton Forshee at Billerbeck Abbey, but Cettie had no illusions. Rand would kill him heartlessly now.

Part of her wanted Rand to do just that. The feeling of rage and revenge was hot in her breast . . . but those emotions, the same ones that had thrummed through her off and on all night, were not naturally hers. They came from the Myriad Ones—in particular, the one who'd tormented her since she was a child. The ghost with no eyes. Most of the time she barely acknowledged its presence lingering inside her. Sometimes dormant. Sometimes furious.

Of all the people they could have faced on such a night, had the poisoner school *known* that Caulton Forshee would be there? Was it coincidence or purposeful? Was it perhaps fate?

If she didn't act quickly, Rand would reload his pistols and murder Caulton before her eyes. She saw it would happen, knew it down to her bones. And so she kicked Caulton in the stomach. As soon as he bent double, she made the tempest tilt and shoved him overboard. He landed on the cobblestones below, then lifted his head and looked up at her in surprised disbelief.

There was no one left on board to oppose her will, so she commanded the Leering to rise quickly and head east.

Rand threw the bodies of the other two mastons overboard and then came down, the pistols once again holstered in his belt. He walked to the edge of the railing, gazing down at the bodies lying in the courtyard.

He scowled. "We needed to kill that last one," he said. "We shouldn't leave him alive."

She felt the anger throbbing in his heart. It was an intense rage, the kind that was pitiless. He yearned to go back and slit the man's throat. Something told her it was a boon he had not seen Forshee's face.

Perhaps she was not so happy to see Rand again at all. Perhaps she had never truly known the man.

She thought once again of that ring.

"The mission," Cettie reminded him smoothly, keeping her feelings of relief veiled. She'd outwrestled her ghost *and* Rand. But resisting their emotions had drained her. She quieted her heart, hiding her true feelings deep inside.

She had to keep them hidden. If she didn't, she knew they'd kill her.

According to the Minister of Wind and the majority of doctors, the source of the cholera morbus is miasma, a term meaning pollution. It is the rank, fetid air of places like the Fells that causes it. They claim it is transmitted by the lungs and that the wealthy who have succumbed to the disease were infected by workers who originally came from the world below. This theory imagines the affliction as an invisible spore that gets breathed in and expelled in a cough or a sneeze.

If that were true, then why did the citizens of Kingfountain also suffer from it? Their air is far cleaner than ours. To test the spore theory, I have performed two studies. First, I've used Leerings to establish a connection between the hospital and the sky manor Fog Willows. These Leerings transport air from the manor's altitude to the Fells—specifically, the hospital. I do this for the sickrooms, for those suffering and dying from the disease. No improvement in the patients has been noted, other than a general observation that the hospital smells nicer.

The other experiment I conducted was among cesspit workers. Those who dig out the deep latrines beneath the tenements. I imaged that their population would be the most susceptible to the cholera morbus, as they work primarily in the dark underground, which has the most noxious air.

I could not find a single case of the cholera morbus among these lowliest of laborers. Nor did I catch the disease myself from being there.

—Adam Creigh, Killingworth Hospital

SERA

CHAPTER FIVE

RETRIBUTION

Sera had seen Lord Welles in all his guises. Smug, indulgent, grand-fatherly. He could also be cunning, urbane, and vengeful. The look on his face as he entered the council room that evening was all wari-ness. His cunning eyes went from face to face, noting the identities of those assembled. It was not the full privy council, just the four other ministers—Lord Scott, Minister of Thought; Lord Halifax, Minister of Law; Lord Prentice, Minister of Wind; and Mr. Durrant, the prime minister—and Sera herself.

The door shut behind him, but Sera caught a glimpse of the offi-cers of Law who'd fetched him from his manor in Lockhaven before it closed.

Lord Welles's hair was fully gray now, and he'd lost some of his vigor, but he was no less imposing.

"What is the meaning of this?" he demanded, striding into the room with a persona of power. He'd been prime minister himself mul-tiple times.

"If you'll take your seat, Richard," Durrant said, indicating a chair, "we can begin."

"Why were officers of Law sent to bring me to a council meeting?" Welles said. "And at such an hour." He put his hands on the table. His eyes darted to Sera. Did he suspect what she now knew?

"Sit down, Richard," said Allanom Scott, his expression quite severe.

A sheen of sweat had formed on Welles's brow. Whatever he was feeling, Sera knew it wasn't pleasant, but he didn't hesitate to take his seat.

It was late evening. The empire had brought the war to Kingfountain, and so most of the fighting happened while the empire was asleep. She was weary and tired from the previous days and weeks and months of strenuous work, but this meeting—this reckoning—was long overdue.

Mr. Durrant walked over to a nearby table where two Leerings had been positioned, covered by a sheet. After lifting off the sheet, he hefted one of them—each weighed at least twenty pounds—and carried it over to where Lord Welles sat. The former prime minister looked shocked at first, for these particular Leerings were rarely brought out in public, but his expression settled into a grimace that matched that of the stern stone face in front of him. Mr. Durrant then shifted his attention to the other Leering, which bore the guise of the first empress, Maia, and moved it in front of Sera. The magnitude of the occasion seemed to be weighing heavily on Welles. His brows were creased and his look full of determination.

"Put your hands on the Leering in front of you, if you please," said Durrant, folding his arms and staring imperiously at Lord Welles.

The Minister of War snorted, leaning back in the chair, as if the Leerings were radiating uncomfortable heat. "What is this about, Durrant? Revenge?"

Sera reached out and put her hand on the one in front of her. The stone was cool to the touch. Comforting. It was her connection to all the leaders who had served before her.

"There are some questions that you must answer," Sera said in a dignified, formal tone. "And they must be answered truthfully."

He met her gaze, his lip twitching slightly. "What do you expect you will find, Empress?"

She met his steely eyes with her own firmness. She'd sent thousands of soldiers to their deaths during the war. She'd wept on her pillow until she couldn't breathe. She was no longer the child this man had manipulated and condemned. She'd seen firsthand what could happen when someone in power trusted the wrong person. The King and Queen of Kingfountain had died for their mistake with General Montpensier.

"Put your hand on the Leering," she ordered him.

How it must have galled Richard Welles to be forced to obey. Nevertheless, he raised his hand and set it on the stone. His eyes locked with hers as she invoked its power, binding the two Leerings together. His forearm trembled as the magic seized it. He would not be able to let go until she released him.

"Proceed, Mr. Durrant," Sera said.

"State your true name for the council of peers. I command you to speak truthfully, on pain of death. May the Mysteries enforce this measure."

Sera had every confidence they would, having seen someone else suffer the ultimate price for lying while touching the Leering. For some people, death was preferable to an uncomfortable truth.

"Richard Foulton Welles," said the former prime minister disdainfully.

"Are you or have you ever been an agent of General Leon Montpensier or an Espion of Kingfountain?"

Lord Welles sat forward in his chair, a look of outrage on his face. "No!" he thundered angrily. "That you would accuse me of treason is not only preposterous but a grave insult! What possible benefit would it give me to join our enemies in any fashion?"

"You are not accused of treason, Lord Welles," said Mr. Durrant. He gave Sera a smug nod. He'd expected such an outburst.

Lord Welles, his cheeks twitching, sat back, struggling to regain his composure. "Then why have you put me in this ridiculous position?"

"Are you in league with Lady Corinne, formerly of Pavenham Sky?"

"No," Welles snapped.

"Were you in league with her in the past?"

"Of course," he answered. "But only before she was unmasked as a traitor. You can ask any of the officers in the Ministry of War, and they will tell you that I have been relentless in my pursuit of her arrest."

"We have," said Mr. Durrant, starting to pace.

"Have what?"

"Have asked your officers. And judging by your business dealings, you and Lord Lawton were partners in many ventures, many schemes."

"There is no dishonor in that," Lord Welles said, his face turning red. "I did not profit extensively from any of his military contracts. There was not even a whiff of corruption during my terms of prime minister. Do you accuse me otherwise?"

"Not at all," said Mr. Durrant. "Your largest source of income is the construction of sky ships. Highly profitable efforts. Not many men can afford to be in that business. You made sure of that."

Welles was starting to calm down. Recover himself. Sera watched him with interest.

"My business dealings were all within the purview of Law. I know that other men are jealous of me." He gave Durrant a glare. "But my dealings were all permissible according to the laws at the time. So I ask you once again, why am I sitting here with my hand atop a rock?"

"We're getting to that," Durrant said. "We just had a few loose ends to tie up first. While your business dealings were entirely *legal*, as you said, they were not always ethical."

"If you are attempting to hold me to the same standard as Brant Fitzroy, bless his memory, then you will find yourself disappointed by me, and nearly every other person in the empire."

"A truer statement could not have been spoken," Durrant agreed. "Which brings us to the purpose of this meeting. Did you have an extramarital affair with Pauline Bellisle, wife of Lieutenant Bellisle of the Nineteenth Dragoons?"

The look of shocked surprise on Welles's face was all the indictment needed. He blinked rapidly, his skin turning pale. He adjusted his posture as a sickly look of shame settled over him.

"It was so long ago," Welles said, his voice barely audible.

"So you admit it happened?" Mr. Durrant spoke firmly.

"Yes," came a half-strangled reply.

"The same Mrs. Bellisle who divorced her husband following the affair and is now the wife of Admiral Hatch, who was arrested on charges of espionage months ago?"

"Yes," Welles ground out. The look of mortification on his face, the swelling anger that followed the confession—both showed he was undone.

"That same madame is a hetaera, we have discovered, and has been in league with Montpensier for many years."

Lord Welles looked surprised again. "A hetaera?"

"You did not know this?"

"I did not! If I'd suspected her, I would have reported her to the Ministry of Thought for an investigation. I swear it!"

"And did you continue this liaison during either of your terms as prime minister?"

"No! I swear it."

"No need to swear, Mr. Welles. The Leering will affirm the truth of your words."

Sera waited for Welles to react to the new title Durrant had used. It was a foreshadowing of what was about to happen. But the man didn't seem to have heard it. He still seemed to be reeling from the confession he'd made before the other ministers.

"Do you understand why you have been summoned to appear in front of a council of your peers?" Sera said, speaking at last.

He looked at her and then away. "Because of the charge of adultery," he said.

"Not only that," Durrant said. "And as I understand from those assembled here, your voice was the strongest in the impugning of Her Majesty's character for her brief indiscretion with a young officer. And it was just that: a small indiscretion. Your mistake, on the other hand, was a major lapse of moral judgment. The hetaera, who has been apprehended, had been intercepting correspondence within the Ministry of War for years. A memo she altered led to the demise of Lord Fitzroy, and we can only guess at what other damage she wrought. Had the facts been known sooner, this would have barred you from becoming prime minister." Mr. Durrant shook his head, walking closer. "The strength of a nation derives from the integrity of its homes. And integrity is measured by conduct, not by professions of honor. Well did the ancients say that no man can purchase his virtue too dear, for it is the only thing whose value must increase with the price it has cost us. Our integrity is never worth so much as when we have parted with our all to keep it."

"You are a fine one to sermonize," Lord Welles snapped. "But I never knew of her involvement with the hetaera order. Is that why I am here? So you can gloat over me now? Smother me in platitudes?" The anger in his eyes was fearsome. He rose from his chair, his hand still fixed to the Leering, and turned to Sera. "So this is your revenge, Sera? My, but you've been a patient cat to wait this long before showing your claws! You would do anything to bring me down. I saw it in your eyes when you began your rise to power. Beware, daughter of *Richard* Fitzempress! He was a weak man, and the weak spawn the weak."

Sera had prepared herself for harsh words. She'd known this wouldn't be easy. But even still, his words hacked at her like swords.

"How dare you speak to Her Highness in such a way," said Allanom Scott, rising from his chair, his voice throbbing with outrage. His eyes were full of accusation.

"What is to become of me?" Welles demanded, raging still. He looked at the others in the room, loathing evident on his face. "Am I to be made a martyr to the cause of sanctimoniousness? What if she uncovers your sins next? Hmmm? Yes, I accused her. Yes, I was a hypocrite! But are we not all so? And in this time of bloody and violent war, you would cast down one who has given his blood, sweat, and breath to preserve this empire? After all I have done?"

"Yes," said Lord Halifax implacably. "Because you *knew* better, Richard. How many officers have you demoted or discharged for the crime of adultery? How many courts-martial have you presided over while your own conscience surely seared you? Would it not make the empire howl with outrage if you were pardoned while they were made to suffer?"

"I didn't know she was a hetaera!" Welles pleaded.

"We suspected that," said Lord Prentice. "We know it for *sure* now that you've said it while touching the Leering. Otherwise, you'd be facing a more serious judgment."

Sera removed her hand from the Leering, and the power binding him fell away. Welles's shoulders sagged as he pulled his shaky hand away from the stone.

"Mr. Durrant wasn't trying to preach to you," Sera said. "He was trying to help you see *why* we were doing this. In the middle of a war. In a time when we need you most. To prove to you, as well as to our ancestors, that we prize integrity above all. We will not part from it, no matter what the cost. To us . . . or to you. And what you've done has injured the empire deeply and cost people their lives."

Sera took in a deep breath. "Richard Foulton Welles, you are hereby stripped of your lands and titles. Your businesses will be forfeit to the crown. You are stripped of your admiral's pension forthwith."

She watched him flinch with each pronouncement. There was no feeling of animosity toward him. In fact, she pitied the man.

"Because of your age and the unlikelihood that you will find suitable work, you will be granted a midshipman's pension. You are hereby banished from Lockhaven and from owning or piloting a sky ship. News of your disgrace will be published in the gazettes tomorrow morning."

"Please," Welles said, trembling, his eyes watering. "Can you not . . . ?" His words choked off. Then he stopped. Whatever he would have pleaded for, he fell silent. He hung his head in misery. The look he gave her, she would never forget it. He'd aged a dozen years during the brief interview. She watched him leave, beaten and disgraced, and took no pleasure from it.

After the door shut, she turned to Mr. Durrant. "Prime Minister, I'd like officers to escort him from Lockhaven and ensure he does no harm to himself. Also, have someone keep watch on him for the next few months. Our enemies may attempt to win his allegiance."

"As you've commanded, so it will be done," Durrant said, nodding. "Well, gentlemen. Thank you for joining us this evening. We will announce our decision at the privy council meeting at sunrise."

The other lords rose from their seats, looking weary and haggard. Sera thought Lord Prentice also looked a little guilty.

Allanom Scott approached her and clasped her hand. "Nearly all men can withstand adversity," he said with a sniff. "But if you want to test a man's character, give him power. Perhaps that is why we need more *women* to rule over us."

"Will he be all right, do you think?" Sera asked.

Allanom sighed. "He has nothing left to lose. That will either make him meek . . . or depraved. I will look in on him in a few weeks. See which direction he may be leaning. With your permission, of course?"

"You have it," Sera said with admiration. She knew the man did not care much for Welles—his request sprang from a genuine wish to help guide the other man toward virtue. "Good night."

He followed the others out of the chamber, leaving her alone with Mr. Durrant.

"Well done, Sera," he said, dropping into his seat at the council table. His shoulders drooped as well.

"We could have humiliated him in front of the entire privy council," Sera said.

Durrant nodded wearily. "I think this was the most appropriate, given the circumstances."

"With his fall, there is now an opening in the peerage," Sera continued. She gave him a meaningful look.

"What?" he said with a chuckle. "*Lord* Durrant?"

"I think you have more than earned it," Sera continued. "I would like you to draft up the papers."

His lips pressed together, and he drummed his fingers on the table. "I must obey you in all things, Sera, save this." He shook his head no. "I will not be made a noble. By you or anyone." A sly smile crossed his mouth. "It would ruin my reputation with the masses."

"You're serious?"

"Quite. Although I appreciate the gesture. And while I am exhausted, I'm not addled. I thought you might attempt something like this. I had a little speech prepared, but I find I can't recall it at the moment. I'll look it up when I get home and recite it to you in the morning."

His manners had always made her laugh. "Why have you never married, Durrant?"

"I am nearing sixty, Your Majesty. Ugly and balding, too, and I have yet to find a woman who's willing to put up with my recalcitrant ways. No, I'm not a fit husband for anyone, I think. But I am fit to be your prime minister. If you'll still have me."

"I depend on you," Sera said, and meant it. They'd been through the forge together. Through trials and missed chances. He'd worked tirelessly on her behalf in waging an all-out war against the traitor

Montpensier, who'd usurped power from her husband's family. She glanced down at the ring on her finger, which brought a stab of melancholy. Trevon was alive, or so she'd heard, but no doubt he was locked away in a dungeon somewhere. How that must smart for a man who so loved to travel, to see every part of his world.

Forcing the dark thoughts away, she looked at Durrant once more. "I'm grateful we finally caught the spy Montpensier sent. Who would have thought? Admiral Hatch's wife has been a hetaera all along."

Durrant nodded. "She won't reveal where the poisoner school is located."

Sera sighed. "At least we've learned it's not in Pisan, but it could truly be anywhere in their kingdom. This war might carry on for years before we locate it. If only we could find the Cruciger orb."

"Probably the very reason it was stolen," chuckled Durrant. "Get some rest. You look weary, and tomorrow will be an especially trying day."

"Why do you say that? Is there news you haven't told me?" The weight on her shoulders bore down even more.

"Yes." He paused a moment, his eyes twinkling. "Your mother wants to see you."

CHAPTER SIX

PRINCE KASDAN

With so many matters of intense importance to address, Sera didn't see how a meeting with her mother could possibly rank. Her mother always seemed to want something—to be added to the privy council, to have her stipend increased, or to complain about some wrong done to her by a petty aristocrat. It exasperated Sera to no end, but Durrant reminded her it had been a long time since she had last spoken to her mother. He was right, which was how she found herself agreeing to dine with her mother the following night.

Durrant nodded his approval and promised to see to the arrangements.

Thoughts about the impending meal were quickly driven from Sera's mind the next morning as she began the daily onslaught of meetings and obligations. Though she was always quick to make her wishes known, she allowed the officials she'd chosen a good deal of autonomy in how they fulfilled them. Things happened too quickly in war, and she didn't want Admiral Grant, the new lord high admiral, to feel he had to wait for orders if a situation called for an immediate reaction.

So many times it felt that victory was at her fingertips, only for a fluctuation of the weather or the ineptitude of a less seasoned officer to get in the way. Though the rift she'd created between the two worlds had given her a decided advantage—they could use it to fly into Kingfountain, but their enemy was forced to rely on the dwindling number of mirror gates—Montpensier's underwater ships continued to elude her fleet. Sera lived in a constant state of anxiety from one day to the next. Casualties continued to escalate, and she suspected she lost a soldier for every one or two who were killed on the other side. It was a grisly arithmetic.

But she had known this would happen. The Mysteries had warned her a blight of war would come to punish both worlds. She could not stop it. Even if she pulled her forces out of Kingfountain, Montpensier would continue to attack. The remaining mirror gates could be destroyed, certainly, but then their access to other worlds would be curtailed. For good. She did not wish to be the leader who isolated their world forever.

No, the war must continue until Montpensier was defeated. He was a cunning foe, a relentless force to be reckoned with. She could remember sitting across the table from him during dinners at the palace of Kingfountain, trading barbs and deflecting his insults. If she'd known then the impact the man would have on her life . . . she'd have lunged across the table with a knife and stabbed him in the heart. Maybe not, but it was a fancy she sometimes permitted herself.

After the privy council meeting, where the news about Welles was greeted with surprise, Sera went to her secret sanctuary inside the palace of Lockhaven. From this control room, she could access every Leering in the City, even though Lockhaven itself was now leagues away. The guards greeted her, and after exchanging pleasantries with them, something she made a point of doing because her father had not, she sequestered herself in the inner sanctum. She was to hold a conference with Prince Kasdan, her husband's younger brother, via Leering. Kasdan was married to the daughter of the Duke of Brythonica, their chief ally in the war.

Sera loved the inner sanctum, the only place in the empire where she could be at peace, where no one would interrupt. Sera arranged herself on the couch beside the Command Leering and placed her palm on the cool stone.

The magic soaked into her, and she could sense Lockhaven's position hovering over the sea near the ruins of the mirror gate that had once stood there. Ships of all sizes and makes filled the air around them, ferrying items and soldiers through the enormous rift in the sky. The constant flood of supplies, fresh soldiers as well as recovering ones, and war material never stopped. It was impossible to quantify the effort that went into sustaining the war. Merchants on both sides had been enriched beyond belief. Others had been ruined.

Like your husband, a voice whispered in her head.

She focused her wandering thoughts on the matter at hand and reached through the Leering to connect with Admiral Grant's hurricane, the *Pleasance.*

The high admiral's personal secretary greeted her from the Leering. He would provide the conduit for Sera to communicate with Kasdan. Her field of vision expanded, giving her a panoramic view of the admiral's private quarters, which were untidy and full of heaps of correspondence. The dim light was a reminder that when it was morning at home, it was dark in Kingfountain. Her view changed suddenly, and she saw Kasdan and his wife, Marie Elysabeth Penthievre. Kasdan was quite tall and striking and his wife more diminutive, which had always made Sera, who was small in stature herself, partial to her. A little boy raced past them, waving at the couple as he left the room. They gave him a fond look as they approached the Leering hand in hand.

"You look well, Kasdan," Sera said by way of greeting. "If a bit tired. You both are overdue some rest, I think. I'll try to keep this brief. Who was that little boy?"

"That was my nephew, Curtis, the little scamp. No need to apologize, Sera," said Marie Elysabeth with a bright smile. "Your time is precious to us as well. We have some news." She stroked Kasdan's arm, looking up at him with a glimmer in her eyes, and Sera knew.

"When is the baby due?" she said. She knew, from her own experience with communication between the realms, that the magic worked differently in Kingfountain. Whereas she could see them plainly, as if they stood opposite her, the Leering on their end rendered her visible to them through a sheen of fine mist, a peculiarity that came of Fountain magic interacting with the Mysteries.

"We're not sure," Kasdan said. "The midwife thinks seven more months? It's difficult to predict. But we are pleased and grateful."

"I'm happy for you both. We need more good news these days."

"I agree," said Marie Elysabeth. "Unfortunately, that is all the good news we bring today." Her smile faded, just slightly.

Sera respected how close they were, how neither dominated the conversation. She knew that Kasdan and Marie Elysabeth were full partners in every way. The Penthievres had been ruling Brythonica for several generations, and while the duke led his forces in the front, his daughter and son-in-law ruled the duchy in his absence.

"What news, then?" Sera asked, preparing herself to be disappointed.

"We had word that Trevon was seen in Leoneyis, hidden in a farmhouse. We dispatched men immediately to raid it, only to find he'd been smuggled out the night before. The farmer didn't know who the prisoner was, only that he was bearded, dressed in soiled clothes, and looked feverish. But upon further inquiry, and after he was shown a painting of my brother, the farmer confirmed it was him."

"The night before?" Sera said, her voice breaking. How many times had it happened? How many times had they come so close to rescuing her husband, only to fail?

Marie Elysabeth reached out to touch the Leering as if she could transmit her tenderness through the stone.

"I'm so sorry, Sera," Kasdan said wretchedly. "We acted as soon as we could. I think Montpensier has to move him constantly and only among his most trusted men. The reward offered for his rescue would tempt any ordinary man. There are hunters scouring the woods for signs of their trail. I had so hoped to give you good news tonight." He shook his head in muted frustration. "I'm sorry."

"It's not your fault, Kasdan," Sera said, mustering her resolve. "That he's still alive is hope enough. That blackguard has already done enough damage to your family. I know you are doing your best to find him."

"We won't stop trying, Sera," said Marie Elysabeth.

"I know. Any other news? Has there been any sign of Cettie Pratt? How fares the war from your perspective?"

"Of your friend, nothing. I'm sorry. As to the war . . . bloody and bloody difficult," said Kasdan with a sigh. "We have brought the fight to Montpensier, but that comes at a price. Leoneyis is his homeland, and he knows every river and every hill. And he's paying pirates to ambush our sky ships. I fear he's also convinced some of the other rulers to pull back from supporting us and look to defend their own borders. Legault has withdrawn fully. Occitania continues to increase its demands in return for its cooperation."

That concerned Sera greatly. "How so?"

"The Prince of Occitania recently withdrew one of his regiments from the front to attack Montpensier's lands in La Marche. The general is not there to defend them, so the prince decided to carve up a portion for himself while we continue the attack. He's demanding we ratify his conquest."

"Selfish man," Sera said disdainfully.

"I agree," Marie Elysabeth said, her eyes darkening. "Ancient squabbles bubble up during times of uncertainty. Long ago, Brythonica used to be part of Occitania. I think the good prince sees this as an opportunity to increase his own power at the expense of others'."

Sera let out her breath. "This alliance we have with Occitania is precarious. We all agree in the adage that the enemy of my enemy is my friend. But that does not make us friends for long. Surely the prince realizes that if we fail to overthrow Montpensier now, the general will wreak havoc on Occitania later."

Kasdan smirked. "I think he is betting that you won't allow that to happen."

Sera rubbed her hand along the Leering's surface. "I'll talk to Lord Halifax and see how many supply contracts we have with businesses supporting Occitania. It might be time to shift some of those elsewhere."

Kasdan and Marie Elysabeth exchanged a smile.

"I think that might do some good," Marie Elysabeth said, her eyes twinkling.

"What is the state of the widows and orphans?" Sera asked next. She always wanted to know how the war was affecting those most impacted by the devastation.

"Sufficiently grim, Sera," Kasdan said. "I imagine it is a mounting concern in your world as well."

"There are so many to look after," Sera agreed. "If there is anything we can do to help, do let me know."

"There is one thing. Find a cure for the cholera morbus," said Kasdan. "It is devastating our cities. People are afraid to even touch the corpses for fear of the contagion."

"Touching a corpse won't cause someone to contract it," Sera said, shaking her head. "I have it on the authority of Doctor Creigh that it is not transmitted that way."

Marie Elysabeth nodded. "And no one else would know better. But people are superstitious. Because the victims' deaths are so horrific, they feel it is a curse from the Fountain. Some think we've been cursed for our alliance with *you*. No amount of reasoning will work. If a cure can be found . . . it would be advantageous to all of us."

"I will ask Adam for an update on the situation. He's studying the disease at Killingworth Hospital right now, in the part of the empire most affected by it. He does so at great personal risk."

"We will fight on, Sera," Marie Elysabeth said. "General Montpensier's crimes are inexcusable. He will be brought to justice." Kasdan pulled up her hand and kissed her knuckles. She gave him a fond smile.

"I just wish so many innocents did not have to suffer for one man's ambition," Sera said, nodding in agreement. It was time to let them get some sleep. "I bid you both good night. And thank you for sharing your good news. I'm so happy for you both."

She meant it, and yet her earnest well wishes were somewhat tainted by her own unhappiness. She'd never taken off her wedding ring, nor did she wish to, yet she could not ignore the fact that Trevon's current imprisonment was not the only obstacle between them. What would happen if they did rescue Trevon? He was the heir of Kingfountain, the rightful ruler of his empire, just as Sera was the rightful ruler of *her* empire. She could not imagine abandoning her people to serve Trevon's, much as she could not imagine him doing the same. Leading up to their marriage, they had spent three months at a time in each of the realms. Could two vastly different and competing worlds be ruled in such a way? She'd asked herself that question over and over again since the day she was made empress, and her heart still told her no.

Should she manage to free Trevon from his imprisonment, it might mean an annulment of their marriage. The thought gave her a bitter taste, but it didn't mean she'd stop trying to save him. She'd never stop. Even if they wouldn't be together.

"We're sorry it had to be tainted with such ill news," Marie Elysabeth said, interrupting her thoughts and giving her a knowing look. "Let us hope our next visit brings better tidings."

"I hope so as well. Good night."

"Good night, Sera," Kasdan said.

Pulling away from the Leering, she squeezed her hands into fists, determined not to lose hope. She trusted the Mysteries. She'd been guided by them during her time as empress.

Trust. Believe.

She knew she couldn't see the future. She couldn't see past the next few hours of meetings and interruptions. And then there was dinner with her mother to consider. Sera sighed. One thing at a time.

⌇

The rest of the day fled past, giving Sera little time to nurse her grief and sadness. Not that she wanted to anyway. Before she knew it, she realized she was half an hour late to dinner. She walked down the corridor with Durrant, who stopped at the door of her room with her.

"I've a meeting with Lord Halifax, which I'm late to," he said. "Good luck." He gave her a knowing wink.

"Are you sure you don't want to switch with me?" she asked.

"No, not particularly. Your mother is a sweet soul, bless her heart. She'll likely plead again to be on the privy council. I can't tell you how many times Lady Florence has importuned me on her behalf. I still am of the opinion that one should be on the council for a reason, for a purpose or advantage one brings to the council as a whole. I'm afraid I just don't see one in this case. But do let me know if I'm wrong!" He chuckled to himself.

"I'll meet you after dinner, then, and we can commiserate." Durrant turned to leave, but Sera caught his sleeve. "One thing. Remember to ask Lord Halifax about our trade agreements with Occitania."

"I haven't forgotten our conversation," he said, nodding. She'd told him of her decision after her conversation with Kasdan. She'd suspected he wouldn't need reminding. He remembered everything. Her guards opened the door for her, and Sera entered to find her mother sitting primly at the small table. There was a young maid with her, who quickly rose and curtsied. Sera had never seen the girl before. Her own maid, Becka, was also present, and looked hugely relieved to see her. It wouldn't have surprised Sera in the least to learn her mother had arrived hours in advance of the dinner and forced poor Becka to entertain her.

"Hello, Mother," Sera said, striding into the room.

Mother turned and looked at her, the expression on her face one of reproof for being made to wait so long.

"You're here at last," Mother said with a toss of her head. "I was beginning to think you'd forgotten."

After all she had gone through that day, Sera had little patience for her mother's little criticisms. But she swallowed her feelings and joined her at the table.

"I'm afraid the food's probably cold," Mother said. "Shall we send for a replacement?"

Sera had no desire to be trapped even longer with her mother. "No, this will be fine. I eat my meals cold constantly." She raised the silver chafing dish in front of her, and not a whiff of steam came from it. Roasted pheasant covered in some sort of gravy. Another covered dish sat beside it.

"Well, the cooks went through the effort. At least we can enjoy it. Will your servants attend to us?"

"I'd rather not stand on ceremony," Sera answered. "We don't keep many servants anymore. The war efforts have depleted our staff considerably."

"I had no idea," Mother said. She reached out and served herself, and then, as if Sera were still a child, served her next. The portion was much bigger than she would have chosen for herself, but she didn't feel obligated to eat it all. Her mother lifted the other silver dish, revealing a tray of roasted vegetables, and heaped some onto each of their plates.

Sera thanked her, and then Becka, who had filled both of their goblets. The other maid had said nary a word.

"Who is your maid?" Sera asked, looking down at her plate. She was ravenously hungry, and the dish smelled pleasant, exotic even. She took one bite, then another.

"She's new," Mother said. "I adore her. She's not very talkative, but she's a good replacement. The other got married, you know."

Sera wiped her mouth on her napkin and turned to face the maid. "Welcome. I'm glad you could come," she said, addressing the young woman with a little nod.

"There is something I wanted to talk to you about," Mother said, using her knife to cut off a piece of meat.

It was coming already. "What is that?"

"We've spoken of it before. I think, and I know Lady Florence agrees with me, that as your *mother*, I deserve a seat on the privy council."

Sera sighed inwardly. She reached for her goblet to take a drink and noticed her hand was trembling. Perhaps she'd gone too long without food. She clenched her fingers into a fist and tried again, but she trembled so much that some of the contents sloshed onto the tablecloth. What was going on? Why couldn't she control her arm? A spasm shook her stomach.

Mother was busy pushing food around her plate, oblivious to Sera's distress. But then her eyes flicked up, and the look of guilt in them struck Sera like a blow. She understood at once that the meal had been poisoned. That her *mother* had probably done it. There she was, cutting away at her dish . . . not eating a single bite.

Sera tried to speak, but her mouth wouldn't work. She felt tremors spread through her entire body. Blackness began to crimp in around her vision.

In fear, she dragged her arm toward her chest. The Tay al-Ard was strapped to her forearm, beneath her gown. She tried digging her fingers into the cuff of her sleeve, but her body's violent trembling made it impossible.

Then a hand gripped her forearm. A hand belonging to a woman who had suddenly appeared out of nowhere. Sera instantly recognized the face of her enemy, the woman whom she had lived with under confinement in her youth.

The former lady Corinne of Pavenham Sky.

There was a dagger in Corinne's other hand, and she slit the sleeve of Sera's dress open without hesitation, the blade ripping into the skin underneath it with a shock of pain and an effusion of blood. The Tay al-Ard was slick with it.

"Get the maid," Corinne said to the young woman standing by Mother's side. Then she yanked the Tay al-Ard from the straps securing it, holding it in her own palm like a treasure. Her eyes glinted with victory.

Oh no. Oh heavens no! Sera thought with dread as the poison made her lose consciousness.

CHAPTER SEVEN

PRISONER

Sera awoke in utter darkness. Her arm was afire with pain, and it took her drugged mind several minutes to piece together her broken memories. Her mother sitting at supper, endlessly cutting into meat that she wouldn't eat. Lady Corinne's menacing eyes. A dagger slicing into her forearm.

I didn't see it coming, Sera thought with despair. She knew—she'd been warned—that Lady Corinne would attack her, but she'd trusted in her guards, in the safety of Lockhaven, in the Mysteries. And now this.

A sickening dread filled her stomach as she tried to sit up. Her head swam, and dizziness engulfed her. She cradled her left arm to her chest, wincing against the pain. She couldn't move her fingers of that hand, which only added to her terror. After the dizziness subsided, she reached with her other hand to feel around. She was on a cot. There was a scratchy wool blanket beneath her. Her stomach growled with hunger. Sera swallowed, still tasting a bitter residue of the poison she'd ingested.

Carefully, she eased her legs off the cot and felt the hard floor beneath. She touched the fabric of her dress, realizing she still wore the gown she'd had on at dinner. The darkness was not interrupted by even the dimmest light. No windows, then. It was a cell of some kind.

More of the pieces began to slide together in her mind. The traitor was her own mother. It made a horrific kind of sense. The woman had been deprived and treated shamefully by Sera's father. She'd always craved power, status. How many times had she begged Sera to include her? Her father had investigated her mother for years, searching for some black mark in her past he could use to separate himself from her legally, and had come up with nothing. But were there secrets that had remained hidden? It was obvious now that someone in the privy council, likely Lady Florence, had taken pity on Mother and divulged secrets to her. Secrets that had been used to benefit General Montpensier. What had she been promised in return? At what price had she forsaken her daughter?

Sera's heart throbbed with anger. The Tay al-Ard was gone. Lady Corinne had snatched it from her, preventing her from making an easy escape. She had believed, foolishly, that there would be no danger to her so long as she kept it close.

Light. Sera needed light.

But she could see nothing, so she reached out with her mind, trying to sense if there were any Leerings around. To her surprise, she felt one nearby. Sera slowly walked toward it, her hand held out in front of her, letting her senses lead her. Her shins banged against sharp edges, making her wince. Then her palm touched wood. The feel of the surface beneath her fingertips indicated a door. Leaning forward until her forehead touched the wood, Sera closed her eyes and reached out to the Leering with her mind. It responded instantly, and light spread under the crack of the door, revealing the tips of her shoes.

A relieved smile crossed Sera's mouth. With just that little bit of light, she was able to see her surroundings better. It was a small storage room, filled with barrels and crates. The cot looked as if it didn't belong there, as if it had been hastily put in place. The floor was stone and dusty. The air, now that she noticed it, was stale.

She tried to make the Leering burn even brighter, but another will did battle with her own. Another awareness skittered across her mind, almost like a shadow wavering in the light, and Sera pushed away from the door. A creeping fear began to go up her legs. A quick look around the now-illuminated room revealed there were no other exits. The door's handle, she quickly discovered, was locked. She jiggled it a few times, butting against the wooden door with her shoulder. It wouldn't budge.

A few minutes later, she heard the sound of footsteps coming down the hall. The sound carried another feeling—a sense of dread, of menace and malice—that grew with each step. The steps were not hurried or rushed, but they were relentless. Sera backed away from the door again, trying to summon some sparks of courage. Then the light beneath the door was broken by the shadow of her captor. A key jiggled in the lock.

The door opened to reveal a woman with a set of keys around her waist. She held a lantern in one hand, the light revealing a wizened face wrinkled with crags, silver hair, and an expression completely lacking in empathy and concern. It was a vengeful countenance, one that made Sera's heart quail.

"Who are you?" Sera asked in a low, trembling voice.

"I am Mrs. Pullman," came the reply, in a lightly accented voice. The name took her aback. This was the woman who'd tormented Cettie all those years ago.

"I thought you were in jail," Sera said, swallowing, trying to master her fear and apprehension.

"I suppose your little friend told you that," the woman sneered. "I was freed, and I'm the keeper here. I see you are awake now. The mistress will want to know."

"Lady Corinne?"

The matronly woman inclined her head.

"Whatever she is paying you, I can do better if you free me."

A little laugh came from the aged woman. "You think I do this for money?" she scoffed. "I see what you've done, *Miss* Fitzempress, since you rose to power. You'd like nothing better than to lift up the riffraff. Respect them, even. Oh no, we can't have that. I am grateful to be of service in this cause."

There was a strong feeling of evil in the air. Sera sensed hatred exuding from the old woman, so thick and full of bile her own heart shriveled from it. It was then she realized that Mrs. Pullman held a Myriad One inside her. She could feel it, like the hum and vibration of so many bees. Sera put a hand on her bosom and felt the cool metal of her maston chain against her skin.

"So what will happen to me?" Sera asked, her mouth growing dry.

"Whatever the mistress chooses to do with you, I suppose," said Mrs. Pullman.

Then the woman's eyes narrowed, her head jerking slightly to one side, as if she'd heard a voice calling her. She frowned with impatience. "Insufferable man. I must go." She pushed the door closed and locked it.

Sera waited a long time in the dark, her stomach empty and ravenous. She sat on the edge of the cot for a time, and when she could bear the stillness no longer, rose and paced the small storage room. Had Trevon been confined in such a place? She had only been locked in the storeroom for so many hours, and already she was going mad with suspense.

A few hours later, Mrs. Pullman returned with a plate of food and a goblet of sweet-smelling cider.

"Can you send me a doctor?" Sera asked, showing the old woman the ravaging wound on her forearm. Her dress was clotted with blood, and some still oozed down the blackened scabs.

"No, Miss Fitzempress. You're not to see anyone until the mistress arrives. She'll be here soon."

Sera sat back down on the cot, staring at the stale-looking bread and baked nuts on the plate. She put a few in her mouth and felt a rare enjoyment. As she reached for the goblet, she felt a quivering thought not to drink from it.

Poison.

As a trick, it was a cunning one. The cider smelled so inviting, and the salty nuts she'd eaten had only increased her thirst. It took great self-control to set the goblet back down. Staring at the bread, she broke off a piece and slowly chewed it. When her thirst became unbearable, she stopped eating and set the tray on the floor next to the goblet. She pulled up her legs and huddled in the dark space. She had lost her freedom. But not her ability to choose her thoughts.

Help me escape from this place, she thought silently to the Mysteries. For she knew all too well what Lady Corinne wanted from her.

The Leering that bound Ereshkigal, Queen of the Myriad Ones, was hidden in the depths of Cruix Abbey. Lady Corinne had tried to break the seal of that Leering, but she lacked the authority. Sera had that authority, and during her visit to the abbey, she'd learned that Lady Sinia, a Wizr of old who'd come to the empire from Kingfountain, had prophesied that an empress would one day unbind the Leering. The name of the empress, she'd said, was the Angelic One.

Seraphin.

With the Tay al-Ard, Lady Corinne could take Sera there instantaneously. How long would it take Mr. Durrant to start looking for her? He knew about both the Leering and the prophecy, so he would know it was of utmost importance for them to find her immediately.

There were trusted people assigned to Cruix Abbey to keep watch for Lady Corinne's return, but no doubt the woman would be subtle about it. She'd had a year to scheme. Her plan clearly involved taking Sera alive, at least for now. That meant she did not yet intend to kill her, a realization that bolstered Sera's courage.

But what was she supposed to do now?

Lady Sinia had made that prophecy before she disappeared. If it had sprung from the Mysteries, did that mean Sera was *supposed* to unbind the Leering? Or would Lady Corinne threaten her in such a way that she felt she had no other choice?

What if Trevon's life was at stake?

Would she have to sacrifice her own life?

Trust. Believe.

Sera had been the instrument of the Mysteries' power before—through her, they had opened a rift in the sky. If she stood strong in her faith, the Mysteries would save her from this awful dilemma . . . wouldn't they? Or would this be a test of her allegiance to the maston oaths?

As she sat there in the darkness, she began to think back on the words of the tomes she had read. On the lessons she had learned at Muirwood Abbey and throughout her life. She'd been duped before. She'd been deceived by Will Russell and others like Lord Welles. While she could not change her circumstances, she could keep her mind open for direction from higher sources of wisdom.

She didn't know how long she had been in a state of pondering, but she heard the sound of footsteps coming down the hall again. Two sets of footsteps this time. Sera rose from the cot, still nursing her painful wound. The lock released. The door opened.

Sera saw Mrs. Pullman first, but the older woman dragged the door wide, revealing Lady Corinne in the corridor. How things had changed. The former lady of Pavenham Sky, once the most fashionable woman in the empire, was skulking in a cellar.

"Good evening. Or is it morning still?" Sera asked with feigned cheerfulness. "I really can't tell."

"Leave us," Lady Corinne said to Mrs. Pullman. The crags in the old woman's face furrowed deeper, but she nodded and retreated down the corridor, holding the lantern in one hand. The light from the Leering in the corridor was situated behind Lady Corinne. It revealed more of Sera than it did of her enemy.

"Where are we off to next?" Sera asked.

"I have havens throughout the land," Lady Corinne said, her voice betraying no emotion. But there was a dangerous look in her eye—that of someone who was becoming more and more unstable. She stepped into the cellar, her body filling the small doorframe.

"So we do not go to Cruix Abbey yet?" Sera said, tilting her head.

"Not yet," Lady Corinne answered. "All in due time."

"They will find me," Sera said, trying to put some steel in her voice.

Lady Corinne smirked. "Not if they don't know you are missing."

Sera looked at her in confusion.

"Do you think I left this up to chance? Do you not think I've been careful in my preparations? You are my slave, my prisoner. Your life means nothing to me, Sera. I would just as soon drive a dagger into your chest, as I did to Lord Fitzroy. I have enough blood on my hands to fill a river. Even some of yours now." Her smile was deadly. She stepped closer. She glanced down at the floor beside the cot, at the tray and full goblet. Her look darkened. "Drink the cider."

Sera's stomach plummeted. She'd known the cider was poisoned. She'd known it. And she didn't doubt Lady Corinne would force her to drink it. So she kicked the goblet over with the tip of her toe, giving the woman a defiant look.

The splash of liquid, the rolling of the cup on the floor, and then intense silence.

"You shouldn't have done that," Lady Corinne said in a low, husky voice.

In a moment, Sera felt her wounded arm wrenched back, her already deadened fingers cruelly twisted. The pain made her gasp and sag to her knees. She'd never hurt so much in her life. There was the dagger again, held only inches from her face.

Lady Corinne cut Sera from the edge of her jaw up to the corner of her eye before shoving her onto the floor.

The pain in her arm and the fire on her face made her shudder with agony. She couldn't believe this was happening to her, that she was being tortured by the woman who'd once been her caretaker.

"I will cut your pretty face apart if you defy me again," Corinne said, the anger building in her voice. "I know how to hurt you, Sera Fitzempress. You vain little thing. When I am done with you, no one will want you. No one will even bear to look at you. If you think I jest, then test me. I have nothing else to lose. Now get up. Get up!"

Sera had never seen Lady Corinne like this. The contrast between the composed, elegant, and unemotional woman she'd lived with and this ferocious creature was staggering.

Sera quickly got to her feet, even though she felt like vomiting. She was afraid of that dagger.

And what it would do next.

The number of victims of the cholera morbus is increasing daily. They are coming to Killingworth in droves, and some die before they even arrive, their bodies lying untouched in the streets because of fear of the contagion.

If we do not root out the cause of this fearsome disease, I fear it could destroy up to half the population of the Fells. The wealthier families are fleeing because they can. Those who cannot leave walk the streets with handkerchiefs pressed to their mouths. The factories are spending more and more to attract fresh workers and to keep those they have from fleeing in fear. The workers have dubbed their journey from home to the shops the Ghost Walk, and their pay is now called Death Wages. Still, many of them have no choice but to take the risk.

None of my staff has been infected, though we handle the corpses all day long. I believe our rituals of washing must contribute to our well-being. It's not in the air. The cholera morbus is something we cannot see. A silent enemy. A ghost.

—Adam Creigh, Killingworth Hospital

CETTIE

CHAPTER EIGHT
HOTEL VECCHIO

The Hotel Vecchio in Pree was owned and run by Genevese merchants. An ornate structure that rose high above its neighbors, it was both longer and wider than any building Cettie had ever seen—even Pavenham Sky. It looked like a government palace, only larger. Judging from the endless rows of ornate windows, there had to be over a thousand rooms on six or seven levels.

And just as Jevin had said, their commandeered sky ship would not stand out there. A hurricane hovered over it, and a few other tempests were already docked in the landing yards inside the enclosed gardens. Rows of potted trees, each dwarfed and painstakingly sculpted, filled the inner gardens. By the time she and Rand landed beside those other sky ships, sometime before dawn, they had already assumed their disguises as brother and sister.

Cettie was weary but alert as they disembarked from the ship. She locked the Control Leering with a word that would prevent anyone else from commandeering the tempest. Given the hour, the grounds were surprisingly active and busy. Zephyrs streaked up from the ground to the hurricane, which dominated the brightening sky, perhaps bringing provisions for the crew.

"I've never seen such a place," Rand said as they walked side by side across the beautiful garden.

"The Genevese are certainly enamored of their grounds," Cettie answered. "We flew over other gardens like this one, but the hotel is spacious."

"At least we can get some rest while we wait," he responded with a sigh. "I'm weary."

"As am I. Do you know anything more about the rest of our assignment?"

Although he shook his head no, she felt a little throb of unwillingness from the kystrel. They shared an overall feeling of wariness as they approached the grand hotel.

"There are so many people staying here, we will hardly be noticed," Cettie said.

He nodded in agreement. Suddenly a small group of dragoons turned the corner, their uniforms having been concealed by the thick hedgerow. Cettie felt an immediate surge of alarm upon seeing their uniforms.

The group hailed them, seeing Rand in his dragoon jacket. "What regiment are you from, Commander?" one of them asked. Was there a hint of suspicion in his voice?

"Falstaff's," Rand replied with a shrug. "What about you?"

"We're assigned to the Duke of Brythonica," said the foremost officer. "Where'd you come in from?"

"Genevar. Pretty boring. Have you seen much action?" Rand asked.

Cettie reached out with her power to sense their motives. Were the dragoons trying to detain them? How innocuous were the questions? The kystrel revealed they were bored and disdainful of the foreigners around them. They were just seeking conversation with a pair of perceived allies.

"I'll go ahead, Rand, and get our room," Cettie said, touching his arm in a sisterly way, as she'd seen Joanna do. One of the soldiers was eyeing her appreciatively, the kind of attention she'd been trained to seek and recognize.

"I won't be long," Rand answered, taking her cue.

As she walked past the soldiers, she gave the soldier who fancied her—or rather Joanna—a timid look and what she hoped was a coquettish smile. Though she kept walking, she could still hear their voices through Rand's medallion.

"Who is that?" one of the soldiers asked.

"My sister, Joanna."

"Your sister? Truly?"

"She's quite unattached at the moment. I could introduce you."

"I would like that!"

"So where are you gents bound for next?"

Cettie listened in on their conversation for a moment before shifting her attention to the entrance of the hotel. The lobby she stepped into was both immense and elegant, with huge crystal chandeliers, folded curtains that hung from enormous golden stays, and a lushly carpeted floor. A few guests roamed the interior, but she surmised the crowd would be much larger after dawn. There were servants bustling around, preparing for the day ahead, each wearing a satin uniform and powdered wig. After studying her surroundings a bit longer, she made her way to the main counter, behind which hung an enormous board with hundreds of slots for room keys. She approached one of the dozen or so attendants and introduced herself as Joanna Patchett.

"Ah, Miss Patchett, you've finally arrived!" said the greeter with a heavy Occitanian accent. "We'd expected you during the night. You came by sky ship, no?"

"Yes. My brother is also here and will be coming inside shortly. Can I have a key to our room, please?"

"Of course!" He was polished in his manners and very cheerful. "Your accommodations have all been paid in advance, I see. You are welcome to enjoy the breakfast feast at your leisure, though I imagine you are weary from your journey. I will have a manservant escort you to your room at once." He snapped his finger, and a young man of fifteen or sixteen who'd been lounging against the back wall sprang into action. He was given the key to the room and instructions to take Cettie there.

As Cettie followed him to the room, she quickly became lost in the grandeur of the place, the veins of marble in the walls and the winding, though comfortably wide, hallways. All the decorations and cleanliness of the place didn't put her at ease. She kept her senses alert, seeking anything that might be out of place, but that was difficult because *she* felt so out of place. She wore another woman's smile, her stained dress concealed by the ring's magic.

The manservant brought her to a set of wide, carpeted stairs, which could have easily fit a dozen people across. They climbed until Cettie's legs began to ache. They passed a few people along the way, guests who'd already arisen, but Cettie greeted none of them unless she was greeted first. It fascinated her to see such an array of clothing and manners. Though she'd been taught to recognize and wear the various court fashions, it felt different to see them in person.

At last the manservant led her to her room, only differentiated from the identical doors lining the corridor due to the number engraved on the brass placard. The manservant inserted the key, twisted it, and opened the door. She gestured for him to go in first, still innately cautious.

The decor was just as lavish as she'd expect. There were two separate rooms, each with a large bed and an intricately carved dresser, connected by a common sitting room, plus a balcony and a changing room. She reached out with her power to sense the presence of anyone else in the room. Nothing. The young manservant familiarized her with the arrangements, tied open the curtain to expose the view of the gardens below, and then bowed to her.

"Will you bring my brother up here when he arrives?" she asked.

"I will, ma'am. It would be my pleasure." Then he left her.

She was alone.

Even though she was in an enormous hotel, surrounded on all sides, she felt a small thrill of being alone. Alone with her thoughts. Alone with her demons.

No one had told her what to do next. She had no current orders to follow.

Without planning it, she made her way onto the small balcony. She could see the underside of the hurricane above, its planks starting to glow with the rising of the sun. She looked down at the gardens, taking in the whorl-like pattern made from the green foliage below. It was vaguely reminiscent of the kystrel's design.

She knew that Rand was no longer in the garden. She could sense him in the lobby, feeling at ease and a little smug at how much information he was getting from the unguarded officers.

As she stared out the window, she was reminded of Fog Willows and her view from the keeper's chamber in the tower. It caused her heart to constrict. Had Lady Maren really taken a lover? She remembered Clive Francis, her mother's old flame, but an affair with such an ill-chosen man didn't seem in keeping with Lady Maren's character. And yet . . . why would Rand lie about it so offhandedly? And then there was Adam and Anna. That was less of a surprise, though she still felt an angry twist of disappointment in her heart. Anna had loved Adam for years, since they were children, but Adam's interest had always been in Cettie. It seemed a little out of character for him to dote on her now.

But then, didn't people often act out of character? Wasn't that exactly what she was doing? Cettie Pratt who had grown up in the Fells and become the keeper of Fog Willows would blush at Cettie the poisoner.

In the quiet, in her aloneness, she began to grieve again for all she had lost.

Then she sensed a wave of concern coming from Rand, concern because her emotions were spilling subtly into him. Curse the kystrel and the bond it had created! She'd been foolish to believe she was alone. She wouldn't *ever* be alone anymore.

Leaving the balcony, she shut the door behind her and fell onto one of the beds. Why dwell on the past? She couldn't change it. Why be miserable for decisions that had been forced on her? Yet . . . yet . . . hadn't she chosen them ultimately? And wasn't it regret that constantly chafed her heart?

What could she do about it?

Nothing. If she attempted to flee, they'd catch her. She had no resources, no friends. No way of communicating with others without revealing herself to her captors. She was utterly helpless to free herself.

And even if she did?

The authorities would kill her because of the hetaera brand.

Rand had their luggage brought up from the tempest, just two small chests they'd taken from the tempest's previous occupants to support the ruse that they were normal guests. There was nothing to do but wait for further instructions, and so they walked the grounds together, listened to the small chamber orchestra play fanciful sonatas from Pree, and enjoyed the lavish meals provided. Cettie ate sparingly, as she'd been trained to do at the poisoner school.

Their conversations were ordinary, but she could sense his rekindled attraction for her. Behind his cheerful small talk, she sensed that he truly cared about her. That he desired her even. His struggle to conceal those feelings from her convinced her there was something behind them.

And yet part of her didn't trust it. That invisible ring she'd discovered on his hand had surfaced in her thoughts again and again. Was it to conceal his clothing? Or his face? He *felt* like the man she'd known from Gimmerton Sough, but was he really who he claimed to be? It was difficult keeping her distrust at bay. It festered like a tiny splinter.

They parted after dinner. He'd promised to play cards with the soldiers he'd met earlier, and she retreated to their rooms. A fire had been built in the small fireplace in the den, rendering the room pleasantly warm, and lit candles dotted the surfaces. Discarding the illusion of being Joanna Patchett, she sat on a small settee and stared into the flames, dreading and looking forward to when Rand would arrive.

She could hear him speak with the other officers, feel his building impatience to be alone with her. The knowledge of how he felt made her insides squirm.

Finally, only an hour or so after they'd parted, she felt him coming up the stairs. She felt him walking down the hall. She even felt him pause at the door, preparing himself to face her.

When he entered the den, she didn't look at him, her eyes still fixed on the flames. She could make him feel anything she wanted. It was a powerful realization. She could wring his heart until he wept. She could make him desperate. Whispers urged her to use the power that way. To make him loyal to only her. Devoted even. Obsessed. The thoughts droned like bees in her mind.

He waited by the door. "Why are you toying with me?" he asked huskily. A wave of vulnerability washed over her. His vulnerability.

She glanced at him. "What do you mean?"

After shutting the door, he walked closer. "I think you know what I mean. Why are we fighting our feelings? It's madness."

She looked away again. "I want you to take off your ring."

"What?" He sounded surprised.

"I know you're wearing one."

"What does it matter?" he said, and she felt his sudden wariness. He did not *want* to remove his ring. She felt his resistance forcefully.

"It matters to me," Cettie said. "I want to see who you really are."

"What do you mean, who I really am? You know who I am, Cettie." He came around to stand before her. She had to admit that she was attracted to him. He looked desperate, his cheek twitching with emotion. "You know my very soul."

"Do I?" she answered softly. "Take off the ring, then."

He shook his head. "I can't."

"You can't . . . or you won't?"

He gritted his teeth. "It's not that simple, Cettie. I cannot take it off. I . . ." His voice choked off on those last words. She sensed a strange magic weaving in the air. Her ghosts were warring inside her now, trying to make her forget what she'd asked.

"Give me your hand," she said, offering her palm.

The flames in the fire flared higher, startling her. The emotions battling inside him grew more panicked. He didn't want to obey her, but she was compelling him to through the kystrel he wore. She saw the sheen of sweat appear on his brow.

Then he dropped on his knees before her. "Stop torturing me!" he gasped, putting a hand on her knee. "Can't you see that we are one? I feel everything that you feel. Stop using the kystrel against me!"

"I'm not," Cettie said, shaking her head. Part of her longed to cup his face. To kiss him. And yet, she also longed to push him away. Her thoughts began to flutter, darkness encroaching on them. It was her ghosts, the ones who lived inside her. "Just take it off," she said, shaking her head, trying to hear past the buzzing in her ears.

"I can't," he groaned. She felt he was telling the truth. He wanted to obey her, but there was an even stronger force that kept him from doing it.

She put her hand atop his. She could feel the ring on his finger. Invisible. Quivering with power.

Blackness began to shroud her vision. She blinked quickly. She was losing herself again. It hadn't happened often since she'd worn the kystrel. Only when she tried to assert herself strongly against the Myriad Ones' impulses. Was there any point in fighting them if it caused her to lose what little control she had?

84

She felt Rand's other hand move higher up her leg. He was breathing so fast, so passionately. His mouth was just inches from hers.

All she had to do was lean forward . . .

She'd felt passion for this man for years. She was in a hotel in a foreign world. What did it matter after all the horrible things she had done?

But it *did* matter. She knew it down to her core. If she gave herself to this man, she would be giving up more than her body. It would create an inextricable union between them.

But it felt . . . so good.

Her mind was pounding with pain. Why not? Why not submit to her fate?

A whisper penetrated her mind.

Because you do not decide what is right and what is wrong.

It pierced the deepest part of her mind, penetrated the farthest corners of her heart. She *knew* the voice. She'd heard it before. It was the voice of the Mysteries, which she'd never expected to hear again. Yet it had come to her at the most critical moment.

You do not decide what is right and what is wrong.

The echo of it burned inside her with a conviction that shattered all doubt. No person, Cettie or otherwise, could define truth. It existed, independent of belief. Inviolate. Immovable.

Her hand was still atop Rand's as he continued to reach up her leg. He was leaning over her now. Something felt wrong. Inside her mind, she heard shrieking.

Cettie grabbed his wrist, squeezing his hand to keep it from continuing its upward journey. Then, with her other hand, she grabbed for his finger and torqued it up. Her own feelings were bound to his. What hurt she caused him also happened to her. The sudden pain shocked them both.

But it gave her just enough of an opening to wrench the ring off his finger. When she did, she felt a strange gushing sensation as the Myriad

Ones left her body. She staggered from the shock of it, feeling hollow yet full—left alone with her thoughts for the first time in a long, long while. But there was no time to marvel over it. No time to steep in the joy of freedom.

The illusion had melted away. It wasn't Rand Patchett standing before her.

It was a man she'd never seen, his face a mass of knotted flesh. It was a hideous face ravaged by scars. She saw his eyes flare with rage.

"W-who are you?" Cettie gasped.

CHAPTER NINE
THE TRUTH WILL OUT

Cettie sensed a surge of rage through their connected bond just before the kishion's forearm lunged forward to crush her throat. That was all the warning she needed. Just in time, she caught his arm and kicked him solidly in the stomach, knocking him backward. But her defense only kept him away for a moment before he lunged at her again, trying to tackle her against the couch. She had no doubt that he would do anything to hurt her. There was no time for her to contemplate his new face. No time to do anything but fight.

Cettie dived out of the way, finding the hotel den too cramped for her usual maneuvers. She banged her shins against a small table, giving him an opening to grab her wrist and attempt to force her arm behind her back. She thrust an elbow into his cheek, and they both crashed to the floor. He freed her arm, but in the next instant a pillow crushed against her face, hard enough to smother her. She managed to control her fear, her racing pulse. In fact, she blasted *him* with the sensation of being smothered, making him feel that *he* was the one without air. The deception worked, and Cettie bucked and twisted until her hand found his throat, then his chin, then his eye.

The pillow came away, and she wrestled herself free. They were both panting at this point, having smashed each other against most of the furniture in the room. She got to her knees and found him hovering over her. Without hesitating, she struck at his groin with her fist. He blocked the blow and chopped his hand down against the side of her neck. The blow nearly knocked her out, but her training saved her. She leaped up, uncoiling like a spring, and attacked him with both hands in a Bhikhu technique.

He toppled over the back of the couch, and Cettie retreated, hand behind her back, twisting one of her poisoner rings to expose the needle. The reprieve was brief.

"Where do you think you'll go?" he demanded, his face shining with sweat. She felt his anger, his frustration, his inner shame at the scars on his face. "Do you think there is anywhere you could run?"

"Who are you?" she said, breathing fast. "You're *not* Rand Patchett."

He flung a tray at her head, but she'd seen a glimpse of his intent before the action and ducked. He vaulted over the couch, landing a kick to her middle. She flew backward, but didn't stay down. When he lunged at her again, she tried to prick his arm with the needle ring, but he grabbed her forearm and sent her spinning to the floor. As she landed, she rolled, breaking free of his grasp, and hooked her foot behind his leg and swiveled. He came tumbling down as well. She struck him in the face once, twice—then he grabbed her hair and yanked, making her gasp with pain.

"Stop fighting me, Cettie!" he snarled at her.

She tried smacking him across the face with her ring hand, but he blocked it, knowing full well what a poisoner could do. He wrested her hand away, squeezing her fingers painfully, until she managed to get her teeth on his hand and bite hard. He let go, only to grab her around the middle, hoist her off her feet, and throw her across the room.

Her back screamed with pain, and she slumped to the floor. Cettie decided to lay still, to pretend that she was unconscious. It was a risk, because he could sense her feelings, but she did her best to guard her mind. Her back ached. Her hair veiled part of her face. Her ears listened for sounds of movement. He was breathing quickly, wiping his face. They were both sweating.

"Why, Cettie? Why?" he muttered to himself. She heard him approach.

She'd never felt so vulnerable before. Had he drawn a knife? Or a pistol? Had their battle alerted any of the hotel staff?

Cettie feigned a moan and tried, in a lethargic way, to sit up.

"No, no, no," he said, dropping down near her.

Cettie opened her eyes and slammed her hand against his, piercing him with the poisoned needle.

Shock filled him.

He began to lift the pistol he was holding with his other hand. Cettie grabbed his wrist and fought to push it away from her head. She could not. He was still strong, and she watched his finger begin to flex on the trigger. The barrel was pointed right at her face.

She felt his inner conflict. He was supposed to kill her. That's what he'd been told to do if she tried to leave. Yet he couldn't. He cared about her. The feelings were not faked—they were real. She looked past the scars into the eyes, the eyes that were still his, despite the illusion.

"Don't," she begged, still wrestling against him.

And then he slumped to the floor, the toxin finally paralyzing his muscles.

Cettie bound him to one of the armchairs. His wrists and ankles were secured with cords she'd made from the excess furniture and curtains. She'd disarmed him as well, removing the various pistols and blades he'd kept on his body. She pocketed a pistol and a dagger for herself. Then, while the toxin raged inside him, she brought out her poisoner bag and prepared a dose of nightshade. Too much would kill him. The right amount would make him tell her what she wanted to know and rob him of his memories of the confession.

While tying him up, she'd tried to remove her kystrel from his neck, but the medallion had sent a powerful shock through her. She tried again, and this time managed to get it off his neck. A wave of pain, intense and unyielding, washed over her, and only receded when she put the medallion around her own neck—an imperfect solution, to be sure, but at least it was no longer in his possession. Her arm still tingled from the ordeal. Though she didn't want to wear it, not anymore, she couldn't face the pain of attempting to remove it again.

She could sense the kishion's stupor through the magic, but he was aware of his surroundings still. The poisonous agent affected the nerves but didn't make him unconscious.

After her preparations were done, she studied his face while waiting for the poison to wear off. His face was covered in a series of healed scars from burns and cuts. As if a bomb had exploded in front of him. Parts of his dark hair had been ignited as well, leaving gaps and splotches of waxy skin. The wounds were mostly on his right side. From the other perspective, she saw little evidence of it, except for a few small crisscrossing scars. His hands and neck had also been burned. The scars covered much of his body.

Who was this man? His personality and mannerisms were so similar to the Rand she knew. Had she ever met the real Rand Patchett?

She saw his fingers twitch. A little groan passed from his lips.

"You are reviving," she told him. "The toxin should be wearing off. It's a serpent venom."

"I know," he murmured. "I recognize it." He grunted, and she saw him test the bonds, his fingers clenching into fists.

"I have some questions for you. And since I can't trust your answers, I'm going to give you another poison. It won't hurt you."

"Cettie, *don't,*" he said, shaking his head. "I'll answer truthfully. Don't bother with the nightshade."

She shook her head. She felt a strange growing sense of power, as if the Myriad Ones inside her were weakening. "I cannot trust anything you would say to me," she answered, bringing the nightshade powder over to him. She dumped it into her palm and knelt by the chair.

She felt his heart racing, his dread increasing.

"They'll hunt you," he said. "We all will. You know too much. Everyone you love will be murdered. You can't—"

She blew the powder into his face. He thrashed against his bonds, his features twisting with discomfort. He shook his head, trying to get the poison off his face. Cettie stayed rooted to the spot, trying to see past the scars. His voice was exactly the same as it had always been, she realized.

His shoulders sagged, and the fight went out of him. She felt through the kystrel that his mind was addled. He was in a state of hypnosis. The nightshade did not last for long. She couldn't give him any more because of the risk of killing him, so she needed to work quickly.

"What is your name?" she asked, leaning close.

"Will Russell," he replied, his voice dead and passive.

That surprised her even more. Will Russell was the young man who'd deceived Sera all those years ago. She'd met him once, at Muirwood Abbey, when she'd taken to flying with Aunt Juliana's tempest. His disfigurement had dramatically altered his looks, but now that she knew the truth, she could recognize him.

Sera had been told he was dead.

"Where is Rand Patchett? Is he alive?"

"Yes. He's in the dungeon below the poisoner school."

"Why? What use is he still?"

"He's a slave. And I need access to his memories through the kishion ring."

Cettie nodded to herself. "Do you know what our mission was supposed to be? Where we were supposed to go?"

"I was ordered not to tell you."

"Tell me anyway," Cettie said.

"The empress has been abducted. You are going to impersonate her. When Ereshkigal is freed, you will be her vessel. She will rule once again."

"Why me?" Cettie pressed, her heart filling with dread.

"Because you can exist in both worlds without heeding any of the covenants. You are the only person who can pass freely between them."

She didn't know why this was so, or even if it was true, but she wanted to keep the interrogation going since her time was limited. "How do you know this?" Cettie asked.

"I overheard your father." The muscles on his hands and forearms began to quiver. The nightshade was wearing off. Too soon.

Cettie leaned forward, her voice thickening. "Where is Sera being kept?"

"I don't know. I wasn't trusted with that information."

"Tell me."

"I don't know!" he said, his voice becoming angrier. She felt the confusion inside him. The poison's effects were dwindling. He was starting to remember.

"Is what you told me about the Fitzroy family true?"

"Most of what you believe is a lie."

Cettie breathed quickly, her heart pounding in her chest. She felt the room lurch, begin to spin. Those horrible things he'd told her were lies. Twisted words. Half-truths.

"Where is Adam Creigh?" she asked him next, pleadingly.

"Killingworth Hospital. In the Fells." He almost choked on the words. "I've been ordered to kill him if you forsake us."

He began to blink rapidly, his placid look steadily replaced by one of confusion. He jerked in the chair, trying to move his arms and legs.

Then he noticed her crouching in front of him and tried to knock foreheads with her. She backed away just in time.

"What have you done?" he snarled, wrenching against the bonds. It only made the ropes cut more deeply.

She backed farther away from him.

"Release me!" he ordered her. She felt a compulsion rise from him, one that jolted her heart. He was using the kystrel against *her*. How was that even possible? He was the kishion, she the hetaera.

The kystrel's power should have been strong enough to control her. Yet somehow it did not.

"I don't think so," Cettie said, shaking her head. She went to the table and began to collect her things into her poisoner's bag.

"What did you make me say?" he asked. "Let me go right now, Cettie. Please. I need to take you far away. I don't want them to kill you."

"Them?" she said. "Don't you remember trying to kill me yourself?"

"I wasn't going to kill you," he said, shaking his head. His voice was desperate, full of real panic. He was afraid of failing. He was afraid for his own life.

"I find that difficult to believe."

"I know you have Everoot with you," he said. "I was going to heal you. I promise. Please, you have to listen to me. You cannot leave the hotel."

"I'm certainly not staying here," Cettie said. Her heart quivered with dread, but as soon as she said the words, she knew they were true.

"You think we're alone? This hotel is run by the Genevese! They are behind all of the poisoner schools . . . the kishion. Trust me, you will not make it out of here alive without my help. They've already taken the tempest to prepare it for our mission. Please, Cettie!" He strained against the bonds again, his face wincing in pain. "I can protect you from them!"

She whirled around to face him. "I cannot trust a single word that comes out of your mouth. You've lied to me. All along. You are not Rand Patchett."

He closed his eyes, and she felt a throb of anguish inside him. "But I *am* him now. I want to be him. Let me go!" he thundered. He opened his eyes wide with panic. "If you leave without me, you will be hunted like a fox cub. You can't get rid of a kystrel's connection! I will know where you are. And they will know. They will kill both of us, Cettie. And they'll hurt everyone you love. Believe me, I've seen it. I saw what they did to Joanna to make Rand put on the ring."

"What ring?" Cettie said, confused.

"The kishion ring! The one that binds him to me, and me to him." He squirmed more. "I need it back. Where did you put it?"

She hadn't even thought about it after she'd ripped it from his finger. It was somewhere on the floor.

"Free me," he implored. She felt him invoke the kystrel again, saw his eyes turn silver with the magic. A sickening feeling filled the room—he had summoned the Myriad Ones with his power. A revelation unfurled in her mind. There was something twisted about the kystrels—they allowed those who used them great power and control, but there was a price. There was always a price. "Please, Cettie. I couldn't bear it if they caught you. They'll twist your mind."

"But they already have," Cettie said.

He shook his head. "No, they were trying to get you to choose this freely. You are more powerful if you choose it. If you don't, they'll make you a slave. You'll be like the girls in the healing room. Your whole life spent in bondage. And they will kill all the Fitzroys . . . I swear it! They will. Even Phinia and Milk. Every single one of them, just to punish you. And you'll still be a slave when it's over. Please, Cettie. I beg you, listen to me!" She felt his sincerity. But was it real? Or was it just the kystrel's magic weaving a spell around her heart?

"I won't stay," Cettie said, feeling the gooseflesh crawl up her arms. The Myriad Ones were in the room now, converging on her. She felt a shudder. William Russell was trying to stall her so they could mount an attack.

She grabbed her bag and started for the door.

"Don't you dare leave me here like this! At least put a bullet in my skull! Have enough pity to kill me! You cannot let them find me like this! Cettie! No!"

She felt the fringes of her mind go black, but the sensation cleared a moment later. The Myriad Ones had failed to force themselves into her mind. Why? How could that be? Were the Mysteries protecting her, even though she no longer wore a chain?

"Cettie, please! Please!" Will's voice throbbed with emotion. "Don't you care if we all die?"

She looked back at him, feeling disgusted with herself, but the urge to run was primal. Without answering him, she twisted the handle and opened the door.

She took one last look at Will before she turned to leave. His eyes flashed white hot instead of silver. A look of terrible rage filled them. He wrenched one arm so violently the ropes nearly snapped apart. She sensed the power inside him, the full might of the Myriad Ones he'd summoned.

Cettie entered the corridor as the sounds of his cursing blistered her ears.

It was the middle of the night.

And she had nowhere to go.

CHAPTER TEN

RANSOMED

Cettie's thoughts were awhirl with doubt and dread as she slammed the door behind her. She'd been lulled into a system of thinking that was so far from the truth she could hardly tell in which direction the truth lay. If only she could put some distance between herself and her pursuers, perhaps she could reason things out.

But where could she go? The feelings of helplessness were almost overpowering. The corridor stretched in two separate directions, each leading to a stairway, and she didn't even know which way to turn. In moments, the man she'd tied up—Will Russell, not Rand Patchett—would be in pursuit of her. Her vision began to blur as the Myriad Ones attempted to overpower her will.

Help me, she begged in a silent prayer. She didn't feel worthy of an intervention, but she would do anything to escape her tormenters. Death would be preferable to the life she'd been living.

Which way?

She felt a little tug to the right. It couldn't even be described as a whisper. Just a slight nudge. And so she started that way, feeling tears in her eyes. Maybe she should go down to the inner gardens where the darkness would help conceal her. No, darkness wasn't her friend. It was the middle of the night, the peak of the Myriad Ones' power. Anguish and guilt ripped through her, and she tried to stifle a sob, failing.

She made it past the door immediately next to the suite she'd shared with Rand—no, Will—and an older man poked his head into the hallway. He saw the tears streaming down her cheeks. She felt exposed and miserable and looked away from his searching face.

"Is everything all right, demoiselle?" he asked. "I heard a commotion next door."

Nothing was all right, but his words of concern made her slow her flight. She looked at him again, taking in his kind eyes, his grandfatherly appearance.

"Someone is pursuing me," she found herself saying. "I can't stay."

"The young man . . . from your room?" said the older fellow.

Cettie nodded and was about to increase her pace when he opened the door wider.

"The Fountain bid me help you," he said, gesturing for her to come inside. "You will be safe in here."

She stopped when she heard a loud crash from the room she had fled. The kishion was free. Indecision wrenched her insides. This old man might be killed if she accepted his help.

"Monseigneur, I cannot," Cettie said, looking back at her door. She needed to run. Now.

"You *will* be safe here," he repeated, stepping away from the door.

"You will not," she said. There was something strange about the moment, almost a feeling of familiarity. Had she experienced this moment in a dream? She blinked rapidly, realizing her indecision was going to get both of them killed.

The old man gestured with his hand, palm up, silently repeating his invitation. There was a small lamp lit within the chamber, but it was full of shadows, as if he'd been sleeping until the recent disturbance.

Cettie bit her lip, unsure, and then accepted the offer for simple pragmatic reasons. She really didn't have any other choice if she wanted to escape. As she went inside, she heard the door handle jangle in the room she'd shared with the kishion. She'd escaped with not one moment to spare. The old man silently pressed his door closed, keeping the handle pressed down so that the latch wouldn't click.

"Cettie!" boomed a voice in the hallway. Will was furious.

Her heart quailed with dread. She didn't want to fight him again, but she would do it to protect the old man who'd helped her. Leaning back against the wall, gripping the pistol she had taken from Will, she used her free hand to loosen her bodice and feel for the kystrel. Despite what had happened earlier, she was desperate to rip it off. Her heartbeat pounded in her ears. Gooseflesh danced up her arms. The ghosts had followed Will out into the corridor. She swallowed, trying to make herself small. Strangely, the spectral beings did not walk through the walls.

She felt another powerful urge to rip the kystrel off her neck. Breathing quickly, dreading another surge of pain, she gripped the chain and tugged. Nothing happened this time. She snapped it off her neck.

Cettie saw a shadow come to the door. It stopped at the threshold. The old man's hand still clenched the handle. In the dim lamplight, she saw there was a patch of pure white in his gray hair, just above his ear. Again she had the sensation that she'd met him before in a dream.

She held her breath, staring at Will's shadow, willing it to pass. The kystrel dangled from the chain clenched in her fist.

And then, to her utter relief, the shadow walked away. A sigh slowly escaped her mouth. She lowered the pistol and the medallion. The ghosts had not yet left, but she sensed they were somehow blind to her presence, even the tall one who had always been able to find her. Which was bizarre because she bore a brand on her shoulder that should have summoned it.

She glanced around the room, taking in her surroundings. It was much smaller than the suite she'd been in. Just a connected washroom and two small—

A little boy lay asleep on one of the beds. He was probably eight years old and slept with such an innocent, untroubled face, Cettie's heart melted inside her. Young children had always helped her keep her ghosts at bay.

The old man waited for several more minutes before releasing the door handle. It clicked softly.

"Thank you, monseigneur," Cettie whispered, shaking her head.

"You are welcome," he replied. "Come sit. Rest. You look weary. Are you hurt?" He motioned to an empty chair.

Cettie walked across the room and parted the curtain, staring out at the night sky. There was a balcony there. She wondered if she should climb up onto the roof and find another way down to the gardens below. From there, she could circle around. It might be easier in the dark.

"I think I've trespassed on your kindness long enough," Cettie said. "Thank you for offering me shelter. But I cannot stay."

"But if you go out there tonight, it will not end well," he said simply. "They will find you." His words were filled with the confidence of someone who knew he was right.

She paused at the curtain and gave him a probing look. "Who are you?"

"A friend, if you'll have one. My name is Owen. You are . . . Cettie?"

Will had shouted her name in the corridor, but she had a suspicion the old man had already known it. She wanted to feel distrustful, to second-guess her decision to seek shelter, but she felt . . . peaceful at that moment. This was more than just the absence of anxiety. Despite the danger of her situation, she felt calm, reassured, and at peace. She hadn't felt this way since losing her connection to the Mysteries.

"Yes, that is my name," she answered. "Are you Occitanian?"

"No. I'm from Kingfountain, although I've been to Pree a few times. The Fountain sent me here a few days ago. With my grandson, Curtis." He gestured at the sleeping boy again. "I was planning to leave in the morning. Perhaps we can help you."

The sense of relief was overpowering. Again she felt tears burn in her eyes. "You don't even know me."

"I may look old, but I remember being young," he said, with a wry smile. "Being afraid. Alone. You remind me of someone I used to know. Someone who helped me when I was that age." He nodded to his sleeping grandson. "I came to Pree for a reason, Cettie. The Fountain bid me here. To help you, I think. If you will let me."

"The Fountain," Cettie whispered, shaking her head. He'd said that once before, but she'd been too overwrought to heed his words. The Fountain and the Mysteries were two manifestations of the Knowing. They were one and the same. She'd asked for help from the Mysteries, and this man had been sent to her. She had forsaken her oaths, but if there was a way back, she'd take it.

"You don't have to decide now. Wait until morning. Here, you sleep on my bed. I'll stand watch through the night to make sure that man does not return. We can discuss things after you've rested. Would that be all right?"

She was still afraid, but she accepted his offer with a nod and stepped away from the window. If the Mysteries had truly brought her there, it was time for her to start heeding them.

She stared at the kystrel in her hand a moment, wondering what to do with it.

"Here. Give it to me," he offered, holding out his hand.

"I wish I could destroy it," she said.

"It's caused you pain?"

She nodded vehemently.

He pinned it to the edge of the small table, the whorl design reminding her of a snake preparing to strike. Then he removed a dagger from his belt and, not hesitating once, used the hilt to strike the kystrel. To her shock, it snapped in half, and part of it fell to the floor with a little thump.

She stared at the broken kystrel on the floor, the edges glimmering in the light. Its power over her had been broken too.

How strange that something that had impacted her life in such an immense way could be destroyed with such ease. She also removed the ring she'd been given to disguise herself and set it on the table. She wanted nothing to do with the school she'd been forced to stay at.

As she lay down on top of the mattress and blanket, a heavy weariness washed over her. She could see the boy's face in the lamplight. Then she remembered something as she fell asleep. When the ghosts used to come for her in the Fells, she'd avoid them by surrounding herself with the youngest children. The ghosts could not reach her with them nearby. Was it a coincidence that the grandfather had brought his grandson to Pree?

That thought lingered in her mind just a moment longer. And then Cettie slept.

She awoke to the sound of a child's voice. "Who is she, Papa?"

"Her name is Cettie. Isn't that a pretty name?"

Her eyes blinked awake. The room was suffused with morning light. She'd slept soundly, not stirring once. At least, not that she could remember. Back at the poisoner school, she'd become accustomed to waking up in a different place from where she'd lain down to sleep, especially before she accepted the kystrel, but every moment of the previous night was burned into her brain. Being freed from the Myriad Ones. Fighting with Will. Hearing his threats—the promise he'd made to murder Adam if she revolted. Fleeing the room. Accepting the old stranger's invitation.

"Hello!" the boy said to her sweetly, raising a little paw and waving at her. His hair was long and slightly mussed from sleep. His smile was infectious.

Cettie lifted herself from the bed on her arms. "Good morning, Curtis," she greeted.

He walked over and gave her a hug, the gesture full of an easy, generous affection she hadn't experienced in a long, long while. She stroked his hair and kissed the top of his head.

"Papa said you're coming with us!" he said eagerly, stepping back.

"If she chooses, Curtis. Only if she chooses."

Cettie swung her legs over the side of the bed. The night of pure rest had transformed her. She felt more like herself—her old self. How strange that the transformation should come about so quickly. It was like awakening from a nightmare.

The old man, Owen, stood from the chair, which he'd moved closer to the door to keep watch. "Where do you need to go, Cettie? We can take you there."

"I appreciate your kindness. I truly do. But I don't think you can take me to where I need to go." Worry for Adam welled in her gut, sickening her.

"And where would that be?" he asked.

"I am . . . I'm not from your world," she answered. "I need to get to the empire of Comoros. But there is a war between our worlds."

The boy gave his grandfather a smile and a knowing look.

"We can help you," Owen said. "There are . . . other ways to cross worlds. I happen to know of one. It's in Brythonica, which is not a long journey from Pree. My wife's family is from Ploemeur. I know the way."

The boy gave Cettie an entreating look. "Please come with us, Cettie."

The Fountain had guided them to be at the hotel when she would be there. It had provided her with a way to escape her prison. Gratitude swelled inside her as she nodded. Getting away from Pree would help, but the thought of anything bad happening to these two souls made her cringe. She would not recklessly endanger them.

"Those seeking me will be watching the hotel closely," Cettie said. "I would need to disguise myself."

Owen looked around the room. "I did bring a rather large trunk. You just might fit inside of it?"

She saw it against the wall beside Curtis's bed. "But your clothes, your things."

"All can be replaced," he said with a dismissive wave of his hand.

"Your kindness is overwhelming," Cettie said.

"It is a very small thing. Your life seems to have its fill of troubles. I've survived plenty of my own, and I've learned to trust the whispers from the Fountain. They've led me right thus far. Just as they will for you."

Cettie's heart panged again. "I hope that's still true," she said, feeling a horrible surge of guilt.

"Isn't it a miracle that we are even here? That there is enough air to breathe? That a burning sun keeps this world perfectly warm . . . just as it does on your planet? On both worlds there is water to drink and food to eat. And good people that we can call friends and family." He reached out and mussed up Curtis's hair. "Do you think there is anything this child could do that would stop me from loving him?" He gave Cettie a piercing look, one that cut her straight down to her soul. "He might get into a little mischief. He might even do wrong. But he's mine. And I will always love him." He beamed down at the little boy, hooking his arm around the lad's neck. The boy smiled up at his grandfather with pride and love and hugged him around the waist.

Owen reminded her a little of Fitzroy. Older, more experienced, but they shared a deep wisdom, something she'd always admired in Fitzroy.

That thought made a shiver run down Cettie's spine. The way Owen loved Curtis was the way her father, her *true* father, had loved her. In the beautiful morning sunshine, she felt close to him in a way that transcended reason. As if he were in the very room with them.

Can you see me, Father? she thought into the stillness.

She felt a rush of warmth inside her that felt like an answer. Cettie hung her head and began to cry softly.

"Well, let's get this chest emptied, shall we, Curtis?" Owen suggested. She could tell he'd made the suggestion to give her a moment to gather herself. Together, the man and the boy heaved the chest up onto the bed. It was long, long enough to fit Cettie if she curled up inside it. When they opened it, she saw a pile of folded clothes, an extra set of boots, a sword and scabbard. Owen unfastened his belt and slid it through the scabbard. It was an older sword, different from sabers the dragoons used. But it was the scabbard that made her stare. It bore the symbol of a raven, and she felt chords of magic emanating from it as Owen buckled it on. It was a melodious sound, pure and powerful.

As he finished cinching the belt, it struck her with powerful certainty that this man knew how to use that sword. She had no doubt of it.

"Let's leave some clothes in there so it's comfortable for her, Papa," said Curtis. He gave her a knowing smile. His childlike innocence made the world seem brighter than it had just yesterday.

"You can get me back to my world?" Cettie asked, the thread of hope growing thicker. "They will try to harm those I love."

Owen nodded. "Trust me. We can get you home faster than you think."

The idea came to me this morning during my walk. Regardless of what time I am abed at night, I always awaken before the rising of the sun and take a brisk walk in the tenements surrounding the hospital. It gives me time to think, to ponder, to wrestle with the issues from the previous day.

I know the officers of Law use a map of the Fells in their efforts to hunt the Fear Liath that was set loose here. They mark the streets where victims are found. The idea came to me to use the same tool to keep track of the victims of the cholera morbus. If I understand their commonalities, perhaps I can discover how the disease is carried. A certain type of food they eat, perhaps. Something they drink. I already know it cannot be the air they breathe.

I fear that if we do not find the source of the plague soon, there will not be enough boxes to bury them all in.

—Adam Creigh, Killingworth Hospital

SERA

CHAPTER ELEVEN

MR. BATEWINCH

Mrs. Pullman brought food twice more, as well as the sickly sweet cider that Sera refused to drink. Her thirst had become an intense, powerful urge. It made Sera suffer in a way she had never suffered before. Her arm was still throbbing, the wound a nasty reddish black, and the cut on her face pulsed with pain. Confined in her little room, hurting and parched, Sera could do little else than wonder what Lady Corinne would do to her next.

Being in the dark made her lose all sense of time. It felt like she had been there for days, but it couldn't have been that long, could it? The lack of water would have killed her.

The isolation was its own kind of torture. Her thoughts spooled in dizzying circles as she tried to think of a way to escape. She'd tested each portion of her little cell, looking for weakness. But she lacked the strength to pry anything open. Thankfully, there were no rats scuttling in the dark. Sera wondered if she could overpower Mrs. Pullman, but how? One of her arms was practically useless. She worried a physical scuffle with the old woman would end in humiliating defeat.

So Sera reached out to the Mysteries, asking for a way out of her predicament. She focused on the idea of escaping, willing something to happen to change her fortune. It was tempting to grumble inside about her condition, but surely Trevon had experienced worse, and his abduction had lasted more than a year already.

If he can bear it, so can you.

The thought gave her strength, and it made her feel closer to her husband than she had the past year.

More time passed, she wasn't sure how much, when she heard a noise coming from beyond the door. Acting on instinct, Sera scooted closer to it, though she did not yet have a plan for how to best Mrs. Pullman. It struck her that the steps sounded different now.

A pulse shivered in the air, and the Leering outside the door spilled light into the corridor. From the crack beneath the door, she thought she saw a different pair of shoes—a man's set. Was this someone who could help her? The feet shuffled a bit, as if the person were searching for something.

Sera sat up and knocked on the door. "Can you hear me? Help!"

"Goodness gracious, who is that?" asked a gruff voice. The steps drew quickly to the door, and the handle jangled. It was still locked.

"Can you hear me?" Sera asked, hope flooding her chest.

"I can. Who is this? Who locked you in here?"

"Mrs. Pullman locked me in here."

"Who the devil is Mrs. Pullman?"

Sera could tell the man was befuddled by the situation. She had to think quickly. "She's the keeper of the manor."

"No, the keeper at Gimmerton Sough is Mrs. Rosings." The handle jangled again. "Who is Mrs. Pullman?"

Sera closed her eyes. "Who are you, good sir? What is your name?"

"I am Mr. Batewinch, the steward of Gimmerton Sough."

Sera bit her lip to prevent herself from squealing. She knew that name. Cettie had told her about him, about his arrival at Gimmerton Sough with the Patchett siblings. So she was at Gimmerton Sough, which she knew Lady Corinne owned. That made perfect sense. At least the woman hadn't stowed her in some far-flung part of Kingfountain. She was still home. There was still hope.

"Mr. Batewinch, please listen to me," Sera said in a trembling voice. "I am Sera Fitzempress. I was abducted by Lady Corinne Lawton, who is a traitor to the empire. My life is in grave danger. Please, you must free me and contact the ministries immediately. There is a Control Leering here at the estate, is there not? You must contact them at once and tell them where I am."

"Y-your Majesty?" Mr. Batewinch said with utter confusion in his voice. "You're the empress? I don't understand. Is this some trick?"

Sera wanted to reach through the door and clutch his shirt. Instead, she took a deep breath to calm her emotions and spoke as quickly as she could. "No trick, Mr. Batewinch. I know your name. I know you were Admiral Patchett's steward. That you've tried to look after his children, Joanna and Randall, as best you can. Please, sir, you must help me. Your keeper may be an imposter. Her real name is Mrs. Pullman—the same Mrs. Pullman who used to work at Fog Willows. She's been feeding me, but she's in league with Lady Corinne. Please! I beg you, send for help immediately."

"Your story sounds a little far-fetched," said Mr. Batewinch. "But either way, a young woman shouldn't be kept locked in the cellar. One of the serving girls told me she'd seen Mrs. Rosings carrying food down here and feared someone was being confined as a punishment."

Sera felt a gush of gratitude for the faithful servant who had reported it.

"Please summon help," Sera said. "You will see that I'm not lying." She thought a moment. The nearest officers would be at the Fells, but Fog Willows was closer. "Can you tell me . . . is Lady Maren at Fog Willows still?"

"Of course. And so is Master Stephen."

"Send her word right away. She knows me, she would vouch for me."

"All right, miss. I won't delay. Whatever trouble you are in, I'm sure we can work it out. Are you really the empress?"

"I am, Mr. Batewinch. I swear by the Mysteries."

"No need to do that," he said. "I'll return promptly. I don't like the idea of anyone being confined in there. This won't do."

Sera's gratitude was overpowering. She leaned her forehead against the door, listening as Mr. Batewinch's footsteps went down the corridor. Then the sound was gone, and she was once more bathed in silence.

Turning, Sera leaned back against the door, her stomach in knots. She nursed her sore arm and regretted not asking Mr. Batewinch to bring her some water. If only she could break the door with her fists. If only Mr. Batewinch had been hale enough to do so for her.

Trembling with anticipation, she waited in the stillness. The steward had left the Leering alight, so she focused on the band of light glowing beneath the door. Each minute felt like ages, but the worst was over. Soon she'd be on a zephyr rushing back to Lockhaven. Lady Corinne had the Tay al-Ard, which made her even more dangerous, but Sera would thwart her, defy her, hunt her down, and bring her to justice.

She heard the sound of footsteps again and recognized the tread as that of the shoes she'd heard earlier.

"Mr. Batewinch?" she called.

"Yes, I am returned." He sounded out of breath. "I couldn't get the Leering to work. I couldn't reach anyone. I don't know what's going on."

"She's controlling it," Sera said, her frustration growing. She scowled, made a fist with her good hand, and struck the door. It only made her fingers hurt.

"So I fetched a crowbar," Mr. Batewinch said. "I'm going to force the door open. Stand back, if you please."

Sera's fury turned to joy. She was to be freed after all. She stepped back, her heart beating double time in her chest. The sound of the metal biting into the wood, the wood crunching beneath the assault, thrilled her.

"Give me a few moments," Mr. Batewinch wheezed out.

Another sound of footsteps mingled with the other noises.

"Someone is coming!" Sera warned.

The crunching stopped.

"Whatever are you doing in the cellar, Mr. Batewinch?" said Mrs. Pullman in a calm drawl.

"I'm rescuing some poor soul you've locked up down here," he answered. "I see you've got the keys . . . I order you to unlock this door at once."

"Do I tell you your business, Mr. Batewinch?" said Mrs. Pullman.

"Unlock this door at once!"

Sera felt a growing sense of dread as an oily feeling seeped toward her, sapping her hope and dimming the bright light coming in from under the door. Her pulse quickened as a spasm of fear shot through her.

"Who are you?" Batewinch demanded, his voice trembling.

"You mean nothing to me," said Mrs. Pullman in a dead, merciless voice. Sera heard her shoes approaching, slapping the floor one after the other, slow but sure. The light of her lantern only appeared to increase the shadows in the corridor.

Then Sera heard a thump, the sound of a body thudding against a wall, and a horrible hissing wheeze. Somehow she knew it was the sound of a man struggling to breathe.

"Let him go!" Sera said, pounding on the door. Then she shrieked as Mr. Batewinch's body collided with the other side of the door with a solid thump. The body sagged to the floor, blotting all but the edges of the light.

This darkness wasn't just the absence of light. She felt the presence of the Myriad Ones, a power she'd not felt since taking the Test at Muirwood Abbey. Sera stood back, swallowing her fear, trying to repel the dark power radiating from the other side of the door.

She heard what was unmistakably the sound of a heavy object striking Mr. Batewinch's skull. A gasp escaped her lips. When the key went
into the lock, Sera tried to radiate bravery and strength, but her knees
were knocking together.

Mr. Batewinch fell back into the cell, his eyes open, his chest still.

Mrs. Pullman stood in the frame of the door, her face in shadows.
She gripped her lantern in her hand. Power and strength emanated from
her despite her wizened frame, dark, dark, dark.

"You killed him," Sera whispered.

"Everyone dies," Mrs. Pullman answered, her tone flat and uncaring.

Sera steeled herself. She remembered the words to banish the
Myriad Ones. To gain power over them.

Sera stood firm and began to say, *"Banirex—"*

Mrs. Pullman rushed forward and clamped her hand around Sera's
throat, cutting off the words. With inhuman strength, the old keeper
pressed her against the far wall of the cell. Sera tried wrestling the hand
from her throat, but the woman's grip was stronger than iron. She
couldn't breathe.

"That only works," Mrs. Pullman sneered, squeezing harder, "on
some of them."

Spots began to dance in front of Sera's eyes, but just when she was
certain she'd suffocate, Mrs. Pullman suddenly released her grip. Sera
dropped to the floor, gasping for breath. The spots still crowded her
vision, but she blinked rapidly, trying not to faint.

Mrs. Pullman dragged the body of Mr. Batewinch into the cell and
left it in the middle of the floor.

"Now you have company," said the old woman with a gleam of
malice.

Sera stroked her neck. She could still feel where the old woman's
fingers had dug into her skin. There would be bruises for certain.

Mrs. Pullman slid the crowbar out of the steward's limp hand. She turned to leave, only to swivel back around when she reached the doorway.

"Who are you to rule over us?" Mrs. Pullman said in a low, callous way. "You're weak. Powerless. You don't deserve the gilded palace you live in. What work have you ever done in your whole life? Your luck was to be born. That is all. Any mewling brat can be born. Our queen will soon rule in your place. All will kneel before her, out of dread, out of fear. You've had your chance, false empress. Now another comes. You are not worthy to lick the ground at her feet."

The words were calculated in their malice. Designed to weaken someone's will, to damage their sense of self. To make them feel unworthy of anything good.

Everything she'd said was a lie.

Sera could not help but think of Cettie as a girl, at the mercy of this cruel old woman. The image made her hate Mrs. Pullman even more.

"Not if I can help it," Sera vowed, staring at the old woman with a look that promised vengeance. "You won't kill me, Mrs. Pullman. Without me, that Leering will be closed forever."

"She knows your weaknesses, child," said Mrs. Pullman with a smile. "You will open the tomb of Ereshkigal. You'll have no other choice."

CHAPTER TWELVE
THE ADMIRAL'S DAUGHTER

The darkness was even more suffocating with a dead body in the room. *Poor Mr. Batewinch,* Sera thought. Lady Corinne had left so many bodies in her wake. She remembered the day she'd found Mr. Skrelling's body rotting on the beach below Pavenham Sky. The horror of seeing Lord Fitzroy's body flung off a balcony to an angry mob below.

Lady Corinne could slice Sera's body like so many ribbons. She could poison her, torture her, cripple her. But she could not break her will. Only Sera could do that.

She'd learned much from observing people through the Command Leering in Lockhaven. Not all who lived in the City were miserable. Even the most oppressed woman, scrubbing dirty clothes in a stagnant fountain, could still whistle and sing while she worked. Many of her people, no matter how poor, had a resilience that made her heart proud of them. She, too, could be strong. Determined.

But the prophecy says you're the one who will open it.

Sera huddled in the dark, considering the words Sinia had uttered so long ago. Sera did not *want* to release such an evil being, but events seemed to be drawing her inexorably toward some fate. Would she be forced to free Ereshkigal in the end? Would they twist her feelings for someone she loved to make her yield?

What had Corinne done to Cettie? Was she also being tortured, or would she be used against Sera in some way?

Would they harm Trevon if she did not fall into line?

Her arm throbbed, her face itched, and her throat craved a drink— sensations that had only grown keener with each passing hour. She leaned back against the wall, struggling to suppress a growing sense of dread.

What would you have me do? Sera thought into the blackness, reaching out to the Mysteries. *Guide me, lead my steps. I will do what you wish of me. No matter what it may cost me.*

In the quiet stillness of the cellar, she waited, straining for an answer. Some form of direction.

It came, but in a most unexpected form. She had the intuition that perhaps Mr. Batewinch had a flask or a waterskin on his person.

That would mean searching a dead man. She shuddered at the thought, but her thirst insisted she try. She crept forward on her knees, reaching out with one hand. When she touched his body, it was unnaturally cool. The life force within him, the soul that had caused his body to generate heat and breath, was gone. She fumbled in the darkness, using only her right hand. A jacket? Pockets. She searched them, finding a few coins, a silk handkerchief. There was a little box made of metal. When she opened it, the strong sweet odor of peppermint filled her cell.

She had to struggle with the body to turn it over to check the other side, a horrific task. Some papers, which she couldn't read in the dark. And then, in his pants pocket, she discovered a penknife, something one used to sharpen a quill or a pencil. The blade was folded down and not very long. Excitement thrummed inside her.

Using her teeth, she released the blade, which snicked into place. She instantly thought of the wooden doorframe. She rose and carried the penknife to the door, feeling the edges where the latch fit into place.

JEFF WHEELER

The blade plunged into the soft wood easily. Sera bit her lip and began scraping away.

She worked at it for hours, digging and twisting, and breaking off little pieces of bark. Time had already lost all sense of meaning to her, but she felt urgency to complete the task. Occasionally, splinters would jab her fingers. She ignored the blood, carving and gouging and prying at the wood until the large piece on the other side of the bolt came free.

Her efforts were rewarded when the door swung open.

Her first instinct was to light the Leering and see her way out, but she stopped herself, knowing that Mrs. Pullman, as the keeper of the house, would sense it. She could pass the Leering in the dark, however, and its eyes would be blind to her. Gripping the penknife in her good hand, she slowly walked down the corridor, bumping into barrels along the way. Her senses screamed at her to run, lest Mrs. Pullman return, but her logical mind knew it was best to walk slowly, keeping aware of her surroundings. And so she continued to walk slowly, one foot in front of the other. At the end of the corridor was another door, but this one wasn't locked. Sera twisted the handle and sighed with relief when it opened.

Darkness greeted her on the other side. No windows were nearby, but the lack of any glowing Leerings indicated it was nighttime. Sera carefully shut the door behind her and stepped forward until she reached a set of stairs. She climbed them swiftly, her ears keen for any sound that would reveal danger. Every muscle in her body was taut with dread.

After mounting the steps, she found herself in another storage room and continued to bump into crates and chests. She had to feel her way from wall to wall until she found the door. After turning its handle, she was greeted by moonlight pouring in through a high window. Her eyes, sharpened by the hours she'd spent in the dark, could make out the details as if it were the brightest day. There was a corridor, carpeted, which led in two different directions. Which to choose?

She paused at the doorframe, listening for sounds. Hearing none, she took a right and quickly found a dead-end and a locked door. So she

118

reversed her path and went the other way. The gauzy curtains fluttered as she passed them, and the moonlight through the windows continued to light her path.

The corridor deposited her in another hallway. She quickly looked both ways, her heart pounding with excitement and fear. She brushed her wrist against her mouth to remove a sheen of sweat from her upper lip.

From what Cettie had told her about Gimmerton Sough, and from what she remembered from attending a ball long ago, it was not a vast estate. If Sera could find her way to the landing yard, she could steal a zephyr and be off. Or, barring that, hide until the zephyr post came.

Light.

Sera froze, watching as the yellow gleam of a lantern rounded the corner, heading her way. Mrs. Pullman held a lantern in one hand and carried a tray of food in the other.

Sera quickly backtracked, trying not to scuff her shoes on the carpet or make any sound at all. Her heartbeat, already worried, now beat frantically. She had passed a staircase going up and decided to take it. If Mrs. Pullman were heading to the cellar, she'd soon know that Sera had escaped. That meant she needed to find a place to hide, a place where the keeper could not use the Leerings' eyes to track her down.

As she mounted the steps, she kept her eyes fixed on the approaching glow of the lantern beneath her.

Which was why she didn't see Joanna Patchett coming down the stairs until they collided.

~

Joanna gasped with fear, but didn't cry out. Neither did Sera.

"Are you hiding from Mrs. Rosings?" Joanna whispered. A band of moonlight revealed her concerned expression to Sera. She was wearing a white nightgown and shawl.

"Yes," Sera whispered back.

Joanna nodded and gripped her shoulder, tugging her upstairs. "This way. I'll hide you."

Sera followed, and they turned the corner on the curving stairway just before Mrs. Pullman arrived at the bottom of the steps.

"Who's up there?" Mrs. Pullman's voice rang out.

They both froze on the steps. Joanna pressed a finger to her own lips, a signal to be quiet.

"You get to bed right away," Mrs. Pullman snapped. "If I catch you in the corridors, you'll be dismissed."

Sera had a rush of uncomfortable intuition. If Mrs. Pullman hadn't been carrying a tray, she would have followed them up the stairs. The light retreated.

The last time Sera had seen Joanna Patchett was at one of the balls she'd held in Lockhaven. As Lady Corinne's popularity and influence had waned, Joanna's had risen proportionately. She was a charming and affectionate girl, a gossip, and Sera had always liked her because she'd befriended Cettie.

But wasn't it odd that Lady Corinne had chosen to hide Sera in Gimmerton Sough, a floating manor that she owned and had leased to the Patchett siblings? Moreover, Joanna and Rand were the children of dead admiral Patchett, who had been a close friend of Lady Corinne's husband. Could Joanna be trusted?

"This way," Joanna said in a low voice, guiding Sera down the hall.

Sera stopped, shaking off the other woman's hand.

Joanna stopped and looked back at her. "Do you want to get caught?"

"Where are you taking me?"

"To my brother's room. He's gone right now. No one goes in there. She won't be able to find you."

"Why do you say that?"

Joanna drew closer. "It's one of the Mysteries. I can't explain it. Just trust me. She can see into almost every room in the house. Except that one."

That meant there were no Leerings in it. If Joanna recognized her, she hadn't indicated it. The dark may well have kept her identity secret, for the moment. Sera decided she had no choice but to trust Joanna, so she nodded. When the lady of the house turned and walked down the hall, she followed her to a closed door. Joanna opened it, revealing yet another dark room.

"I'll light a candle. Give me a moment," Joanna said.

Sera stood at the entryway, trembling with worry. The room smelled of leather and a musky scent.

There was a strike of sparks, then a taper was lit, which was used to light a candle.

"Come inside. Quickly. Shut the door."

Sera hesitated a moment and then did so, pressing her back against the door, ready to flee if need be.

"What has she done to you?" Joanna said, holding up the candle. "You've got blood on your dress. And your cheek is—"

The light had finally revealed Sera's face. Joanna's eyes bulged in surprise.

"Your Highness!" she gasped.

"I've been abducted," Sera answered, concealing the penknife behind her back. She didn't truly trust Joanna. Her surprise seemed genuine, but she'd been deceived before.

"What? How?"

"Lady Corinne brought me here. You didn't know?"

"Certainly not! The servants have been acting strangely all day. And Mrs. Rosings said the steward fell ill suddenly. I was on my way just now to check on him. Something doesn't feel right. I never thought . . . I'm in total shock."

Sera glanced around the room. "Where's your brother?"

Joanna shrugged. "I don't know. He's been gone for several days. But that's not unlike him." She continued to gawk at Sera. "Look at your face. Did Mrs. Rosings do that?"

"No, it was Lady Corinne," Sera said. "They were keeping me in the cellar. Mr. Batewinch tried to call for help, but the keeper has tampered with the Control Leering. She . . . she killed him. Mrs. Rosings isn't her real name. She's Mrs. Pullman. She used to be the keeper of Fog Willows years ago."

Joanna's face lost color, and her mouth dropped open into a little O when Sera revealed poor Mr. Batewinch's face. "Mrs. Pullman?" she said at last. "She came by recommendation of Lady Corinne, who told Mr. Batewinch to hire her."

"That doesn't surprise me," Sera said. "So you knew nothing of this?"

Joanna shook her head quickly. "I thought you were one of the servants out wandering the hall at night. I know Mrs. Ro—well, whoever she is, doesn't like it. The servants don't like her, but she's always been very pleasant to me. I . . . I can't believe we were living with someone like that all this time."

Sera's trust was growing, but her instincts urged her to take care. They told her that all was not as it seemed. "Are you a maston, Joanna? Did you pass the Test?"

Joanna hung her head. "I did not."

"Can you . . . I know this sounds strange, but can you open your nightgown a bit? I need to see if you're wearing any jewelry. A medallion specifically."

Joanna's eyebrows bunched at the request. "I have a locket my mother gave me. How did you know?"

Dread grew in Sera's heart. "Can I see it, please?" She adjusted her grip on the knife.

Joanna set the candle down on a nearby dresser. Sera watched her closely, concerned that the other woman might attack her if she relaxed her vigilance. Joanna unbuttoned a few buttons on her nightgown, revealing a golden chain and locket. Sera's heart raced. Was it a kystrel?

Joanna pulled the locket out of her bodice. The candlelight made it gleam. It was the size of a gold coin with decorative edges.

"It was my mother's," Joanna said, angling it toward the light.

"Can you take it off? I'd like to see it more closely."

Joanna reached behind her neck and worked at the clasp. When the chain dropped away, falling into Joanna's cupped hand, Sera nearly jumped out of her skin.

"Here," Joanna said, handing the locket over.

That surprised Sera. She'd learned from the Aldermastons that a hetaera never removed a kystrel willingly unless she was giving it to someone else who planned to use it. Sharing it that way would expand her power. As Sera took it, she felt no energy or magic emanating from it. The metal was warm, but only because it had been against Joanna's skin. Sera turned it over, seeing the worn and antique facade. Although there were decorative patterns on it, none of them contained the whorl-like symbol of the kystrel.

"How did you know I had it?" Joanna asked.

"I thought it was . . . something else," Sera said.

The sound of a key entering a lock came from behind Sera. She whirled and heard the mechanism click into place, locking them in the room. She grabbed at the handle, trying to twist it, but she was too late.

They were trapped.

CHAPTER THIRTEEN

HER GRACE

"What are we going to do?" Joanna whispered as the light from the candle flickered. Sera stared at the door, the barrier, and felt like screaming in frustration. This door was even sturdier than the one in the cellar.

"I don't know," Sera said, her voice sounding miserable even to her own ears. But she would not give up hope. There were other servants in the house. Could they be alerted? She rubbed her forehead, feeling the weariness, pain, and fear weigh on her. She still wasn't sure she could trust Joanna.

"Here, sit down. There is so much blood. Let me see if I can wash some of it away. I think there might be some water in that pitcher. There's a towel by Rand's shaving bowl."

"Water!" Sera said greedily, seeing the pitcher on a nearby dresser. She rushed to it and thankfully, mercifully, it was still half full. She didn't care how old and musty it was, she drank deeply from it, finding relief at long last. Never had a drink been so refreshing. Joanna stared at her as if she were slightly daft, but didn't comment on it. There was still plenty of water left after she was done.

"Here, let me help you," Joanna said. She poured water into the shaving bowl and dipped the towel into it. Sera sat on the cushioned seat by the table. It struck her that this was where Joses must have shaved Rand every morning—before the valet's death. As part of her fruitless search for Cettie, she had heard multiple reports of that fateful day, the day before Cettie vanished. Joses, Cettie's childhood friend from the Fells, had been killed by the Fear Liath in front of her eyes. The mental anguish must have been excruciating.

Where are you, Cettie?

The sting of Joanna's ministrations as she wiped away the encrusted blood on her cheek jolted her from her thoughts.

Wincing, Sera asked, "Did your brother get a new valet after Joses died?"

"No," Joanna answered. "It's hard to find someone of quality these days, especially with the war going on. All the young men are off fighting. His room's a mess, as you can clearly see, because of it."

"How is Rand? Is he still considering public office?" Sera asked, scrunching her nose. She hadn't kept up with the Patchetts much since Cettie's departure, other than hearing about the brother's failed attempt at politics. And talking would help distract her from the pain.

"Do you really want to talk about my brother?" Joanna said with a hint of doubt. "I'm tending the empress in my brother's chamber because my keeper is holding us both hostage and killed our steward. This may be normal for you, Your Highness, but I'm a little rattled."

"This is not normal," Sera agreed. She looked up, meeting Joanna's eyes. "It's hard to trust anyone these days. When I first met you, it was at Pavenham Sky. Do you remember?"

Joanna squeezed the towel over the basin and then dipped it again in the water. "I remember it well. You were being snubbed by everyone during one of Lady Corinne's teas."

"You remember that?" Sera asked.

"I said I wished the war had never started. Cettie once told me that you met Prince Trevon there in disguise. He'd dropped a tray and made a mess. Your missing husband."

The words stabbed into her, but she shook off the pain. "That's right. It was him. In disguise. A good disguise can make a prince into a pauper, an enemy into a friend. And so you can naturally understand that I'm more than a little concerned about your loyalty."

"Now we're *really* talking," Joanna said with a small smile. "I'd suspect me too, I suppose. The last time I saw Lady Corinne was when she came here a year ago to thwart my brother's political ambitions. I was devastated when Pavenham Sky fell. And I've lived in dread that Gimmerton Sough may suffer the same fate. She owns it, after all. Why did the one manor plummet to the earth and not the other?"

"That's not very comforting," Sera said.

"It's not supposed to be. I don't even like this house. It's gone dark again."

"What do you mean?" Sera pressed.

"When we first moved here, things were strange. The Leerings didn't work very well. I didn't pass the Test, you know, but I did *take* it. This estate was full of . . . dark beings. Mr. Batewinch couldn't control the main Leering. No matter what he did, the dark ones kept coming back and haunting our halls. Until Cettie came. For some reason, the Leerings obeyed her. I was grateful to her for that, and for what she did for Rand. He was very low back then. I feared he'd try to kill himself."

Joanna finished scrubbing at Sera's cheek. "Well, I think I got the rest of the blood off this scratch. But your arm is an entirely different mess. You were stabbed?"

"Lady Corinne did it."

"I never would have thought her capable of such an act," Joanna said. "She was always so mild, in person. But she was very cunning. I don't know why she made me part of her set. It was almost as if . . ." She hesitated, shaking her head.

"Go on," Sera pressed. Joanna was trying to pick the bloodied dress away from the wound, but it was a dried, wrinkled mess.

"I don't want to make this worse. I'm not a doctor. Maybe if I just cut away the sleeve? I'd need a knife, though."

"I have one," Sera said, realizing she was still gripping the penknife in her good hand. She wanted to hand it over, but her feelings of distrust throbbed to life again. Sera paused, taking a deep breath, and stared into Joanna's eyes. "I have to ask you a question first. Do not lie to me, Joanna. If you help me escape, I will reward you and I will forgive any past treachery, but I need to know if I can trust you."

Her words had shaken Joanna. The young woman blinked rapidly, her eyes large in the dim room, but then she nodded in agreement. "What do you want to ask me?"

"Are you a poisoner?"

Joanna flinched. "A poisoner? Are you serious?"

"I am very serious," Sera answered. "Look me in the eye and answer me."

"I'm not, Sera. Truly. I'm not. The only way I even know what one is because Rand's told me about them."

"Rand?"

She nodded vigorously. "He . . . he knows things. From the Ministry of War, I think. He told me once that he thought I'd make a good poisoner. I thought he was jesting."

She was so convincing. Her words felt true. But Sera still wasn't convinced. The medallion Joanna wore didn't have the traditional markings, but hetaera often gave their kystrels to someone else to wear. She knew, from the spies they'd captured, that hetaera had brands on their shoulders. Even Empress Maia had carried the mark on her shoulder.

"You don't believe me," Joanna said, shaking her head. "How can I prove myself loyal to you, Sera? I know my brother and I will be ruined if I do not help you. Believe me, I don't want that. I'll do anything I can to prove myself to you."

Sera sighed. "Can I see your shoulders?"

"My shoulders? Why?"

"I cannot tell you. But if you want me to trust you, then do as I ask."

"That's a strange request to make."

"I know." Sera sat still on the stuffed chair, staring at Joanna with an unflinching gaze.

Joanna shrugged and opened more of the buttons on her night-gown. She then slipped the fabric down on her right shoulder, revealing the pale, unmarked skin.

"The other one too," Sera said.

Joanna lifted the fabric up again and then turned and pulled the nightdress down on the other side. "What do you think you'll find?" she asked curiously. She gave Sera an arch look from over her shoulder. There was nothing. Nothing but . . .

Joanna was about to pull the nightgown back up, when Sera stood up from the cushioned seat. "Wait."

The young woman paused, confusion on her face. "What is it?"

"Something on your neck," Sera lied. "Look away."

Joanna's brow wrinkled. She turned her face away from Sera, who took up the wet towel. There was a slightly different coloring on Joanna's shoulder. It had almost escaped her notice, but the candlelight had revealed it. Sera raised the moist towel and dragged it across the spot. The discoloration wiped away, revealing a brand. The fountain lily Sera recognized from the shoulders of the other hetaera they'd caught.

Joanna's hand seized Sera's wrist, her grip punishing, and pulled it away. As if nothing had happened, she lifted the gown to conceal the brand again and buttoned up her nightdress. She turned to face Sera, her expression angry but not alarmed.

Sera licked her lips and shook her head slowly. "You are very good. I *almost* believed you."

Joanna cocked her head. "I knew it would be hard deceiving you, Your Grace. I hoped it would work."

"How long?" Sera demanded.

Joanna's eyebrows wrinkled in a mute question.

"How long have you infiltrated the empire? I'm assuming when you first arrived with your brother." Sera stopped, looking askance at Joanna. "Or is he really your brother? He's not, is he?"

Joanna smirked. "No, we just pretend to be siblings. I may as well tell you. The irony is delicious."

"What do you mean?" Sera asked.

"Randall Patchett is being confined at the poisoner school where I was trained. He believes he's making a sacrifice to save his younger sister's life. He doesn't know that she's being held at another school. The Rand you know is Will Russell."

Sera started. "He didn't die?" It struck her that this other part of the war, silent and full of layer after layer of deceit and trickery, had been in motion for years.

"You're beginning to see now, aren't you?" Joanna said smugly. "We began recruiting Will when your father sent him away. Nothing chafes a man more than being robbed of his inheritance . . . or his opportunity for glory. He was a prime target. His feelings of revenge against you and your father were fierce. The accident on the sky ship . . . it ruined him. He'd always relied on his looks, but his face was mangled, scarred. Everyone thought he was dead, but we were waiting for him beneath the waves. Will is a kishion now. He can't wait to see you again. We promised him his revenge, and he will get it."

Sera felt revulsion at the words and the callous way Joanna delivered them. "So he never cared for Cettie. It was a ruse, a plot."

"You're very astute, Your Grace," Joanna said.

"And what about you?" Sera pressed, trying to subdue her outrage and anger. "How is it you both look like the Patchett siblings? Is it magic?"

"I cannot tell you, Your Grace. It's a *Mystery*." She smiled condescendingly. "As for myself, I'm here to keep you under guard until Corinne returns."

"Is that even who she is?" Sera demanded. "Or is it another trick? Another deception?"

Joanna's brow narrowed. "I'm not at liberty to divulge *all* of our secrets, Your Grace. This game would have been more fun if I'd fooled you. If you think cutting me with that little knife will do you any good, I'd like to disabuse you of that notion. You cannot hurt me. Though if you feel the need to try, by all means, do so."

Sera felt a little foolish brandishing a penknife against someone who'd been given years of training as a poisoner. Rather than allow Joanna to twist it out of her hand, she dropped it on the floor, listening to it rattle as it landed.

"Where's Cettie?" Sera asked.

Joanna gave her a long, probing look. "She's on her way back to Lockhaven as we speak. She's a hetaera now. And a poisoner. She will become you."

Sera closed her eyes. Not her friend. Not her confidante.

"We've been preparing her for a long time. It was all so innocent at first. She didn't know that by befriending you, she was helping us overthrow the empire."

"Is Trevon alive, then? Is he part of this too somehow?" She wished she could punch Joanna in the mouth. Her earlier feelings of helplessness had returned. She was trapped once again. Deceived and betrayed.

Joanna smiled knowingly. "He plays a part in this, yes. We need him alive for now. Just as you are needed for the illusion to be perfect."

I have been developing my map of the disease. I've hand-drawn a map of the streets around Killingworth Hospital. I've walked these streets a hundred times and so their names are familiar. Some streets are straight, others crooked. Each building is a square or rectangle on my map. Within each of these, I have tallied the number of victims whose lives have been claimed by the cholera morbus. There are lines in factories too, but I've noted that most of the tally marks are in the tenements and houses.

What am I missing? There seems to be an unusual grouping of tally marks on Marshall Street. Is there something about it that causes so much death? I can't say how many times I have walked down this street. Seen the women scrubbing clothes in the fountain Leerings. Watched the pigeons strut along the rooftops. Listened to the clack of carriage wheels on the cobblestones. Marshall Street is four blocks away from Killingworth Hospital. I go there every day, knocking on door after door, asking how many have died. How many are sick. Another scratch. Another tally.

And the sun goes down once again.

—Adam Creigh, Killingworth Hospital

CETTIE

CHAPTER FOURTEEN
THE GROVE

The jostle of the carriage wheels on a patch of uneven ground roused Cettie from her slumber. The noise of the hooves and the rhythm of the wheels had made it easy to nod off. The boy sat next to her, staring out the window, a peaceful look on his face. Across from her sat the man who had rescued her from the Hotel Vecchio in Pree. After they'd put enough distance between themselves and the hotel, he'd freed her from the chest, leaving her unharmed but for a sore neck.

She felt a weight on her lap and noticed someone had set the scabbard with the raven sigil across her lap. Once again, she noticed the subtle melody it exuded. It radiated magic. She lowered her hand to the smooth leather scabbard and felt her skin tingle.

Cettie became aware that she'd been relieved of the aches and bruises from her fight with Will. She rubbed along her forearm. No pain, not even a little spot.

Her eyes lifted and met Owen's. He was smiling knowingly at her.

"What have you done?" she asked him. It was as if she'd been healed with Everoot.

"I found that scabbard when I was younger. It has certain powers. I thought they might be useful while you slept."

Cettie rubbed her eyes. "I'm sorry I fell asleep."

"Don't be. You've missed some excellent scenery, but that is all. We're approaching Brythonica. We'll be there by nightfall."

"I wish I hadn't," Cettie said. "I would like to know more about you. You've been very kind to me."

Owen shrugged. "There's too much to tell." He folded his arms. "The story would fill a book. But now isn't the right time. Are you nervous about returning home?"

Home. The word brought a pang of guilt. She didn't deserve to go *home*.

Cettie looked down. "I think so, yes," she stammered. "I wonder what will happen. I've disappointed so many people. I . . . I wasn't always like this. I was deceived. Led down a dark path."

Owen said nothing, just looked at her with sympathy.

"Perhaps I shouldn't have left like I did. I'm afraid of what will happen to my friends. The people who trained me threatened to kill them."

"I imagine they did." His eyes narrowed slightly. "There is no greater fear than that of suspense. Your mind begins to imagine the worst."

"It's true," Cettie said. "But I've seen some of the worst. It's not an idle threat. My return will lead to many troubles."

"So what if it does? You'll face them."

Cettie sighed and nodded. If she could do something to help Sera, the empire, then it was worth the risk of being executed by her own people. In any case, she couldn't predict the future. She wasn't a harbinger anymore. The last vision she'd had was the one of the attack on Fitzroy—the one that had set her down this path.

The carriage began to slow, and there was a thump from the driver's seat.

Owen slid across the seat to open the window. "What is it?"

"Road blocked ahead, sir," shouted the driver from above. "Soldiers."

"Whose?"

"Occitanian."

"Is everything all right, Papa?" Curtis asked. His brow wrinkled.

"It will be fine," Owen said comfortingly. The carriage continued to slow.

Cettie felt her stomach clench with dread. She had her poisoner bag on the seat beside her, plus the pistol she'd stolen from Will and the dagger she always carried. She would not let anyone harm the old man and his grandson.

"What are we going to do?" she asked him, her voice becoming firm.

"We're going to reach our destination," he answered. "Just a minor delay. I wouldn't worry."

"I *am* worried," Cettie said. She leaned toward the window and tried to look ahead. It was a military blockade. Pickets had been erected to block the road. Horses were tethered to them, and there were twelve, maybe thirteen, men assembled, dressed as soldiers and armed with muskets and sabers. She glanced at the other two passengers.

"It's all right," Owen insisted. Then he reached for the Raven scabbard. "But just in case."

The carriage slowed to a halt. Cettie heard the soldiers talk to the driver, but their voices were garbled. Owen looked at Curtis and smiled. "Stay in here with Cettie. I'll talk with them. Don't come out of the carriage, all right?"

"What will you do, Papa?"

"I'm just going to talk to the soldiers. Don't worry."

"I'm not worried."

"I know you're not. Take care of Cettie for me?" He looked at her as he said it.

"I will, Papa!"

"Good. Stay in here." Gripping the scabbard in one hand, he opened the carriage door and stepped outside without hesitation. One of the soldiers shouted at him to return to the carriage, but he did not heed the man.

Cettie put her arm around Curtis and pulled him closer to her. She watched as Owen disappeared, and then she slid along the bench to get a better view. Though she couldn't hear what was being said, he was addressing the soldiers in low tones. They had all gathered around the carriage now, and some had their weapons aimed at it.

The captain of the soldiers had an unfriendly look on his weather-beaten face. "So you claim this is your daughter and her child?" he said, loud enough to be heard through the open window. He craned his neck, looking around Owen at her and Curtis. "I think you are traitors and spies!"

"Please let us pass," Owen said calmly, speaking louder in response to the captain's bluster. "We are doing the Fountain's will. Stand aside."

"You are not in charge here, old man!" the captain snapped. "Seize the carriage. Arrest them."

"I don't think that is a wise choice, Captain," said Owen, drawing the sword from the Raven scabbard.

"You think I'm afraid of an old man?" the captain sneered. "I said seize the carriage. Driver, come down at once, or you'll be shot."

Owen's shoulders sagged. "I'm afraid, Captain, that I can't let you do this."

"You're daft! Bind him in irons, I say."

Two of the soldiers approached Owen, one of them carrying irons. Cettie stared, wanting to use the power of the kystrel to save him. Even though Owen had broken it, she wondered if she could still invoke its power—although doing so would likely bring Will down upon her.

Just then, Owen swung the scabbard around and struck one of the two men in the temple, dropping him to the ground. The other froze, staring at him in shock, and Owen kneed him in the stomach. A gunshot rang out, the explosion jolting the cabin and startling the horses, who neighed in terror and bucked. The air was instantly hazy with smoke. Cettie was about to charge out and join the commotion, but she felt Curtis tug on her arm.

"Papa said to stay inside."

"He may be hurt," Cettie said.

The boy only smiled. "He isn't."

Some of the smoke cleared, at least enough to see. She watched in awe as Owen whipped his sword around, cutting the arm of a man armed with a musket. The soldier promptly dropped his weapon, backing away as he winced in pain. Another gunshot sounded, and Cettie gasped, afraid the old man's streak of luck had finally ended, but the shot missed. The captain raised his own pistol, aiming directly at Owen's face, and pulled the trigger.

Cettie nearly screamed out. At that close range, he couldn't have missed. But the pistol jammed, and the captain, snarling, shook it and tried again. Nothing happened, so he threw down the pistol, which fired and hit one of his own men. Bellowing with anger, he drew his saber and charged at Owen. The two exchanged quick blows before the captain was pierced in the breast by Owen's longer sword. He groaned and dropped to his knees, trying to stanch the blood.

Another shot sounded, then another. But none of them hit Owen, who dispatched each soldier, one by one, until the last wisps of smoke abandoned the scene.

Cettie stared in disbelief, watching Owen stand there with a bloodied sword in one hand, the scabbard in the other as he watched his attackers scatter. The captain, shivering with fear and still on his knees, looked up at the old man in dread.

Owen wiped the blood on the captain's coat before sheathing the blade. He walked back to the carriage, opened the door, and whistled for the driver to go on.

The carriage lumbered past the pickets.

～

Sera had told Cettie about the beauties of Brythonica. The beach made of sea glass, the berry fields she'd visited with Trevon. It was a lush and green land, full of hills and groves and open farmland. She watched the scenery pass until sunset, when the shadows grew thick enough to obscure the way forward. The air held a sweet fragrance—was it eucalyptus? The driver slowed, but he knew the way, and there was only the one road to follow.

"Are we going to Ploemeur?" Cettie asked.

Owen shook his head, saying nothing. When she'd asked him where he had learned to fight so well, he'd remained equally silent.

Soon the carriage entered a dense wood. Shadows filled the carriage, and night sounds—the clicking of unseen insects and the hooting of owls—filtered in through the open window. The breeze had also become noticeably cooler. Cettie's companions sat comfortably in the silence, but she sensed a presence waiting for her in the woods. Her nerves went taut, her worries growing. In her experience, darkness had always brought the Myriad Ones. Yet she felt a little safer in Owen's presence, and not just because of his swordsmanship.

After some time, Owen lifted his sword pommel and used it to tap the roof. "Stop here, please."

The driver obeyed, and the carriage slowed to a halt.

They were in the middle of the woods, and the feeling of sentience Cettie had picked up on originated directly to the left of the carriage. She clenched her hands together, subduing a shudder, and shot a worried look at Owen.

"We'll walk the rest of the way," Owen said. "We're almost there."

He opened the door and disembarked, then helped Curtis down the long jump before extending a hand to Cettie to help her down as well. His palm was weathered and rough, but it was also warm and comforting. As a child, she used to hold Fitzroy's hand, and that simple connection had given her courage to face the unknown.

"Wait for us here," Owen said to the driver. "We'll be gone an hour or so."

"As you say, my lord," said the man from his perch.

"This way," Owen said, leading her and Curtis through the trees. He was guiding them directly to the source of the feelings.

"What is this place?" she whispered, her throat tightening.

"It's the gateway back to your home," he said.

"It feels . . . dangerous," Cettie said.

"It *is* dangerous," Owen answered. "As long as you're with me, you'll be safe. But the magic here is powerful. That you can sense it means you're Fountain-blessed."

She gave him a sharp look. "Fountain-blessed? Like in the stories?"

"They're not stories," Owen answered.

"But how can *I* be Fountain-blessed?" Cettie asked. "I'm not from this world."

"Come and see."

She mustered her courage and followed him. There was no trail, but she didn't need one, nor did she need Owen to guide her. She could sense the magic of the place—ancient, powerful, and dangerous—both drawing her to it and warning her away. She felt a vivid sense of wrongness being there, like a Leering was trying to bar her entry. Somehow Owen's presence prevented it from affecting her.

They reached a small grove, and Cettie heard the lapping sounds of a waterfall. Through the parting of the trees, she saw a myriad of stars—the sky was absolutely swollen with them. There was a shambling oak tree nestled amidst dark shapes she assumed were boulders. Water was streaming from the base of the tree. As they approached, she saw a smooth stone plinth and a metal bowl that gleamed silver in the starlight.

Her breath slowed as she stared at the strange place. She was positive she'd never been there before, and yet it felt strangely familiar. It was an eerie sensation. As she peered into the blackness of the boulders—a cave, she realized—she remembered the Fear Liath and trembled violently.

Owen put his hand on her shoulder. "Nothing will hurt you here. Stand near me."

She sidled closer to him, trying to calm herself.

"Curtis. Fetch the bowl and fill it with water."

"All right, Papa." The boy obeyed promptly and went to the plinth. He lifted the bowl, which was heavy for someone of his size, and grunted as he carried it to the darkness at the mouth of the boulders. She heard the sound of the water sloshing inside the bowl. It quickly filled. Then the boy, weighed down by his burden, began to approach.

"Watch," Owen whispered to her. "But you might want to cover your ears."

Cettie quickly did so.

The boy tipped the contents of the bowl onto the plinth. She could hear the water splashing onto the surface, see the stone turning slick. After quickly setting down the bowl, he rushed to join them. And then a crack of thunder split the sky, so loud that she cowered. The boom shook her ribs, her heart, and momentarily deafened her. A high-pitched squeal came, followed by a vibrating thrum of magic that was so deep and pervasive she could only describe the sensation as being plunged underwater. It felt as if the whole world were a musical instrument, and some giant hand had plucked the strings.

And then it began to hail.

Cettie dropped to her knees as the huge chunks of ice slammed into the grove. They came in torrents, the ice hissing as it smashed into trees and boulders. Yet none of it touched her, or Owen, or Curtis. All three stood in the maelstrom, protected by a power she did not comprehend. After the storm, things settled peacefully.

Light filtered into the grove, accompanied by peaceful music and the chirping of birds. The light, which reminded her of a sunrise, came from the cave made by the boulders. Lowering her hands from her ears, she stared at the light. It revealed the hidden colors of the grove, the moss on the tree trunk of the massive oak, the thick clumps of mistletoe drooping from the laden branches. The boulders could be seen as well, glistening and wet, the ice nearly melted already.

"Come," Owen said, reaching his hand for hers. She took it, feeling childlike again. Then he turned toward the boy. "You can go back to the wagon and return to Ploemeur. Thank you, my boy."

Curtis smiled, gave them a little wave, and left the grove while Owen and Cettie walked hand in hand into the cave. The budding light began to sting Cettie's eyes, and she winced, squinting, trying to see what lay beyond.

They entered the cave, which had expanded enough to accommodate them, and stepped through a rift into another world.

They had traded darkness for daylight. The familiarity of her surroundings shocked her. She saw the enormous oak tree with limbs so heavy that they dragged to the ground in places. It was the sentinel oak tree beyond the walls of Muirwood Abbey. She had gone there after taking the Maston Test.

Muirwood! Her heart soared with relief.

She heard a crackling sound in the detritus surrounding the oak, the noise of someone approaching. She turned to find a pudgy man in breeches and stockings and a waistcoat holding a gnarled walking staff capped in gold.

"Well, my boy," said the newcomer, his voice accented and husky. "You came at last. Good of you to bring our *little sister* along. I was beginning to worry you'd been distracted by the berry fields."

"Hello, Myrddin," said Owen with a fond smile, and the two men embraced.

CHAPTER FIFTEEN

RENEWED

Just like the grove, which felt familiar despite being unfamiliar, she almost felt she knew the strange man who had joined them. His outfit was from an older era, as were the square buckles on his shoes. He had dark hair, streaked with gray, a prominent nose, and an excited manner, bursting with energy.

She felt out of place. Had Owen and this man truly been expecting her? How did they know each other?

"I am also called Maderos," he said to Cettie, holding his paunch and bowing slightly to her. "It is good to see you again, little sister."

"Have we met before?" Cettie asked, growing more confused. She was in a familiar place, yet with strange company.

"We have, although you won't remember it. Owen calls me Myrddin out of habit, I suppose. The *pethet*." He grinned at Owen and butted him with an elbow. "But in this world, I am a wayfarer, a prophet, a beggar, a fool. And here you are again. You've been to this grove before, no?"

Cettie cast her eyes around it, feeling so insignificant next to the towering tree. "I have been here. After taking the Maston Test."

"Yes, the Test!" Maderos said, beaming. "That was when we met."

"But I don't remember you," Cettie said, shaking her head.

"No, of course you wouldn't. But even though you do not remember, it is nonetheless true. We made a bargain, you and I. Now it is time for me to live up to my end of it."

A chill swept down Cettie's spine. What could he mean?

"I will tell you," Maderos said, as if hearing her thought. "But first . . . you must make a choice. Every choice has its consequence. It is like this staff." He hefted it in his hand and offered it to her. "If you take one end, you get the other end too. Choices, consequences. Sometimes we know what they will be. Other times we do not. The consequences may surprise us. Or hurt us. We accept both ends when we pick our actions. Is this not so?"

Cettie thought about his words a moment, then nodded solemnly. The Mysteries emanated from him, from the grove itself. She felt safer than she had in years, yet at the same moment, she felt a heavy doom weighing on her.

"So I offer you a choice, little sister. A choice between two sticks to pick up. You must choose one of them." He arched his feathery eyebrows at her.

"What are they?" Cettie rubbed her arms.

"One choice is to forsake everything you are and have become. A hetaera, a poisoner, a harbinger, a daughter, a sister, a keeper, a friend. I will take you to a distant land where no one knows or would recognize you. You may start over again. Find what you will, become what you will . . . whatever you choose. You will not remember who or what you are now. That is the consequence. But you will be free to be whatever you choose. Cut off from the Mysteries, from your oaths, from your obligations. That is the first choice."

Anonymity had its allurement. She'd assumed that by returning to her world, she would face the demands of justice. That she might even be executed. He was offering her a way out.

"And the other?" she asked him.

"I will be truthful, little sister. It will be a harder life. Your enemies will seek to kill you. They will chase and hunt you. Just as they'll do with your friends. And you will chase and hunt them in return, to protect your empress. Rather than forget everything, you will be given a Gift of Wisdom that allows you to remember everything you've ever done or said. That will bring painful memories as well as sweet. You must accept both. And you will be a chosen one, a warrior of the Medium. An Oath Maiden." Cettie saw Owen smile when that term was mentioned, and a knowing look came on his face, which confused her even more. "You will be given powers and gifts to help you in your calling. It will not be easy. And so, little sister, you must choose."

He set his staff in front of him, putting both hands on the golden knob at the end.

Cettie stared at him, then at Owen, feeling perplexed and shaken. One of the paths seemed so much easier than the other, and she was so, so tired of life's demands. But it would mean she wouldn't remember the Fitzroys, or Sera, or even Adam. She would lose all sense of herself and the experiences that had formed her.

Her mind and heart tugged her in opposite directions. What an awful choice to have to make. She felt herself growing sick with worry. What if she chose wrong? What if her choice filled her with endless regret?

"Only you can decide, little sister," said Maderos.

"How can I?" Cettie asked. She looked imploringly at Owen. "How can I know which is the right one?"

Owen gave her a sympathetic smile. "I cannot choose for you. But I've come to recognize the right path usually is the *harder* one. You'll never climb a mountain and reach new heights if you keep taking the easy path down."

What he said made sense. In the deepest part of her heart, she knew what she should do. The difficulty of it cowed her, but she knew losing her memories would be the selfish course. It would serve one person, *her*, and it would limit the greatest good she could do for others. She regretted her decision to join the poisoner school. If she could atone for it in some way, she was willing. Even if the cost was her life.

That thought filled her heart with peace and her eyes with tears. She knew what she needed to do, no matter the heartache. No matter the pain.

"I'll do it," she whispered, choking. She sniffed and shook her head. "I will do what I must to regain the trust the Mysteries had in me." She looked up at Maderos. "I will serve."

An approving smile appeared on his face.

"Kneel, little sister," Maderos said. "You will close your eyes. Open yourself to the Knowing as you learn this Mystery. Never reveal it. Guard it in your heart as a treasure."

Cettie knelt in the scrub, feeling the brittle twigs and fallen leaves snap beneath her weight. She adjusted her poisoner's bag so that it was behind her, hanging from the strap around her shoulder. She closed her eyes, obedient to Maderos's words.

"There will come a Dryad to you," Maderos said, his voice soft. "They are the guardians of memory. The guardians of the portals between the worlds. There is one watching this tree, and another watching the one in the grove you just left in Brythonica. Do not look at her, lest she steal all your memories, until *after* she has kissed you. When she has, you may open your eyes. And you will remember. To become an Oath Maiden, you must accept certain oaths. In doing so, you will be granted special power. If you forsake them, the consequences are dire."

"I will accept them," Cettie said in a firm voice.

"Hold out your hand," Maderos said. "Put it over mine." She heard the clacking of stones, and when she tentatively reached out, she felt several pebbles in his rough palm. She laid her open hand over them.

"These are the five oaths. There will be four more later if you are faithful to these. Never slay a man with pistol, arquebus, or arrow. In return, you will not be slain by such. Never take a life unawares or out of revenge. Never hearken to greed or take a bribe. Never swear an oath falsely. Never refuse to serve when the Mysteries compel you—even at the peril of your life or loved ones."

As Cettie heard the oaths, her heart tingled inside. She felt a swelling of power, of the magic of the Mysteries embracing her. It felt right. It felt like she had, in truth, returned home.

"I swear it," Cettie said forcefully.

"Just say, *yes*, little sister. That will suffice."

"Yes," Cettie said.

Maderos retrieved the stones. "Remember the oaths you have taken. If you stand true to them, nothing you are called to do will be impossible. But if you lose heart, as you did before, you will be overwhelmed by darkness for good. This is my warning to you, little sister. Now be still. Do not open your eyes until after the Dryad's kiss."

Cettie clasped her hands together, feeling the breeze ruffle the hair on her neck. The woods smelled so clean, so pure. She heard no other sounds than that of nature, not even the breathing of the others. She felt alone, as if the others had left.

"Are you still there?" she asked.

Silence met her. Then she heard a snapping twig from near the tree. The compulsion to look slammed into her mind. But she squeezed her eyes shut, clenching her fists too, and withstood the onslaught. Her ears strained to hear another sound—then she started when another crack filled the still air, this time much closer. She felt someone approach, and her arm hairs stood on end in anticipation of being touched. Her breathing had quickened, and so she focused on slowing it down. *Do not panic,* she told herself. She knew she was safe.

Fingers brushed through her hair. She willed herself to remain perfectly still.

Soft lips brushed against her mouth.

Cettie opened her eyes, looking into the amber eyes of the Dryad girl. And then the memories came crashing down on her, an avalanche that buried her in emotion. Cettie pitched forward, catching herself on one hand. Memory after memory, each knife-sharp and keen, slashed through her skull. The Fells, the slappings Miss Charlotte had given her. Mrs. Pullman's cold menace and burning resentment. The sound of Joses's laughter. Her fear as he went off to steal food for the other children. Flying on a zephyr for the first time. Holding Fitzroy's hand. Adam Creigh's faltering confession of love.

And then there were the memories she'd forgotten. The ones the Dryad had stolen from her in this very place. Cettie gasped as she realized that she *did* know Maderos. She'd met him in this grove on her last visit, and he'd advised her of her role as harbinger. It was he who'd Gifted her with that ability. Her arms and legs trembled as the memories continued to rush through her, opening her eyes.

She was chosen. A precious vessel of the Mysteries, of the Knowing. She'd had her first vision there. It had shown her Fitzroy's death in Kingfountain, her own betrayal of the Mysteries, and her decision to stop fighting Lady Corinne and the kishion and stay at the poisoner school. She'd sobbed at the thought of losing her father, of losing herself, and yet she'd accepted the role. It was part of the Knowing's plan, part of its reconciliation of the infinite choices mortals made. Father had undoubtedly faced his own death with courage. Could she do no less?

The Dryad had stolen her memories of the vision, of what she had chosen to do, for the poisoner school would surely have killed her if they'd known she intended to destroy it.

Memories. More memories. The ground felt like it was spinning, and her shoulders sagged as she struggled to stay conscious. Memories came of her childhood. She saw the deed Mr. Pratt had signed, giving her up, saw someone hand an infant to the tall, handsome man in a dragoon jacket. But still the memories went back further, before it was even possible for her to remember.

She remembered her birth in this very grove.

The labor had started in Brythonica. Her father was there—the kishion. A woman who wasn't Lady Corinne—yet *was*—lay beneath the oak tree, groaning. The woman screamed in agony as the labor continued. Cettie saw it all, saw the blood and the taut nerves, the clenched hands, the sweat. And as Cettie came into the world, a silver bowl full of water was poured on the plinth. There was thunder, hail, and a vortex opened between the worlds.

The Dryads had seen it happen. They were both silent witnesses to Cettie's birth.

A child born between two worlds. It had never happened before.

A child who was heir to both.

Cettie watched her father lift the babe, a wild, triumphant look in his eyes. He pressed his lips against her bloodied scalp.

A vessel. A vessel to give Ereshkigal for her rebirth. One who could cross from one world to the other without permission, without covenants.

A destroyer of worlds.

And yet . . . and yet . . .

One crucial meeting had changed her life's trajectory. Lord Fitzroy had put a stop to the chain of events that would have ruined her life and her soul. He had guided her away from an awful destiny prepared in advance by her parents. Had she been brought to the poisoner school as a young girl, raised to know nothing but cruelty and want, they would have won her loyalty.

Cettie hunched down, doubled over, pressing her cheek against the carpet of decayed leaves, and wept in gratitude for what Lord Fitzroy—her true father—had done. He hadn't known. But he'd listened to the tiny prick of conscience that night in the Fells, when she'd asked him to adopt her. He had unwittingly chosen a different fate for her.

Cettie walked up the hill toward the abbey, her arms folded, her eyes finally dry. She remembered how foggy her mind had felt the last time she made this journey, years before. The visions had started soon afterward, catching her completely by surprise. She hadn't remembered accepting the Gift of Seering. She hadn't remembered she'd willingly become a harbinger.

Today, when she'd awoken with her memories, Maderos and Owen had been gone. Without any instructions, she was left to follow her heart, and her heart told her to seek out the Aldermaston of Muirwood. She had no idea what would happen next, but she followed the impression and had started on her way.

As she neared the outer borders of the abbey, the Leerings warned her not to approach. The brand on her shoulder felt as if it had been burned into her skin anew. Cettie unwove the Leerings' protections with her mind, not dispelling them, just making a little path for her to cross, as her father the kishion had done years before with his kystrel. After crossing, she slid the protections back into place.

She felt a smile rise on her mouth as she took in her familiar surroundings. As she advanced, she saw the cider orchard, the pond. Soon she could hear the laughter of the students enjoying a pleasant afternoon. Then there were the archery butts, one of the places she'd liked to go to think. The abbey could be seen above the trees, beyond it all, and Cettie felt a strong pull from it. As if the stones welcomed her home.

When she reached the common lawn, some of the students looked at her in confusion. She was an adult now, no longer as young as she'd been. No longer one of them. To Cettie's eyes, the students were like unmolded clay. And so had she been.

She reached the Aldermaston's manor and went inside. No one spoke to her or questioned her. The poisoner's bag thumped against her back. What was she to do with it now?

After turning the corner, she approached the Aldermaston's study. That was usually where he was at this time of day. She paused at the threshold, her hand resting on the cool metal handle. Whatever was going to happen would happen. If the Aldermaston rejected her, if he turned her in to the Ministry of Law, so be it. She twisted the handle and pushed the door open.

Thomas Abraham sat at his desk, poring over an ancient tome, his glasses pinched at the end of his nose, his wrinkled brow showing his intense focus.

She quietly shut the door behind her.

He looked up from the tome and squinted, his eyes not strong enough to identify her without the glasses. He pushed them back up to the bridge of his nose, and she saw his cheeks go pale and slack, his eyes widen suddenly with fear.

"Have you come to kill me, Cettie?" he whispered.

CHAPTER SIXTEEN

ABDUCTED

Cettie's heart panged with regret that the Aldermaston's first instinct was one of survival. She hastened to reassure him.

"No, Aldermaston," she said, her throat tightening. "I've come to make amends. To suffer whatever consequences may be suitable. I was abducted and taken to the world of Kingfountain against my will. I was deceived." She sighed. "But I willingly accepted a hetaera's brand, though I regret it to my shame. I am to be the Mysteries' tool to help Sera. Aldermaston, she has been abducted from Lockhaven. I fear her maid has also been replaced with a poisoner. There are schemes at work right now that would overthrow the empire. I wish to help. And so I've come to you first, so you may judge my intentions."

His look had changed and shifted as she related her tale. He seemed surprised, and she had no doubt he was worried for Sera, but he also looked . . . relieved. A sheen of sweat had formed on his brow, and he withdrew a handkerchief from his vest pocket to mop it. Then, stuffing the handkerchief back in his pocket, he rose and walked around the table that separated them.

Cettie wondered at the action, until he put his hands on her shoulders and looked her in the eye. "My dear lost one, you have returned? Truly?"

Tears began to spill from her eyes. She hung her head, racked with guilt, and nodded, only to be pulled into a bearlike embrace.

"I'm so sorry," she mumbled, but his affectionate embrace nearly smothered the words.

"My dear, dear Cettie," he said, sniffling himself. He pulled away, looking confused. "How did you get here? By what means did you cross the worlds?"

"There's that old oak tree," Cettie explained. "The tall, crooked one, outside the boundaries."

"The sentinel oak," the Aldermaston said, nodding in understanding.

"It's a gateway." Cettie's memories of it were so sharp, so piercingly clear. The details of her life had all bloomed in her mind. "There is another place, a similar place also with an oak tree, in a grove in the other world. A portal opened and brought me here. I met a man named Maderos." She breathed out slowly, trying not to slur her words. "I had met him before, only I'd forgotten—"

"Maderos, the wayfarer?" the Aldermaston said in surprise and recognition.

"You know of him?"

"Yes! Well, there have been records left of him from previous Aldermastons. He is unlike other men. He is a special gift from the Knowing who has aided our world for centuries . . . perhaps longer."

"Is he mortal?"

The Aldermaston shook his head. "No, not in the way you and I are. He's a Dryden, a being who exists in the mortal world and yet has progressed beyond it. There is no easy way to explain them, other than they are emissaries of the Knowing. They are charged with assignments, delegated with authority, and they intercede in the mortal world at pivotal moments. There are records of his past visits. When he appears, it is always a portent of great danger."

"Yes, it must be," Cettie agreed. "I never told you, Aldermaston, but after I took the Test, the Mysteries led me outside the grounds of the abbey to banish a Myriad One that had tormented me all my life. My memory of that moment was taken away, but I recall it clearly now. It was Maderos who gave me the Gift that allowed me to see the future."

"The Gift of Seering," the Aldermaston said, nodding vigorously. "No one has had it in over a generation."

"I have it," Cettie said. "The last vision I saw was of Lord Fitzroy's death. I . . . I could not bear the thought of losing him, and wished to prevent it. I was deceived by Lady Corinne. She is my mother, Aldermaston. My birth mother. But Lady Maren is still my true mother, and Lord Fitzroy my true father. I . . . I feel so terrible about what I've done. If you could tell her that I've returned. That I am sorry. If she never wishes to see my face again, I will—"

The Aldermaston shook his head, confusing her. "I cannot do that, Cettie. You don't understand. Stephen Fitzroy has been searching for you since your capture. He's used the family's shipping interests to conduct searches in both worlds."

Cettie stared at him in disbelief.

"It's true, my dear. I will tell them you have returned, and I assure you, they will embrace you as I did. Stephen has come to Muirwood many times, along with Caulton Forshee, to ask for my advice on where next to search for you."

Cettie's eyes widened. "I came across Caulton days ago, in Genevar."

The Aldermaston held her gaze. "He was there looking for *you*."

Her knees buckled at the news. "I'm afraid, Aldermaston. I'm not who I was. Nor am I what they made me. I'm a poisoner . . . a hetaera . . . a criminal of the empire, but I don't wish to be any of those things."

He hooked his hand around her neck. "You are much more than that, child. I must send word to the Fitzroys and my contacts in the ministry at once. If the empress has been abducted, as you said, then we've reached a critical hour."

"She has been taken, Aldermaston," Cettie said. "But I believe I know where to find her." If Will was in league with her mother, then Gimmerton Sough would be the first place to start looking for the missing empress.

∾

Cettie walked the grounds of the abbey, reminiscing about the years she'd spent there as a student. She walked by the cottage she and Sera had shared in Vicar's Close. The plants had been changed in the garden, but the cracks in the plaster and loose shingles on the roof were all too familiar. She saw her old teacher, Mrs. Romrell, who had inspired her in the study of mathematics. Mrs. Romrell's warm, affectionate greeting indicated she either didn't know about Cettie's misfortunes or did not judge her for them.

Cettie walked around the abbey several times, reveling in how different it was from the poisoner school in Genevar. The Leerings on the walls protected the students but didn't trap them inside. The abbey wasn't a prison. While the poisoner school was well appointed and pleasing to the eye, it was a cold place. It lacked the aura of safety, of peace, of goodness that permeated the air she now breathed. Each time she circled the grounds, the abbey felt more welcoming, and she felt a greater sense of belonging.

As the sun began to set, she saw a tempest appear in the distance, skimming the tops of the trees. She recognized it as the one she'd flown so many times on her errands to Lockhaven. The Fitzroys. Her heart lurched as it drew closer, racing toward the abbey at full speed. Her temples began to throb, and nerves made her queasy with apprehension.

She walked swiftly across the lawn toward the landing yard, where she watched the tempest come to rest. Who would be in that tempest? Stephen? Lady Maren? They'd come swiftly upon getting the news, that much was clear.

As she neared the underbelly of the tempest, she caught sight of movement on the deck just before the rope ladder tumbled down. Cettie froze as she watched the rope sway and then settle. She clutched her hands together, biting her lip, watching for the boots to appear, and they did. Stephen. It was Stephen who hurried down the rope ladder. When he reached the grass, he whirled and saw her.

It startled her how much he looked like Father.

A broad smile lit up his face at the sight of her. He charged across the gap between them and wrapped his arms around her, heaving her off her feet, as he twirled her around before setting her down.

"It's you! By the Mysteries, I know it is!" he said with pure delight.

"Stephen," she murmured, her throat seizing so quickly the name choked off.

He put his hand on her face, as if reassuring himself she was really there, then kissed her other cheek. He started laughing, though the laughter hitched with tears. They embraced, both of them crying.

"You came back," he whispered, squeezing her harder. "How? How?" He pulled back, his broad grin making her heart melt. She had never hoped to see Stephen greet her with such genuine joy and affection. "Caulton sent word . . . that you saved his life. You were in Genevar only days ago. How did . . . well, it doesn't matter. None of that matters. You are back. Thank the Mysteries. I thank them with all my heart. We must return to Fog Willows at once. Mother needs to see you herself. She was too afraid . . . afraid it would be a trick, a deception. She couldn't bear to lose you again."

"I'm sorry, Stephen. I can't tell you how I regret—"

He held up his hand and shook his head curtly. "No, I beg you. Whatever happened, you will say it when you are ready. We have bent all our efforts to try and find you, Cettie. My lost sister. When Mr. Sloan told me what you'd done . . . how you'd paid off my debts. I can't even begin to tell you how grateful I am to you. You saved Fog Willows, Cettie. With Anna so ill at the time, our family would have been ruined if I'd been under a deed. The estate would have been seized by someone else or plummeted to the ground. Mother told me all about Lady Corinne and her lies. You're not the only person she's deceived, but now her tricks have been revealed to all. You saved us, Cettie. I want to hear nothing of regret or guilt."

Cettie cringed at his words. "But I am guilty, Stephen."

"Whatever it takes," he said, pressing his forehead against hers, "we will defend you. If we must hire a fleet of advocates, so be it. You are home. Corinne may have taken the last year of your life away, but she did not rip you out of our hearts. You will always be my sister, every bit as much as Anna and Phinia. Do I make myself clear, Cettie Saeed? You're a Fitzroy. You're one of us. I'm only sorry it took me so long to realize it."

Cettie wept again, hugging him tightly, feeling the warmth of his embrace soothe the hurts and the anguish she still carried with her.

After the embrace, she looked at his face. "You've truly been searching for me?"

"With all the intensity of a man possessed by the fiercest determination," he said. "I've employed Caulton and Aunt Juliana to help me, and others too. One of my agents learned that a zephyr was seen flying over Genevar. It was not known where it landed, and anyone who asked too many questions was silenced. But that gave me another clue of where to look. Genevar, it seems, has been benefitting enormously from this war. Caulton said that he saw you in your attack at the warehouse." He met and held her gaze. "He felt your power and warned me that you might be a hetaera. I didn't pledge to help you lightly, Cettie. Whatever has happened to you, we will face it as a family." Her throat was thick again, her heart aching with relief and gratitude. "When the

Aldermaston's message arrived, with his assurance that you were hale, I came immediately." He glanced over her shoulder. "Ah, here he is."

Cettie turned, her heart still brimming with appreciation, and saw the Aldermaston approaching them.

"Welcome, Lord Fitzroy," the Aldermaston said.

Stephen smiled wistfully. "That title will always belong to my father. Stephen will do well enough, Aldermaston." He reached out and they firmly shook hands. "Thank you for returning her to us."

The Aldermaston put a hand on each of their shoulders. "I come bearing news. I received word from Lockhaven that the empress disappeared several days ago. Prime Minister Durrant has kept it a closely guarded secret. Not even all of the privy council knows. Her maid, Becka Monstrum, was apprehended. They found an invisible ring on her finger, just as you said they would. Her form changed immediately as the disguise was stripped away. She bore the lily mark on her shoulder. As soon as she was revealed, the young woman attacked the soldiers sent to arrest her. It took six men to subdue her and four young mastons from the Ministry of Thought to overpower her and her kystrel. One of them ripped it from the chain around her neck. She's been incarcerated in Lockhaven and is now being interrogated by the Ministry of War."

Stephen grinned at Cettie.

"Well done, Sister."

"Did they send officers to Gimmerton Sough?" Cettie asked. She couldn't help the pang of worry she felt for Shantelle. What would happen to her? The young girl had made bad decisions, just as she herself had, but there was more to her than her worst choices. "I believe Sera was taken there."

"Yes, officers were dispatched as soon as your warning about her maid was verified."

"Gimmerton Sough?" Stephen asked.

"Yes," Cettie said. "Rand is part of this cabal. In fact, I know that Rand is an imposter. He's really Will Russell. I think Rand's sister may also be involved. If they're not careful, Sera could be . . . she could be killed."

The Aldermaston shook his head. "No, they need her alive. We believe their goal is to liberate Ereshkigal. Only Sera can."

Cettie gave him a fierce look. "That is their goal. I was to be the vessel. They planned to send me to Lockhaven to impersonate Sera. The maid was part of the trick."

"Then we don't have any time to lose," Stephen said. He hooked his arm around Cettie's. "We fly to Gimmerton Sough."

The Aldermaston shook his head no. "The Ministry of War is sending zephyrs to come fetch her. Mr. Durrant wishes for her to be brought to Lockhaven at once."

Stephen narrowed his gaze. "I'm sorry, Aldermaston. But she stays with me."

"I implore you to see reason. You cannot simply take her away when—"

"I can, and I will," Stephen said. "If they want her, tell them where to meet us. Gimmerton Sough."

CHAPTER SEVENTEEN
GIMMERTON SOUGH

They did leave Muirwood Abbey, but not before the Aldermaston pressed a new chain into Cettie's cupped palm with an entreaty to wear it at all times to protect herself from the Myriad Ones that would seek to reclaim her. Gratitude burned in her heart as she clenched the chain and symbol in her fist. She didn't feel worthy to put it on, but she honored the Aldermaston's request, nonetheless.

She and Stephen boarded the tempest, and he offered her the helm with a look of encouragement.

"Come, Cettie," he said. "We both know who is the better pilot." Once again, she was struck by how much her almost-brother had matured in her absence.

The peaceful feeling that suffused the abbey and its grounds had melted away the negative emotions that still plagued her. It was like a terrible night was ending, brought to heel by the first rays of dawn. She stood at the helm, her hands gripping the spokes of the wooden wheel mounted there. All it did was give the illusion of a ship—the power came from elsewhere.

It came from the Knowing.

Her mind whispered to the Leering, *We must away.*

The tempest vaulted into the sky, making Stephen grip the handrail in surprise. A smile spread on his mouth as the tempest began to rush with the breeze, leaving the grounds and the majestic abbey awash in colors painted by the sinking sun.

As they raced to Gimmerton Sough, Cettie revealed her story to Stephen. She told him of the poisoner school in Genevar. Of the Leerings that summoned serpents should anyone attempt to leave the walls. Of the young women she had met, each snatched from a life of misery and despair. Of the tests of courage, combat, and duplicity she'd faced, guided by her father, a kishion, and the garden keeper named Jevin. She ended with the information of how she'd discovered Rand Patchett, who they'd known, had in truth been Will Russell.

Stephen listened with uncanny patience. He'd changed so much since Father's death. There was stone dust on his jacket, and his hands were callused from working at Dolcoath mines. Even his pose, hands clasped behind his back, made him look more like his father. The son had finally accepted the mantle of his master.

In return, Stephen shared the news about their family. Lady Maren's health had declined since news of her husband's death. Not sickness— just a deep melancholy that was getting worse. Anna had been restored to good health, but she too grieved for Father. She was anxious to see Cettie again, to embrace her as a sister. Phinia and her husband, Malcolm, were expecting their first child. If it was a boy, they would name him Brant.

The tidings brought joy to Cettie's heart, but she couldn't banish the memory of Will's threats. Corinne would seek revenge for her betrayal. Fog Willows needed protection, and she said as much. Stephen assured her that the Ministry of War would supply watchmen and keep the estate under guard.

"Can you tell me what's become of Adam?" Cettie finally asked, her heart twisting with pain. She'd saved requesting news of him for last.

Stephen's expression became more somber. "I haven't seen him recently, Cettie. He runs a hospital in the Fells called Killingworth. The empress bestowed it upon him. They say he works day and night, that he accepts any patient, even those who cannot afford to pay. He's still trying to find the cause of the cholera morbus. He has some notions about the air and has connected some of the Leerings in the hospital to Fog Willows—with our permission, of course. He claims there are certain airs that are lighter than others. I don't understand it, but then the Mysteries of Wind were never my strong point. I'm sure you'd comprehend it." He smiled at her.

Cettie clenched the spokes of the helm. She so desperately wanted to see Adam. At least to apologize to him and to return the book of drawings she'd smuggled away from the poisoner school. Perhaps Will had stolen it on one of his visits. Or maybe even her father, the kishion, with his mask of invisibility. A powerful longing filled her heart at the mere thought of Adam, but she had no expectation that he'd take her back. She didn't deserve it.

It was strange and wonderful to be talking to Stephen in such an open, frank manner. He had truly accepted her as family.

"Father would be so proud of you," she told him, feeling it in her heart.

His lips pursed, and he looked away, shrugging slightly. "I never did much to make him proud," he said softly. "I wish it were otherwise."

"If the Myriad Ones can see us . . . can torment us," Cettie said, "then why wouldn't the ghosts of those we love also be able to see us?"

He looked at her and smiled. "Perhaps you're right. The night is upon us. I think we're almost there."

They were indeed. Cettie recognized the feel of the estate as they approached—the same darkness she'd sensed soon after the Patchetts had taken up residence. Zephyrs patrolled around it, and still more were fixed in the docking yard. They were Ministry of War ships, Cettie saw, bearing the paint and colors of the admiralty.

"Of course they arrived first," Stephen said, gazing warily at the ships. He didn't need to speak his fear aloud—Cettie knew they were taking a risk. "Let's get closer."

As Cettie maneuvered the tempest toward the docking yard, two of the zephyrs peeled away from their orbit of the estate and rushed at them. Cettie felt the tempest's Control Leering pulse as the other ship tried to wrest control of the vessel away from her, but she shoved her will against theirs and prevented it.

Identify yourself.

"They're hailing us," Cettie said to Stephen.

He put his hand on the wheel, joining his thoughts with hers.

This is Stephen Fitzroy of Fog Willows.

Do you have the girl with you? Is that her at the helm?

Stephen frowned. *It is.*

Land your tempest in the docking yard at once.

We will obey.

Cettie's unease grew, but she slowed the tempest and carefully maneuvered it down to the docking yard as she'd done so many times before. The zephyrs hovered above them, and she saw some blue-jacketed dragoons approach on foot with arquebuses in their grips. The weapons were aimed at the tempest, at *her*.

Stephen unfurled the rope ladder and climbed down to meet them, showing a brave face despite their aggressive approach. Cettie followed him down and was instantly surrounded.

"We'll be taking her into custody," said the lieutenant, who bore the rank on his shoulders.

"Have you found the empress?" Stephen demanded. He stood between the soldiers and Cettie, his hands raised defensively.

"She doesn't appear to be here," the lieutenant said. "We're conducting a search of the grounds."

"Who is in command?" Stephen asked.

"Colonel Forsgren."

"Take us to him at once," Stephen said in a tone of command.

The lieutenant hesitated, looking at Stephen as if to gauge how seriously to take him, but then he nodded. Surrounded by an armed escort, they crossed the yard and entered the manor.

Though Cettie knew she was in danger of being revealed, and arrested, that was not the main source of her uneasiness. The manor was alight, and yet she felt great darkness there, much like the time she'd visited at Mr. Batewinch's behest to clear the house. As they crossed the threshold, she sensed a prick of awareness on the back of her neck and saw a Myriad One half-hidden in the shadows. It eyed her balefully, hatred emanating from it like a furnace. She was grateful she'd put on the chain earlier.

As they marched down the corridor, Cettie glanced back to see if the creature followed them. It did not.

They reached the sitting room, where the keeper of the estate, Mrs. Rosings, conferred with a gray-haired officer with the markings of the colonel rank. As soon as Cettie looked at Mrs. Rosings, she saw the woman's nostrils flare. A smug little smile pressed on her proud mouth. She recognized Cettie, as well she should, but there was more to it. It was a cunning look.

"Colonel Forsgren," Stephen said, nodding. "A word, if you please."

"Good evening, Lord Fitzroy. The trail is cold. I've men searching the estate, but we've no sign of Her Majesty. The keeper tells me that Mr. Batewinch disappeared mysteriously the other night on a zephyr. He hasn't been seen since, and she has no idea where he went. I've ordered a hunt for the man. Sadly, I don't think we're any closer to finding our empress. I was about to disband the search."

Cettie felt a discordant note in the colonel's words. She recognized the sound, the feeling. A kystrel was at work. Cettie gazed at Mrs. Rosings, feeling her certainty grow.

She leaned over to Stephen and whispered in his ear. "The keeper has a kystrel."

A look of annoyance flashed across the colonel's face. "Is something amiss?"

Stephen glanced at Cettie and then turned back to the colonel. "Colonel, arrest this woman." He gestured at Mrs. Rosings. "She's part of the plot."

Anger pulsed into the room. Cettie felt a wave of blackness smash into her mind. As if Stephen's words had summoned them, the Myriad Ones began to draw in from the corridors, converging on the room from many sides.

"Young Fitzroy, I see no reason—" Forsgren began.

Cettie was not going to wait for the trap to spring. She stepped forward suddenly, grabbing Mrs. Rosings by the left hand. With her thumb on the top of the hand and her fingers digging into the fleshy underside, she twisted the woman's arm, making her gasp in pain. A look of hatred swelled in her eyes. Cettie felt the woman's fingers and discovered the hidden ring, the one she was using to alter her appearance.

Cettie twisted the ring off, and the illusion melted away.

The image of Mrs. Rosings was gone.

It was Mrs. Pullman.

$\rightleftharpoons$

Cettie looked into the face of her nemesis, the woman who had tortured her during her early days at Fog Willows. The woman's craggy skin, drawn taut with dislike, and the fury blazing in her eyes showed she remembered Cettie well—and hated her still. A gasp of shock came from Stephen's mouth. Colonel Forsgren stared at the woman in disbelief and confusion. "What is the meaning of this?" he asked.

"Mrs. Pullman!" Stephen said. The two had been close once. The old keeper had won him over with her solicitous behavior, hoping to make him into his grandfather's image. In her absence, he'd fashioned himself after a much better role model—his own father.

"Let go of me!" Mrs. Pullman snarled.

Cettie released her, watching as the old woman chafed her bony wrist.

The light from the Leerings flickered, and the cloud estate jolted in the air. A decorative table fell over with a smash. Shattering noises came from beyond, and dishes were jostled out of place. Cettie felt the magic that had suspended Gimmerton Sough in the air for centuries begin to fail. The harmonious song, which was imperceptible to the others in the room, became discordant and began to fade into silence. When it did, the estate would fall.

The feeling of downward motion rattled everyone, causing grunts of surprise and looks of alarm. Then the lights from all the Leerings winked out, plunging them into complete darkness. Screams of terror erupted from the household servants. The estate was sinking, reminding Cettie of the day of the Hardings' ball. The Hardings had lost their remaining fortune in a failed speculation, something that had caused the whole estate to jolt alarmingly, but it had been saved by Lady Corinne and her husband, who'd bought the manor. Of course, they'd engineered the whole thing apurpose. Cettie had been but a child then. She'd not understood the Mysteries at all.

"We're sinking!" Colonel Forsgren shouted. "To the zephyrs!"

"Where are they? I can't see anything!" Cettie didn't know the man's voice, but there was no mistaking his panic.

Standing by Stephen, she reached for his arm and felt it in the pitch black. He squeezed. They began to plummet in earnest, the feeling making Cettie's stomach lift in her chest.

"We die together, little one," Mrs. Pullman said in the dark, audible despite the screams that now filled the still air.

Cettie felt the Myriad Ones in attendance now, raging through the dark sitting room, feeding on the terrified minds of the victims about to perish.

Would there even be enough time to flee to the sky ships? In the dark?

Cettie squelched the feeling of panic rising in her gut. She could save the manor. She knew she could. Closing her eyes, she sought out the Command Leering. *Obey me,* she thought. *Brighten.*

A muted glow emanated from the wall Leerings, hidden behind translucent panes of glass. In the dimness, she saw the frantic faces of the people gathered around her. Only Mrs. Pullman looked resigned. Had she known she was to die? Was this her final act of revenge?

I am the keeper here, Mrs. Pullman thought, her words sharp as razors in Cettie's mind. The lights began to fade.

Cettie saw the keeper's key fastened to a strap around the old woman's frail waist. Moving forward, she knelt and grabbed for the key. Mrs. Pullman's fingernails raked across her hands as she fought to keep it in her possession.

You took it from me once! You won't again!

Cettie felt the manor's fall accelerate. The lights flickered, off and on, off and on, and shouts and screams continued to pierce the gloom. Some officers were staggering, trying to find a way out—a way back to the ships—but they could not keep on their feet for long. They would never make it in time. Mass chaos filled the flickering interior of the manor, and the Myriad Ones flitted from shadow to shadow, feasting on the despair. Despite the painful gouges on her hands, Cettie wrapped the strap around her own palm and tugged, trying to break the cord.

Mrs. Pullman's thoughts crashed against Cettie's. *It's mine! Mine!*

The Leerings faltered again, plunging them into blackness. She felt someone brush past her, and suddenly Mrs. Pullman's thoughts grew confused.

Get off! Get off! the old woman shrieked in her mind.

The cord snapped, freeing the key. Cettie heard it thunk against the wood floor and begin to slide away.

Light! Cettie pleaded, invoking the Leerings again.

The pale illumination that resulted was enough for her to see Stephen grappling with the old woman, holding her away from Cettie.

Mrs. Pullman's nails were tipped in blood, and her long fingers groped to scratch at Cettie again.

On the floor, sliding away from them, was the keeper's key. Cettie lunged after it, sliding a pace before she grabbed it up.

Squeezing the metal in her hand, Cettie bowed her head and beckoned the Control Leering to obey her. To halt the descent of the mansion. She invoked her memories of the Hardings—Sir Jordan's booming laughter, Lady Shanron's joyful parties. The dancing and gaiety that had been enjoyed by so many. She felt the Leerings throb to life in response. Her memories of the time before, when Gimmerton Sough had been a true home, seemed to feed the Leering. The lights became blindingly bright. Cettie focused on her order, willing it to hold firm. Then she felt Stephen's will join hers, adding his thoughts to invoke the Control Leering to obey them. The fall began to slow, but Cettie knew they might be too late to stop it from happening.

Slow, slow, slow, Cettie pleaded, invoking the Leerings, commanding them in the name of the Mysteries.

"What's happening?" someone shouted.

"It's slowing!"

Cettie felt the power of the Leering fade again, displaced by the power of Mrs. Pullman's kystrel. The discordant tune was harsh in her mind. The lights began to fade. The key was in her hand, yet it struck her that a key was little more than a symbol, a delegation of authority. The key had made it easier for Mrs. Pullman to control the estate, certainly, but the real power came from her kystrel.

"Stephen!" Cettie cried out. "The kystrel! Around her neck! Hurry!" A cluster of Myriad Ones gathered around her. A prickle of gooseflesh crept up her arms as their dark energy closed in on her, the flashing lights illuminating them.

Fear started to press in on her, but she remembered what Maderos had said to her. She was a tool of the Mysteries, and the Myriad Ones would control her no more.

Banirexpiare! she thought at them, invoking the maston word of power.

The Myriad Ones screeched in painful obedience. Their shrieks were like storm winds inside her mind.

"No!" Mrs. Pullman groaned.

Cettie turned and saw Stephen yanking on the old woman's medallion. Magic pulsed out of the kystrel. Mrs. Pullman was using her force against him, trying to compel him to obey. Cettie knew how kystrels worked. The old woman was flooding him with the feelings of his childhood, reminding him of the little favors she'd done for him, the preference she'd always shown him. She had been a mother-like figure to him while Lady Maren had so frequently been ill. His eyes were wild with conflict.

"Take it!" Cettie begged him. "Remember, Stephen. Remember. She poisoned Mother."

He locked eyes with her, frowned, and then broke the chain. As the links snapped, Mrs. Pullman slumped to the floor, exhausted, weeping.

There was no more resistance from the Control Leering. Cettie used the Leerings beneath the estate to see the ground rushing toward them. So close. *Too* close. She blinked with terror, using all her will to slow their descent. Power rippled inside her. Every Leering in the manor joined together in a unity of purpose.

Cettie felt the slowing sensation, but in her heart she knew it was too late. Stephen drew away from the old woman and crawled to her amidst the tumbled furniture. His hand closed on hers, and he bowed his head, lending her every ounce of his will.

It wasn't enough.

Cettie felt the collision as the base of Gimmerton Sough impacted the grassy plain beneath it. The jolt sent everyone sprawling. Dust and debris began to rain down on those who hadn't made it out of the chamber. Cettie and the others began to cough. Groaning timbers sounded like thunder. At any moment, the ceiling would collapse on them.

Only it didn't.

The estate had stopped falling.

Cettie willed the Leerings to shine, and they did. A fog seemed to linger in the air, but the dust began to settle. No one had kept on their feet. Her heart jumped into her throat when she saw Stephen was grievously injured. He lay still, a giant piece of plaster or stone next to his head. She saw the blood pooling around his head, saw the ragged fall of his chest, heard the wheezing of his breath. The dust made her want to sneeze.

Her mind flashed to another day, another injured young man. Joses. He had died in front of her. Her memory of that day was dagger-sharp from the Dryad's magic. She could remember every smell, the feeling of the cool mist on her face, the terror as the beast hovered over her, the anguish at her failure to save her friend.

Was she to lose Stephen in the same way?

Fumbling with her dress, she reached into the secret pocket in her vest. There, inside a watertight pouch, she withdrew the little stub of Everoot she'd been given at the poisoner school. She pressed it against Stephen's bleeding scalp. It might not be enough. It wouldn't be if he were already gone. She didn't beg for Stephen's life, although she wanted to.

Your will be done, she said, closing her eyes, holding the small patch of moss to the wound.

She felt the Everoot's magic fill the air, its song thrilling and lovely beyond description. The wound closed over, and she could see color rise to her almost-brother's chalky brow.

Stephen sat up, as others were beginning to do. He touched his forehead and looked surprised to see his fingers weren't stained with crimson.

He looked at Cettie and smiled weakly.

"You saved us," he whispered.

The intruder arrived after midnight. The hospital admits serious injuries at all hours, so this was not a surprise. That he ended up in my office, holding a pistol to my face, stunned me. He was a rough man, a man with scars riddling his cheeks and upper lip. His eyes were filled with a fervor that bordered on madness. I stared into those eyes, trying my best to keep calm, and it struck me that I'd seen them before. Had I passed this man on the streets? Had someone he loved died in my care? Why would he want revenge on me?

I asked him what he wanted. He said he'd come to kill me, to put a bullet in my brain. I told him, calmly as I could, that a bullet wouldn't kill me. That he should put the weapon down. Smirking, he told me that his bullet would. He knew I was a maston, and he'd killed many of us. I realized then that this was no ordinary drunkard or poppy slave of the Fells. He knew of the Mysteries. And that meant that his pistol, likely from the other world, would indeed kill me.

I asked him why he wanted me to die. That was the last question I asked, for then I held my breath. The Leerings in my chamber, connected to the estate of Fog Willows, were already at work, bringing in purer air from the clouds. I reversed the Leering, sending the air in the room away.

All the while those eyes stared at me. He was going to kill me. He would relish it. He said he was killing me because of Cettie. That she had sent him to murder me. How did that make me feel, he wondered, to know that she had sunk so low? I did not respond. I was holding my breath.

Until he collapsed on the floor, unconscious.

—Adam Creigh, Killingworth Hospital

SERA

CHAPTER EIGHTEEN
THE FELLS

A knock sounded on the door. Sera strained against the ropes securing her wrists and ankles, but the gag stuffed in her mouth prevented her from screaming. Through the crack in the door of the closet where she'd been imprisoned, she could see Joanna, still in her nightdress, standing by the door. Lady Corinne nodded to her once and then vanished without a trace, wrapped in magic.

Joanna undid several buttons on her nightdress, mussed up her hair, and then opened the door with a feigned lethargy.

"Yes?" she mumbled and then stiffened in feigned surprise.

"P-pardon, miss. I mean, I beg your pardon, Miss Patchett."

"Who are you?" Joanna asked, stifling a yawn. She stood in the doorway, blocking the view of the darkened interior. There was enough light streaming in from the hallway for Sera to see Joanna's face, but not that of the man she was talking to.

"I didn't know you were here . . . I mean, I'm terribly sorry. I have orders, miss, to search every room. I've been down all the rooms on this side. This was the last one. I'm sorry, miss, but I need to search it."

"You need to search my room?" Joanna said. If Sera had not known better, she would have believed the girl was truly confused. "You have a dragoon's jacket."

"Yes, miss. I-I am a dragoon."

"What's your name?" Joanna asked, inclining her neck. She flicked some hair off her shoulder. Sera bit into the gag, trying to grunt—anything that would reveal herself.

"My name is Baird, if you please. It's my duty, miss. I must inspect every room, every closet."

A throb of fear welled in Sera's heart. Though she wished more than anything to be freed, she knew this young man would have no hope of rescuing her. Lady Corinne would kill him—if the girl posing as Joanna did not do so first. His life meant nothing to them. Sera wrestled against her bonds, but they'd tied her up securely.

Why was Gimmerton Sough being searched? Had a servant gotten word to the Ministry of War?

Go away, Sera thought to the dragoon, willing him to hear her. *Forsake your duty this once. You cannot save me. You will die if you come into this room. There are* two *of them. You will die. Go. Please go!*

"If you must, Mr. Baird," the girl posing as Joanna said, opening the door wide, letting more light spill into the dark room. "Do you have a rank? My brother was a dragoon, you know." Her voice had a sultry quality to it now.

Sera watched as the young officer took a step forward. She saw the shine of the polish on his black boots. His blue dragoon jacket. He had fiery red hair and a look of worry on his flushed cheeks. As well he should.

Please go. Please go! Sera willed, gazing at him through the crack. *Go!*

He hesitated on the threshold, his head cocked sideways.

Joanna stood at the edge of the door. Although Lady Corinne was invisible, Sera imagined she was poised nearby with a dagger, ready to pounce on the young man as soon as he entered the darkened chamber.

Sera's insides writhed with worry. She stared at the soldier's innocent face. This was a young recruit, hardly a man at all. So many had already died in the war, the soldiers were getting younger and younger. He'd probably just passed the Test at one of the abbeys of the realm.

Please, heed me! Sera thought. *Go. Leave. You must.*

"Aren't you going to come in?" Joanna asked, a little smile lighting up her face.

The young man was clearly racked with indecision. Did he hear her, or was he merely reacting to the social prohibition that prevented women and men from being alone together.

His cheeks were still aflame with color. Was it embarrassment or some other reaction? Sera couldn't tell, but she willed him to step back into the corridor.

"I'll be back later, miss," he said, then retreated into the hall where Sera no longer could see him. "I think you should dress first, miss. And I'll bring my officer with me. Sorry to disturb your sleep."

Sera exhaled her pent-up breath, nearly sobbing in relief. Joanna stood at the precipice, and Sera could see she was wrestling with what to do next.

"Lieutenant!" the young man shouted out in the hall. "Lieutenant, can you come here, please?"

"Allow me to change," Joanna said, then shut and locked the door. Once she'd done so, she lit a lamp and set it on the table. Lady Corinne reappeared, a dark look on her face.

"He wouldn't come in," Joanna said, shaking her head. "Foolish boy," she added with derision.

Wise boy, Sera countered in her mind.

Joanna looked around in frustration. "This is Rand's room. I need a dress."

Lady Corinne cocked her head. "We're running out of time. They're coming."

"Who?" Joanna asked.

"Mrs. Pullman just told me that the Fitzroy tempest has landed in the yard." She paused, her head still inclined. "It's Stephen Fitzroy. And *she* has come too."

"Really?" Joanna asked in excitement.

Who did they mean? Anna? Lady Maren?

"It's time to leave," Lady Corinne said. "Get your bag."

Not again, Sera thought in despair. Her rescuers were practically standing outside the door. She was grateful the young man had retreated, but she wished he would return with more soldiers. With his lieutenant and Stephen and enough men and women to defeat her captors.

Corinne opened the closet door, and she and Joanna grabbed Sera's arms and hauled her to her feet. With her ankles tied together, she wobbled, her knees weakened by the strain of her position on the floor.

"Where are we going?" Joanna asked.

"Somewhere they won't search. Somewhere they *can't* search. We need to bide our time and arrange for the right leverage. But first, we must cut off a stray thread."

"Who? Mrs. Pullman?"

Lady Corinne nodded. "I've wanted to see her die for years. Ever since . . ." She stopped herself, perhaps seeing Joanna's hungry look, and swallowed the secret. Sera wondered at the crack in composure. Corinne had lost the self-control she'd shown at Pavenham Sky. Her secrets were starting to spill out now after having been bottled up so long.

Why did Corinne hate Mrs. Pullman? It was an unintentional slip, but Sera had caught it and clung to it.

"What are you going to do?" Joanna asked.

"Let Gimmerton Sough fall," Lady Corinne said with malice in her voice.

Joanna's eyed widened with awe and respect. "How?"

"I own the deed of this place," she said. "The keeper works for me. Her mind is so wrapped up in knots, she'll want to die. She knows she'd be tried for murder anyway. Why not die now, on her terms, destroying her enemy as well?"

Her enemy. Who was Mrs. Pullman's enemy? Cettie? Could she be the woman who'd arrived with Stephen?

Did that mean her friend was still faithful to her? Hope flickered to life in her heart but was quickly doused by the realization that Cettie and Stephen and all the soldiers in the manor might be about to die. She wished more than anything to buck and fight, but it would do no good. If she truly hoped to defeat them, she would wait for her opening.

"Here, on the bed," Lady Corinne said. The two wrestled Sera to the edge, keeping their tight, punishing grip on her arms as they made her sit. Lady Corinne drew the Tay al-Ard from a pocket in her skirts. Joanna eyed it hungrily. There was competition between the two women, she realized. Yes, they worked for the same ends. For now. But Sera could sense a deeper rivalry. Lady Corinne's fame and power had waned while Joanna Patchett's had risen. No one wanted to give up power or influence, even if it was simply part of a cover.

Sera waited, wishing she didn't have the gag in her mouth. She heard voices beyond the door. Were the soldiers conferring with each other? They were waiting for Miss Patchett to dress. How long would they wait before they knocked again?

How much time passed, Sera didn't know. Minutes? A quarter hour? More? But then light began to flicker beneath the door. Lady Corinne glanced at Joanna with a secret smile.

Sera's stomach lurched as Gimmerton Sough began to plummet. Cries of worry and alarm filled the air. Bodies thumped against the door, then the wall. Joanna's eyes glowed with silver light. The manor was rushing down, ready to shatter on the plain below. Sera feared for her friends, she feared that the landing would cause another earthquake for her people. The damage wrought by Pavenham Sky's fall was still felt, a year later.

Joanna's grip on Sera's arm tightened. And then the Tay al-Ard yanked them away, adding to the delirium of confusion. They were gone.

When they arrived at their destination, the sudden horrible smell was overpowering. Sera remembered this stench from her time in the house on Kelper Street. Some days, especially after it had rained, she would get a whiff of it while walking past the vents that led to the cesspits below the houses. The smell of sewage and trash had a strange, sickly sweet stench, one that instinctively made her want to gag and cover her nose with a handkerchief. In other parts of the City, she knew, the smell was unbearable.

This—this was so much *worse*.

They were standing on a little narrow square of wood at the bottom of a set of stairs. Lanterns hung from hooks on the walls, casting light on the support timbers and floorboards above their heads. The sound of rakes scraping through sludge sent shivers down Sera's back. Human filth covered the ground, which created such a noxious vapor the air was almost unbreathable. Sera felt her gorge rising but couldn't cover her mouth with the bonds and gag.

There were grunts from a man, followed by the loud bark of an order, then a slap and the cry of a child.

"What is this awful place?" Joanna said, a look of horror and disgust on her face. She turned to Lady Corinne in surprise.

Sera looked at her as well and did a double take. A different woman was standing there. Gone was the prim and composed look of Lady Corinne of Pavenham Sky. This woman, though still handsome, was quite a bit older, with silver in her hair and wrinkled skin around her eyes.

"Ack! Visituhs!" shouted a grimy man as he approached them, dragging a shovel or rake behind him.

"Mr. Trimble," Corinne said with a slight bow.

The man was filthy from head to foot. Muck was splattered on his pants, his boots. He wore gloves, but they were the working kind, not the velvet sort favored by the upper classes. His long beard was caked with the filth, and as he extended his arms wide, he showed them a grin that was missing at least one tooth.

"It can't be her!" he bellowed with a nasty look. The right part of his head was shaved, and his long dark hair and beard were riddled with gray. His eyes had a cunning look. "Thar she is! My precious Tyna has returned home! Look how fancy you are! Is this a social call?" He leered at them.

Sera felt her skin crawl.

"I need to use the lockroom, Trimble," Corinne said. "Just for a day or two."

"What? Only a day or two? You haven't brought me more workers?" He ambled up the few steps to the landing and leaned his rake against the wall. His boots were oily in addition to being filthy. He looked over Sera with a sneer and grabbed her chin with his befouled gloves. "Who is this pretty little bird, eh? All trussed up and gagged. Look at her face. Did her father carve her up like this?" He laughed, and Sera felt a hideous sensation swell in the room, more powerful even than the stench.

"The lockroom, if you please," said Lady Corinne.

"Of course, of course! I could put her to work, you know, Tyna. Make her scrape the muck like the children. You can't know how hard it is to find workers now with this cursed war on. Mostly girls on my crew now anyway. How old is this one, seventeen? I like 'em young."

He leered at her again, and Sera shuddered. Glancing at Joanna, Sera saw the other girl had a growing look of revulsion. Joanna did not look contented to be there. Her eyes narrowed with distrust.

So this was not part of the plan, then. Sera would try to use that.

"This way, my dears. You follow Mr. Trimble this way. Watch your step, if you can!" He cackled with glee and tromped down, hoisting his awful rake and trying to clear a path ahead.

"Cut her ankles loose," Lady Corinne ordered.

Joanna reached inside her bag and withdrew a gleaming dagger. She crouched by Sera's feet, wincing at the specks of filth that had already collected on their persons. She sliced through the bonds, freeing Sera's legs at last.

"Walk," Corinne ordered, pushing her down the steps. Sera's hands and mouth were still bound, and she had little choice but to follow. As she gazed down at the miserable gallery, she saw children scraping the muck. Some as young as seven or eight years old. They were filthy, their faces smeared beyond recognition, their clothes soiled. It struck her that they were made to work at night so that people wouldn't see them. This work was the lowest of the low. Her heart ached at the realization that her programs for the poor had not gone far enough. Young children should not be doing this sort of work. And then she noticed that each had an ankle chain, and the chains were fixed to rings that lined the support posts.

Were they in the City? Or the Fells?

Mr. Trimble escorted them to a room with a door made of iron. He pulled out a large ring of keys and jiggled one of them into the lock at the door. As he pulled it open, the hinges squeaked and groaned. Some of the children shuddered and looked away from the terrible noise, working with their little rakes to clear the sludge.

Joanna was walking in her slippers, wincing with utter contempt with each step she took. The pretty silk was soiled and soaked through. It was obvious she cared much less for this assignment than she had impersonating the fashionable Joanna Patchett. By the time they reached the room, Mr. Trimble had already lit a candle. The horrible stench clung to Sera's skin, her clothes.

"Welcome to the lockroom," he said, setting his rake aside as he swung the door open. There were chains fastened to the walls, pegs holding manacles of different sizes, most of them small but many large enough for adult men. The floor was dirty cement. He went to a wall and, wrinkling his nose, picked one. "There . . . this should fit 'er. Do you mean to lock up both of 'em?"

"I am *not* staying here," Joanna said under her breath.

"Yes, you are. We'll discuss it later," Corinne shot back.

"Come in, come in." Trimble gestured with his hands. Sera entered the dark cell. There were no windows, no light at all except for the half-melted candle. There were no Leerings at all in there, or in the cesspit.

He came forward and crouched by Sera's feet. His filthy gloves lifted her dress, exposing her ankles and shoes. He clucked his tongue. "Shoes this fine could fetch a fine price on the street, Tyna, even dirtied as they are. Can I have 'em?"

"Not yet," Lady Corinne said, her expression hard and guarded. A different woman. A different face. Was this a disguise? Or could it be that Lady Corinne was the disguise?

"I should be grateful to have such a pair as these. Such weak, skinny legs." One of his hands went up her leg, making her wrestle against her bonds and try to jerk away. His hand clenched around her calf muscle, pinching hard enough to make her flinch and cry out against the gag. He brought the manacle around her ankle and secured it with one of the little keys on his ring.

He then jiggled her leg, testing the grip and making sure there wasn't room for her foot to escape. As if proud of his handiwork, he straightened and looked down at her, his bushy beard so close to her face her skin itched.

"Got a lot of spirit left, this one," he grunted. "Who's she? That dress is pretty fine as well, 'cept for the blood. Need help taming 'er?"

"I can manage, Mr. Trimble," Lady Corinne said. "I just need her kept here in the lockroom for a couple of days."

"Want me to feed 'er? That'll cost extra."

"No need. Thank you, Mr. Trimble. You may go."

Sera felt a pulse, a throb of the Mysteries, and then the man huffed, wiping his narrow nose on his forearm. He looked Joanna over, grunted, and then grabbed his rake and made his way back to the open iron door.

"She won't get away from me," he said as he stood in the doorway. "None of them ever get away from me."

After he had left the cell, closing and locking the door behind him, Joanna whirled on Corinne. "Why this place?" she asked, her voice shaking in rage. "Of all your hideouts, why this one?"

"Because they will not find her here," Corinne said.

"This is horrible!" Joanna snapped. "I cannot stay here, not dressed like this! I've never smelled anything so revolting in my life. Take me somewhere else."

"I don't have time!" Lady Corinne said, her face betraying a flash of anger.

The two women stared at each other, poisoner against poisoner. Sera felt they were on the verge of attacking each other.

"I cannot stay here. Not like this," Joanna said. "I'm in my night clothes."

"But you can. And you will. Take her dress if you must. Or make yourself appear to be clothed. Do what you will! But you must wait with her until the preparations are done."

Joanna's eyes flashed with anger and resentment. Then she turned on Sera, still gripping the knife in her hand. "I'll have your dress, then. At least until I can find something better. I wish there were a poisoner school here."

"There will be soon enough," Lady Corinne said. "Don't leave her unguarded. Mr. Trimble has his . . . *fits*."

It was said with a voice of experience that made Sera go cold.

CHAPTER NINETEEN

THE INVISIBLES

Corinne left them, and Joanna promptly untied Sera's wrists so she could take her dress. Left only in a dirty shift, Sera felt even more vulnerable. Her eyes had grown used to the darkness, but she didn't think she would ever get used to the smell. The scraping noises had recommenced as soon as Mr. Trimble had left them, bolting the door behind him. The only light emanated from the fat stub of a candle.

While Joanna squeezed into Sera's bloodstained gown, Sera worked at the gag that prevented her speaking. The knot behind her head was difficult to maneuver with her shaking hands, but she picked at it with the fingers of her good hand.

Joanna stared at her arms, at the fabric barely reaching her wrists, her nose pinched with disgust and anger. She reached behind her back, trying to secure the buttons, but it would not be easy without a maid.

The knot loosened, and Sera ripped the gag from her mouth. Freedom at long last.

"Corinne's plans are falling apart," Sera said after rubbing her jaw.

Joanna turned and scowled, still struggling with the buttons.

"Have you considered what will happen to you when the ministries find us? I think they will. It's only a matter of time."

"I didn't tie the gag well enough," Joanna said with a sharp look.

Sera scooted herself back, her ankle beginning to throb from the manacle secured there. "Hear me out. You and I both know Corinne . . . possibly better than anyone else. Her behavior has been more erratic of late. Surely you've noticed."

"And what of it?" Joanna asked. "Do you think you can persuade me to let you go?"

At least she was talking. It was a start.

"It would be to your advantage if you considered it," Sera said. "If you're caught, you'll be executed. No other outcome is possible. I don't know if you fancy being hung on a gallows, but I imagine it's not very pleasant. That is the fate of traitors and spies. But if you help me escape, I promise that you will not be killed."

Joanna snorted. "I'm sure you'd find a comfortable cell for me, Your Majesty. But no thank you. Not even you could protect me from them."

"Who?"

"I've said enough." She turned away, hiding her troubled expression as she continued to paw the buttons. Sera's frame was smaller than Joanna's, so the dress didn't fit very well.

"Here, let me help you," Sera offered.

Joanna turned, startled and suspicious.

"That dress isn't meant to be buttoned up by one person," Sera explained. "I'll help. Come closer. I can't go anywhere. You think I can break this chain with my hands?"

"You might try something foolish."

"I'm trying to survive this ordeal," Sera said. "Nothing more, nothing less. Come closer. I doubt I could best you even if I had a weapon."

"You couldn't," Joanna said archly. She approached and sank lower, low enough that Sera could reach the buttons. She moved her hair out of the way.

Sera tugged at the fabric and managed a few buttons on the top and the bottom, but they strained against the eyelets. There was no way she could close the gap.

"There," Sera said with a sigh. "That's the most that will go in."

"Thank you," Joanna said.

She started to rise, but Sera gripped her hand firmly, stopping her. "You said I couldn't protect you from them," Sera said in a low voice. "Who did you mean? The poisoners?"

Joanna gave her a dark expression. Still looking into Sera's eyes, she reached down and wrenched her hand loose, sending a searing pain into Sera's shoulder.

"Your empire has hunted us for generations," she hissed with a menacing voice. "I'm a hetaera, Sera. I did it willingly. Do you think the Ministry of Thought would allow you to protect me?"

"I'm the empress," Sera said, gritting her teeth. "I can."

"You couldn't even protect yourself," Joanna said with disdain. "It wasn't that difficult getting to you."

"You're lying," Sera said, shaking her head. She tried to wrench her arm back to end the pain, but she couldn't. "It takes time to subvert someone. To manipulate them into doing what you want."

"It happens a lot faster than you would think," Joanna said, letting go of Sera's hand. "Even the scrupulous ones. I've been working on Stephen Fitzroy. If he survives the fall of the manor, I've no doubt I'll get through to him. Every person will fall if the enticement suits them. Your empire has been corrupted beneath your very nose, Empress. You need look no further than your own father."

Sera's heart boiled in anger. "And you need look no further than Brant Fitzroy. Not everyone falls. He didn't."

Joanna shrugged. "One man doesn't make much of a difference."

"Sometimes it can make all the difference," Sera said. "If it is prison that you fear, then we can make another arrangement."

"I don't fear your prisons," Joanna said. Then she looked around the cement floor stained and smeared with muck, her nostrils flaring. "It doesn't matter. Your promises are nothing more than smoke."

"How little you trust," Sera said, shaking her head.

"Well, it was trusting that got you into this mess in the first place," Joanna said slyly. "Your own mother delivered you to us on a silver platter. Besides, I knew I might die ere this assignment was finished. It's the risk we all accepted with the brand. Even Cettie accepted it. Yes, your pious little Cettie is one of us now. We will gain back what was lost. What was ripped away from us by the first empress. You *will* restore our true queen to us, Sera."

"You are mistaken," Sera said. Maybe Cettie's involvement was a lie after all. Lies were the coin these people used. "You cannot force me."

"We'll see," Joanna said, smiling. "I'm not going to stay in this sludge pit any longer than I have to. I need some air. And since I can't have you trying to escape, I have just the remedy for you." She twisted a ring on her finger, exposing a needle. Before Sera could react, Joanna jabbed it into Sera's shoulder. There was a sharp bite of pain and then fog. Sera felt herself slumping.

How long Sera was unconscious, she didn't know. The poison left her groggy and lethargic. The small candle had burned out, leaving her in utter blackness. She was aware of sounds, of movement, of the dragging of chains. Still, she couldn't move. Her muscles were too rigid and heavy.

She was thirsty again, and her stomach gnawed with fierce hunger. Her body ached, not just because of her wounds, but from the cramped posture and the iron manacle's grip on her ankle. Her thoughts were dark and brooding.

In her sluggish haze, she called out in exasperation to the Mysteries.

Why did you let this happen to me? I have tried to be good, to change from the selfish princess I used to be. I want to do your will. Why must I suffer these degradations? If I'm meant to die, then why not just end it now?

Silence met her mute entreaty. This did not surprise her. For while she'd felt the power of the Mysteries many times, had even been given words to speak on its behalf—like the Gifting she had performed for Lord Fitzroy on his deathbed—she knew she couldn't force an answer to come. So she waited in the darkness.

As she began to tremble, her muscles coming back to her again, she thought she heard a whisper in her mind. A fleeting whisper, so faint it could hardly be discerned over the clanking chains in the other room.

With ordinary folk like you and me, if our pleas to the Medium are sometimes granted, beyond all hope or expectation, we had best not draw conclusions that we have earned such treatment. If we were stronger, we might be less caringly handled. If we only had more courage, we might be sent with far less help to defend even more desperate posts in the thickest battles of life and death.

She'd read those words in a tome years ago, while studying at Muirwood Abbey. The sentiment hadn't made much sense to her at the time, but something about the passage had lodged in her mind.

She was comforted by the words, strangely enough, and felt as if they were the answer to her silent plea. Her experiences were for a purpose in a greater cause. The certainty of this thought gave her strength. Warmth unfurled inside her, and she lifted herself up, dragging the heavy chain a few inches across the floor. She leaned against the stone wall of the lockroom, conviction burning inside her.

If we only had more courage . . .

Sera's mind lunged at the thought, grasping onto it. *Send me,* she thought. *Send me into battle.*

A key fit into the lock, and then the iron door groaned and opened. She saw Mr. Trimble smack a boy on the back of his head and bark at him to get in. The children were all assembled outside the lockroom.

One by one, they entered and took their places along the wall. There were fifteen . . . no, eighteen children in all. The big beast of the man struck some of them as they entered the room. The punishments seemed arbitrary, and she saw each child cringe in anticipation of being chosen.

"Get in, get in, you little blighters," Trimble sneered.

Each child was in chains, she saw, and several of them were bound together. A ritual then unfolded before her light-stabbed eyes. Under the overseer's watchful eyes, the children fastened themselves to the manacles fixed to the wall. None of them could run away, she saw. They were bound to each other, then to the wall. And Mr. Trimble held the keys.

The ritual complete, the children sat shoulder to shoulder in the cramped room, some of them within reach of Sera. Those nearest her were looking at her in curiosity. She was bigger than most of them, but a few of the youths were teens. They all had a starved, wasted look that put her in mind of the stories Cettie had told her about growing up in the Fells.

"I'll be checking each one," Trimble said. "No mistakes, or I'll cuff you with my key ring. Ya hear me?" He staggered into the room and gave an exaggerated yawn. "It's morning, my little pups. Time to sleep. All snuggled and warm, *heh heh*. A litter of pups. Litter, that's all you are."

Trimble went from one end of the room to the other, testing each of the manacles. He'd even tested Sera's connection to the wall. Once he was through, he removed the chains attaching the children to one another. He was precise and methodical. There was no hope of escape.

Sera's heart throbbed with pity as she looked at the children's grimy faces. These were nothing more than slaves. Nothing her government did had touched their ruined lives. How could it? They lived below the streets, away from the seeing eyes of the Leerings in the fountains above. And she had a feeling Mr. Trimble wasn't the only one engaged in such a trade.

Her attention was roused when Mr. Trimble suddenly smacked one of the children. "I saw that look! Don't you sass me! I won't stand for it! I won't!" He smacked the child again, the noise making all the rest of the children flinch. The boy was weeping, shoulders hunched, trembling.

She clenched her fists, trembling with rage, wishing she could command a dragoon to beat him.

"And you!" he said, lurching toward another boy. He struck him too. "I saw you slacking at the end. Hardly pushing your rake at all. You think I'm jesting? That I won't fix a millstone to your ankles and throw you into the river outside town? If you're not going to work, I'd just as soon drown ya! What good are you to me?"

"I'm sorry!" the boy wailed. "I'm-I'm sorry, Mr. Trimble!"

"You'd better be sorry! I won't abide laziness. None of it. You want to eat, you must work. You work harder tonight, and you'll get your bread tomorrow morning. Mind that, lad. You better mind that."

The boy looked devastated at the thought of missing a meal. But he didn't complain. None of them did. They were terrified.

He finished unlocking the extra chains and left them all in a heap on the floor. Trimble looked from face to face, rubbing his scraggly beard, his eyes wells of menace. He was looking for something. No one met his eyes, all heads were bowed low.

"You," he said at last, pointing to a little girl. The feeling of misery and despair in the dark, fetid room increased, making Sera's stomach ill. "It's your turn. Up. Stand up!"

The little girl rose, her chain dragging against the stone. Everyone looked away from her, their expressions both guilty and grateful. They were thankful they had not been chosen.

The awfulness of the moment seared Sera's heart. She found herself standing, pushing herself up against the wall before she could even think.

Mr. Trimble turned at the noise, spotting her. "What are you doing?"

"Go," Sera told him, her voice trembling.

In two steps, he was in front of her. He slapped her face without hesitation. The sting shocked her, his violence terrified her, but she did not turn away. Staring at him again, she repeated her command—"go"—directing her will against his. "Leave them alone."

Rage and fury filled his eyes. He hammered his fists against Sera, who pulled in her elbows to protect her body from the assault. Blow after blow struck her. He was screaming at her, but she couldn't hear his words—the pounding of her heartbeat deafened her to them. She didn't understand why, but his blows didn't hurt.

"Leave!" Sera yelled at him, and again he went wild, striking her over and over. The blows hit her back, her ribs, her shoulders, but something gave her the strength to stand against it, to endure it. She'd never been beaten before, not like these poor waifs. Not like Cettie.

She saw the wild madness in his eyes, the uncontrollable anger. He would keep beating her because she had spoken up. She had challenged his authority in front of the children. But she wouldn't stand aside. She wouldn't abandon these children as so many others had done.

His blows slowed, and she looked at him, her teeth chattering. She was full of emotion, full of defiance. "You cannot make me cry," she told him, shaking her head, sagging against the wall.

His look of rage only intensified. He was consumed by the Myriad Ones. She could feel their heavy presence in the room. Their host might not recognize her, but they did. And they wanted to break her.

Sera stared into his face and thought the command word. *Banirexpiare.*

It was as if she had punched him back without using her fists. Mr. Trimble staggered backward, a slack look on his face, his jaw hanging wide.

The Myriad Ones who'd inhabited him dispersed. Sera stared at him, her breath coming in shallow gasps. Her arms were throbbing now in pain.

"Go!" Sera commanded him.

He stared at her, knees quaking, and then walked out and slammed the iron door, fixing the key in place and locking it. He'd left his lantern on the middle of the floor.

All the children stared at her in wonderment.

"Who are you?" one of them asked in a whisper.

"I'm Sera," she answered, trembling anew at what she'd endured. She hadn't backed down. The bruises and aches from the beating she'd endured were beginning to surface. Her stomach had never felt so sick before.

"Sera? Like the empress?" It was the little girl who spoke, the one who'd been chosen for punishment.

"Yes," Sera answered. "I *am* the empress. And I will see that each one of you is freed from this filth."

CHAPTER TWENTY

SECRETS

In the dark of the cesspit, there was no way to tell day from night. The children slept fitfully, some of them—the ones who were closest—nestling into Sera's warmth. She could hear all the little noises they made, the weary sighs, the whimpers, the shifting on the dirty stone floor. Every moment, she felt more resolved to help them.

When Mr. Trimble returned, much later, he carried a lantern in one hand and an iron truncheon in the other. Sera's eyes widened when she saw the weapon, and a tingle of fear swept down her spine. Her arms and shoulders still throbbed from his earlier beating. Children lifted their heads at the noise of the door grating open. Every last one of them was terrified of him.

Sera struggled to control her expression, but she was relieved to see Joanna follow the brutish overseer into the room. She had purchased a new outfit, one appropriate for the Fells. The fabric was dark, the gloves black, and the bonnet had a veil pulled back. She carried a large parcel under her arm.

"Come on, you rats," Mr. Trimble snarled. "Up. Up and get ready. I brought your breakfast. You can eat while you walk. We're going to another pit tonight." He passed around a bucket of water, with a ladle gripping the rim. The children ate and each took a long drink. When it was Sera's turn, she started to gulp it down.

He scanned the crowd of children, his gaze coming to rest on Sera. A brutal, menacing look twisted his blunt features into an even uglier mask. He set the lantern down and then tapped the heel of his hand with the truncheon.

"Thirsty, lass? Feeling feisty again?" he asked Sera. She could sense the Myriad Ones crawling inside him once more.

She stared at him boldly, refusing to look away. He stepped forward, giving Sera a better view of Joanna. The other woman's brow had wrinkled in concern.

"Take the children and go," Joanna told him.

"I don't take orders from you, wench," Mr. Trimble said.

She glared at him. "You *will*, or you'll find yourself on the ground clutching your manhood in agony."

Trimble's eyebrows lifted. "Ah! Or I can bash your brains in with this?" He hefted the truncheon.

Joanna stared at him, her eyes turning silver in the dark. A feeling of dread and menace filled the room. Sera gazed at her in amazement as the oppressive feelings Mr. Trimble had brought into the room scattered.

"By all means, try it," Joanna said. A pulse of fear exuded from her, and Mr. Trimble's composure began to wilt. The children cowered from her, their fearful expressions showing the effect it had on them as well.

"Come on, rats! Come on!" He tucked the truncheon under his arm and dragged the chains he'd left on the floor. "Lock up your ankles, you vermin. Come on, you know how. Get moving, get moving!"

The frightened children obeyed, one by one, and Mr. Trimble unlocked them from the wall once they were chained to one another. From chain to chain they went, their eyes wary and tired. Some of them glanced hopefully at Sera, and she burned their faces into her memory. Of course they moved the children at night, when gangs and the Fear Liath ruled the streets. That would change, she vowed. If she had to use the Ministry of War to tame the Fells, she would. Distracted by the war, she'd allowed the lawlessness to go on for too long.

The sound of the dragging chains made her shiver with dread as the children marched out the door. Trimble frowned at them, cuffing a few for no reason at all, and Sera seethed.

Joanna watched the procession pass. She had a little frown on her mouth, and her nostrils flared. Trimble was about to fetch the lantern, but she told him to leave it.

His bearded face twisted with displeasure at the order, but he didn't defy her. After he left, he shut the iron door of the lockroom behind him. The silver glow faded from Joanna's eyes.

"I brought you another dress," Joanna said, bringing the parcel closer. "It's not fancy."

"I don't need fancy," Sera said. "And it's cold down here. Thank you."

Joanna untied the knot that held the parcel closed and quickly opened it, revealing a plain gray dress with lacings on the back instead of buttons. The rich wool looked invitingly warm, and Sera sat up, dragging her ankle chain to get closer.

With deft fingers, Joanna unfolded the gown and moved to help Sera put it on over her shift.

"Are those bruises?" the poisoner asked suddenly, her brows lifting in surprise. Sera could see them on her upper arms.

"I probably have them all over," Sera said. "Trimble beat me after you left."

Joanna fetched the lantern and shone it on Sera, who winced at the bright light.

"He *did* thrash you," Joanna murmured, her voice angry. Then a little twist quirked her mouth. "It's probably your first."

"Yes," Sera said, nodding. "My father was cruel, but he wasn't brutal."

"Yes, he was cruel," Joanna said. "And egotistical and easily manipulated." She helped Sera pull on the dress. It felt good to have a layer of wool on. The cloth felt like a protection, even though she knew it wouldn't stop a man like Trimble.

"My father wasn't always like that, you know," Sera said.

"Power corrupts," Joanna said, nodding in agreement.

"You have a great deal of power," Sera said. "You've been groomed to take Corinne's place, have you not? The way she brought you to Pavenham Sky and let you rule the girls."

"You're observant for a royal," Joanna said, pursing her lips and tightening the lacings in the back. At least it didn't come with a corset.

"I've had a lot of time to think, lately," Sera answered. "Do you know where they are keeping Prince Trevon?"

"And why would I tell you that?" Joanna asked, brushing her hands together and rising.

"I'm only curious."

"That you are. But you're asking me to divulge a secret. I won't do it."

Sera shrugged and leaned back against the wall. "And so we wait here in this cesspit until Corinne returns. How gloomy."

Joanna gazed around at the dank room. "It wasn't my first choice either."

"Do you know Corinne's history? How she was turned? I heard from Lord Fitzroy that she was lost for a while during a visit to Kingfountain. Did it happen then?"

"No," Joanna scoffed. "That was a ploy to get her governess fired."

Sera wrinkled her brow. "Truly?"

"You saw her true face, Sera," Joanna said. "Corinne is the *mask*. She rarely reveals herself like that. She's much older than the part she plays."

"Still, she's a handsome woman," Sera said, her mind whirling. "Trimble called her by another name. Tyna was it?"

"I brought you a few rolls to eat," Joanna said, reaching into her pocket and producing a little bag. As she opened it, the delicious scent of fresh bread made Sera's mouth water. "Eat them, I've already had a share."

Sera knew it for a dismissal, but she didn't object. Not yet. She needed those rolls. She devoured them, the soft, slightly sweet bread heavenly in her mouth. Not even the smell of the cesspit could totally ruin the taste.

Joanna paced the room, looking at the chains fastened to the walls, the filth everywhere. Her nose flared with disgust, and she shook her head.

As Sera ate, she continued to ponder the mystery of Lady Corinne's true identity.

The Tay al-Ard can only bring you to a place you've visited before. Tyna knows Mr. Trimble. She knows about his fits. Because she's experienced them herself. How many bruises did he give her?

The pieces of information whirled around her mind, struggling to fit together into a larger picture, as she finished every crumb in the bag. She was missing something, she knew, the key to unravel the situation. Joanna continued to pace, looking more and more disgruntled by the forced captivity.

"Tell me who Tyna is," Sera asked in a soft voice.

Joanna turned and smirked. "Why should I do that? We may as well talk about the weather."

"I sense a storm coming," Sera said, giving her a thoughtful look. "Her plan isn't working. That's why we're both down here."

Joanna frowned and turned away.

"You were supposed to take her place. But she made Gimmerton Sough plummet to the earth. It's shattered into rubble by now. What does that mean for you? It means you are expendable."

"If you don't stop talking," Joanna said, an angry glint in her eye, "I just may poison you again to make you be quiet."

Sera fell silent. Doubt, uncertainty, suspense—those dark emotions were preying on Joanna's mind, and Sera had just stirred them up like a hive of bees. It didn't take a kystrel to realize that.

Then it came to her, a bolt of intelligence, a memory that made sense of everything. The Mysteries had given her the nudge she needed.

"I know who she is," Sera whispered, her heart beating fast.

"What are you talking about now?" Joanna asked.

During their years together at Muirwood, Cettie and Sera had become very close. They'd shared stories from their childhoods with one another. Sera had told Cettie of the day her father had saved her from falling out of a tree—the last time she'd felt loved by him. Cettie had told her of her life in the Fells, a wretched existence Fitzroy had saved her from. Over the years, they'd shared everything with each other. Cettie had once told her, in confidence, about Lord Fitzroy's lost love. The story itself wasn't much of a secret. It was fodder for gossip among the elite. But Cettie knew something most of the others did not. She knew the woman's name.

Christina.

My precious Tyna has returned home! She could hear Trimble's voice in her mind. *Look how fancy you are!*

Trimble was roughly the same age as Christina, though the streaks of gray and leathery skin made him look older. He knew her because they'd once been chained together in this very lockroom.

Fitzroy had searched for Christina for years. He'd searched the Fells, never to find her. Of course not, because she had been sequestered underground in the worst of places. She wouldn't have known he was searching for her. A woman who'd served at Fog Willows, and charmed the heir to the estate, had been reduced to scraping human refuse. What a bitter fate. Because of Mrs. Pullman?

No wonder she'd wished for revenge.

Yes, the pieces were fitting together snugly.

"The look on your face," Joanna said, interrupting the flow of thoughts. "I don't like it."

Sera turned and looked at her. "I know who she is," Sera said. "Tyna." Then another realization struck her. "Mr. Skrelling almost learned the truth about her, didn't he? He found out Corinne was Cettie's mother, but if he'd asked the Cruciger orb different questions, he might have learned she was just an imposter. Like you."

"We're *all* imposters," Joanna said smugly. "Including you. Your mother had an affair with an officer from the Ministry of War. I should call you Sera *Pratt*."

Doubt stabbed inside Sera's heart. She'd feared the truth about her parentage ever since Lady Corinne had cast doubt on it when she was a child. But Joanna's words didn't feel right. It didn't match the certainty of the convictions she'd felt earlier.

"That was investigated and proven false," Sera said.

"But how do you know?" Joanna asked, her voice throbbing with mischief.

"This isn't about me," Sera said, shaking her head. "I didn't choose to be empress. The position was bestowed on me. I have touched the Command Leering, and it has obeyed me. I don't think it would have if my blood were tainted."

"Are you so sure?"

"I am, actually," Sera said. "Your words are only intended to make me doubt myself. But doubt and belief cannot coexist. One must drive out the other."

"A fancy speech, Your Highness," Joanna said. "You're just unwilling to accept the truth."

"And what do you know of truth?" Sera shot back. "You are living a lie. You aren't Joanna Patchett. You've only been trained to impersonate her. To know her mannerisms, her way of speaking. You use magic to disguise your face. Who are you really? A servant who lost her place? An urchin who was starving and dreamed of a better life?"

Something in Sera's accusations must have struck home because Joanna flinched, her smug look fading.

A spell of quiet passed between them.

"You don't know what it's like to be poor," the young woman said in a strained voice, full of vengeance, full of despair.

Sera stared at her, gauging her emotions. They were genuine, she decided, not wrought by a magical amulet.

"You're right, I don't," Sera said. "But be honest with me. If someone takes my place, *pretending* to be empress, do you think the inequality will change? It won't. Did Christina use the wealth she accrued from Pavenham Sky to free other children bound in chains? No. She garnered more and more power. Not to heal the wounds. But to murder. You've seen yourself what I have tried to do as empress. It hasn't been enough. It won't be enough until there are no longer any starving children, until there are no longer any more desperate individuals who sell themselves or their offspring in deeds of servitude."

Joanna was staring at her. Something was changing in her face. Was her resolve weakening?

"Show me who you really are," Sera said. "Show me your real face."

Silence.

Joanna's voice was just a whisper. "I don't want to be *her* anymore."

"Show me," Sera asked.

She watched as the illusion melted away. Standing in the fashionable Joanna's stead was an average woman with a round face, a slightly pointed nose, and brownish-blond hair. Ordinary. Simple. And then Sera understood, and her heart ached. Joanna's glamorous life was everything she'd dreamed of—only it wasn't real. Reality would always be preferable to a pretty dream.

"Help me," Sera pleaded. "Help me get back home."

"If I do, they will kill me," the woman said, her voice trembling. "I swore an oath that I would suffer myself to die before betraying them."

"I absolve you of that oath," Sera said.

The woman pretending to be Joanna frowned.

"Can you unlock the chain?" Sera asked, holding out her leg.

"I can," came the reply. There was a look of hesitation. Of distrust. Then the woman nodded and started forward.

That was when Christina appeared. How long had she lingered there, invisible and ready to strike? Long enough to witness the conversation. Long enough to see the betrayal.

"Look out!" Sera warned.

Joanna turned, and the two poisoners faced each other. A knife appeared in Joanna's hand, the silver blade gleaming in the lantern light. The pallor on her cheeks showed that she knew she'd been compromised. There would be no arguing, no pleading. One would have to kill the other.

Joanna flung her blade at Christina's head, just as the other woman raised a pistol. Christina dodged at the last instant, and the blade arced past her face.

An explosion sounded in the lockroom, so loud it deafened Sera. She clamped her hands over her ears, but they were already ringing painfully. Hazy smoke filled the room along with the pungent odor of sulfur and powder.

Joanna sank to her knees, her mouth gaping in shock. She was fumbling for something in her dress, and Sera watched in horror as the girl's skin began to blacken and shrivel. She gaped, trying to speak, her mouth working until her skin began to come off in flakes. Before Sera's eyes, Joanna's limbs and body desiccated until she slumped onto the floor, nothing but dust and a heap of clothes.

Christina lowered the smoking pistol.

"What-what was that?" Sera stammered, shuddering, her ears squealing with pain but hearing again.

Christina walked forward and revealed the Tay al-Ard strapped to her arm. "A special poison," she said, her eyes hard and angry. "A rare poison. Deathbane."

I am writing this note from Lockhaven, where I delivered the man who was sent to kill me. He had a kystrel around his neck, which I removed after he fell unconscious at the hospital. Prime Minister Durrant informed me, after the man was interrogated, that he was a former Ministry of War dragoon who'd been presumed dead. His death, it seems, was staged, and he was instead shuttled off to Kingfountain to be trained in the art of subterfuge.

His true name is Will Russell. Yes, the very one who was involved in the disgrace of Her Majesty. He is in chains and under guard. I have asked to see him, to learn what I can of Cettie's whereabouts. He seemed to know quite a bit about her. But my petitions have been in vain. I cannot sleep. I can find no rest. Did she truly send him to kill me? I don't want to believe it.

I don't know what to believe anymore. There's a knock at the door. I must go.

—Adam Creigh, writing from Lockhaven

CETTIE

CHAPTER TWENTY-ONE
LURKING BENEATH

It started as her visions always did, with a strange feeling of aloofness, a drifting away from consciousness, and the tingling power of the Mysteries coursing through her body. Cettie forgot where her physical body was as the vision subsumed her, wrapping her up and lifting her away. She found herself gliding over the foam-tipped waves as if she were a gull, the rustle of the sea and the wind filling her ears.

Then she noticed the shadow beneath the water, staining the sea like a drab of ink. The vision sucked her below the surface. She involuntarily flinched, even though they could not harm her—her spirit self wasn't drenched after all, nor did she need to breathe. The colors beneath the waves shifted as the brilliant light of sunrise stabbed through the water. She'd barely noticed the position of the sun, but the knowledge of its timing came, supplied by the magic that had brought her there. She was a harbinger—a seer of things to be.

Below the waves she saw an enormous ship, one that dwarfed any she had seen before. It was one of Kingfountain's special seacrafts, the type that could disappear entirely beneath the water, but the size rivaled that of a hurricane sky ship. There were over a hundred smaller vessels trailing in its wake. The surface was polished like pearl, with little sigils and carvings in the hull. Whether it was made of wood or stone, she didn't know, but it glided through the water at great speed.

In a blink, her vision brought her on board the massive ship, where she saw military officers and sailors walking around with purpose and responding to orders. Her consciousness was whisked to the command area, where a man with a brooding face and a haughty expression stood with his hands clasped behind his back. He wore a saber and a brace of pistols at his belt. His military jacket was adorned with medals. She'd never met this man in person before, but she'd seen him in her other visions, heard about him from Sera and Fitzroy.

General Montpensier.

"Lord General," an officer said, hurrying toward him, "we passed the mirror gate at Salize. Our bearings are true. We've crossed over into the Dahomeyjan waters." They spoke a foreign tongue, but Cettie could understand their language through the magic enfolding her.

"Good, very good," General Montpensier replied with a curt nod. "I want all in readiness for the night attack. We must reach Lockhaven before their dawn."

"Sir, but how will we reach the flying city from the sea?"

The general's smile was cunning. "I will not tell you, Commander. But trust me, we will shatter it. Have everyone ready."

"What about the rest of our surface fleet stationed at Leoneyis?" the commander said, perplexed. "Admiral Grant will find them today for certain."

"It's no matter. The fleet is lost. But they are a diversion, nothing more. They keep his eyes fixed away from us while we destroy the seat of their government." He rubbed his mouth, and Cettie could see the nervousness in his eyes. He projected confidence, but his mannerisms showed he was fatigued and desperate. He knew his maneuver risked all.

The commander looked at Montpensier in disbelief. His general had just forsaken a great number of his brothers- and sisters-in-arms.

"Go," the general ordered with a snarl, and the commander left.

After he was gone, another man approached the general. He, too, wore a military uniform, but Cettie could sense the kystrel nestled beneath his jacket.

"What is it?" Montpensier said in a low voice.

"We lost one of ours," said the man grimly.

Montpensier scowled. "Who?"

"Russell."

"Killed?"

The man shook his head no. "Captured."

"By the Fountain!" Montpensier cursed. "Why didn't he commit suicide?"

"We don't know. He lost consciousness. When he revived, we saw he was in an interrogation cell."

"Disaster," Montpensier snarled. "Evacuate the poisoner school in Genevar. Get the prince out of the dungeon immediately. Or kill him. I don't care. Her plans are unraveling faster than a seaman's first rigging knot."

"Lady Corinne still has the empress," the man said, his voice revealing a throb of anger.

"If I held Her Beloved Majesty, the empress, I'd wrap chains and a cannonball to her ankles and drop her into the sea. The other traitoress, well, she should never should have escaped to begin with! Reckless! Evacuate the school. Send word at once."

"Yes, my lord," said the man deferentially. But Cettie saw the distaste in his gaze, the contempt for the man he served.

Someone jostled Cettie's shoulder, rousing her from the vision. She gasped as the vision melted away. There was a young officer standing before her, a look of unease on his face. The pistol in his other hand was pointed at her. Three more officers stood guard, weapons at the ready.

Cettie rubbed her face with her hands as the world came back into focus. She cast a look around the room. It was a small waiting room, with dark wainscoting and a few padded benches to sit on. There were no windows to reveal the time of day, but it had been well past midnight when the tempest arrived at Lockhaven. The moment they disembarked, she'd been arrested by the Ministry of War. They'd wished to lock her in irons, but Stephen had intervened and sworn on his honor that she was trustworthy. She'd saved many lives from perishing at Gimmerton Sough, but the looks on her custodians' faces, and the gun pointed at her, showed they all feared her.

"Miss, the prime minister is ready to see you," the young officer said. "You dozed off."

"Thank you," Cettie said, her mind still rushing from the vision she'd seen. She got to her feet, and the dragoons encircled her. Her poisoner bag had already been confiscated.

After a brief journey through a series of short corridors and doorways, she entered the prime minister's chambers through a secret door. She could hear Stephen's and Durrant's voices as she approached.

But she was shocked to find Adam Creigh in the room as well.

Her astonishment was so complete, her mouth went dry. He looked fatigued and concerned, and more careworn than she'd ever seen him. But he'd also never looked so handsome. She longed to reach out and touch him, to beg his forgiveness—but that impulse was rivaled by an even stronger instinct to flee, to run far away. All her memories of him flooded back, brought to crystalline vividness in her mind. Her heart was afire in her chest.

When he saw her, he didn't seem to recognize her at first. But then his eyes widened, his fists clenched, and the muscles at the corners of his jaws went taut. No, he'd not been expecting her arrival. Her cheeks burned under his gaze.

"Ah, there she is," said Durrant, who looked more tired than all of them. "Welcome, Miss Cettie. We meet under rather perplexing circumstances. Lord Stephen has vouchsafed for your conduct. Gentlemen, put the pistols down," he added, gesturing to the soldiers escorting her.

"I'm sorry, Prime Minister," one of them said. "But our orders come from Admiral Grant himself. You're not to be left unprotected."

"I can hardly walk ten feet without stepping on one of your boots," Durrant complained. "Your protection is highly inconvenient. But do as you've been ordered."

"Cettie," Adam said, drawing her eyes to him. Oh, how she longed to talk with him, just the two of them, and forget the past—no, forget the *world*. He wouldn't want her back, but she needed to make amends. To see him happy again. He deserved someone like Anna, someone who had been faithful to him all the while. Not Cettie. Never her.

And yet she still wanted him. Her burden would be to always want him.

"Young man, you'll get your turn with her," Durrant said, interrupting him. "But as *I* am the prime minister, I insist on mine first. If you would, my dear, approach the Leering on the pedestal over there with me? I would like you to put your hand on it. It is a Truth Leering."

"I know," Cettie answered. It had the carved face of a frowning man with curly hair and deep-set eyes. She felt the magic of the Leering, sensed its purpose, and even heard the gentle hum coming from it. She nodded in obeisance and walked over to it. Stephen gave her an encouraging nod. Adam stood transfixed, his look darkening as he watched her. Did he hate her?

After she reached the Leering, she put her trembling hand on it. The soldiers crowded around her, blocking her view of Adam. Under these circumstances, it almost came as a relief. Still, she felt the loss. Durrant stood opposite her, then placed his hand on the other side of the stone facade, invoking the magic, locking them together. It was a strong bit of music, but she instantly saw how to dismantle it. If she'd wanted to, she could have pulled her hand away. She didn't.

"State your true name, if you please."

"My legal name is Cettie Pratt, but I am the natural daughter of the woman masquerading as Lady Corinne and a kishion, her lover, who is my father. I do not know his true name."

Mr. Durrant's brow furrowed even more. "I did not know this."

"Although the real lady Corinne had no natural children, this woman bore me in a nexus of sorts between our world and that of Kingfountain. I am a daughter of both worlds. I was deceived by my natural mother, my father. I have become something I once abhorred. If I could change it, I would. I cannot. But still I hope to be useful to Sera. The Mysteries have *called* me to be her protector. I had a vision, Prime Minister. Just now. While waiting for you to see me."

"You have?" he asked, his brows lifting in wonderment.

"My powers have not worked since I was abducted. But they are working now."

Durrant looked at her firmly, his face devoid of expression. "What did you see in your vision?"

Cettie swallowed, feeling her composure rattled by the knowledge that Adam was listening to her. Judging her. She wished she could see his expression. "It was sunrise," she began. "The vision opened over the ocean in the world of Kingfountain. Then it went beneath the waters. General Montpensier has a fleet of ships that can move unseen from above."

"We know this," Durrant said.

"One of the ships is the size of a hurricane."

Durrant's eyes widened. "*That* is news."

"I overheard him speaking to one of his underlings. I don't understand the context, but it sounds as if our admiral, someone called Grant, is about to discover a fleet of ships and destroy them. I surmised that the admiral believes Montpensier is with that fleet, but he's not."

The look of surprise on Durrant's face said much. She was revealing information she could not have known.

"They passed a mirror gate at Salize. There was something said about Dahomey as well."

Durrant nodded. "Go on."

"They plan to attack Lockhaven. The underling doesn't understand how it will be done, but Montpensier seems convinced they can do it, even from ships beneath the waters."

"Salize is the name of a rock formation off the coast of Legault. It is connected to the ruins of Dochte Abbey off the coast of Dahomey!"

"There's more. After the general spoke to the underling, a kishion approached him with the news that you've captured Will Russell."

"How could word have traveled so fast?" Durrant exclaimed.

"Will Russell has been in disguise among us for years and there are many ways they transfer messages. He took the place of Rand Patchett. His sister, I believe, is also a hetaera. They assigned Will as my kishion."

There were a few grunts of surprise at that. Cettie pressed on boldly. "They've ordered the evacuation of the poisoner school in Genevar. That is where I've been held since I was taken. From what they said, Prince Trevon is being held there."

"Prince Trevon! His location has been changed constantly," Durrant said. "This is good news."

"He's being kept in the dungeon."

"It was *your* information," Durrant said, "that revealed Sera's maid as an imposter. Do you know where the empress is?"

Cettie bowed her head. "I don't. I'll do all I can to help make things right. I am loyal to the Mysteries, Prime Minister, and to Sera. But I know that I must earn back the trust that I once held. Trust is so fragile, but let me do what I can to mend it."

"So you know where the poisoner school is?"

"I do. Well, one of them. There is more than one. But it makes sense to me that they'd keep Trevon guarded at the one my mother knows best."

Durrant rubbed his mouth with his free hand. Neither had pulled away from the Leering yet. "Is there anything you are concealing from me? Is this information intended to deceive us away from your true aims?"

Cettie felt the throb of the Leering, compelling the truth from her. "No. I've been completely honest with you."

"I can sense that," Durrant said approvingly. "Your cooperation will, of course, provide leniency for when we must face the truth about what you've let yourself become." He sighed and removed his hand, which freed Cettie to do the same.

"Now *I* will be truthful to *you*," Durrant said. "Lockhaven is trapped here. It has only ever obeyed Sera. We cannot budge it from its position without her. Which means we are helpless against Montpensier's fleet if they have already made it through the mirror gate. We must begin evacuating immediately." He looked her in the eyes. "You are the only person who can find the poisoner school in Genevar. Well, you and that scoundrel Russell, but I don't suspect he will be willing to assist us."

"He has a ring on his left hand—" Cettie said.

"We know. We discovered it after the good doctor brought him here. It was also invisible, like the one worn by Becka's imposter. At least he won't be able to use it to resume his disguise. He is guilty of the most heinous treason. No, Cettie, if your vision is true, then you need to help rescue Sera's husband." Durrant started to pace. "It is already day in the other world. You'll have to fly to Genevar in full daylight. They'll know you're coming. I don't imagine there are many sky ships that fly over its massive walls."

"No, there aren't. I will do as you command, Prime Minister."

"How many soldiers do you think should accompany you?"

Cettie looked down. "They will kill as many of us as they can. We need sharpshooters. Dragoons to clear the way from zephyrs. But once we go inside, they'll be useless. I will go in alone."

"No, you will not," Adam said, stepping around to the prime minister's side, a look of fierce determination on his face. His jaw was clenched again. "I will go with you."

CHAPTER TWENTY-TWO

BROKEN HEART

While all the preparations for the operation were underway, Stephen did not leave Cettie's side. She was grateful for his reassuring presence, and as they stood together in the landing yard where the zephyrs and soldiers were assembled, he wrapped his arm around her shoulder and pressed a kiss into her hair.

"Mother will be anxious to hear back from me," he said. "I would go with you too," he said, "but I cannot risk Mother and Anna's safety at Fog Willows should anything happen."

"I will be less worried if I know you are all home safe," Cettie said. She glanced at Adam, who was talking to some of the soldiers. He had a medical bag slung across his shoulder.

Stephen noticed her looking at him. "I suppose the two of you will have a much-needed talk," he said.

Cettie nodded, dreading it. Desiring it. She'd tried to argue against including him on the mission, but his argument that Trevon might need a doctor had swayed the prime minister. Ultimately, the choice had not been hers. He had vowed he would go with her into the deepest parts of the poisoner's school. She had no intention of letting him fulfill that promise.

"He's a good man," Stephen said. "I think he'll do the right thing. In the end."

She looked up at him, then lowered her eyes. "I don't deserve him. Tell me truly, Stephen, does Anna still love him?"

He flinched. She knew the truth without it being spoken. It didn't surprise her. Not at all.

"His heart has been constant," Stephen said softly, emphatic.

"Which I do not deserve," she answered. "If I can, I am going to persuade him to return her affections. They belong together. I want them both to be happy."

Stephen did not look convinced, but he didn't argue with her either. Maybe he thought, deep down, that she was right.

"It looks like they are nearly ready to depart," he said, rubbing her shoulder. "Be safe, Cettie. We'll be waiting for you at Fog Willows."

She pursed her lips. "I'm not sure the prime minister will let me go once this is over. But I should like to see Mother again. And Anna. And even Phinia. Tell them all how sorry I am."

An officer approached her with a stern expression. "It's time to depart, Miss Cettie," he said, bowing his head to her. Her eyes darted to Adam. He was watching her and Stephen, his arms folded, his expression inscrutable. He wasn't happy, that much was clear.

"Thank you," Cettie said to Stephen and kissed his cheek. He squeezed her hand and stood by as she followed the officer.

"You'll be riding with me and Doctor Creigh in that one," said the officer, gesturing to the zephyr that Adam stood beneath. "My name is Captain Dumas."

"Thank you, Captain," she said. There were around twenty soldiers in all, in three zephyrs. As she approached the air ship, she couldn't help but think again of the last mission she'd been on for the empire, the day she and Will had gone to the Fells to capture the Fear Liath. The day Joses had died.

When they reached the rope ladder dangling from the sky ship, the captain said, "After you," while he and Adam held it steady for her. She didn't need the help, but it was gallant all the same.

After mounting the ladder, she boarded the vessel. The other soldiers who would be accompanying them were already aboard, along with the pilot. The Leering lights in the landing yard lent a bright glow to the scene, almost as if it were daylight. Looking over the side of the zephyr, she saw the other ships readying for the journey and noticed that Stephen still stood below, hands clasped behind his back in a posture that made her think of their father. Of Fitzroy. Her throat tightened.

Then Adam appeared up the rope. He gestured for her to sit down by him on one of the benches, and she did. She felt like a tangled mess of nerves. It was so wonderful to see him again. Yet so painful too. She remembered every word of the letter she'd written him to sever their engagement. At the time, under the sway of the Myriad Ones, she'd meant every word.

"Mr. Cochran," the captain said, looking up at the pilot. "Take us through the prism cloud. Then give control of the zephyr to Miss Cettie, who will guide us to Genevar." He turned to Cettie. "We've sent word ahead to the *Serpentine* to rendezvous with us on the way."

Aunt Juliana's ship. Cettie was pleased by the development. It would be good to see her aunt again. And if she had the chance, she would like to apologize to Caulton.

Their zephyr led the way. Other soldiers had crammed onto the bench with them, which did not give her and Adam the privacy she'd hoped for, but the noise of the exposed wind would make it difficult for them to be overheard. They were on their way now, heading toward danger. This might be her last chance to speak with him. As she looked at Adam, taking in his fatigue and bedraggled appearance, she regretted again that he was coming. He'd not slept that day.

"I've not seen the prism cloud yet," Cettie asked, breaking the silence between them.

"You'll see it shortly," he answered. "When you came to Lockhaven, you might have missed it because it looks like a cloud during the day. At night, it's a pillar of fire. It's colorful, like the light that comes from a prism. Those buildings over there are blocking it, but watch . . . there it is."

Cettie gasped at the sight. It was like a rosebud almost, with layers of colored petals. The center of the vortex was a bright patch of natural sunlight, which came through the whorl and shone into their world. It was nearly as big as Lockhaven itself, and Cettie watched in wonder as a hurricane passed through from the other side.

"My goodness."

She couldn't take her eyes off the prism cloud. It looked familiar to her. Not because she'd seen it before, but because part of her awareness had. She now had access to memories that weren't her own. These memories felt different from those she'd accessed through the Myriad Ones, and they sounded different too. They were steeped in the Mysteries.

The zephyr raced toward the rift, followed by the other two on its flanks.

The colors became more vivid and pronounced as they rushed ahead. She could see the sky in the other world, the clouds and even a seabird. She gripped the edge of the seat as the zephyr approached the broken veil between the worlds. Her heart beat fast in anticipation of what it would feel like. She remembered racing through a mirror gate in a zephyr with Lady Corinne and her father.

She should have leaped overboard and plunged into the sea.

As they approached the fiery maw of the prism gate, the magical chorus of energy was so loud that it vibrated within her chest. Cettie turned her face away, shutting her eyes, the noise of the cacophonous music so penetrating she felt insignificant in its presence. It was power, true power, in all its glory. Sera had accomplished this feat? It amazed her. It awed her.

As soon as they were through, the song of power began to fade. When Cettie once again became aware of herself, she had a hand pressed to her heart and tears in her eyes. She squinted because they had passed into full daylight. Looking back, she saw the inky black of night falling behind.

They were over the sea, but she could see masses of land in the distance. A few seagulls cruised above the waves below them, and the other zephyrs dipped through the prism cloud to join them.

"Where are we?" Cettie asked Captain Dumas.

"Off the coast of Occitania," he answered. "We'll head west here to reach Genevar. The *Serpentine* will be watching for us. Would you like to take the helm, miss, and lead the way?"

"Not yet," Cettie answered. "When we get a little closer."

Captain Dumas nodded and gave orders to the pilot.

Cettie gazed at Adam and saw he was studying her face. She wished her powers allowed her to read his mind. He looked conflicted. No wonder. Honorable man that he was, he probably felt it was his duty to reaffirm their engagement. That was just the sort of thing he would do.

"I have something for you," she said, keeping her voice low. They'd returned her poisoner bag to her after she'd passed the test with the Truth Leering and earned Durrant's trust. She opened the bag and withdrew the book he'd given her after they'd both passed the Test at Muirwood Abbey.

His eyes widened with recognition when he saw it. "I thought you'd lost that."

Cettie gently stroked the leather-bound cover. "I was afraid Anna had taken it," she said, then shook her head no. "I should have trusted her integrity more. It was stolen from me because it meant something to me to lose it. Because it came from you." She offered it back to him.

He took it, his expression softening. He opened it to a random page, gazing at the notes alongside the sketches. Then he closed the book and handed it back to her.

She kept her hands folded in her lap, refusing to take it. "It's yours, Adam. You lent it to me. I'm grateful that I could finally return it."

"I want you to have it," he said.

"Adam," she said, leaning closer to him. She tried to keep her voice steady, only partially succeeding. "I lost Joses because I let him come with me that day. I couldn't *bear* it if you were harmed because of me." She blinked and licked her lips to moisten them.

"They've already tried," he replied, his voice husky. "They will try again. It's no secret where I work. I accept the risk. I cannot let you do this alone."

"I'm not alone," Cettie said, her heart aching. "The Knowing is my shield. My friend. My tutor. My protection. I want you to stay with the zephyr until the school is secure." She put her hand on his wrist. "Promise me."

"I won't," he said forcefully, shaking his head. "I'm a doctor, Cettie. If any of these soldiers is injured, I will rush to aid them. Or the prince. But I will not let them take you again."

"They won't take me," Cettie answered, shaking her head. "They'll kill me."

"And I would rather you not die," he said.

She breathed in through her nose. Just touching him was painful. She took her hand away. "I made oaths to the Medium, Adam. I have powers now I didn't have before. I don't exactly understand them, but I can feel them. I have sworn an oath to be Sera's protector. She is in great danger. They will try to twist her mind, like they did with me." She took a quick breath. "What I'm trying to say is . . . we cannot be together, Adam."

Her words caused him physical pain. He flinched. "Why not?" he whispered.

"We cannot go back to what we were. It wouldn't be fair to you." She swallowed, trying to muster her failing courage. "You deserve someone like Anna Fitzroy. Someone who is *worthy* of your loyalty. I am not."

Her words were breaking his heart. She stopped speaking, not wanting to cause him even more pain. She looked down, her throat bulging, her own heart twisting painfully.

His fingers clenched the book in his hands, his knuckles going white. She'd never seen him so discouraged or depressed. It was for the best, she believed. There would be less pain now to remove the festering splinter. Then he could heal. Then he could love again. She believed it with all her heart. She wanted the best for him—and even if she redeemed herself, she could never reverse the wrongs she'd done to him.

It was several minutes before he mastered himself enough to speak. His voice sounded anguished. "I still want to go with you. I don't want you to face your enemies alone."

She looked him in the eye. "You're not a killer, Adam." She pressed her lips together, giving him a warning look. "These people *are*."

Cettie had taken over the helm. The wind felt wonderful in her face and hair, almost as if it were renewing her. The memories the Dryad had restored to her did torment her at times, but they also brought tender moments back to life. Like the afternoon that Fitzroy had taken her out in the zephyr to test the storm glass. It had been one of the happiest moments in her life, filled with the thrill of discovery and the feeling of belonging to someone.

Adam was asleep, arms folded, head ducked low, and so she did her best to keep the zephyr riding low and smooth, not wanting to jostle him awake. The tenderness she felt toward him at that moment nearly suffocated her. But she'd done the right thing by insisting the relationship was over. She was sure of it. The last thing she wanted him to do was take unnecessary risks for her. To mourn for her if anything happened at the poisoner school or afterward. She wanted only for him to be happy. To choose someone better to love.

Focusing on piloting the craft kept her mind off Adam, off what might have been had life turned out differently for them. She kept the zephyr low as she sped along the coast toward Genevar. The waves crashed on the shore or against the ragged rocks jutting like teeth from the water. Her favorite part was when they glided above a building wave as it crested. There was magic in watching the water curl, turn white at the edge, and crash in a roar and tumult. Skeins of seaweed decorated parts of the ocean, and in the distance, she could occasionally spy the masts, rigging, and bulk of ships far beneath them.

It was at just such a moment, as she watched a long, powerful wave forming, that she saw the tempest rise from a hidden cove in the rocks. She had sensed the *Serpentine* moments before it came into view.

Aunt Juliana's mind pressed against her. *There you are, you little scamp,* she thought with a throb of warmth. *Genevar is just around the bend, Cettie. Lead the way.*

Hello, Cettie, added Caulton Forshee, his thoughts joining in. *Thank you for sparing my life.*

She's still a little scamp. But I love her.

I know, Julie. But try to be civil.

I'm always civil.

A smile came to Cettie's face as she heard their banter. How she'd missed them. She remembered seeing Caulton lying on his back, his eyes shocked, as he'd watched her at the warehouse. She'd saved his life.

She was hoping she could save more.

As if in response to her thought, Adam joined her, standing shoulder to shoulder. Memories of the day Joses died began to hit her again, like the waves against the shore beneath the zephyr. She found herself blinking back tears, unable to bear the thought of losing another friend. Someone she had loved with all her heart and, despite herself, always would.

CHAPTER TWENTY-THREE

INTO THE VOID

The last time Cettie had approached Genevar by sky ship, she'd been in Lady Corinne's zephyr. The city had not started shooting at them, but this time she was greeted with the pop and crack of bullets as she brought the zephyr in from the bay.

Captain Dumas ducked, and Cettie brought the zephyr streaking higher before he could give the order. She saw the worry in his eyes but also the determination.

"I wasn't sure how we'd be welcomed," he said to her, one hand grabbing a railing, the other keeping the hat on his head. "Now I know."

The huge outer walls, which formed intersecting angles like a giant star, were nearly a hundred feet thick in places, meant to withstand a sea assault. But Genevar was vulnerable by air, and so they'd always had peace treaties with the empire to protect their interests. That they were firing on the incoming vessels indicated the erstwhile truce might be over.

The other zephyrs and the *Serpentine* were quick to follow Cettie's action and rose higher. A few bullets thudded against the hull, but soon they were out of danger and soaring over the walls. She saw smoke bloom from the wall cannons below, but could not hear the thunder. The wind whipped through her hair.

Below stretched the city's cramped houses, the angled roofs with the curved-clay tiles. It was an ancient land, a place where trade had been king for centuries. It was the poisoners' lair now. Did they operate with the permission of the government? By the welcome they'd received, Cettie imagined they did.

"How far to the poisoner school?" Dumas asked, gazing at the mass of buildings.

"It's deeper inland, far from the shore," Cettie answered, "where there is more space between the estates. There are Leerings in the walls of the poisoner school that prevent people who are not part of the order from coming or going. Flying in from above is our only option."

"We don't know what to expect, do we?" Dumas said, frowning.

Cettie shook her head. "Just get me down into the courtyard and hold the walls."

"Are you a maston?" he asked her pointedly.

Cettie hesitated, but in her heart she still was. And the Aldermaston had given her a chain again. She nodded.

Reaching for his collar, he unfastened one of several decorations that were pinned on like brooches. She saw the maston symbol interwoven in the design. "This is part of the Mysteries of War," he said. "Fasten it to your collar. When I speak and give orders, you will hear them in your mind. This will also allow me to hear you. It's a captain's tag, so be careful with it. There is a tiny Leering hidden beneath the design."

"Thank you," Cettie said. She secured the pin to her collar.

"It only works when it's invoked. Be ready. If you need help when you reach the dungeon, tell me, and I'll send men down to assist you."

Cettie thanked him again and continued to pilot the zephyr across the city. Thanks to the Dryad, her memory was precise. She recognized the landscape, knew exactly how to reach their destination. But as they drew nearer, her worry increased. What would be waiting for them at the poisoner school?

She glanced back at Adam, who was looking overboard, gazing down at the city. He'd rested on the short journey, but the weariness was still plain on his face. Oh, how she wished he hadn't insisted on coming. She couldn't bear it if any harm befell him.

Then she saw the distant hill where she'd spent the last year.

"There it is," she said, her stomach fluttering with nerves. She recognized the walls, the taller buildings that rose into the sky. It was such a peaceful looking place, hardly distinguishable from the other expensive villas in the area. There were fruit orchards and parks and walking paths. From their vantage point, the snakes were hidden. So were the poisons.

"Which one?" Dumas asked.

Cettie pointed and described it to him. "It's a square series of buildings with an open courtyard in the middle. The plants growing in the center are all poisonous. Do not touch them. Stay away from the rooftops as well. Poisoners are trained to jump from roof to roof. If one gets into a zephyr, you'll all be killed."

"Thanks for the warning," said Captain Dumas. "We'll roam around the perimeter. I guess we should drop lower and see what happens?"

Cettie nodded and willed the zephyr to descend sharply. She guided it in a zigzag path, making it difficult for sharpshooters below. But no weapons fired against them. She glanced at Adam, and he met her gaze in return. Was that fear in his eyes? It was hard to tell what he was feeling. As they approached the school, she saw the upper grounds appeared to be abandoned. There were no signs of people in the courtyard below. In her mind, she heard the meal gong sound, saw the girls walking from their garden beds to join together for a meal.

Could that be the explanation?

Cettie looked at the pilot, who was gazing down with nervous eyes. "Are you ready to take the helm? I'll jump over the side when we're low enough."

He nodded and joined her.

"This is Captain Dumas," the captain said, invoking the Leering at his collar. "Arquebuses at the ready. If anything moves down there, other than us, shoot it. Keep the *Serpentine* back until we are in position. Ready, lads. Do your duty."

They dropped down toward the inner courtyard from above. Cettie could feel the Leerings embedded in the walls respond to their arrival, sending out a warning blast of fear to those inside the compound. A chill took hold in her heart. She could sense the evil of the place. Her confusion and disillusionment had masked it before. But fear did not own her—she was determined to prove herself once and for all, and that determination filled her with energy and purpose. She slung the poisoner bag over her shoulder and remembered her oaths, one by one. Thinking on them brought her a small degree of comfort. She was going into the enemy's lair, a place where truth was twisted, but she would remember herself.

"Still don't see a soul," Dumas muttered.

Was it truly abandoned? Was the Leerings' warning just an automatic reflex, a protection invoked even if no one was there? The zephyr came down low enough that Cettie could see the flowering leaves of the nasturtium flutter. She put her hand on the edge of the zephyr, coiled and prepared to spring.

She saw the table where Jevin played his hautboie in the mornings. The sun was rising now, squelching the shadows. But that wouldn't help in the darkness of the dungeon, where Trevon was being kept, if, indeed, Montpensier had been talking about this poisoner school.

"Can I bring a lamp with me, Captain?" she asked.

He nodded and ordered one of the dragoons to hand one to her. She took it and looped the strap of her poisoner bag through it. Her heart was thundering, but she tried to appear calm. She still did not see anyone in the compound. The zephyr hovered over the stones.

Cettie vaulted over the edge of the sky ship and landed on the ground. She heard a cry of warning from above and whirled, just as Adam landed from the other side of the zephyr. The two of them were the only ones who'd made the jump.

Her mouth pinched with anger. "Get back on the zephyr."

He shook his head. "I already told you. I'm coming with you. The Mysteries are telling me I should go."

Cettie looked up and saw Captain Dumas staring at Adam in shocked surprise. He clearly hadn't ordered him to join her.

She squeezed her hands into fists, not certain what to do. She couldn't force him back on the zephyr, and she'd pledged to listen to the Mysteries—if he was truly supposed to be there, she couldn't refuse his company. She closed her eyes, trying to hear the Mysteries' direction through an avalanche of conflicting feelings.

All is well.

That was the only message she could discern. She would have preferred a different answer, but she went with the one she had been given. Opening her eyes, she looked up at Captain Dumas and nodded for him to go. The zephyr launched into the sky. She saw the other two flying in wide arcs around the walls. The *Serpentine* lumbered overhead, blotting out the sun, its shadow falling on her and Adam.

"Stay close to me," she told him. She saw his nervousness, but he was a brave man and always had been.

"I intend to," he answered.

꙳

As Cettie reached for the door handle to the building connected to the underground chambers—including the place of healing where the Everoot had cured her so many times—she tried to sense the presence of hetaera magic. She hadn't sensed any yet, which made her wonder if the school had truly been abandoned. Surely there were underground tunnels allowing escape.

She gripped the handle, turned it, and pushed it open. Darkness, so dark her eyes could see nothing. The windows had all been shuttered. She walked inside, listening for any indication she was not alone. Her senses were on a knife's edge, but they did not pick up on any strange sounds or smells. She entered the classroom, giving her eyes a little chance to adjust.

Every detail of the chamber was just as her memory had left it. The wicker chairs, the padded bench. There were oil lamps hanging from iron pegs. All were darkened. She stepped in after her eyes had mitigated the darkness. She walked deeper into the room, Adam following close behind, seeing the things for the first time.

Steady lads. Eagle eyes, all of you. She heard the captain's order in her mind.

She walked softly, trying to mute her steps. At the other side of the room was another door. Pausing there, she tried to sense if anyone lay behind it. She felt nothing. So she twisted that handle too and ventured deeper into the dark. Retrieving the lantern from her satchel, she invoked its light, illuminating the corridor beyond.

There, at the far end of the corridor, was the stairwell going down to the healing chamber. The place that held the Leering covered in Everoot. It was the deepest part of the school, though she imagined the dungeon lay even deeper. She'd never been there before.

With a shivering heart, she walked toward the stairs. She heard the noise of Adam's boots behind her. Her mouth was so dry she wished she'd brought some water. It was painful to swallow.

The door.

Cettie put her hand on it, and she immediately felt life emanating from beyond and below. There were people down there, sparks of life, each with their own sad tune.

"There are others here," she whispered over her shoulder. "Be ready."

Cettie twisted the handle and then started down the steps. She heard moans coming from below, frightened whispers. The light from the lantern chased back the gloom, revealing that the door to the healing room had been ripped off its hinges. A huddled mass of people covered the benches in the room. None of their feet touched the floor. The Leering below was still working, dripping water from its surface, which pattered into the basin of the fountain.

She kept coming down the steps, scanning everything, trying to make sense of it. She recognized some of the servants who had once obeyed her. They stared at her with horror and fear, as if she'd come to kill them all. What had they been told?

Then she noticed the serpents writhing on the floor. Some were even coiled at the foot of the steps. So the slaves were trapped by their fear. They couldn't escape, nor had they been taken.

"There are people down here," she said, speaking to the pin at her collar. "Trapped. Serpents everywhere."

Be careful, the captain said. *How many?*

Cettie went down the steps, seeing the huddles of people. There were probably no more than twelve, each one trying to stay above the floor. How long had they been left in the dark? Some winced away from the light of her lantern. As she got closer, she saw there were dead bodies on the floor, sprawled out in painful poses. Snakes hissed at her light as she approached.

"I see a dozen. Some are dead. Do not come closer yet."

Aye. We're standing ready. I won't give orders until you learn more.

"I'm here to help you," Cettie said in a calming voice as she reached the lower steps, just above the coiling snakes. She'd mastered her fear of them at the school. The students had all been taught to lift and handle them so they could touch them without being bitten.

As she was about to stoop and clear the stairs, she sensed the invocation of power. The eyes of some of the people huddling on the benches began to flash silver. She felt their kystrels flare to life, sending terror at her, terror that would freeze and bind her limbs.

There was the crack of a gunshot—behind and above. From the courtyard.

She felt Captain Dumas's thoughts suddenly wink out. He was already dead.

CHAPTER TWENTY-FOUR

OATH MAIDEN

Cettie knew the sensation of terror all too well. How many times had she fallen victim to it? She had learned at the poisoner school to confront her fear, and all her other feelings, and to capture them within the medallion she wore around her neck. That medallion had given her the ability to control her emotions. And that was what most people craved—to be in control of themselves, of their circumstances, of their fate. But control was only an illusion, and one with a steep price.

The kystrel had made her its slave.

Terror beat into her now, bringing back the fears of the young girl who'd hidden from ghosts only she could see, but she could not hide from it, nor would she have. The light from the lantern began to dim. How many Myriad Ones slunk through the shadows?

"Welcome back," said a hateful voice that she recognized at once. Gone was the facade of caring and wisdom. Jevin's glowing eyes stared at her from the benches. Her mentor. Her deceiver. The menace in his words told him all she needed to know. The man who'd been so solicitous, so kind, intended to kill her.

She felt a hand grasp her wrist. Adam.

He took the lantern from her, and bright light flared from it. Adam held up the lantern, standing on the stairs in defiance.

And Cettie's terror cringed away from her stronger sense of purpose, just like the Myriad Ones cringed from the light.

Banirexpiare.

The thought came from her and Adam together, their minds joined as one. Shrieks of pain split her mind, a keening sound that rumbled like thunder. The light was a shield now, a barrier the shadow beings could not pass. It grew brighter and brighter as her will and Adam's united. The brightness revealed that the Leering with the Everoot had been stripped bare of the mossy plant. None of it was left. The craggy face of the carving seemed to be weeping at the loss.

The snakes hissed and retreated from the brilliance, seeking shelter in the shadows. Taking a deep, heartening breath, Cettie stepped into the room.

The first kishion rushed at her, his pistol aimed for her head. He pulled the trigger, but the mechanism jammed. Anger contorted his face. He tried shaking the gun and aimed for her again as she approached him. The trigger went. Nothing happened. Swearing a foul oath, he threw down the pistol and drew a dagger from his belt. This he shoved at her chest, trying to stab her heart.

Cettie felt as if the world slowed. Magic coursed through her, heightening every sense, connecting her to every person in the room. She stepped to the side on instinct, the dagger going wide, and then brought her knee up into his stomach. Her arms moved in unison, performing a Bhikhu technique that Raj Sarin had shown her—the *butterfly hands*—and when she struck the kishion, she felt an explosion of power erupt from her palms. The man was thrown from his feet as if he'd been struck by a battering ram, his arms pinwheeling as he sailed backward. She felt his bones breaking, and then he lay sprawled on the floor in agony.

"Kill her! Now!" Jevin thundered.

A dagger sailed toward her head, but it seemed to come no faster than a feather dropping. She caught it midair and tossed it aside, moving forward and springing up, her legs scissoring to kick the man in the face. Again she felt a swell of power, an amplification of her abilities. As a hetaera and poisoner, she'd had access to the toxic but occasionally useful knowledge of the Myriad Ones, but now she could draw on memories from a thousand lifetimes of strong warriors, Oath Maidens all.

Three of them attacked her at once, leaving only Jevin, who grabbed one of the prisoners by the collar and hoisted him off the bench.

The beard and scraggly hair and tattered clothes hid the man's identity, but then she recognized him. Trevon. She needed to get to him while he was still alive. She had to save him for Sera.

The raw fury on her attackers' faces showed their hate, their willingness to crush her life. One of them, she realized, was her weapons instructor. Another, a hetaera student she recognized, tried to tackle her, but Cettie sidestepped at the last moment. She was all elbows and feet, blocking strikes, dodging blades. Another enemy raised a pistol and fired again, and this weapon froze just like the last one. The oath magic was protecting her. She brought them down, one by one, striking with more strength than she had ever done before. She was the Mysteries' vengeance. Its power rippled through her arms, her hands. For the first time in a long, long while, she felt at one with herself, totally at peace in the vortex of a raging storm. Around her, the attackers peeled back, struck and injured, bones breaking, vital organs bruised. The other poisoner in training was among the fallen.

She'd thrown her old master to the ground, but he was up again a moment later, trying to destroy her. She caught his fist and flipped him onto his back with jarring force. His eyes glazed over, and he slumped, either unconscious or dead.

"We trained you *too* well," Jevin said. He held Trevon around the waist, pressing a dagger to his throat.

"Trevon," Cettie said, walking toward them.

"Ah, not so close!" Jevin warned, jabbing the point of the dagger into his hostage's throat. Cettie saw a trickle of blood.

Trevon's eyes burned into hers. He begged her to save him with his gaze. His skin was raw, his eyes feverish, so different from the courtly man she'd known. A vivid memory surfaced in her awareness—the first time she'd suspected Sera and Trevon's arrangement was not merely a political one was on a walk the three of them had taken in a garden in Lockhaven. The couple had bantered with a sweet familiarity, and she'd caught Sera looking at Trevon with longing. She'd asked Sera about that secret smile later, and her friend had actually blushed. Trevon had clearly been brought very low. But he was still alive.

Cettie kept walking, slow and sure.

"Your father is up there, destroying the soldiers you brought with you," Jevin said. "And then he will destroy you. You failed us, Cettie. We would have made you our queen, but you betrayed us. And so you will die."

She could hear shots being fired outside, their noise muted by the thick walls. Still she advanced.

"You want him dead?" Jevin challenged, jutting out his chin. "Do you really want to tell your precious friend that you let her love be murdered? You have the power to stop it, Cettie. You have the power to make a mark on both worlds in a way no one else can. Destiny brought you to us, Cettie. You were born to be our vessel, our *queen*. Accept your birthright, and I'll spare his life."

She vaulted at him. Words were his best weapons. He lied and deceived with every breath. They all did. Talking to him would only give him more power.

While she had no doubt he would do as he threatened, she had a small bit of Everoot left. If she could free Trevon quickly enough, his wounds would be healed.

Jevin's eyes widened with surprise at her attack. He started to cut Trevon's neck, but Cettie's hand grasped his forearm and prevented the killing blow. Power radiated from him—a strength his thin frame belied. She tried to pry his arm away to free Trevon, but it was like pulling on a tree.

Darkness was at Jevin's core. An unearthly darkness. A darkness she recognized.

His visage twisted with anger. "You cannot defeat *me!*" he snarled. His silver eyes burned with malevolent power. Yes, her ghost was inside him, the one that had tormented her for so many years. His agent—his servant—his master. Had it always been connected to Jevin? Had he been a secret tormenter for so many years, in league with her eyeless enemy?

She slammed the heel of her hand into his face. His head hardly budged. Then he suddenly released Trevon and, dropping the knife, seized her throat with his hands. She pummeled him, trying to break his grip, but her blows were ineffective. The strength she'd felt earlier was draining from her. The magic was shrinking, failing, as her lungs struggled for air.

She kicked him once, twice, trying to break the chokehold. She was on her back, not even sure how it had happened. Spots danced before her eyes.

"You are nothing! Nothing! You forsook them for us, and now us for them. What are you but a false traitor? Die! Die!"

Then, just when Cettie felt consciousness start to dance away from her, Adam smashed the lantern against the side of Jevin's head. The blow broke the man's nose, leaving an angry, weeping welt across his nose and eyebrow. It knocked him off her. Cettie could breathe again.

As she struggled to rise, trying to shake off the fog of unconsciousness, she saw Adam standing before her. The glass from the lantern had shattered, exposing the white-hot light of the Leering fastened to the iron. Jevin covered his face, the light seeming to scald him, or perhaps it was the creature inside him. He swore at them, oath after oath.

Trevon had staggered to his feet, holding his neck with one hand, trying to stanch the bleeding, and a pistol with the other. His arm was shaking, but the pistol was aimed at Jevin's head.

The villain jumped as the blast boomed. The bullet ricocheted around the room, missing Jevin, who had leaped into the fountain around the Water Leering. Blood dribbled down his face as he stared balefully at them. Cettie felt an invocation of magic, a word of power uttered in his mind.

Kennesayrim.

A whorl of magic engulfed him. A conduit opened, just for a moment, a shaft of dark light pulling him away. It had a peculiar sound to it, like a certain set of chords played by instruments. Then the fountain was empty, and the song had ended.

He had escaped with his life, and she knew he would never stop hunting her until one of them lay dead.

Trevon sank to his knees, the smoking pistol falling from his hand. His fingers were smeared with blood, and his pale face went slack.

Adam rushed to him, catching him before he fell.

"It's Trevon," he said to her, setting the prince down.

Cettie nodded, still reeling from the fight. She felt bruises forming on her neck. Her vision had blackened at the edges, but she managed to cling to consciousness. Trevon tried speaking, but his words came out as gurgling gasps.

"Shhh," Adam soothed, working frantically to stop the bleeding.

Cettie found her pouch with the remaining stub of Everoot and quickly removed the little patch of moss with speckled flowers. The lamp illuminated it in her hand. The craving to use the magic on herself was strong, but it felt wrong, so she endured her own pain.

Some of the other prisoners were beginning to gather around now that the snakes had been repelled by the Leering's light. Cettie felt no threat from any of them, just fear and budding hope. They'd been prisoners there. Slaves. They would be grateful to escape.

"Here, let me," Cettie said, bringing the moss closer.

"What is that?" Adam asked, his brow wrinkling.

"Trust me," she said. He backed away at once, still pressing his fingers to the bloody wound. Cettie touched Trevon's jaw with the moss. Tingles of magic shot down her fingertips into Trevon's body, and she saw him shudder and groan in relief. The frantic spasms passed, and soon he was breathing cleanly again, his chest rising and falling.

The magic winked out, and Cettie saw nothing left of the root in her hand. As Adam pulled his hand away, he gasped in shock.

"The wound is closed?" he said in surprise.

"It's a healing plant," Cettie explained.

Trevon tried to sit up and, with a little help, succeeded.

"I'd almost given up hope," Trevon gasped. "Sera? Is she alive? I must know the truth."

Cettie and Adam exchanged a look, then Cettie put a comforting hand on the prince's shoulder. "We don't know, but we think so. She was abducted by Lady Corinne a few days ago."

"Abducted?" Trevon said. "I've been in isolation for months. I don't even know how much time has passed since . . . since . . ." His chest began to heave. "Since our wedding."

"It's been over a year, Prince Trevon," Adam said.

"A *year*?" he said incredulously. He looked heartsick, bereft.

Cettie's eyes caught a couple of familiar faces among the prisoners. She almost did a double take. Rand and Joanna Patchett. The real Rand and Joanna Patchett. How strange that she'd never met them.

"Randall Patchett?" Cettie said, looking at him.

"Do I know you?" he answered, confused. He shot a worried look at his sister. "You seem . . . familiar. I've heard your voice." He rubbed his brow in consternation.

She rose and walked toward them. So much to explain. But there wasn't time. Not yet.

"I must go," she said, turning back to Adam. "I must stop my father."

"We're all going," Adam said with determination as he rose. "Can you stand, Trevon?" When the prince nodded, Adam gripped his hand and pulled him to his feet. "All of you, come with us." Adam grabbed the broken lantern, still alight, in his other hand and carried it with him.

Cettie strode ahead, feeling fatigued and drained. The superhuman magic that had filled her moments before was gone. If she'd lain down, she would have fallen asleep in moments.

But she trudged up the stairs, hearing the report of weapons through the walls. With Captain Dumas dead, there was no way to find out what was going on outside. Her father had the magic to turn invisible. He could shoot every dragoon, one at a time. The urgency of the situation lent her strength to mount the stairs faster. Adam brought Trevon after her, and the other freed prisoners followed them, anxious to be away from the dungeon.

Cettie rushed up to the main level and ran toward the door leading to the courtyard. She sensed the magic of a kystrel just beyond it, the power whirling like a storm. The door burst open suddenly.

No one appeared in the doorway, but Cettie could sense her father's presence. The magic was cloaking him. She sensed its power, felt its threads weaving the illusion—and, with a twist of her mind, she unraveled them. The illusion dropped away, revealing her father standing in the doorway, one hand clutching a pistol.

He stared at her in surprise.

Just as a bullet hit him in the back of the head.

His eyebrows arched and then his legs crumpled, and he fell backward. Standing behind him, pistol in hand, was Aunt Juliana.

"Got you this time," she muttered darkly, lowering the weapon. Only then did she notice Cettie standing before her.

"I was coming after you," Juliana said. Her tempest, *Serpentine*, hovered above the courtyard behind her, its rope ladder swaying in the wind.

Cettie stared down at the body at her feet, the eyes still blinking, his mouth moving but no sound coming out. He was still alive, paralyzed. His eyes were haunting, frantic, desperate. His whole body began to quiver.

"Daw . . . tur . . ." he choked out.

Daughter.

She stared at him in shock. The hate and revenge that had motivated him throughout his cursed life was spilling away now, trapped beneath limbs that would not move as he directed them. Blood pooled behind his head on the cobblestones. He was dying. He was helpless.

Cettie felt anguish seeing him like that. There was no illusion this time. No forgery. He was truly dying. She had no Everoot left to save him.

"Daw . . . tur . . ." he whispered again, his voice fading.

He was *not* her true father. Not in any of the ways that mattered. But she didn't hate the man who had given her life. Not even for shooting Fitzroy.

She pitied him.

"Save . . . mmmgghh!" His eyes fixed on her in desperate pleading. He was going into the beyond, to face whatever punishments awaited him. She could see the torture in his eyes.

Cettie knelt and took his hand in hers. She squeezed it as she watched the embers of life flicker within him.

His struggle lasted only seconds more. Then his final breath came out in a wearied gasp.

Cettie bowed her head. She was not sorry he was dead. But she was grateful to have been with him at the end. And even more grateful that she hadn't been called upon to kill him.

"The Genevese are coming," Juliana said urgently, glancing behind Cettie. "We must go. We must get the prisoners to safety."

Cettie noticed a bulge in the pocket of her father's coat. Her head tilted sideways. Carefully, she reached her hand into his pocket.

And found the Cruciger orb.

CHAPTER TWENTY-FIVE

WIZR

All of the prisoners of the poisoner school were brought aboard *Serpentine*. Cettie checked each one, inspecting for invisible rings, brands, or kystrels. The zephyrs continued to patrol the skies while the prisoners were secured on the tempest. Before the last was loaded, cracks of musket fire began to assail the zephyrs, which they responded to by rising vertically into the air.

"Get them on board, now!" Juliana barked. "We're leaving."

The last few prisoners were hurried up the ladder, Cettie and Adam climbed up after them, and then *Serpentine* vaulted into the skies. Cettie clung to the railing, looking below as the sky ship cleared the walls. Cavalry riders lined the road leading to the poisoner school. Some wagons hauling cannons could also be seen farther off. Another quarter hour, and there would have been too many enemies to fight with such a small force. The Genevese were clearly incensed at the intrusion into their lands. There would be consequences.

The ordeal in the dungeon beneath the poisoner school had left Cettie completely drained. She felt no connection with the Mysteries at all, numb even to the magic of the sky ship. The fatigue would make her useless unless she kept busy. Amidst the commotion on deck, she spied

Caulton Forshee gazing at the Cruciger orb, studying it intently. Adam attended to the injuries of the new passengers. Some had been bitten by the serpents. Others bore injuries that spoke of their poor treatment in confinement. Her heart throbbed as she watched him treat each of them with solicitous care.

Trevon sat alone, arms folded, his look dark and depressed.

She went to him, sitting down nearby, and he looked at her with eyes full of suspicion. "You fought like a Fountain-blessed," he told her. "You're not the girl I once knew."

She clasped her hands together and gazed down at them. No, she wasn't. She was someone entirely different. "I'm not," she agreed, "but part of me is. I'm glad we found you, Prince Trevon." In the past, he had asked her to call him Trevon, without the honorific, but they would need to rebuild their friendship for her to do so again.

"Where are we going? Lockhaven?"

"I think so," Cettie replied. "What do you know about what has happened?"

He pressed his hands against his face and shook his head. "I know that General Montpensier betrayed my father. He killed my family."

Cettie shook her head, and he looked at her in surprise.

"One brother, as I understand it, survived. He's leading the revolt against Montpensier. He married the Duke of Brythonica's daughter."

Trevon's eyes widened. "Kasdan?"

"I believe so. I only heard this news recently. Sera has been meeting with him."

The look of relief on his face transformed him. "That contradicts what Jevin told me. I . . . I don't know what to believe anymore."

"Jevin?" Cettie asked in surprise. "What did he tell you?"

"That all my siblings were dead."

Cettie shook her head in disbelief. "It's not so." She paused, then added, "You saw him disappear through the fountain with the Water Leering, did you not?"

"I did see that," Trevon agreed. "It was a ley line."

Cettie scrunched her eyebrows. "What is that?"

He pursed his lips. "It's part of Fountain magic," he explained. "They run through the palace in a few spots as well. You can travel from one spot on a ley line to another instantly. Only the Wizrs know how to use them."

Cettie blinked. Jevin was a Wizr? He hadn't just used his kystrel against her. She'd sensed a stronger power at work. Something even darker.

Trevon's gaze became brooding once again. "He told me that my marriage to Sera was annulled by the empire's privy council."

Cettie shook her head. "No, that's not true either."

A look of hope surfaced on his face like a sunrise, but his features dropped again the next moment. "And my wife was kidnapped? By Lady Corinne?"

"Lady Corinne abducted me as well," Cettie said. "I followed her . . . ignorantly. We crossed a mirror gate into your world. I was brought to the poisoner school. The one we just attacked."

Trevon's mouth opened in understanding. "I remember hearing about your crossing." He paused. "I've been moved around so frequently, I hardly know one direction from another. But it looks like we were at the poisoner school at the same time, at least in part. Sometimes I heard voices. Once or twice, I thought I'd heard yours. But I couldn't be sure of anything. I was always kept apart from the others. In isolation." He shuddered and wiped his mouth. "I can't believe an entire *year* has gone by."

Caulton approached them and clapped a hand on Trevon's shoulder. He'd tucked the orb into his pocket as he arrived. "How are you feeling, my lord?"

"Most grateful," he replied, although he didn't look it. "Which mirror gate do we cross?"

Caulton shook his head. "There is an open rift between the worlds now. Her Majesty opened it. They call it a prism cloud. You'll see it soon. We're heading there now."

"Sera did what?" Trevon asked, just as Cettie put her own question to Caulton. "Did you find her?"

Caulton's eyes narrowed. "She's in the Fells."

Why would Lady Corinne have taken Sera there?

"Do you mean Sera?" Trevon asked. "How could you know that?"

"It's one of the Mysteries, so I cannot divulge it."

"I'm sick to death of being left in ignorance!" Trevon said. "Your religion is too secretive."

Cettie worried that Caulton would be offended, but he didn't appear to be. "I'm afraid I agree with you, but this is also a state secret. Julie wants to know if we should go directly there."

"Durrant wouldn't like that," Cettie said. "What of the fleet?"

"What fleet?" Trevon asked again, growing more agitated.

Cettie put her hand on his knee to soothe him. "Montpensier has brought a fleet of underwater ships to attack Lockhaven. He's come in person. Lockhaven cannot move without Sera."

Trevon looked confused, but he must have decided to leave his questions about Sera's power and accomplishments for a later time because he asked, "But what can they hope to do? Our ships cannot fly."

"Montpensier has something planned. We don't know what it is." She glanced back at Caulton. "Where is the fleet now?"

"It has already crossed over," Caulton said. "We have tried communicating with Lockhaven, but it is as if they cannot hear us. The zephyrs are having the same trouble. It's night on the other side of the rift, but I doubt they are all abed."

Cettie felt a growing sense of dread. "So we have a choice to make. Do we go to the Fells or try to reestablish contact with Lockhaven? Maybe we'll have an easier time of contacting them once we cross back to our world."

Caulton shrugged. "It shouldn't make a difference. We've used Leerings to speak between worlds before."

"Our first priority must be Sera," Trevon interjected. He may have missed the pivotal events of the last year, but his loyalty clearly remained with his wife. "If she's in the Fells, we must go there first. The Fells are enormous, though. How will we find her?"

"Trust me, Prince Trevon. It will be much easier now," Caulton said with a smile.

~

A hand lightly touched Cettie's shoulder, rousing her from a dream. She blinked, disoriented, and saw Adam crouching over her. The dream had been strange and dark, but she felt comforted by the hum of the sky ship's magic. The short rest had done much to restore her body—and her connection to the Mysteries.

"We're nearly at the prism cloud," he said. "I didn't want to wake you, but I thought you'd want to know."

"No, thank you. I'm grateful you did." She sat up on the bed and brought her legs down to the floor, shaking off the disorientation.

The door to the chamber stood open. Aunt Juliana had told Cettie to use her own quarters for a rest.

She gazed up, a little surprised to see Adam still standing there. "Has there been any word from Lockhaven?" she asked.

He shook his head no. "Concerning, isn't it?"

Cettie massaged the edge of her nose. "It wouldn't surprise me if Lady Corinne can intercept messages. Or block them."

"How are you feeling?" Adam asked, folding his arms. He looked thoughtful, but also wary.

"A little bruised, I think," she said, stroking her forearm. "But I've been through worse."

He shook his head. "That's not what I meant. Your father was killed in front of you." He took a step closer, his eyes full of compassion. "He was trying to speak to you. How are you handling that?"

Now she understood. His concern for her feelings struck a deep chord inside her.

"I haven't let myself think very much about it," she said. "I share his blood, but he was not my true father." The memory of his dead eyes struck her forcibly. It brought back a cascade of other memories, crisp from the Dryad's kiss. Training with him. Wanting to earn a curt nod from him, a look of respect. She shuddered at those sentiments now. Her memories were so sharp they cut her.

"I didn't want to cry," Cettie said, the words coming out in shaky gasps.

"Grief comes and goes in waves," Adam said. "Sorry to have burdened you. I was worried about you."

She shook her head slowly. "It's not your fault. It's his. He may not have been wicked once, but he made his decisions." She licked her lips, her heart a mixture of mostly unpleasant feelings. "Thank you for asking. That was kind of you."

He shrugged. "We'd best get up on deck," he said. Then a small quirk of a smile tugged at his mouth. "I have a hospital in the Fells now."

She blinked rapidly, trying not to weep. "So I heard. I'm proud of you, Adam Creigh. Lord Fitzroy would be too." She gripped the edge of the bed, trying to steady herself. "Were you with him, when he was shot?"

"No, I was still at the palace," he said. "Sera asked me to wait there. She'd had a strong impression from the Mysteries. I tended to his wounds."

Cettie's brow furrowed. "He wasn't killed at once?"

Adam shook his head. "No. He would have survived the gunshot. He asked me to give him a Gifting. Sera was part of it. We knew then that he was going to die, only we didn't understand how." His expression clouded with sadness. "When the Espion came, we were all injured. He ordered me to go, to save myself. I almost couldn't do it."

Cettie felt the tears running down her cheeks. She couldn't stop them now. The situation had come to life in her imagination. The two men she loved most, facing death together.

"But I did. Lady Corinne killed him in the end. She said something to him. I recognized the tone of her voice, but I couldn't make out the words. I was outside on the balcony, trying to get away. I saw them throw his body out the window." He frowned and rubbed his chin. "I don't know why I told you this just now. I should have waited."

It was her fault. She'd thought so all along, and he'd just confirmed it—she'd brought Fitzroy's assassins to Kingfountain with her. Adam had almost been killed too. Her heart felt like a stone. She didn't think she would ever forgive herself.

She wiped tears on her wrist. "I'm grateful you did," she said thickly. "And I'm sorry you had to endure that. It's my fault."

He gave her a compassionate look. One she didn't deserve. "You take too much on yourself, Cettie."

She pressed her lips firmly together, but rather than dispute his words, she continued to dry her eyes. Rising from the small bed, she smoothed the blanket she'd rumpled and fluffed the pillow. She turned, seeing Adam still standing in the doorway, waiting for her.

I don't deserve your kindness, she thought. *But I am grateful for it. Maybe you do.*

Her heart leaped into her throat, and she looked into his eyes in shock. Had she heard his thought? It had been so faint, just a little feathery brush against her mind.

"Shall we?" he asked, gesturing to the door.

Cettie nodded. He let her pass out of the room first. The quarters were so close that her sleeve brushed against him as she passed, sending a jolt through her.

We cannot be together, Adam Creigh, she thought in consternation as she walked to the small stairs leading up to the deck. *Not after all I've done. You deserve someone who hasn't made these mistakes. Someone more like you.*

Whether or not he heard her, she didn't know. His expression revealed nothing.

When they reached the deck, she could see the prism cloud looming in the sky, a black void that showed some winking stars in the night sky beyond. A weave of brilliant colors separated the two skies. She spied Trevon gazing at it in wonderment. The other passengers, the slaves they'd freed from the poisoner school, had all gathered around too. Cettie didn't think she would ever tire of seeing such a display.

On the other side, she saw Lockhaven poised in the night sky, massive and foreboding, its walls illuminated by a thousand Leerings.

She glanced at Aunt Juliana at the helm. Her aunt met her gaze.

"Still no word," she said with concern. "They cannot hear us coming."

Then a hurricane sky ship lumbered into view, crossing through the prism cloud in front of them, blocking their view of the floating city. Its hulking size dwarfed them. Cettie felt a throb of warning in her mind, an instinct from the Mysteries.

"It will try to stop us!" Cettie shouted to Juliana. "Evade it!"

CHAPTER TWENTY-SIX

INSURRECTION

Juliana responded swiftly, and the tempest lurched to the left, banking sharply. The zephyrs followed them, copying their maneuver. Cettie grabbed the nearest railing to steady herself, and Adam collided with her before he, too, could grab the bar. Cries from the other passengers caused a commotion on deck.

"Caulton!" Juliana shouted. "Get them belowdecks!"

A voice came from the Leering at the helm of the tempest.

"This is Lord Welles, admiral of the hurricane *Farragut*. You will yield *Serpentine* upon my orders. Dragoons—escort them to the landing yard on *Farragut* at once."

Cettie and Juliana looked at each other in concern. The Control Leering had been used to address both them and their escorts, and from the way Juliana was wrestling with the helm, Cettie could tell other minds were attempting to take control of the ship.

"We are under orders from Prime Minister Durrant," Juliana said in reply.

"You will obey my orders or suffer the consequences," Welles said.

"Get them below, now!" Juliana said. Caulton nodded and began leading the rescued prisoners belowdecks.

"Come along. Come along," he said, his voice revealing his concern.

The leviathan-sized hurricane came closer. Cettie grimaced, feeling the wrongness of the situation. Something had happened after they'd departed Lockhaven. She was not sure what Welles was about, but felt certain he was not acting on the prime minister's orders.

"They're trying to pull us alongside her," Juliana said with gritted teeth, her knuckles white against the wheel.

"Is Lord Welles still the Minister of War?" Cettie asked Adam, who quickly shook his head.

"No, he was relieved of command days ago." Anger flashed in his eyes. "His disgrace was in all the gazettes. This is an insurrection."

The zephyrs had closed in around the tempest. She could see some of the dragoons' faces. A few had shouldered their arquebuses and were now aiming at *Serpentine*. But not all of them had fallen into line. Cettie glimpsed the concern, the hesitation to obey the order.

"What do we do?" Juliana whispered. She looked ready to defy the command.

The last of the passengers, all except Prince Trevon, were filing down the steps belowdecks. Cettie watched them go. Caulton then returned on deck.

Cettie stared at the much larger ship with determination. "Maybe Welles allied himself with Montpensier after being stripped of command."

"Then I don't think we'd be wise or safe to board the *Farragut*," Juliana said.

"You would be unwise not to," came Lord Welles's voice from the Leering. That meant Welles was listening to them.

Cettie looked at Juliana. "Do as he says," she said, but she slowly shook her head no.

Juliana smirked and nodded. The tempest leveled off and began to head straight for the hurricane. Cettie saw the huge polished length of its side, the massive masts that jutted out like dragon wings. "We'll come. But where is Prime Minister Durrant? We were acting under his authority."

"I understand. All will be explained upon your arrival. Wise decision, Captain. I don't think you'd want your ship destroyed around you."

Adam looked at Cettie, his eyes wrinkling in concern. She put her finger to her lips.

"I'm sure you have a fine explanation," Juliana said in a tone that indicated otherwise. She watched the zephyrs, one on each side of them, the other trailing behind. Some of the crew had already been killed in the previous skirmish. She wished she could communicate with those who were hesitating. But there wasn't time. Cettie unfastened the pin that Captain Dumas had given her.

"What are you doing?" Welles bellowed in surprise. Had he felt a loss of connection?

They were almost at the hurricane when Cettie nodded vigorously.

"Grab onto something!" Juliana shouted.

Cettie reached out with her mind and took control of all three zephyrs at once, blocking their pilots from the controls. It taxed her mind, but her sudden move had surprised them. All three began to drop from the sky, the dragoons shouting in fear. Cettie felt them wrestle for control, but she repelled their attempts. The Mysteries coursed through her again, the power swelling.

The *Serpentine* banked sharply and began to pick up speed. Cettie heard the discordant strands of music from the other ship as it sought to control their vessel. She released her grip on the zephyrs and countered those on the hurricane by blasting their minds with a stronger chord of power. The big ship began to list.

"Into the gap!" Cettie said, pointing.

Smiling fiercely, Juliana increased the speed of the tempest. Now that Cettie had released her hold on the zephyrs, the pilots reclaimed them and stopped their fatal dives toward the ocean below. Two of the zephyrs immediately resumed pursuit. The third had stalled in the air, the soldiers vying for control.

"You are mad!" Lord Welles thundered at her. "We will shoot you down. A tempest cannot defeat a hurricane!"

"That's true," said Aunt Juliana. "But a hurricane can't outrun a tempest!"

As the tempest shot past the hurricane, cannons began to fire at them from their nests along the big ship's hull. Juliana banked sharply, then arced up and above the other craft. The sky ship was designed to attack ships below, especially those in the waters. Its strongest vulnerability was from other ships above itself.

One of the cannonballs struck a zephyr, which had come in pursuit. The sky ship's hull shattered, and the dragoons plummeted toward the ocean. Cettie felt sorry for them, but there was no time to help.

Sera's disappearance must have been revealed to Lord Welles. So too, perhaps, had word of Montpensier's imminent attack. Had her theory been correct? Had he truly made an alliance with the enemy?

It was treason. But perhaps, in his mind, he'd justified it.

Serpentine passed through the prism cloud, and suddenly all was dark, all was night. Lockhaven gleamed like a jewel in the sky. Other sky ships hovered around the floating city, illuminated by Leerings on board. Behind them, the lumbering hurricane began to turn, to swivel in pursuit.

Cettie reached out with her mind and quenched all the Light Leerings aboard the *Serpentine*. She hurled the pin she'd been wearing overboard, lest they use it to track her.

"Where next?" Juliana said.

"The Fells," Caulton said. "There's no other choice now. If Welles has seized authority over part of the military, then he can stop us from reaching Lockhaven. The only person who can countermand him right now is the empress herself."

"Fly low," Cettie said. "They'll have a difficult time following us in the dark. They may know we're going to the Fells. But they won't know where. We have hours until dawn."

"Then we'd best hurry," Juliana said with determination. "I never liked Welles much anyway."

The eastern sky was a pretty shade of violet, announcing the imminent sunrise. The *Serpentine* had been intercepted twice during the night, both times by zephyrs, but Cettie had forced the smaller ships to land. Her power in the Mysteries had grown as the night waxed on. Her strength and vigor were returning. The little rest had done her good, but something else was giving her strength. Filling up her reservoir of confidence and determination. She glanced at Adam, who stood near her, watching the roofs of the buildings pass below them.

They had arrived in the Fells, dark and loathsome, and full of memories, but it felt more bearable with him beside her.

He's not yours, she reminded herself. *Not anymore.*

"There's Killingworth," Adam said, his voice betraying a hint of pride.

"Where?" Cettie asked eagerly.

He pointed to the building, one of the few already lit. It had been a manor once, and still had a weathered look to it. The lights were a welcome sight after flying in the dark for so long.

"It has a hundred beds," he said. "Four other doctors, and a dozen nurses. We could be twice as big and still not have enough resources to help the people." He glanced at her. "But we try."

Proud of the man he had become, she put her hand on top of his and squeezed it. When their skin touched, she felt another jolt of awareness go up her arm and quickly pulled her hand away.

He looked down at the Fells, his expression inscrutable.

"That way, Julie," Caulton said, standing near her by the helm. Prince Trevon, no longer dressed in his prison scraps, thanks to Caulton, stood beside them. This was no royal outfit, like the ones Cettie had seen him in on his previous visits to her world. He looked like an ordinary man in need of a shave and a barber. His eyes were fixed on the Cruciger orb. After their run-in with Lord Welles, they had agreed there would be no secrets between them. They were already at a disadvantage—no need to worsen their odds by hiding important information from one another. Trevon was utterly intrigued by the device.

"She's still there," Caulton said, shaking his head. "I've been watching the orb constantly. I don't think Lady Corinne knows we're coming."

Cettie wouldn't count on that. She lowered a hand to her poisoner bag, comforted by the feel of it. Cettie had prepared different toxins for the confrontation with her mother. Nothing fatal—though she didn't doubt Corinne would kill her without a second thought, she didn't want to kill her mother. With any luck, there would be no need. She had a poisoned ring that could stun someone for hours and a packet of nightshade dust.

More lights began to appear throughout the city. Many workers arose before dawn to report to the factories. The ships under Welles's control would have an easier time of following them now. But she heard a soft, distant song in the air, and she knew they were being protected by the Mysteries.

"There!" Caulton said, pointing at a ragged tenement building. The windows were all broken. It was a dark, gaping maw, a place of disease and death. No light emanated from it, but even from this height, they could smell the stench of the place.

"What is this place?" Juliana said in disgust.

"I've been in this neighborhood," Adam said, wary. "Marshall Street. The cholera morbus has claimed several victims from this area, so many of the buildings are abandoned now. People are afraid to live here."

"That makes it a good place to hide a royal," Juliana said. The tempest slowed and came to rest above the filthy street. The smell emanating from the gutters was horrible. Even in her life in the Fells, Cettie had not been to such a vile place. The tempest came to rest just above it.

Cettie looked at Adam. "Please stay," she pleaded.

He shook his head no. "I'm not leaving you to face her alone."

"None of us are leaving you, Cettie," Juliana said, brandishing a pistol. "You must get it out of your mind. We go together or not at all."

Caulton nodded in agreement, one hand on his hip, the other holding the dimly glowing Cruciger orb. Prince Trevon stepped up beside him.

Her heart shrank. She didn't want to lose any of them.

"I'll tell those down below that we're going," Juliana said. "They'll be safe on *Serpentine* if we keep it high enough."

When she returned, Adam hefted the broken lamp he'd carried out of the poisoner school and nodded for Cettie to lead the way. They unfurled the rope ladder, and she climbed down first. The air was chill, and fog began to gather in the streets. Why was that? Had the temperature dropped so much that mist had gathered in the air?

Or was something causing the fog?

Her keen memory flashed back to the day Joses had died. Yes, she felt a presence. The same presence that had haunted her life since that long-ago day in the grotto at Dolcoath. She looked up at Adam, still standing at the edge of the sky ship.

His eyes narrowed. "It's here," he said, acknowledging her reaction.

The Fear Liath had found her. Adam swung over the railing and climbed down the ladder quickly. The Light Leering in the lamp glowed—a beacon. A promise.

The fog swirled around her ankles, obscuring the mottled, grimy cobblestones. The rank smell in the air made her want to gag. *Courage,* she told herself. The Fear Liath had not come there by chance. The beast had defeated her once before, and no doubt her mother hoped it would best her again.

One by one, her companions descended to the ground. Her chest felt like a hand had reached in and squeezed her heart.

Adam looked back up at the tempest. "What will we do with the ship?"

Juliana, weapons in each hand, invoked the ship's Control Leering, and the tempest lifted up higher, protecting the passengers in the hold. It would draw attention from the sky ships searching for them, but if they succeeded in saving Sera, that wouldn't matter. The fog had coalesced, and now the other side of the street was hazy. It was like a cloud settling over them, swallowing them up.

"That's the building," Caulton said, orb in hand, gesturing.

Cettie pushed the poisoner bag behind her. She could sense the Fear Liath's mind, its evil, lurking in the shadows and the mist. It was not trying to prevent them from entering the building. What was it doing, then? Why had it been posted as a guardian?

She didn't know, but that didn't stop her from moving forward. She led the way into the building. The light from Adam's lantern chased away some of the gloom.

The door had already been ripped off the hinges, probably for use as firewood. Heaps of charred wood had been stacked in the main hall. The building looked like it had once been a factory tenement, but it was abandoned now. Pieces of sky showed from holes in the roof overhead. The rubbish and debris on the floor made walking a dangerous act. She tried to move quietly, but the others hadn't had her training. They were making too much noise.

What would her mother do when she realized they'd come? Would she try to kill Sera rather than release her? Cettie breathed in through her mouth, unable to fully block the stench, and shoved aside the distracting thoughts. Caulton pointed to an iron trapdoor beneath a broken wall. The ground around it looked like it had been trampled by a lot of people.

"She's still down there?" Cettie whispered.

Caulton nodded once.

Cettie licked her lips. "Is Lady Corinne down there? Can you ask it that?"

Caulton stared at the orb, and she felt his nudging thoughts.

"Yes," he answered, then squinted. "And no. The orb shows that it's someone who is disguised as Lady Corinne."

So Cettie's mother was waiting for them. Or would they catch her by surprise?

Adam raised the lantern higher, and Cettie bent down and pulled on the handle of the trapdoor. Trevon joined her and helped her set the heavy piece of metal down gently. An overpowering odor of human refuse filtered up to them. Stairs led down into the darkness.

A snuffling noise sounded behind them, by the broken door they'd used to enter the building. Cettie whirled, seeing a hulking shadow in the mist.

The Fear Liath had found them. Was it going to attack them now?

"Its weakness is light," Cettie said to Adam. "That makes it vulnerable."

The miasmic fear of the creature had permeated the air. Everyone looked tense, on edge, fearful. Aunt Juliana held up her pistols as she turned to face the creature.

She sent it so we won't think clearly, Cettie realized. The creature was part of a trap. She had no vision to guide her of what would happen next. No notion of how they might avoid the trap but save Sera anyway. And so she started down the steps into the darkness. Adam followed her with the light, and the others followed him. The room beneath them was a huge cesspit. She'd been terrified of them as a child. The entire lower floor of each building in the Fells was used to hold human waste. She saw angled slats in the upper walls and filth staining the walls below them. The other buildings emptied into this one, it seemed. There was evidence of rake marks. Some broken handles. The lowest of the low scraped dung for a living.

"By the Mysteries, the *smell*," Juliana said, gagging.

"Over there." Caulton pointed to an iron door set against the far wall. Cettie could sense a kystrel at work behind it, amplifying the feelings that were already natural. Loathing, disgust, dread, hopelessness. That room emanated every terrible thing. And Sera was inside it.

Cettie led the way to the door. It was locked. She sensed the presence of . . . of children. Like the ones she'd cared for and protected in the Fells. The ones who'd kept her ghosts at bay, if only for a while. Her Dryad-kissed thoughts brought all those desperate moments back to her.

Children? Her mother was using children to torment her?

Cettie felt the injustice keenly. She had to clench her fists to stop from pounding on the door in anger. Once she had mastered herself, she reached into her poisoner's bag for the thin bar and tools she'd need to unlock the door. In a moment, she'd released the tumblers. Acting quickly, she returned the tools to her bag and opened the door.

The faces of the huddled children beyond gazed at her fearfully. They were chained to the wall. Each one was gagged. Some had tears streaming down their cheeks. Her heart quailed for them. And then she saw Sera lying on the ground, unconscious and possibly drugged, her dark hair covering part of her face. She wasn't wearing a royal dress anymore, but her gown wasn't soiled or ruined.

The feeling of dark magic—*kystrel magic*—hung in the room, mixed with something else. The power of the Mysteries, and perhaps even that of the Fear Liath upstairs. The kystrel music drowned out the others, making it impossible to discern the various strands. Someone was invisible. Cettie held up her hand to those behind her, warning the others to stay back.

"I know you're here, Mother," Cettie said into the void as she stepped into the room. The light from Adam's lantern pushed back some of the murk. He stood behind her in the doorway.

Nothing. Not even a sigh of breath.

"Do you see her?" Trevon whispered. When she didn't answer, he pushed closer. "Sera!" he gasped out.

"Stay back," Cettie warned, approaching the body. What was her mother's plan? Why hadn't she spoken? Not seeing her made the anticipation so much worse. She was being toyed with. Manipulated.

Some of the children were choking on their gags as they sobbed. She could see the warning in their eyes. The plea for rescue. Her heart broke for them, for the forgotten children. These slaves chained to the wall. It would all be perfectly legal of course—their deeds had been signed away, signed away again and again. Her heart quivered with outrage.

Cettie walked closer to Sera, keeping her movements careful and deliberate. Still, she heard no sign of her mother. Nothing to strip away the advantage of her invisibility.

"Father is dead," Cettie said, hoping to provoke a sort of reaction. A betrayed gasp. Anything. "Did you know?"

There was no answer. Cettie had reached Sera's crumpled body. The conflicting magic continued to whirl around her.

"Sera?" Cettie said, crouching down and touching her friend's arm. She kept her eyes roaming, looking for any sign of a threat.

Sera's head lifted slightly, some of the dark hair falling away. She'd changed a little since they'd last seen each other. But her face was as familiar to her as . . .

No.

Cettie realized it was wrong. An illusion. It wasn't Sera on the ground at all.

The Fear Liath roared as the illusion vanished. Sera melted away, replaced by Cettie's mother. As Lady Corinne's hand gripped Cettie's wrist, a rush of magic seized them both and sent them hurtling away.

She's sleeping in the captain's room. I must talk to her, but I don't wish to wake her. She needs the rest. Is this even real, that she's here? That I'm here on a tempest rushing back to our world? She's so weary, so broken-hearted and consumed by guilt. I want to know what happened to her. To hear the full truth, no matter how bitter. I need to know if I could trust her again.

I don't know how to describe my emotions. I've never felt so conflicted before. And yet . . . when I look at her face, I still see the young girl Lord Fitzroy brought up from the Fells. And now we're going back there. Why do we keep coming back to our origins? Why does the past torment us so?

Sleep, Cettie. I will wake you when we reach the prism cloud. For now, I can only wonder what they did to you. These enemies have no mercy, no spark of compassion. You've lived among them. How much of them is still a part of you? I wish I knew. I wish it could be different. That we didn't have to endure so much. If I had been there instead, could I have prevented it? I don't know what the Knowing wants. Sometimes, I think it asks too much of us.

—Adam Creigh, on the Serpentine

SERA

CHAPTER TWENTY–SEVEN
QUEEN OF THE UNBORN

When the whorl of magic from the Tay al-Ard ended, Sera was left dizzy and anguished. She was still trussed up with strong cords, arms wrenched painfully behind her back. They'd waited in the darkness of the lockroom for a miserable amount of time, the only light the illumination of Christina's silver eyes. She'd disguised herself as Sera and put a ring on Sera's hand that had made her invisible—and then jabbed her in the neck with a poisoned ring to make her limbs go slack and her mind fog with a stupor.

Sera had heard Cettie's voice through that fog. She'd struggled to rouse herself, to scream a warning. But the poison had pinned her limbs in place. She'd simply lain there, limp and passive, as the trap was coiled and sprung.

The dizziness faded, and Sera looked around, trying to determine where the Tay al-Ard had taken them. Her heart sickened with dread. She recognized the stone walls, lit by burning oil torches set in iron rings. Felt the looming danger of the Prison Leering.

Cruix Abbey.

No, Sera thought in dread. She had suspected fate would bring her there. But she wasn't prepared for it.

She'd thought it would be well protected. She'd tried to ensure it was so.

It wasn't.

Her worries were distracted by the pain of two bodies crashing against hers. Her legs were crushed. The drug had faded, but not enough that she could even yelp in pain. She heard grunts and gasps and then, in the flickering light, saw Christina and Cettie writhing on the ground next to her, grappling with each other.

The Tay al-Ard went spinning away on the ground, the metal making a scraping noise as it rolled away from the combatants. Light from the torches reflected on its metal surface. If only she could get to it!

Sera's entire body felt as it were made out of lead, so slowly did it obey her. She bunched up her aching legs and scooted herself across the floor toward the magical device. More cries of pain filled the air as Cettie and Christina grappled. Both were in her peripheral vision, and Sera marveled at Cettie's skill. Though her friend had always been talented with the Bhikhu style of fighting, this . . . this was unlike anything Sera had witnessed before. Christina was struck in the face, in the neck, only to return the blows.

Sera scooted herself forward again. With her arms behind her back, her wrists throbbing, it would be difficult to grab the Tay al-Ard. But all she needed was to touch it, to grasp it, and it could take her back to Lockhaven. Sweat popped out across her entire body as she strained to move just inches at a time.

A gasp of pain. Cettie was leaning forward now, her arm twisted behind her back. But she jumped forward into a roll, unwinding the hold, and swept her leg back to knock Christina off her feet. Her advantage gave her a moment to lunge toward the Tay al-Ard, but she was stopped short by the other woman, who'd already regained her feet.

Sera heard footsteps coming down the tunnel leading back to the Aldermaston's rooms. Help or additional foes? She would rather not be there to find out. Grunting herself, she moved closer, until her head bumped against the device. It rocked a little and then held still.

Cettie flung Christina off and reached out for the device. Her fingers almost brushed Sera's head, but Sera was still invisible. She couldn't see her own body.

And then Cettie's face contorted in pain. She'd been stabbed or injured in some way, though Sera hadn't seen how. She slumped onto the stone ground, her arm still extended, her fingers listless. Her eyelids quivered and then closed.

Was she dead?

Burning anger filled Sera's heart. More desperate than ever to stop Christina, to bring soldiers to this place, she inched a little closer to the Tay al-Ard. A shadow appeared on the floor, approaching her. She blinked in recognition. It was the Aldermaston of Cruix!

"You didn't kill her, did you?" said the Aldermaston in a stranger's voice. The Aldermaston she'd met didn't speak her language—this one didn't even have an accent.

"No," Christina panted, rising to her knees. "She almost reached the Tay al-Ard."

"Where's the empress?" the man asked, his voice angry.

"Somewhere . . . on the floor. Nearby," Christina said, gasping.

"Apokaluptis," the stranger said, and Sera felt a breeze brush across her. She was visible again, the magic tamed.

The disguised Aldermaston chuckled and knelt, quickly picking up the Tay al-Ard himself. She'd been so close . . .

Then his disguise melted away also, revealing a man with a short beard and cunning eyes. He wore a black cassock and had a musical instrument strapped around his shoulders.

"You did well," he said, looking at Christina and giving a small nod. "We almost lost her."

Christina nodded in return and stood.

"Hello, Your Highness," the man said, still squatting near her. "My name is Jevin Toussan. I'm pleased to meet you at long last."

"I can't say I return the sentiment," Sera whispered back.

Jevin smiled at the insult. He looked to be in his midthirties perhaps. Maybe forty at the most. "I imagine not," he said. "But that's no matter. You are here at last. That's what is truly important."

Christina rose, rubbing her wrist as if it pained her. Cettie was still immobile on the floor.

The bearded man met Christina's gaze. "The kishion are coming. It's time."

"How are they coming so quickly?" Christina asked, her brow wrinkling.

"The ley lines," Jevin said, but the word was incomprehensible to Sera. He tucked the Tay al-Ard into his pocket and then helped lift her into a sitting position since she could not use her arms. Part of Sera's dark hair fell across her face. She stared up at the man.

"I won't release her," Sera said forcefully, feeling the dark menace of the Prison Leering brush against her thoughts. There was a yearning there, a yearning to be free, to end the entrapment.

Jevin eyed her keenly. "I think you will." Then he rose and turned back to the entrance.

Sera, sitting upright, gazed around the entombed space. The walls were part of a natural cave that existed within the mountains of Cruix Abbey. The ceiling was vaulted, not because it had been built that way, but because nature had created it so. A crack ran along the apex where the slanted rocks joined together. Hollows had been carved into the rocks, forming benches where ossuaries had been made to store the remains of the dead. The space was neither cramped nor large. It was a cave within a cave, deep within the mountain itself, where no light could reach them. If not for the sputtering torches, all would be pitch black. The Leerings carved into the walls had been disfigured, the faces smashed by chisel and hammer.

That was different. That was new. It meant she couldn't use them to summon help.

Sera swallowed. Cettie lay nearby, her arm still outstretched. Cettie, who had been missing for over a year. Who had been abducted and concealed. She still looked like her friend, but the fight might have been staged for her benefit. Sera didn't know what to believe. The webs of deceit were too thick.

The kishion came noiselessly. Sera felt them before she saw them, and her blood ran cold as they arrived from the corridor. Five . . . eight . . . ten. Then more. They walked into the room, coming around in a circle, and then stood near the shadowed alcoves of the ossuaries. All in all, there were twelve of them. Jevin made thirteen. One of them caught her eye deliberately. He had awful scars on his face, but they didn't conceal his true identity.

Will Russell.

A little smirk twitched on his face. He knew she recognized him, and it amused him. Then he looked at Cettie, and his eyes narrowed with anger.

What do I do now? she wondered in the darkness. She gazed at the others, trying to see if she recognized any of them. But she did not. Then their eyes all began to glow silver as their kystrels burned to life. Darkness began to dim the torchlight. They were using their dark power to invoke the Myriad Ones. How were they getting past the barriers of the abbey above?

The revelation came like a slap. The kishion had carried the beings inside. They were willing vessels. Fear crept up her spine.

How could she, one person, hope to stand against them?

Cettie's fingers twitched.

"You *will* open the Leering," Jevin said in a menacing voice, his hands clasped behind his back, much like Fitzroy used to do. The two men might share that mannerism, but it was clearly all they shared. "We both know that only you can do it. That you were *meant* to do it."

The sickly magic made Sera begin to tremble. She'd never felt so abandoned, so alone. *Please,* she thought to the Mysteries. *Help me!*

"A prayer, Empress?" said Jevin, his voice full of menace. "You think that will help you now? Now, when you are kneeling before the altar of the Queen of the Unborn?" he said, holding out one hand in a reverent gesture to the Leering.

Sera felt a strangling feeling in her throat. She could sense the Myriad Ones gathering around her. Were she not wearing a chain, she would have been completely vulnerable to them. She tried to utter the word of power to banish them, but her mouth would not work.

Banirexpiare, she thought instead, since her lips could not utter it. Nothing happened.

Jevin chuckled coldly. "They're already banished. *Here.* Among the dry bones. Where else would you send them? A farrow of pigs? It is night still. The stars reign. Even the moon blushes to share its light. It is the moment of our greatest power."

Sera wilted inside. There were no dragoons to command. No zephyrs that could reach her in time. If Durrant knew where she was, he would have sent legions to protect the abbey. No one was coming. She was alone.

Cettie's head began to lift. Sera glanced at her erstwhile friend. Cettie's eyelids were quivering. But a look of relief dawned on her face when she saw Sera. A little smile.

"Don't . . . be . . . afraid," Cettie whispered.

"Ah, our little *traitoress* is recovering from the poison already," Jevin said with a look of disgust. "Christina. Would you help your daughter up?"

The woman bent down and hoisted Cettie up onto her knees, but the poison was still ravaging her body. Her limbs were slack, without strength, but her eyes were alert. She gave Sera a fierce look. Her lips moved without sound.

"Anthisstemi," Jevin hissed. Another jolt of power shook through Sera. Her weariness fell away, all her senses sharpening. Cettie appeared to be restored as well—she sat up taller on her knees and turned to Sera and said, "They're coming."

Who was coming?

"No one is," Jevin said with a mocking tone. "Lord Welles has started an insurrection. Many of your people are still loyal to him. Your *mother* persuaded him yesterday to join our cause." He gave Sera a knowing look. "Hetaera can be so very . . . persuasive. He believes he will be granted governorship of certain lands on this side of the mirror gate. A governor, not a prime minister able to be dismissed by the whims of the privy council . . . or a peevish young woman. You destroyed him, Your Highness. You tarnished his pride, his sense of self. It made it all the easier to seduce him in the end. In doing your duty, you played right into our hands. There are no sky ships coming. The friends you left behind in the cesspit will be killed by the Fear Liath. As will all the children. Unless . . ."

He raised his eyebrows in a tempting manner. "Unloose her. Free our queen willingly, and perhaps we'll be merciful."

Sera swallowed again. The thickness that had blocked her speech loosened. It was strange, as if Jevin had loosened some sort of invisible noose he'd held around her neck. She felt his power, felt the firmness of his mind. But Sera had always been stubborn too.

"I won't do it," Sera said, shaking her head. She tried to wriggle loose of the bonds, but they cut into her skin. Her wrists were swollen, and her fingertips hurt from the lack of circulation. The cave had an earthy, mineral smell—the smell of death.

Jevin sighed. "Then I'm afraid you will have to be convinced. Christina?"

Sera's courage began to waver, but she would not be cowed by his cruelty. "What are you going to do? Torture me?"

"No," Jevin said with a menacing voice. "We'll torture your friend. That's much more painful, isn't it?" Sera's eyes widened with horror. "A pity Mrs. Pullman didn't live to do it herself. She would have relished the opportunity."

Christina had a firm grip on Cettie's arm, but when two of the kishion approached, she relinquished her to them. One of them was Will. They grabbed Cettie's arms to control her, but Cettie didn't fight them. All her attention was on Sera.

"Whatever happens, they're coming. Don't save me. I accept thi—"

"Silence!" Jevin snarled, and Cettie went mute. She couldn't say a word, and the throbbing power of the Mysteries filled the air, awful and wrong.

"There *is* no one coming," Jevin said, his cheek twitching with barely controlled anger. Sera caught a glimpse of his rage, as if a furnace door had been cracked open . . . just a little, exposing the white-hot flames within. It quickly shut, and his calm facade was restored.

"You're lying," Sera said.

"I have no reason to," Jevin said with an incredulous look. "We've won. Despite all your resources, all your power, all your *goodness*, we managed to bring you here where we wanted you. Your fleets are in disarray. General Montpensier is about to destroy Lockhaven. And the Queen of the Unborn will return in all her glory and majesty. What happens next is on your conscience, Sera Fitzempress. You chose suffering and death for your people when you chose to fight back. How easy to sit on your velvet chair with your velvet *stool*, giving commands but not living the consequences. The suffering. Well, now you get to experience it for yourself. What should we use first? Black henbane? Cettie is a poisoner. She already knows how this will feel."

Sera's heart wrung in misery. Would Christina deliberately poison her own child? Cettie continued to look at Sera with purpose and determination. Though she could no longer speak with words, those eyes did it for her. They were not the cruel eyes of Jevin, or Will, or Cettie's mother. They were full of compassion. Of acceptance.

Whatever happens, they seemed to say. *I accept it. Don't let them deceive you.*

The two kishion gripped Cettie hard, prepared for a struggle. She did not give it to them. Christina, coldly, reached into her own bag and produced a small vial. She nodded to the two men, and they forced Cettie's lips open. She didn't resist as her mother poured poison into her mouth.

CHAPTER TWENTY-EIGHT
PRICE OF BETRAYAL

Sera couldn't look away. She was transfixed by the scene, by her own feelings of helplessness. Why was the Knowing letting this happen? She didn't understand. Then the pain and convulsions started. It was like Sera could feel them herself as she watched her friend's eyes squint, her body begin to tremble. The spasms became more violent, and the two kishion dumped her onto the floor to writhe and quake.

Groans came from Cettie as the poison ravaged her. Jevin must have released her voice, knowing the sounds she'd make would wring Sera's heart. Tears pricked her eyes. Whatever Cettie had done, she knew her friend's heart. She did not deserve this.

"Stop it," Sera shouted, unable to wipe the tears away. She looked at Jevin accusingly, but he seemed to be relishing the experience. His expression was hard as stone, yet there was a flicker of triumph in his eyes. He met her gaze, and she felt the awful darkness swirling inside him.

"Release the binding," he commanded her.

"I won't," Sera replied, shaking her head, her voice trembling.

"Another, then," Jevin said. "Earworm. Now."

Christina reached into the poisoner bag and withdrew another vial, this one metallic in color. The two kishion grasped Cettie's head, holding it to the floor while her mother poured the vial into her ear. Sera watched helplessly, and then the shrieks of agony started. Sera tried to rise, to come to her friend's aid, even with her own hands lashed behind her back, but Jevin intervened. He closed the distance between them, then gripped her shoulder and shoved her back down on the floor.

"If you want this to end, then you know what to do. Release the binding!" he shouted at her. The anger in his voice struck her heart like shards of glass.

Cettie had said *they* were coming. Could she wait? Could she endure watching Cettie's suffering, knowing she had the power to end it?

Do you?

Lies. These people told nothing but lies. If Sera released Ereshkigal from her prison, the kishion would likely kill her and Cettie both, and then the vengeful being would be unloosed on the world. Wouldn't countless more be killed and made to suffer?

"Have you no sympathy for your friend?" Jevin asked in a low voice, between the screams and the gulps for air.

"Have you no soul?" Sera countered.

"Look what you are doing to your friend. She suffers needlessly." His lips pursed. "Acetane powder is next. You cannot understand, Empress, how it makes one itch. These poisons will all kill her. But not soon. Slowly. And you will watch her die in the end if you do not stop it. The powder."

Sera tried to sit up again, her heart wrenching in pain as she witnessed yet another round of Cettie's suffering. Hers was an empire to command. Yet she felt powerless.

Help me, she pleaded to the Mysteries. *Do not make me endure this. Send aid. Please!*

As Sera watched Christina reach into the bag again, she felt a slight tremble in her heart. A feeling, from the Mysteries, that she was not alone, that her plight was not unnoticed.

But it wasn't over yet either.

As Christina withdrew a bag of powder, it struck Sera that while Jevin was a heartless villain who would no doubt allow Cettie to die, Christina was her mother. Surely that meant something. Was this task so easy for her, despite the cold look in her eyes?

"Christina," Sera said. Then her voice choked off, the invisible lash around her neck tightening.

Free me, she begged in her mind. *Let me speak.*

The strangling feeling began to loosen. Jevin's brow twisted with surprise. Beads of sweat trickled down the side of his face.

"You are her mother," Sera said hoarsely, her voice panting. "Why do you let them control you like this?"

"She is not under our control," Jevin said with disdain. "She is a hetaera! She *rules* us all."

"You are their *slave,*" Sera said, fixing her eyes on Christina's. She strained to rise again on her knees. "Can you not see that? Every woman in this room is in bondage. Even your queen."

"Be silent," Jevin warned.

"You were taken from someone who loved you. Someone who searched for you for *years.* Mrs. Pullman sent you to the Fells. Do you not remember who you once were? Who you truly are?" Sera felt power pulse within her as she spoke. The words came to her, unrehearsed, revealing information to her as she said them. It reminded her of the Gifting she had pronounced on Lord Fitzroy before his death. "Your love of music. Don't you remember it? How you would watch him play the cembalo? Music connected you. Music does that."

Christina was staring at her, eyes widening. The small leather bag in her hand hung in the air.

"He never betrayed you, Christina. He was true. No, *you* betrayed him. He knew you would come to him. I understand it now. I gave him his last Gifting." The memory of it would never leave her. *You will see her face before the end.* "Even at the end, he was concerned about you. You were the one who drove a dagger into his heart, but he forgave you with his dying breath."

"Be silent!" Jevin shouted, backhanding Sera across the face. The blow rocked her on her knees.

It must have cut Sera's lip, for she tasted blood in her mouth, but she didn't flinch. She turned her gaze back to Jevin. "You cannot abide the truth, can you?"

"It isn't the truth!"

Sera turned back to Christina. "You are surrounded by kishion," she said. "You're too strong for them. They never meant for you to survive this day. Your part in their plan is ending. And you will be murdered just as they have murdered your sisters. Is that not the consequence of defying the kishion? Obey or die."

Christina was staring at Sera, her mouth a frown. "I die either way," she said. "I cannot expect mercy from you."

"You can," Sera said.

"It's you who've killed my sisters," Christina said. "Those you've caught."

"I haven't. All are imprisoned, yes. But I've not executed any. Any who say otherwise have lied."

A quirk of a smile wavered on Christina's mouth. "Imprisonment. Like our queen."

Sera tried again to wrench free of her bonds. "There must be consequences, Christina."

"There are," Jevin said, looming over Sera with fists clenched. "You have a silver tongue, Your Highness."

"Yours is forked."

"You think to turn her heart? It's not possible. She is one of us."

"Only because you *made* her that way," Sera said. "She obeys because of threats. Because you've warped her mind to obey your will. I will not yield, you black-hearted villain. You can make her kill her own daughter. And me. But what will that do? As long as Ereshkigal remains in her prison, I am content to die. I know the same is true of Cettie." Then she turned back to Christina. "You are just as helpless as I am. I can prove it. Command them as you will, Christina. Watch the last illusion fail."

Silence.

Jevin's eyes smoldered with fury.

Christina looked up and saw what Sera did—the kishion were walking closer, surrounding her, their eyes full of menace. Cettie wept silently on the ground, the convulsions growing less and less.

There were too many of them, Sera saw. They had brought enough to best her.

Christina's eyes looked haunted. If she'd tried to invoke her kystrel, she had failed. No power came to save her. No ability to sway emotions. No inhuman strength. She was alone, stripped of her power, in front of her foes who had presented themselves as friends.

"Do you understand now?" Sera said sadly, gazing at Christina. "They didn't come to free Ereshkigal, only to bind her once again. To force her to do their bidding. You were their tool."

Christina looked around in growing panic, watching the kishion surround her. No doubt the poisoner's mind reeled at the prospect of facing so many enemies. There was no way she could win. No way she could survive the trap they'd set for her.

Sera watched Christina draw a dagger. No doubt it was poisoned.

"Kill her," Jevin said flatly, unconcerned.

Christina whirled and threw the dagger at him. Sera watched the blade go straight for his chest, only to stop in midair a few inches in front of him. It hung, suspended, then struck the stone floor, making a jarring sound as it settled.

Not just a kishion—a Wizr.

Jevin looked indifferent.

One of the kishion fired a pistol, and Christina lurched forward. Blood stained the front of her gown. Smoke filled the room, and the echoes of the blast nearly deafened Sera as several other pistols were fired. Haze filled the space, bringing with it the stench of the fumes. Sera's ears rang painfully.

When the smoke had cleared, she saw Cettie kneeling over her mother's body. Christina's eyes were still open. Blood oozed from the corner of her mouth.

Jevin walked over and grabbed a fistful of Cettie's hair, yanking her back and shoving her toward Sera. Blood dripped from Cettie's ear. She looked at Sera with grieving eyes, but she did not look surprised.

"I'm so sorry," Sera whispered, her own ears aching in sympathy. She didn't know what the poison had done, or if Cettie could even understand her.

"You haven't ruined my plans," Jevin said, pacing in front of them. "She was going to die anyway. As you said."

Sera closed her eyes. The pieces were fitting together in her mind now. "You could never trust her. Not fully."

"No," Jevin agreed. "Hetaera cannot be trusted. But they can be controlled."

"And what do you want to use that demon queen for?" Sera snapped. "Do you not see the risk in freeing such a being? Will she not turn on you next, Wizr?"

"Turn on *us*, you mean?" Jevin said, gesturing to the other kishion who had gathered around. "I think not. We have power over the kystrels, my dear. They cannot harm us. So yes, we wish to set her loose on the world. To remake it after our own order."

"She does not make, she destroys!" Sera said.

"Yes, she is like fire!" Jevin said, eyes gleaming. "Fire purges. Allows new life to be born from its ashes. Fire can be controlled, and so, too, can her power, once you understand the principles of how it burns." He smirked. "And I understand it."

"You'll destroy the world," Sera muttered.

"There are other worlds to visit," he said slyly. "Other cankers to spread. The Knowing obeys the strongest wills." He stood over her once more, glaring down at her. "Yours is no match for mine."

Sera glared back at him. "We will see."

"If the death of the sewer children doesn't rack your conscience, what about the deaths of fellow believers? You know from your cursed tomes that Ereshkigal has power over fire. She's burned Cruix Abbey before. How fitting that the empress's heir should be here when it burns again!"

Sera closed her eyes.

"You will yield!" Jevin shouted at her. "Every student, every woman, every child, every servant, every tome will be destroyed unless you obey me! I will burn them all to ashes while you watch." Smothering darkness emanated from his words as he yelled at her. She wanted to cower, to flinch, as the blackness attempted to subvert her will. "You think you are strong, Empress? You cannot stop me! The Mysteries and the Fountain are mine to command. What power do you have?" he asked, crouching before her. "Nothing! You have nothing. You are nothing!" She felt spittle strike her face.

You are my daughter.

She heard the words in her mind, felt the tender throb of the Mysteries.

Sera looked him in the eye. "I will not yield," she whispered.

Jevin's face contorted with rage. He grabbed Cettie and hauled her up. Her body was so ravaged by the poison she couldn't stand. He held a dagger to her neck, his eyes wild and fierce. "I'll shed her blood and make you drink it!"

Sera believed he would. She felt the vortex of pure evil inside him. But even though the dark energy raged around her, she felt the quiet stillness in her heart.

Sera bowed her head and closed her eyes, refusing to watch. Cettie was prepared to die. So was she.

"I will only release the Leering if the Mysteries command me to. Not you."

"I am the Mysteries!" he bellowed at her. There was bitterness and misery in his voice. And anger unlike anything she'd experienced. The furnace door of his wrath was open now, and Sera could feel it. He would do as he said he would do. There were no feelings that would soften him. It wasn't anger that drove this man. It was pure, malevolent hatred.

Sera squeezed her eyes shut even tighter, pleading with the Mysteries to know their will. She would do what they wanted from her. No matter what happened.

She heard a gasp of breath, and then a body fell next to where she knelt.

"Go up to the abbey and gather them," Jevin raged. "Every last one of them. Put them inside the sanctuary. Bar the doors. We'll burn them all. Kill any who resist."

"So be it," they said in a collective whisper. There was a gleeful emotion behind the words that made Sera's stomach wrench.

CHAPTER TWENTY-NINE
THE DOOM OF CRUIX

The kishion had all left the Leering chamber, leaving Jevin alone with Sera and Cettie. He paced in front of the Leering itself, then reached out his palm and touched the stone, bowing his head in deep concentration. Was he communing with Ereshkigal? Then he dropped his hand and pulled out his musical instrument. He began to play it, and a strange power wove through the room. His melody was haunting, foreboding, and it sent a chill through Sera's heart. A loud cracking noise emanated from the Leering.

"Can you hear me, Cettie?" Sera whispered, shifting despite her discomfort to get closer to her prostrate friend. "Are you alive?"

Cettie's head lifted slightly, her pale, drawn face revealing the anguish she felt. She nodded slowly and moved one arm toward Sera. She started to drag herself closer. "Let me try to free you."

"I don't think we can make it out of here," Sera said, keeping her gaze fixed on Jevin.

"Help is coming," Cettie said.

"But will it come in time?" Sera wondered. "They're going to murder everyone here at the abbey. I cannot stop it. Even if my arms were loosed. I won't release her, Cettie. Even to save the innocent. There are many more lives at stake." Sera sighed. "I cannot *bear* this much longer. I may die of a broken heart before they kill me."

"No," Cettie said. "You will rule and reign. I've seen it, Sera. Believe me."

Sera bit her lip. "It's hard to believe right now. So much suffering. So much death. How could the Knowing want this? How could it allow it?"

Cettie was staring at her sympathetically. "I had my crisis of faith too, Sera. I failed, but you must be stronger than I was. Even now, I serve the Knowing's will. It knows what will happen, Sera, it always knows. It knew I would choose to forsake it. But it also knew my most desperate hour and sent help. I don't understand it . . . but I've come to trust it. It will not lead us astray."

Sera felt a small throb at the words. She nodded her head slowly. "I'm so grateful you're here with me, Cettie."

Cettie smiled. "I will do everything in my power to ensure you survive this, Sera Fitzempress." She had pulled herself so close that her arms were nearly touching Sera's lap. "I'm going to cut your bonds. My mother has a pouch. It will be damp to the touch. Hidden in a secret pocket. There is moss inside it . . . a powerful magic. It can heal us. Get it. I lack the strength."

Sera slowly turned, trying to shift so that her back was to Cettie. But she kept her gaze fixed on Jevin, who still stood by the Leering, head bowed as if in some sort of trance as he played the hautboie.

Cettie started to work on the bonds. The pressure of tugging on them made her wrists hurt all the more, but Sera bit her lip and endured it.

"It's growing louder," Cettie said.

"What?" Sera asked, straining to hear over the sound of Jevin's song.

"The music."

That confused her. "I don't understand."

"Not the song Jevin is playing. Remember our days in Vicar's Close? I hear the magic as music, Sera. Chords . . . strains . . . measures . . . it's beautiful. It's growing louder. It's stronger than the magic Jevin is weaving. There's singing this time too."

"I hear nothing," Sera said. Were the students at the abbey singing?

"It's not from this world," Cettie said, grunting. "I'm so tired. Almost finished."

"What does it say?" Sera asked.

"It's not in our tongue. The words, I mean. I can't explain it. It's been so soft, but now it's louder. They're coming, Sera. They're coming."

The bonds fells away from Sera's wrists, and she gasped with the relief from the constricting pain. Blood flowed back into her fingertips, causing pinpricks of agony, but she knew the pain would lessen. Sera started to crawl toward Christina's body, making her movements deliberately slow.

Sera felt hope flare to life inside her. Jevin had the Tay al-Ard in his pocket. She'd seen him stuff it there. The other kishion were gone. With Cettie healed, they'd stand a chance to overpower him together.

She licked her dry lips again, arriving at the corpse. She quickly began her search, rifling through Christina's skirts.

At first she thought the dampness seeping through the gown was blood, but she had discovered the wet pouch. She carefully withdrew it from the pocket.

Then a voice startled her.

"You forget that Leerings have eyes," Jevin said coldly, turning around, his own eyes glowing silver as he put his instrument down on the floor.

Sera quickly tried to untie the knot on the pouch, but an invisible force yanked her off her feet and dragged her across the floor by her ankles. Jevin closed the remaining distance between them with a few quick strides. He yanked the pouch out of her hand, his face mocking her.

"Still you resist," he said, looming over her, squeezing the pouch in his hand. A look of fury blazed in his silver eyes. He threw the bag aside and dropped down, grabbing her throat with his hands and squeezing. She couldn't breathe.

Sera tried to bat his arms away, but he was impossibly strong, more so than such a slight man should be. His fingers dug into her skin. She arched her back, trying to claw at him with her fingers. As spots of blackness began to dance in her eyes, he finally let go, and she twisted away, gasping for breath. He walked over to Christina's body and fetched a small vial from her poisoner's bag. Cettie was crawling toward her, on her knees, but she slumped to the ground, exhausted.

"You don't know true pain until you've swallowed Kyanos," he said, strolling back as if he hadn't a care in the world. "It tastes a little like almonds. Have a bit!"

He knelt by her, twisting off the cap of the vial, and grabbed her by the back of the neck. Sera grabbed his wrists and tried to make him drop the vial, but he overpowered her and forced it to her lips. She jerked her head to the side, smelling the odor he'd described.

"Drink it!" he snarled. "I won't let it kill you. You'll only wish you were dead!"

As he tried to force the contents of the vial down her throat, she bit his hand so hard he flinched and jerked away, dropping it. The pasty ichor drained out. "You can't make me!" Sera shouted at him. "I won't give in, no matter what you do."

He nursed his hand, massaging the bite marks with his thumb, staring at her balefully.

"You . . . cannot . . . force me to do as you'd like," she said, trying to scoot back toward Cettie. "I'm not a puppet dancing on strings as you are. Those things inside you, squirming about, filling you with hate. They control you, Jevin. This is not who you really are."

He rose, still massaging his hand. "But you *are* a puppet, Empress. Only you do not see the hand controlling your strings. The invisible hand." He said it mockingly. "The *intelligence* behind the Mysteries . . . that is what controls you." He glared at her, his eyes full of wrath. "You trust it blindly, Sera Fitzempress. You cannot question it. You cannot make demands of it. How sorry I am for you, to follow something so blindly. In such ignorance."

Sera glared back at him.

"You put your trust in vapor. A shadow. It never reveals itself, yet it murders innocents just as we do. How many have been put to death for not following it blindly? You believe the Knowing cares about you, about the world, but we are nothing more than particles of eternity. Playthings that live and then die. Existence is meaningless. This shell I wear," he said, gesturing to his body, "it goes to the worms. The Knowing cannot stop us from murdering the people we've gathered in the abbey. It's not because it chooses not to interfere. It's because it *cannot!* It is victim to its own laws. It cannot intervene against free will. I will prove my words with fire, and you will see that I speak the truth. The Knowing will not stop me from destroying Cruix Abbey. It didn't stop her then," he said slyly, looking back at the Leering, "and it cannot stop me now."

She didn't hear the kishion return, but she saw them appear from the black stairs above. Her heart was racing as she felt the inevitable approach of destruction and death.

"It is done, my prince," said one of the kishion to Jevin.

He turned and looked down at Sera. "Your last chance, Miss Fitzempress. Release her. Or you will watch them burn."

She felt a hand touch her arm. It was Cettie, her eyes full of hope. Cettie, who'd told her to trust. To believe.

Sera turned back to Jevin. "I will not unless the Mysteries command it of me."

"Blind faith. *Unthinking* blind faith," Jevin muttered. "I must strip away your self deception, my dear. The universe wrenches everything into chaos. Watch as Cruix Abbey is consumed. Again."

Sera clasped her hands together, squeezing them tightly. In her heart, she issued a final plea.

I will face this awful thing if it is your will. But if you would stop this atrocity through me, then let it be done. I would sacrifice myself for my people.

Her thought went out, carried into the aether.

Jevin gazed down at her with contempt.

"Conflagrare," he said spitefully, invoking a word of power.

A feeling of peace came over Sera's heart. And then a wind began to howl inside the cave, the noise of it shrieking through the enclosed space. The kishion all turned, many with worried looks. Jevin's expression shifted to a frown of concern. The noise of the wind grew louder, louder, until it made it impossible to hear anything, and a gust of wind blew out the torches. Bits of rock began to crumble and patter to the floor, and then a jolt struck the mountain—a wrenching earthquake that shook the very rock they stood on. Sera fell forward, grateful her hands were unbound so she could catch herself on the rough floor. She smelled dust and smoke, felt the impact of rocks tumbling from the ceiling and smashing onto the cave floor. Cries of terror sounded.

The blackness was absolute and terrifying, but Cettie finally reached her in the darkness. The two held each other as the room tilted and bucked. Cettie was sobbing. Sera felt a strange peacefulness despite the tumult.

Then she felt something touch her head. She couldn't see in the darkness, but she felt the reassuring bulk of a hand. Knowledge flooded her mind. Knowledge of Leerings and how to construct them from the elements themselves. Leerings that could make sky manors, and even an abbey, fly. Rocks slammed down all around her, pulverizing one another and spattering their debris all around. One of them smashed into Will Russell, killing him instantly. Another crushed a kishion's legs, trapping him and making him moan in pain. But none touched her.

Sera began an incantation in a language she'd never heard nor spoken before. The words came to her, borrowed from another mind. A mind she now recognized as that of Empress Maia.

A thundering crack sounded from above. Groans of pain filled the air, only to be silenced by crushing rock. The building above them had lifted into the air, exposing the inner cave to the night sky. Starlight flooded in to relieve the darkness as the hulk of rock rose higher into the jewel-strewn sky. Sera's heart melted with relief, and she could see the look of wonder on Cettie's face as the abbey rose higher and higher.

"There! There!" Cettie whispered in awe, pointing to the sky.

Sera didn't understand what she saw, but it was an unraveling of sorts—the opening of a flower bud, the unfurling of banners. A prism cloud had opened above them, one that seemed to fill the entire sky overhead from one end of the horizon to the other. Streams of orange and pink light came, like the sun did when piercing clouds. Its radiance was beyond any words. There were flying cities coming through the rose-tinted portal, cities larger and more majestic than Lockhaven. Then she heard it, the music that Cettie had described to her. A chorus of ten thousand sung in brilliant harmony, dousing her with a wave of emotion so powerful it wrenched tears from her eyes.

She was gazing at a portal to Idumea. It made everything she ruled in the empire seem squalid, inferior, base. It reminded her of the vision she'd seen in the oceans of Kingfountain—her glimpse at the Deep Fathoms. But this wasn't just a glimpse. The sky had opened wide.

"I can't . . . can't believe," Sera gasped, clutching Cettie harder.

"The song," Cettie said. "Can you hear it now? Can you?"

Sera did hear it, but she could hardly speak through the tears in her throat. She nodded, her bones shaking from the vibrations. The myriad of stars twinkled still. The veil within the universe had broken.

But not even the lights and grandeur of Idumea could prepare her for the sensation of the Knowing touching her heart. She heard its voice. Not as a thundering command. Not as a wind or as the roar of a raging fire. Not as the deep rumble of the ocean during a storm crashing against the surf. It was a still voice, a mild voice, as if it had been a whisper. It pierced her to the deepest part of her soul and made her entire body tremble.

Sera.

And what startled her even more than her name being spoken was that she felt she recognized and knew the voice. Like a memory she'd only forgotten.

CHAPTER THIRTY
JUDGMENT DAY

Sera and Cettie clung to each other, gazing in wonderment as Cruix Abbey floated toward the broken veil. Sera trembled from head to foot as the power of the Mysteries coursed through her. In her heart, she'd feared the abbey would burn as it had centuries ago. Instead, it had ascended to another realm of existence—to Idumea itself. Radiance came down from beyond the veil, washing over the mountainside, making it seem as if it were kissed by dawn. She saw the rubble of the cave around them, strewn with the bodies of dead kishion. The Prison Leering was untouched, but a kind of steam radiated from it. Fragments of boulders were all around, but none were near where she and Cettie knelt.

There were no words to describe how she felt. Her entire being was suffused with such love, tenderness, compassion—yet those words were insufficient. Language wasn't suitable for what she had experienced. Not even the greatest poet in the realm could have articulated it. It left her breathless, heaving quiet sobs as her emotions swelled to the point of bursting and beyond.

Cruix Abbey entered the rift. Cettie dug her fingers into Sera's arms as the power built to a crescendo of sorts. Then the fold closed in on itself, the petals closing, and the vision came to an end.

"No, no!" Sera wept, not wanting it to be over already.

The fold closed to a single point of light, a star that shone brighter than any other. It was so white hot it made her wince, yet she could not tear her eyes from it. That single point, blazing through the expanse, sent down a shaft of light that struck the ruined ground where they knelt. Both Sera and Cettie lifted their arms to cover their heads, their joy replaced by a jolt of sudden terror. Then the star was gone.

And they were no longer alone.

Sera saw three personages standing a few paces from them. The one in front was a middle-aged man with a heavy paunch and waistcoat, breeches, and a gnarled staff with a golden knob at the top. Behind him stood a man with silver hair and a sword and scabbard belted to his tunic. Next to that man stood a radiant woman whose eyes glimmered like the stars above. Her gown was of a different time.

"Well done, little sisters," said the foremost man, coming forward at a quick pace. The other two, flanking him, did the same. "Well done indeed. Let me introduce myself, Your Majesty. That would be proper given the circumstances. My name is Maderos. I'm sometimes called Myrddin as well. This was not the first time the false priest of Toussan and his instrument have needed to be thwarted. When he was learning to be a sexton at a sanctuary, he discovered a hidden book that quickly corrupted him." He looked at Cettie and bowed his head. "Well met again, my friend."

"I know the two men," Cettie murmured softly. "They serve the Mysteries."

The woman spoke next. "My name is Sinia," she said in a beautiful voice.

Sera gaped. "Lady Sinia? Of Brythonica?"

The stately woman smiled and bowed her head slightly. "Yes, Your Majesty."

"I am Owen Kiskaddon," said the silver-haired man.

"He's the one who saved me," Cettie whispered. She bowed her head to all three and made a gesture of reverence.

"*Tusk,*" said Maderos. "We are your fellow servants. Please . . . stand. There is much you need to know and little time in which to tell it. The mirror gates between the worlds will break asunder soon. You must be warned."

Sera wanted to rise, but she only had the strength of a newborn kitten. Holding on to Cettie, she tried to stand, but her legs wouldn't allow it.

Lady Sinia approached them both and gently placed her hands on their heads. "*Anthisstemi exulpo,*" she said, and strength filled Sera once again, allowing her to rise on her own. Cettie rose as well, and the two huddled close to each other.

"Thank you," Sera said. She stared at the otherworldly beings. Maderos, Sinia, Owen—these were legends from the past. She'd heard about them from Trevon during their time together. Stories from a bygone age of kings and vassals and epic battles.

"If you would, Lady Sinia," Maderos said, gesturing for her. "She may hear it better coming from you."

Sera noticed that Sinia wore an old, pitted key on a strap attached to her girdle. She had long blond hair, smooth and flawless, and a kindness that radiated from the depths of her person.

"You are the Lady Sinia from the stories?" Sera said, shaking her head in wonderment. "The Duchess of Brythonica?"

"I am," Sinia replied. "I came to this abbey many centuries ago and left a prophecy for you."

"I was the one you spoke of, then?"

Sinia smiled. "Yes. In my former life, I was a harbinger. One who is blessed with visions of the future. Or the past. Like your friend," she added, nodding to Cettie. "I saw that the day would come when Ereshkigal would need to be released from her prison."

The words caused Sera's heart to flutter with dread. The entire mountaintop had been wrenched loose, but the Leering was still there, steaming, roiling, seeming about to burst.

"Was I supposed to release her, then?" Sera asked in confusion.

Sinia caressed her cheek. "Not then. Now."

"Help me understand," Sera said, shaking her head.

"You did your duty well, daughter of Maia. When Ereshkigal was bound, it was for a fixed time. The first empress knew that the day would come when she would be released from her prison. When she would seek revenge on the empress's family and persecute believers. You are the one foreseen to come, Sera. Your time to rule was chosen a thousand years before you were born."

"A thousand years?" Sera gasped.

"That was the duration of her confinement. What was foretold by harbingers since the days of the first noble kings. A vision seen by the First Father himself."

"But why release her?" Sera asked, staring at the Leering with growing horror. "Why not *destroy* her?"

Sinia gave her a knowing smile. "She *will* be destroyed, Sera. But not yet." She put her hand on Sera's shoulder. That simple comforting gesture was more than her own mother had ever given her. "Someone else will face her . . . and destroy her. I've seen it. If you do not free her now, she'll return stronger, after the one who is meant to dispatch her is already dead. I know what is being asked of you, Sera, but these travails you have endured—and endured so *well*—will give you the strength to become the empress you were meant to be."

"But if I release her, she will do unspeakable evil *now*, among us," Sera said. "I don't understand, Lady Sinia. Why must I allow it? And not just allow it, *cause* it."

"There is no harm in asking questions," Sinia said. "I, too, have had to face choices that I knew would cause pain to others . . . and to myself. You've had a glimpse of Idumea, Sera. It, too, was once a fallen world. A world where the innocent suffered and wicked men and women ruled. But Idumea was redeemed at last. Paid for with a price." She held out a hand and gestured to Maderos and Owen. "We were chosen, from our times, because of our service to the Knowing. Each of us has suffered heartache like you have. We have seen the innocent betrayed. The Knowing sent us to help you. To prevent Ereshkigal from overpowering you. I tell you, Sera, she only has as much power as we give her. With your determination to remain faithful, you have blocked her power over you. This you must teach to your people. Too much knowledge has been kept from the masses in your world. It has been cloaked in the Mysteries. It is time that everyone understood it."

Sera's heart felt like a fire burning inside her chest. All her life she'd believed it was wrong to live in the clouds while the people below suffered. Now, she understood, better than ever, that fixing this wrong was to be her purpose.

Sinia stroked her hair. "Do you understand now why you were chosen? Why the Knowing allowed you to be taken into the depths of the Fells? So that you might learn for yourself what is happening in your realm. So the scales might be removed from your eyes. The soul of each child is precious to the Knowing, no matter their birth. No matter their station." She gazed then on Cettie with a look of love and acceptance.

When Cettie started to weep, Sinia enfolded her in her arms. "Your parents chose murder and destruction, but their choices did not make you any less precious. The worth of a soul is its capacity to become something greater." She kissed Cettie's hair. "Your true father, your loving father, pleaded that my husband, Lord Owen, might be sent to ransom you." She turned her head to face her husband, the silver-haired man, who nodded in agreement.

"I was pleased to do it," he said.

"He still lives?" Cettie asked, her voice choking.

"Death is not the end," Sinia said. "It is only another birth. He was faithful to his oaths. He has received his reward. Now he waits for the rest of his family to join him. You will meet again, Cettie. A wise Aldermaston—an Aldermaston from Muirwood—once said, it will be no greater miracle that brings us into another world to live forever with our dearest friends than that which has brought us into this one to live a lifetime with them." Sinia gazed up at the sky with a far-off look in her eyes. "It is not the Knowing that destroys and murders. There is always a choice, and humanity is constantly seeking to destroy itself. Hate, above all, is the greatest scourge. The Knowing permits hate to endure and even prosper for a season. Then the season ends. I have witnessed these patterns through the many lifetimes I have served. Autumn is ending. Winter begins. She must be loosed, Sera, but just for a season. Then spring, I promise, will return again."

Sera's heart understood that what Sinia told her was true. She did not understand it by reason alone. Logic would have told her that she should never release Ereshkigal, but a gentle whisper ensured that the woman's words were true. She had felt the Knowing herself. And everything she'd experienced had been affirmed in the words of Sinia. She needed to trust what she could not see.

"Is that why the mirror gates will close?" Sera asked, thinking of Trevon. He was a prisoner still in Kingfountain. Would she ever see him again? "Because I must free her?"

Lady Sinia shook her head no, her expression becoming graver. "For too long your worlds have violated the covenants between them. Like two siblings who hate each other and are determined to fight. You've both plundered other worlds to enrich yourselves. The Knowing is longsuffering. Warnings were given but not heeded. Too many have suffered because of the violence between your realms. Because of the poverty inflicted on others. We have been commanded to close the portals between the worlds, save a few, which allow us, the Unwearying Ones, to travel between the realms. You have seven days to bring your people safely home, Sera, and return to Kingfountain those who wish to depart. The worlds will be shut up then. Only those given permission will be able to cross."

Sera's heart was pained at the punishment. She and Trevon had dreamed of uniting the realms under their leadership. Their union had only brought more bloodshed. She winced at the punishment, but she could not deny it was just.

"My husband," Sera stammered, feeling her throat tighten.

"Has been found," Sinia said, lowering her voice. "If the mirror gates were to remain open, Sera, your posterity would someday rebel and destroy both worlds." She shook her head. "The Knowing intervenes to prevent annihilation. Not to cause it." She cupped her hand against Sera's cheek. "It is not blindness to follow and trust a harbinger who can see the future. Who knows what would happen otherwise. If you do this, it will prevent the extinction of your world. Like Idumea, your world, too, may be redeemed. For a price."

Sera mustered her courage. She looked at Cettie, and her friend reached out to take her hand.

"It is time," Maderos said, his eyes crinkling. "Prison has not softened her fury."

"No," Sinia agreed, gazing at the Leering. "There is no water that can quench that fire. Only a gate to shut it in."

"Little sister. Before you release her, a word of warning to your friend." He gazed at Cettie. "Your enemy still lives. He used the Tay al-Ard to flee while his brethren died. He must be destroyed before the seven days are through. You have this charge. If you do not stop him, he will raise another wicked root."

Cettie nodded. "How will I catch him when he has the ability to flee in an instant?" she asked.

Sinia twisted a ring from her finger and handed it to Cettie. "My mother's father made this ring long ago. In another world. It will summon the Tay al-Ard into your hand when you are near him. Invoke it with a thought. You may use that magic to fulfill your role as an Oath Maiden. To do your queen's bidding. And to protect her."

Cettie accepted the ring, staring at the ancient metal and the delicate runes carved into its tarnished band. Then she put it on.

Sera's heart was aching at the decisions she was being asked to make. Releasing Ereshkigal from her prison. Sending Trevon back to his realm to rule in his father's place. Both decisions would cause her unspeakable anguish and despair. Yet strangely, that knowledge didn't sway her will. She was still too full of the Medium, still too certain that what she was doing was right. Clenching her hands into fists, she stared at the Leering and walked toward it. Shimmers of heat radiated from it. Ereshkigal was straining to burst out.

"Stand near me," she heard Owen say to Cettie.

Sera approached the Leering, feeling the furnace blazing inside it. The Leering's eyes were white hot and smoking. Fissures appeared on the stone, but it still held together. Would her hand burn if she touched the rock?

Glancing back, she saw Maderos, Sinia, and Owen standing together, their faces grim but determined. Cettie stood beside Owen, shuddering, though her expression was as undaunted as Sera's heart.

Maderos nodded to her. The time had come.

Sera faced the Leering with defiance in her heart. She put her hand on the stone, and surprisingly, it did not burn. The stone felt strangely cool, the surface rough against her palm. Sera bowed her head.

You will suffer, daughter of filth. Scion of vengeance!

The voice was so much like Jevin's, cruel and full of rage and threats. The promise of destruction and pain. Yet . . . yet . . . it was bluster. That was all.

I invoke this Leering, Sera thought. *Release who you've bound.*

There was a sharp cracking noise, the splintering of rock. The face of the Leering split into a thousand tiny shards, then the cracks deepened, stone began to slough off, and the boulder collapsed at her touch. An acrid smell stung her nose, reminding her of smelling salts.

Sera felt energy prickle against her skin, a tingling sensation that made her think of lightning about to strike. Wind whipped around her as she backed away from the rubble. It moaned through the rocks and crags of the mountain. A wicked cry of glee trembled in Sera's mind. It grew louder and louder and more painful each moment. Sera was forced to her knees, covering her ears, trying to blot it out. The wind ripped at her dress, made her hair flap in her face. This felt nothing like the windstorm from earlier. It felt diseased.

It felt as if it would destroy the very ground they stood on.

Banirexpiare.

Sera didn't know who had thought the word, but it hadn't come from her. The wind was tamed, and Sera looked up. The three Unwearying Ones stood firm. Maderos lowered his crooked staff and made a pouting smile.

"The *pethet* is gone," he said. "She will wander the world, looking for someone to claim. A willing vessel to inhabit."

"Sera, you must return to Lockhaven," Sinia said. "Montpensier's fleet has arrived to destroy it. Many of the sky ships in the admiralty have defected to serve your enemy. But the city will obey you, the true empress. I will take you there."

"I will take Cettie to the imposter," Maderos said. "I know where he is skulking."

The other eyes turned to Owen, who loosened his sword from its scabbard. "I will go to the Fells to stop the monster."

Maderos turned to Sera, his eyes earnest. "Seven days."

His words struck again in the pit of her stomach.

Seven days left to find Trevon. Before she would lose him forever.

CHAPTER THIRTY-ONE
THE EMPRESS REIGNS

Lady Sinia brought Sera to Lockhaven through a power she did not understand. She did not have a Tay al-Ard. She merely took Sera's hand, led her to a small rivulet of water running down the wall of the cave, and as they stepped through it, a yanking feeling similar to ones she'd felt made her lurch and nearly fall into the shallow pool of water in the control room of Lockhaven. Sera looked down, expecting to see the water soaking her skirts, but instead, she saw that the water was pushed away, repelled somehow by their presence.

Durrant was there, pacing with a look of panic, sleeplessness, and despair. His hair was a wild mess. The man looked as if he'd literally not slept in days. When he turned and saw her standing in the pool, he stopped short, his jaw hanging open.

"Sera," he breathed out in wonderment. "Do my eyes deceive me? Or are you a shade?"

Lady Sinia gestured for Sera to step out of the water. She did so and turned to thank the woman for her help, only to see her vanishing in a sheen of mist. Sera wished she could have forestalled her departure. Trevon had always wondered what had happened to Sinia. How he would have loved to meet her. The empress's heart ached, but there was no time to wallow in sadness. Her empire was slipping through her fingers.

"I'm real, Durrant," Sera said. The prime minister was still gazing in shock at her disheveled and injured state.

"My lady, you are . . . an answer to prayer," he said. He gesticulated and turned almost in a full circle. "There is literally not a moment to waste in niceties. Montpensier's fleet will arrive within the quarter hour. We're stranded, helpless, and unable to move or flee. Lord Welles, to make matters worse, has commandeered our hurricanes and taken them to the City. Admiral Grant is coming, but it will be impossible for him to arrive in time. My lady, moments ago, I was certain all was lost. And now"—he wagged his head in disbelief—"you are here. Save us, Sera. Lockhaven will not obey anyone else."

"There's much to tell you and little time, Durrant," Sera said, touched by the look of need on his face. "But do not lose hope. Warn the privy council that I've returned."

"How exactly *did* you return?" he said.

Sera looked at him curiously. "Did you not see her? The woman who brought me here?"

"You are the only one I saw standing in the waters," he said, shaking his head.

His words bewildered her. There was magic at work that was incomprehensible, but there was no time to wonder at it. She needed to focus her attention on saving her people. "Go, Mr. Durrant. I will deal with our enemies."

He nodded vigorously, smiling for what was probably the first time since her abduction. "You are here. I'm still in a state of shock. It is so truly good to see you again. We will speak of what happened to you . . . later."

"Go," she said, nodding, and he hurried out of the room to go to the privy council.

Sera, exhausted as she was, felt a surge of vigor and reached out and touched the Command Leering that bore the face of Empress Maia. The affinity she felt for her ancestor had grown immeasurably. Part of her felt as if she herself *were* Maia. Memories that weren't her own seemed to flicker to life in her mind. How many times had Maia sat in this very room during her war against the kishion of her days? The empress had lost her husband during that war. It pained Sera's heart to think the same would happen to her.

Are you with me, Empress Maia? Sera thought as she closed her eyes, caressing the Leering's smooth stone.

She felt a flush of warmth rise in her chest. The Leering activated, and she called forth the view from the eyes of the Leering embedded in the rocks at the bottom of the floating city. Waves undulated beneath them, interrupted by seagulls winging their way beneath Lockhaven's shadow. She could sense, through the Command Leering, the fear and panic of Lockhaven's citizens. Those who could escape by their own personal zephyrs already had. But the floating city was also home to many refugees from the war. She felt their bewilderment, the dread of the news they'd heard. They were preparing for death, trapped in the sky.

She turned her attention to the water, and she saw the hulking form of General Montpensier's ship, gliding beneath the surface like a massive whale. There were dozens of support ships with it, forming an underwater armada against her people. She imagined General Montpensier in that lead ship.

She remembered the uncomfortable dinner parties she'd attended in Kingfountain. How the general would always goad and try to upset her. All the while, he'd been plotting to betray his king and seize the throne for himself. His ambition and dissatisfaction were unlimited. He thought to rule both worlds. Now he would pay the price for his lack of loyalty.

Part of her cringed at the thought of destroying so many lives. But it was her duty as empress to protect her people. She hadn't started this war.

But she would end it.

"Come, General," she whispered. "I'm waiting for you." She would wait until they breached the water before she attacked.

Several minutes later, the massive sea ship finally burst above the waves. White foam crashed against its hull as it reached the surface. Sera narrowed her eyes, watching to see what they would do. The other ships surfaced as well, forming a ring around the main one. Then she saw ant-like men scrabbling on the deck of the huge ship. Partitions were opened, revealing immense cannons that had been hidden in holds belowdecks. Sera squinted, using the magic of the Command Leering to amplify her vision. She saw the cannons being loaded with huge bags of what seemed like powder. Soldiers carried heavy iron balls. These were cannons built to destroy Lockhaven, to break apart the rocks supporting it. The ships had been positioned to fire at the floating city. Even the smaller ships had cannons attached to them. It would be a relentless barrage.

How much of their flaming powder had they brought on the ships to feed the greedy cannons? She imagined the ships were full of the stuff.

"Well, General," Sera said dispassionately. "It's unfortunate that your powder is so vulnerable to flame."

She invoked the Command Leering again and compelled the city of Lockhaven to start gliding toward the fleet, closing the distance between them. Then she invoked the defensive Leerings beneath the city to rain lightning down from the underside. She heard shrieks of fear as fire arced down toward the ships and the sea. The ships could not submerge with the panels open, lest they be flooded.

They'd doomed themselves.

The arcs of fire came closer to the command ship. One of the smaller ships launched a huge cannonball at Lockhaven with a deafening boom. The cannonball smashed into the underside, causing a slight tremor. Sera retaliated with a blast of lightning, one that exploded the small ship with a flash of bright light.

Sera kept her attention fixed on the main ship, though, bringing Lockhaven directly above it. Hail and lightning smashed into the deck. Soldiers scrambled, some diving into the waters to avoid being struck. But there was no escaping. The ship turned into a tower of flame, so bright and hot its jet reached the underside of Lockhaven. Had she been watching firsthand without the Leering, it would have blinded her. Huge black clouds of smoke billowed from the burning husk of the ship lolling on the waves, obscuring what she'd seen. Another ship exploded, hit by bits of burning wreckage. But the mammoth enemy ship had been completely destroyed. Chunks of blazing wood floated amidst the other detritus. Sera could smell the acrid stench through the Leering.

Montpensier's schemes were finally at an end. More explosions came from below as other ships caught flame. Some were trying to flee, but the ocean had become a burning cauldron. Gray and black clouds billowed on its surface and the choppy waves spread the devastation.

A few more ships managed to send cannonballs up, and while most missed, a few did not. Sera sent arcs of lightning toward the surviving ships, but the smoke obscured her view, and she knew she might not catch them all. They would flee for the mirror gates or try to remain hidden beneath the waves. They didn't know the gates would soon be closing.

Within half an hour, all evidence of Montpensier's fleet had been destroyed. She stopped raining lightning down on the ruins of the fleet and ordered Lockhaven to return to its original location over the City.

A message came through the Leering, and she recognized Admiral Grant's voice.

"This is Admiral Grant of the high fleet. We have ships drawing nigh to your position. They should arrive within six hours. Please respond, Lockhaven. Please respond."

His tone was urgent, as if he knew all too well that his ships would arrive too late.

Sera felt a smile quirk on her mouth. She invoked the Leering again. "We are well, Admiral Grant. All is well."

"Your Majesty!" he said in surprise.

"Order those who are loyal to the empire to join your ranks. You will meet us at the City, where we will bring some traitors to heel. We may have to fight our own countrymen, but I hope to persuade Lord Welles to surrender. You are still loyal to me?"

"I am, Your Majesty," he said. "Lord Welles should be punished for this."

"And he will be," Sera promised. "Join us as soon as you can. I'd like the fleet to surround us. And Admiral—order a full retreat from Kingfountain. We must abandon that world immediately."

"Your Majesty, I don't understand," he said, his tone baffled. "We've made great gains. If we press the fight, I'm confident we can conquer them. They've never been this vulnerable before."

He was right, of course. But then, he didn't know what she did.

"Follow my orders, Admiral. Evacuate that world immediately. The remaining mirror gates will all come crashing down. I cannot stop it. It's a punishment . . . from the Medium. Whoever is left on that side when the gates are destroyed will be trapped there permanently."

Silence hung between them for a moment, and she could tell he was wondering how it was possible for her to know such a thing, then he said, "Yes, Empress. I will issue the orders at once."

Sera let go of the Leering and slumped down on the padded bench beside it. She felt the gentle sway of motion. Lockhaven was heeding her, as before. It was moving. As tired as she was, she knew her work was not over. After rubbing her aching wrists, she rose from the bench and left to meet with the privy council to decide what was to be done about those who had committed treason.

～

Sera listened with patience and interest to the council members who were left. The room was only half-full because many had fled for their lives. Some had been ordered to go, by Mr. Durrant, but others had fled surreptitiously. Those who had stayed were the most courageous, the most loyal to her.

Arguments had been made for both clemency and strict justice. Sera gave no indication of her own thoughts on the matter. She wished to hear the arguments of her advisors before deciding. Many on the council were angry. All were grateful that Montpensier's force had been destroyed.

"You cannot pardon Lord Welles," Lady Sanchia snapped after someone suggested that retaliating harshly against Welles was inadvisable since he clearly had a strong bedrock of support within the empire. "The crime he's committed is unpardonable! He broke our trust by siding with the enemy. Treason is a capital offense."

"But if Her Majesty hadn't humbled him, he may not have turned on us," said another lord. "I'm only speaking my mind. He was drunk on power. And we ripped away the bottle."

"You blame Her Majesty?" Lady Sanchia said, aghast. "His downfall was his own doing. He was foolish enough to have an affair with a hetaera mistress."

"Her Majesty deserves no blame," Mr. Durrant cut in. "Do I need to remind you who it was who just saved us from certain destruction?" He sighed, shaking his head. "Your Highness, I think we've heard plenty of options. There are merits to each, to be sure. The question is how do you wish to be remembered? You've been uncommonly quiet. I'm afraid not even I have any notion of what you will do. Your expression is enigmatic."

Sera stroked the soft padded arm of the fine chair upon which she sat. Her wounds still festered. She smelled of the filth of the cesspit. She was in desperate need of rest. But this was more important. Her leadership had been forged for this purpose.

"After I was abducted, I was hidden in a cesspit in the Fells," Sera said. Eyes widened with surprise. Some of the ladies covered their mouths involuntarily with their handkerchiefs. "I witnessed firsthand the cruelty that we do to each other, especially to those less powerful than us. I intend to make some radical changes in our society. To pass laws that will condemn the slavery of children. No more will deeds be bought and sold. No more will people be treated like chattel." She sighed. "Some of my ideas will not be popular. They will stoke animosity and anger. But I intend to take care of our people. Instead of using all of our wealth to build sky ships, I intend to use it to build bridges. I'm not saying we will disband the Ministry of War. But I see now that we erected it to pursue our interests in other worlds instead of improving the lives of our people."

She paused, choosing her words deliberately. She didn't know how the council would react. "Some of you may not feel comfortable in the world I intend to rebuild. Lord Fitzroy had some excellent ideas, and we had only just begun to implement the simplest of them before he was killed. I will continue to pursue his plans with a vengeance and look for more ideas to further improve the condition of our people. We must do this, my friends. And I tell you why. Our enemy is no longer the rulers of Kingfountain. It is the Queen of the Unborn. She is freed from her prison at Cruix Abbey.

"For too long we have guarded the secrets of the mastons, veiling them behind the Mysteries. Keeping the poorest among us in ignorance. These secrets must be shared with everyone, lest Ereshkigal destroy us from within. She will use our own thoughts against us." Sera shook her head. "The war we face now is a battle for our minds. If we do things as we've done them for the last few centuries, then we will fail as a people. From this day forward, the Mysteries will once more be known by their proper name: the Medium. And all children in want of an education shall be given one. We will open new abbeys and new schools throughout the empire."

She leaned forward and placed her hands on the table in front of her. All eyes in the room were fixed on her. Most of the council members looked nervous and worried. Her latest revelation was still sinking in. Ereshkigal, the Queen of the Unborn, had won power in secret by manipulating kings and queens. She'd persecuted the mastons to the brink of extinction. Her return would cause terrible events to unfold.

"I propose an amnesty for the traitors," Sera said. "Those guilty of crimes against us or those who do not wish to live among us any longer shall be exiled. This world is certainly big enough. Our cartographers will choose a location that is wholly uninhabited. These people will be colonizers in a way. They will establish their own society. Rule themselves as they please. We will provide sufficient provisions for them to survive for several years, and then we will leave them be. Without sky ships, they will be stranded. Perhaps Lord Welles, since he sought to be our governor, would prefer ruling such a society to facing charges for his crimes. Those who do not accept the amnesty will be charged through the Ministry of Law. It may take years to try all the cases, but we will grant each person a fair trial and an advocate to speak on their behalf. Those found guilty will suffer the consequences of their crimes, including prison sentences for lesser crimes. Execution for treason or murder."

She leaned back in her chair, looking at their faces one by one. Silence.

Mr. Durrant's brow was deeply furrowed. His mouth was pinched into a frown. "Would the exile be permanent?"

She stared at him. "Yes."

The door to the privy council chamber was thrust open, causing looks of alarm to spread over the small group. It was one of her guards, Lieutenant Wilton.

"Your Highness," he said breathlessly. "A tempest bearing the name of *Serpentine* just hailed us. They're en route from the Fells. Prince Trevon is on board." He struggled to breathe. "He's on his way to Lockhaven now!"

I am back at the hospital with a group of malnourished and sickly children whom we recovered from the cesspit in the heart of the Fells. It is morning, and I am still alive. But I'm deeply worried about Cettie and what has become of her. The monster from the grotto attacked us in that awful place, but the iron door held the beast at bay. It raked its foul claws on the metal door. It howled and raged. Our only light was the lantern I held. Then all went quiet. Sickly, deathly quiet. We waited, unsure, trying to calm the children. But it was still out there. The orb told us it was lurking, waiting for us to emerge.

We unlocked the children from their bonds. We readied ourselves to face the monster. How many hours had we been trapped down there? I have no idea. But we felt, finally, that we should go. That we should trust the Mysteries, which said we should leave. We knew, from the orb, that Sera and Cettie had been transported to Cruix Abbey. We had to tell the government, anyone who would listen. I knew they were both in grave danger.

The monster attacked as we emerged from the locked chamber. I made the lantern I carried as bright as the sun. It charged at us still. I heard Juliana's pistols fire twice. It was too big, too monstrous to be stopped by such a small weapon. And yet it worked. It shrieked in pain and then slumped to the floor. For a moment, I thought I saw a man standing behind it with a drawn sword. An angel from the Knowing, perhaps? I don't know. The beast was dead. I brought the children with me while the others left on the Serpentine. I pray they make it safely to Lockhaven. That the empress, and dear Cettie, may be returned whole and hale.

—Adam Creigh, Killingworth Hospital

CETTIE

CHAPTER THIRTY-TWO

RUINS OF PAVENHAM SKY

Cettie and Maderos stood together on a beach. The sun had not yet risen, but there was sufficient light to see the endless gray waves before them. The water hissed as it lapped up on the shore, stopping before it reached their shoes. Cettie waited at the old Wizr's side, gazing at the scene before her. A giant tree lay on the sand, its massive gnarled roots facing the sea, the bark silver and black from its constant bathing in the salty waters. Sera had described such a sight to her before. It belonged on the beach below Pavenham Sky.

But the estate had fallen. Part of the cliff had been sheared away. Boulders mixed with wall stones on the surf. Seaweed tangles tufted from broken turret windows. Small seabirds skittered around the debris. Skeletal bones from the walls and struts had been washed up on the shore. But some were too heavy to be moved by the sea and emerged from the sand like mammoth Leerings. The wind had a briny but pleasant smell.

What wreckage. What destruction her mother had wrought.

"He is here, Maderos?" Cettie asked, turning to look at him after taking in the whole of the scene. "Jevin?"

"Up there," Maderos said, pointing his staff to an island cliff that rose before them. There were towering trees on the cliff, and she realized that the beached tree had originally come from its grove.

"But why?" Cettie asked. "Why would he come back to these ruins?"

A little smirk lighted on his face. "So many questions, little sister. My friends are always curious. Because," he said, pointing to the little island, "there is a mirror gate here. A small one. Not big enough for a ship with sails. But plenty large enough for a smaller vessel. Yes. Here there is a mirror gate the ministries don't know about."

Cettie gazed at him in surprise.

"Our enemies are cunning, little sister," he said in a mischievous voice. "They find unexpected ways to subvert us. Some they learn about in legends gone by. Others are given to them in evil books."

Cettie nodded.

"Walk with me, little sister," he said, and started at a quick pace along the shore toward the island. "The tide is low. He will not stay here long. You have the ring?"

She nodded, touching it on her finger.

"Good." As they approached the mass of rock, white crests lashed against its sides. A few gray-and-white seagulls hastened away from them as they walked along the shore. The sand they trod was so wet the island was mirrored in ripples on its surface. Looking back, she saw their footprints disappearing into the sand.

"How will we get to it? Do we have a boat?" she asked.

"No, little sister. We just need to bend the water back is all. Like *this*."

He held up his hand and muttered a word she didn't understand. The water receded farther and farther, exposing the ground beneath the surf. Not all was sand. Jagged tidepools, previously covered by the sea, could be seen near the cliffs. As they walked along the wet rocks, Cettie peered into the small little pools flourishing with colorful and strange sea life. How she wished she could stoop and explore the contents, but

Maderos continued hiking along the uneven ground with the assurance and ease of a mountain goat. She had to watch her step to avoid plunging a shoe into one of the pools.

When they reached the edge of the cliff, she stared up at its massive bulk. Rivulets of water trickled down the seaweed-encrusted edges, revealed by Maderos's magic.

"I will hold the waters back while you climb up," the old man said. "Hasten, little sister."

She gazed at the rocks, searching for handholds. She adjusted the poisoner bag against her back and looked up again, trying to pick the best spot to climb.

Then she paused and looked at him. "Thank you, Maderos. For everything you've done for us."

He shrugged slightly. "You may need a weapon, little sister, when you face him. Take mine." He offered her his cudgel staff with the golden knob.

She stared at it a moment and then accepted it. She wound the straps of her poisoner bag around its grooves, securing it for the arduous climb. He stepped away, arms folded, and watched as she began to pick her way up the side of the cliff. Her training at the poisoner school had hardened her muscles and given her the confidence to do such a feat. She felt no fear as she quickly maneuvered up the face of the cliff. The hard climb tested her limbs and made her hot despite the chill of the morning breeze. After she'd gone up a little way, she heard the surf smashing against the stones beneath her. Gazing down, she could no longer see Maderos.

The muscles in her forearms, hands, and calves began to burn as she continued to climb. Part of the rock was slick from the water trickling down from above, reminding her of the water wall at the poisoner school. Had the Knowing presented her with that challenge to prepare her for this moment? She rested at times, drawing on her strength, and then continued. Soon she could smell the trees crowning the small island. With her muscles straining, she finally reached the crest and pulled herself up, pausing to catch her breath. She'd done it. Sitting on the gorse at the edge, she stared down at the waves beneath and felt a touch of dizziness, which she still experienced when at a great height. Then she stared down at the ruins of Pavenham Sky, which she was now more level with. It had sunk a crater into the mountainside. Shattered bits of stone and shingles lay everywhere.

When she was ready to continue, she untied the knots and brought the staff around to help her rise. The wood felt smooth in her hand. She began to stalk through the smattering of thick trees atop the islet. She could hear the faint notes of magic coming from farther ahead, toward the middle of the island. The feeling reminded her of the sound of Jevin's hautboie. She thought she smelled a whiff of wood smoke in the air.

Dawn had risen at last, the sun an orange globe rising over the mountains in the eastern sky, so pale in comparison to the sight of Idumea. She walked purposefully but quietly, trying to mask the sound of her approach.

The feeling of magic grew stronger. Then she heard voices.

"It's time to awaken," she heard Jevin say. "We must go before the kishion finds us. Come now. We must hurry."

Jevin wasn't alone.

Cettie followed the noise, approaching a tighter cluster of trees. It struck her that she, and these others, would be invisible to anyone on shore. She couldn't even see the shattered remains of the mansion any longer, obscured by the tall evergreen trees. *Shui-sa* trees.

"I'm cold," Cettie heard a young woman's voice say.

"I know. We'll build another fire after we escape. Come, lass. We must hurry."

Cettie saw movement through the trees. As she carefully approached, slowing even further to avoid alerting them of her presence, she peered around a tree. There was Jevin in a black cassock and a dark gray cloak. He looked haggard from the events of the night. His eyes were burning, feverish, and he kept looking over his shoulder as though he could sense he was being watched. "Come on, lass. Hurry." He gestured again to a young woman wrapped in a cloak, his expression straining with impatience. Cettie saw dark hair spilling out. Then the girl lowered the cowl, and Cettie recognized her.

It was Becka Monstrum, Sera's maid.

"Where are we going?" Becka asked, her voice worried.

"Where that murderer can't find you," Jevin said, holding out his hand to her. His other hand snaked toward his pocket.

Cettie invoked the power of the ring just as he pulled out the Tay al-Ard. She felt the magic link the ring on her hand to the metal of the device. It was yanked out of Jevin's hand and sailed directly to her, binding itself to the ring on her finger.

He looked up in shocked surprise, a twist of fear on his face.

Cettie slipped the Tay al-Ard into her own pocket and then stepped away from the tree and started toward him.

"You!" he hissed, and she saw the furnace of hate begin to open once more. His momentary fear was blasted away by fury.

"You have failed in your scheme, Jevin Toussan," Cettie said.

He bared his teeth like a wild animal.

Becka, whirling around, saw her. Her eyes widened with recognition, and she reached out a hand.

"Stay with me," Jevin said, gesturing for her. "She is a kishion's daughter. The one you saw murder that young man. Ask her to deny it!"

"Becka," Cettie said. "Get away from him. I've come to save you."

"She won't deny it. She can't deny it. She's the seed of that man! I'm trying to protect you. Come here."

Cettie continued to close the distance between them, brandishing the staff.

"You come at me with a pauper's stick?" Jevin mocked. He drew a long dagger, its blade dusty with poison. It looked familiar to her, from some ancient memory not her own. An Oath Maiden in the past had faced a similar weapon.

"The kishion did sire me," Cettie explained, keeping her eyes fixed on the dagger. "But he is not my father. Lord Fitzroy is."

"And Fitzroy is dead. Murdered. Come, child. Come with me now."

"He will destroy you, Becka, just as he almost destroyed me. He is a deceiver. An accuser. You mustn't believe anything he says."

Becka was on her feet now, backing away from them both. She looked like a mouse poised to flee.

"You think you can best me?" Jevin said with contempt. "I who taught you?"

Cettie gazed into his eyes without flinching. "Yes."

He hefted the dagger, but then turned sharply as he flung it, aiming for Becka instead. The girl screamed in terror. It felt as if time slowed. Cettie rushed forward, spinning the staff. The end of the weapon caught the dagger midspin and knocked it away. Cettie turned, feeling as if she were underwater, and gripped the staff by one end, swinging it around.

Jevin ducked and struck out at her, his face contorted with rage. His hands joined together, he mouthed a word, and she saw lightning race from his fingertips to consume her. The jagged bolts were sucked into the staff, making it hiss and steam. Jevin stared at her in shock. He'd expected his magic to destroy her, but the lightning merely tingled against her skin. Traces of it danced on her shoulder blades.

His spell had been ineffectual.

Cettie lunged at him, striking him in the stomach with the knobbed end of her weapon. He bent double in pain but managed to grab the shaft of the staff. Smoke began to sizzle from his burning hands, and he let go at once, howling in agony.

Power surged inside Cettie. She charged toward him again, striking his collarbone, hearing it snap. Another strike hit his shoulder. He fell, only to roll and get to his feet again. His eyes glowed silver as he screamed at her, trying to grab her, to choke her to death as he'd attempted to do with Sera. Dark shapes hovered in and out of him, Myriad Ones just as intent on destroying her as their host was. Their magic, their envy, their malice hit her like a bludgeon. But she would not yield. She stepped forward into the murk, and struck him again. His body collapsed, fingers clawing at the small shrubs. He tried lunging at her again.

You are nothing! An urchin! You were born in filth and will die in filth!

She could hear the words in her mind. How he transmitted them to her, she didn't know, but she recognized Jevin's voice. His thoughts tried to overwhelm her like floodwater.

You mean nothing. You are utterly worthless. Pathetic! A traitor to anyone who ever mattered to you. No one will weep when I kill you. They'll be grateful you're dead. Just die. It would be better if you just died! Hurl yourself onto the rocks below the cliffs. Just die!

The thoughts held power, and Cettie felt them collide with her soul like fists. These were thoughts she herself had entertained, and he threw them back at her, knowing the injury they would cause. For a moment, she had the urge to do as he said. To give in and give up. But they were lies! They were desperate lies from a coward.

Through some magic or innate skill, he could weave his thoughts into the minds of others. Was it Fountain magic?

It didn't matter, in the end. She would listen no more. She would not allow him to cause any more harm.

Cettie cracked the staff across his cheek before his fingers could reach her. The blow stunned him, made him sag. He blinked rapidly, trying to regain his balance.

He looked dizzy, disoriented. "Who are you?" he gibbered. "Where am I? How did I get here?"

The Medium whispered to her, the voice clear this time, undeniable.

Into your hands is the accuser delivered.

She knew what she had to do.

"Who?" He looked up at her, his eyes sparking with recognition once more. The next moment they blazed silver as he invoked his kystrel to save himself.

Cettie spun the staff over her head and brought the metal knob down on his skull with killing force.

Jevin slumped into the brush, his arms and legs twitching. He choked and gasped a moment, struggling to breathe. She saw his eyes roll back in his head. Then he stopped moving, stopped breathing.

He was dead.

Cettie wiped her mouth on her sleeve, backing away from the body. She glanced over and saw Becka staring at them, aghast.

"C-Cettie?" Becka whispered.

Cettie was winded by the conflict. But she also felt . . . free. As if a fist that had been clenching her mind had suddenly relaxed. She stifled a sob.

"Are you all right?" she asked Becka.

The young woman trembled. She opened her mouth but seemed to struggle for words.

"The man you fear. The kishion who murdered Mr. Skrelling. He's already dead, Becka. So is the woman you knew as Lady Corinne. My . . . my mother. I'm going to take you back to Lockhaven. Have you been trapped here on this cliff since you were abducted?"

Becka nodded. "I was so frightened, Cettie. So frightened. They told me he was coming. That he'd throw me off the cliff if I tried to escape. I've been here for days."

Cettie smiled reassuringly. "Come. You're safe now."

"Where is Sera? Where did they take her?"

Cettie, holding the staff with one hand, took Becka's hand in the other. She felt for an invisible ring on the girl's finger. Thankfully, there wasn't one. She then checked the other hand, just to be sure.

"To Lockhaven. Where I'm taking you. Sera's worried about you. She needs you."

"I would like to go back. They . . . they poisoned her."

Cettie nodded. "I know. And I will make sure that doesn't happen again."

She squeezed her hand.

CHAPTER THIRTY-THREE

FORGIVENESS

The Tay al-Ard brought Cettie and Becka into Sera's private room in the palace at Lockhaven. Brilliant sunlight came through the sheer drapery, revealing the remains of breakfast. Cettie had visited Sera on occasion in Lockhaven, but she'd not been there since her rise as empress. Becka knew the location, and so she was the one who had invoked the magic to bring them there.

Their arrival was noted with a gasp.

Sera and Trevon were sitting on the plush window seat, fingers interlocked. The gasp had been Sera's. She jumped to her feet, her eyes full of bewilderment and joy as she stared at her two friends standing on the ornamental rug. Her wounds had been tended, her clothing changed into something more befitting her station. The same was true of Trevon.

"Becka!" Sera said in trembling relief. The two embraced, tears flowing. Becka was sniffling, but her smile was radiant.

Cettie remained aloof, savoring the wash of warmth inside her.

"Is it really you?" Sera said, pulling away and kissing her friend on the cheek.

"Yes," said the younger girl. "I'm here to serve you, Your Highness. If you'll still have me."

"Have you! I can't do without you." Squeezing Becka's hands, she looked at Cettie, her eyes swimming with tears. A moment passed, and then Sera rushed across the room and drew Cettie into her embrace, tightening her hold until it almost hurt.

Time seemed to melt away. Years were peeled back, stripped bare. Cettie's mind was still perfectly sharp. She remembered their days together at Muirwood Abbey, their little cottage at Vicar's Close with the lavender garden in front. Images flooded her along with the sights and smells from the memories. The times they'd spent together walking the grounds, often hand in hand. The memories seemed to feed a deep hunger inside her. Friends they had been. Friends they would always be. And those memories were joined by ones of the time she and Sera had spent with Trevon and Becka during the prince's visits to their world, picking through the fruit stands on Wimpole Street as Sera bragged about the apples from Muirwood. Those had been such happy days. Days that had made the sun feel brighter.

"Are you hurt?" Sera finally asked, wiping her nose on her sleeve. She caressed Cettie's hair, blinking quickly, drinking her in.

"I'm well enough," Cettie answered, her voice thick after the rush of memories. "Though very tired."

"Trevon, come. Come!" Sera gestured for him to approach and then took his hand in hers when he arrived. He was groomed and dressed as a prince again. But the look on his face said that the good times had ended. He looked crestfallen. There was a heavy expression on Sera's brow as well. A pained look.

"He told me you were the one who saved him in Genevar. We spoke to his brother, not an hour ago," Sera said. "And shared the news. They are ready to welcome back their lost king," she said, her voice trembling. "Every moment we have left is precious to me."

"The marriage?" Cettie asked, her own brow wrinkling in sympathy.

Sera sighed. "We never consummated it, Cettie. The privy council says it will be best to annul it. I cannot go to Kingfountain. Once the mirror gates are sealed, there can be no crossing."

"But what about this?" Cettie said, holding out the Tay al-Ard.

Sera took it from her, fondling the magical device, and offered it back to Trevon.

"It does not work between worlds," Trevon explained. His own eyes were dark with sadness. "Only within them. Tell her about the general."

Cettie's eyebrows lifted.

"His fleet is destroyed, and he with it," Sera said. "Admiral Grant has returned and has offered surrender terms to Lord Welles. We're expecting his capitulation today. If not, there will be more bloodshed. Montpensier's death and our defeat of the kishion will end the war happening within Kingfountain. But there is much anger, many problems to be solved. The kingdom is fracturing. There are still enemies on the loose. They weren't all gathered at the abbey. They need Trevon . . . to heal the breach."

Cettie was pained to hear that news. The way they stood near each other, the way Sera clenched his hand in her own . . . She knew their separation would be painful to them both. Their hardships seemed to have brought them even closer together.

"I'm so sorry," Cettie whispered. But she understood, in a small way, those feelings. She, too, would be separate from the man she loved.

Sera maintained her composure. "We'll do what's best for our people," she said. "You must be famished! Here, eat some of our food. I'll have more brought straightaway. Then you must rest, Cettie. Sleep as long as you need. I'm going to send word to Fog Willows that you're here, safe and sound. I'm sure Lady Maren and the others will come immediately. Juliana is already here."

Cettie's eyes widened. But what about Adam? She didn't dare ask, fearful of what the answer might be. That he wouldn't be coming back.

As if the empress had discerned her thoughts, she said, "Adam remained back at the Fells," Sera said, and Cettie felt her heart drop. "At the hospital. He's rescued all those poor wretcheds who were bound by deeds." Sera's eyes smoldered with anger. "New laws will be passed soon. This treatment of children will not stand. I've asked the lord high admiral to support the Ministry of Law in restoring order to those dark places in our cities. I've commanded the Ministry of Thought to open refuges and orphanages to care for those with no homes. And I've asked the Ministry of Wind to add more doctors to study the cholera morbus and find a cure, once and for all. I cannot solve all these problems in one day. But we will begin. One day the name of the Fells will be only a memory."

Cettie's heart throbbed with gratitude. "Thank you, Your Majesty," she said.

"No," Sera replied, shaking her head. "You will *always* call me Sera."

<hr />

A light touch on Cettie's shoulder awakened her from blissful sleep. She blinked quickly, lifting her head from the pillow in Sera's chamber to find Becka kneeling at her bedside. The girl had changed and bathed, and it looked like her peace of mind had been restored to her.

"The Fitzroys have arrived from Fog Willows," Becka said. "They are anxious to see you. Are you feeling well enough?"

"Yes, of course," Cettie said, sitting up and rubbing her eyes. "I should like to see them very much." The mattress had felt like feathers and clouds, and she'd sunk into its peaceful oblivion. She had no idea how much time had passed. There was still light coming in from the windows, but it seemed to be waning.

"Can I help you change?" Becka offered.

Cettie smiled. "I haven't any other clothes." Then she noticed three gowns folded over the back of a sitting chair.

"Her Majesty thought you might approve of one of these. They're all yours."

One of them, a dark green gown with thick black stripes, reminded her of one of her favorite gowns when she was keeper of Fog Willows. "The green, if you please."

Becka helped her dress and did her hair for her. How strange it felt to have an attentive servant. It made a little feeling of guilt wriggle inside her chest, but it was overpowered by her desire to dress quickly in order to see the Fitzroys again. Once she was ready, she followed Becka through the royal corridors.

"They're in the music room," Becka said.

The sounds she heard coming from the room she approached would have revealed it anyway. The doors were already open, welcoming her. Cettie's heart began to race with nervousness. Above the gentle strains of strings and rushing scales of a clavicembalo, she heard the din of voices in conversation. She thought she recognized the booming laugh of Sir Jordan Harding.

Her stomach began to twist into knots. Becka smiled, touching her arm comfortingly, as if she understood how Cettie felt.

Cettie entered, amazed at the size of the crowd gathered before her. Cettie's heart quickened at the sight. Sera and Trevon spoke with Lady Maren with smiles and nods, while Mr. Durrant, the prime minister, spoke to none other than Phinia and her husband, Malcolm. Aunt Juliana and Caulton Forshee stood nearby, huddled close together. Sir Jordan and Lady Shanron and their children were also present, and Sir Jordan was in the middle of a story about a hurricane—the storm, not the ship—he'd been in off the coast of Florentine when he was a young officer. Her heart swelled at the sight of so many people she loved and cared about. Then it constricted painfully.

Adam was also present, standing beside Anna Fitzroy, and their heads were bent low in private conversation. It caused a prick of pain in her heart, but she plucked it out.

She tried to convince herself it was good to see them together. Her heart was conflicted, but her mind would overrule it. She loved them both and wanted them to be happy.

This would be her penance, the price she should pay.

"Thank you for bringing her, Becka," said a voice at her shoulder. It was Stephen Fitzroy, who had been waiting by the door for them.

"My pleasure, Lord Stephen," Becka said.

Stephen offered Cettie his arm.

"I don't know if I can do this," Cettie whispered, her chest squeezing so hard it was painful.

"One step. Then another," he suggested with a wry smile. "They all want to see you."

"I'm surprised to see the Hardings," Cettie said, taking his arm and entering the room with him. The music did not come from Leerings in the walls. The instruments were being played by living musicians. This was a palace, of course, and could afford its own performers. The music caused just enough commotion that the others hadn't noticed her arrival yet.

"You saved Gimmerton Sough from crashing," Stephen reminded her. "All of the Lawtons' assets have been seized by the crown. They had no children. I believe the empress is going to offer them a fair price to reclaim it. They'll be our neighbors again."

She smiled broadly at that.

Sir Jordan noticed them finally and quickly made their presence known to the others with an ebullient laugh and said, "Well, there she is! Now the set is complete. Does this mean we can eat soon?" Cettie bit her lip as the others all stopped what they were doing. Everyone made way for Lady Maren to hug her first, and Cettie felt tears squeeze through her lashes as she fell into her warm embrace. The subtle scent of her perfume brought back floods of memories.

"I'm so sorry," Cettie said, grief-stricken.

"Hush, Daughter. None of that," Lady Maren said. "You're back. You're back!" Maren kissed her again and again. "You're my child. *My* child. I've missed you. How I've missed you!" Then there were no more words. They just held each other, weeping.

One by one, the well-wishers embraced her. Even Phinia, who had a jealous sort of expression on her face and complained, a little too loudly, that no one had ever made such a fuss over her, and she'd always been *good*.

Adam stared at her from across the room, giving her a relieved and tender smile. He looked so beloved to her at that moment, her heart ached. He nodded his head to her, letting the family have their turn first.

Then it was Anna's turn to greet her. Beautiful, perfect Anna, who swept Cettie into an embrace, blond curls almost smothering her. She couldn't speak—neither of them could.

"I love you, Cettie," Anna whispered. "You'll always be my sister. Please come home. We need you."

The reunion abounded with emotion and goodwill. After each guest had greeted and welcomed Cettie, Sera suggested they indulge in a little dance before dinner. That was received with warm applause and one of Cettie's favorite pieces was chosen: "Sky Ship's Cook." They broke into pairs. When Adam asked Anna to dance, Cettie made herself smile in approval, but she couldn't watch for long. Then Stephen asked for her hand, and she gratefully joined him. Sera and Trevon led the set.

With one exception, it was about as perfect a moment as could be found. A memory, Cettie knew, that she would always remember. And always feel.

CHAPTER THIRTY-FOUR

RUINS

Sera and Trevon walked hand in hand on the abandoned beach beneath the ruins of Pavenham Sky. The sun had set after dinner in Lockhaven, but Pavenham Sky was far enough west that they got to watch it going down a second time the same day. They went slowly, their shoes crunching on the rough sand. This beach was much colder and more melancholy than the beach of glass beads in Ploemeur, but it was important to them in its own way.

"This is where we first met," Sera said, looking up at him. "An auspicious moment that went awry in so many ways."

"Thanks to a clumsy oaf," Trevon said, chuckling to mask the pain in his voice. "I don't know what you saw in me."

Yes, it was painful being there with him, knowing they'd have to part despite the love they'd found for each other. But Sera had learned to lean in to pain. The tide would settle eventually. It always did.

"You caught my eye for some reason," Sera said. "There was something different about you."

"I've never been handsome," Trevon said, "so it certainly wasn't my looks."

"You are perfectly acceptable to me. And although I wish I were taller, I am tall enough."

They stopped near the huge fallen *Shui-sa* tree on the beach. She rubbed one hand along its wet, smooth trunk.

"I used to walk along this shore so many days," Sera said wistfully, "dreaming of a way out." She glanced up at his face. "You rescued me from this prison. I'm grateful, to be sure. But it was this experience that brought about the greatest change in my life."

"What do you mean, Sera?" he asked.

She stared off at the sea, listening for a moment to the crashing of the waves. There was power in water. A certain majesty that couldn't be explained.

"My father is a direct descendent of the first empress. I was always taught that a person's lineage was directly linked to their power. Yet I couldn't work the Mysteries as I thought I should. Failure made me doubt myself. It made me impatient. I was forced to learn patience at Pavenham Sky. I was forced into a state of humility. And yet I learned something else about myself as well. No matter what restrictions they put on me, they could not force my mind to be still. I was sovereign over only one thing, and that was my thoughts. My parents, Lady Corinne, even that loathsome Wizr Jevin . . . they all tried to rule my will. But I could not be ruled by them." She smiled in a sad way. "I wish I'd known that at Muirwood. I would have learned the lessons much faster. I'd have been much less selfish."

Trevon let go of her hand and began to climb atop the dead trunk.

"What are you doing?" Sera asked.

"You've said before you used to climb up here and walk along this trunk. I wanted to see what it was like."

"It's slippery. Be careful."

"If you could do it, Sera, I think I can manage."

He reached the top and then took a few steps toward the massive gnarled roots at the end facing the sea, which were probably three or four times his height. She clambered up beside him. It brought back vivid memories, and she could almost hear Master Sewell giving her a halfhearted warning to come down. At her invitation, he had joined the palace staff.

"Could we go to Muirwood tomorrow?" Trevon asked, turning around and facing her on the log.

"If you'd like," Sera answered. "Do you want to see the apple orchard again before you go?"

"Actually, I was hoping to speak to the Aldermaston," he said. "I have a peculiar question for him."

Sera took a few steps closer. "What kind of question? Can I help?" She'd told him about Lady Sinia and how she had been sent by the Knowing to help them. The tale of her abduction had been solved at long last. Trevon had believed her, and they'd shared the news with Prince Kasdan and his wife, who, come to think of it, hadn't seemed all that surprised by the revelation.

"I'm curious," Trevon said thoughtfully, "if a marriage performed in Kingfountain would still be considered a marriage here in this world. Or would it have to happen *again* to be just as binding?"

Her heart trembled. "What do you mean?"

His lips were pressed tightly together. Then he asked, "What if I stayed?"

She blinked in surprise. She didn't dare even breathe.

He took a step toward her. "Look at this devastation," he said, gesturing toward the ruins spilling around them. "This . . . wreckage that the fissure between our worlds caused. So many lives lost on both sides." He shook his head sadly. "But I fear that we wrought the greater harm. We were the ones who kept trying to attack. To change your beliefs to better match ours." He put his hands on his hips. He looked away again. "When I asked to treat with you . . . back when you were a prisoner here . . . I hoped to free you not only from your confinement, but from what I saw as the confinement of your faith. Yet you turned the tables on me, Sera." He gave her a slow smile. "You asked if I would be willing to give up what I cared about, what I believed in, and adopt your ways. Would it be fair to ask the same of you?"

"I remember that little speech," Sera said, her heart swelling.

"It wouldn't be fair to ask it of you," Trevon said. "My time as a prisoner also taught *me* that. I worried so much about you. I swore if I ever got free, if I ever found you again . . . that I wouldn't let us be parted."

Sera bit her lip, then said, "Trevon?"

"What if I choose to stay?" he asked again. "My brother has proven he is a capable ruler. He's the one who fought for my throne . . . he's the one who has earned it. I think the hollow crown would sit perfectly well on his head. I've been thinking about this since you told me about the closing of the mirror gates." He pressed his lips together again. "I'm ready to make my choice. If you'll have me, I choose you, Sera Fitzempress. I will be your consort. You will be my ruler."

Sera felt such strong emotions she thought the ocean was surging inside her heart. "But we could rule . . . together!"

Trevon gave her a slow shake of his head. "I don't think your people would accept that. At least not yet. So I make no demands. I have no expectations. Whatever is *right*, we will do it. And you will be the most influential ruler since your forebear ascended to her power."

Sera closed the distance between them, wrapping her arms around him and hugging him to her with all her might. "I can't believe you are saying this," she whispered. "I would never have asked you to do it. I wouldn't have dared hope for it."

He pressed a kiss against her head. "I know, love. It wouldn't have happened before the nightmare we went through. But these trials we've seen have bent me into a better shape."

She looked into his face and leaned up on her tiptoes to reach his lips with hers. It was just as delicious as she remembered and stirred up all those familiar feelings in her heart. The surge of relief, of joy, of satisfaction radiated from the tip of her nose to the soles of her feet. She let the wave carry her.

"Are you sure, Trevon?" she asked him after their kiss, stroking his bottom lip with her fingertip.

"I am sure, Sera. But let's ask the Aldermaston all the same. I'm thinking I would like to spend some time at the abbey. Learn what you have learned. See for myself how it matches with the traditions that I was taught. Perhaps I'll take the Test myself someday."

She gripped the front of his coat. "You've given me my heart's desire."

He stroked some hair away from her forehead and then kissed her there. "I know you are good at cleaning up messes. Let me help *you* this time."

It's been two months since I last wrote in this journal. These will be looked back on by others, and what can I say that has not already been said? These words may be of benefit to a future generation who did not live when the mirror gates allowed us to travel between worlds. The histories will reference names like General Leon Montpensier, but they will forget the flawed, ambitious man and only remember his deeds. They will forget the self-sacrifice of Trevon Argentine, who forsook a kingdom to live among people who were bitter and resentful of his homeland.

How can I, with this meager pen, relate such events? I will do my best.

Lord Welles chose exile instead of execution. He and those who speculated on his success have been banished to the island of Tenby. It is in the southern hemisphere on the other side of the world. It will take years before they've advanced to the point where they might be able to cross the seas again. They will have no Leerings for heat, light, or water. It would not surprise me if they made Welles their king, though a miserable kingdom it will be. The courts are still full of cases of treason, and the hurricanes will not disembark to Tenby until the end of the year. While the weather is lamentable here, it is strangely calm and beautiful in the southern sphere. Some of the gazettes have faulted the empress for her leniency. Some people are always thirsting for blood.

Mr. Durrant has been a capable prime minister and has already begun implementing the programs Her Majesty decreed. He is shrewd in his placement of officers. It seems the Ministry of Law has finally earned its turn at the helm of power. Yet the empress and her husband are wise to not let any one ministry control the whole. She seeks advice from all the other ministers as well, forming balance in her judgments.

There is one case that has been of especial importance to me. Cettie has had her trial too. I received word from Mr. Teitelbaum that it will be concluded today. The evidence was presented in secret council. The judgment will be pronounced today at the court of justice in Hyde Street here in the Fells. And so I must forsake my pen again. I would be there when the pronouncement is made. I hope it is fair.

—Adam Creigh, Killingworth Hospital

CHAPTER THIRTY-FIVE
THE VERDICT OF CELESTINA PRATT

Cettie sat solemnly at the council's bench, sitting alongside Mr. Sloan, her advocate. Lady Maren had insisted that the family lawyers represent her case, and she was there as well, sitting on Cettie's other side, holding her hand beneath the table.

The chief magistrate, Lord Wilcom Coy, sat on an elevated seat. Though his judicial robes and powdered wig were immaculate, he had the haggard look of a man who'd made judgment on hundreds of cases in the months since the mirror gates had all failed. Cettie had watched several people burst into tears as their verdicts were read. Many of them had been deemed guilty of conspiracy and would have to forfeit their lands and titles. How they had wept. The wheels of justice had ground them to dust. It was very intimidating, especially with the crowd of onlookers in the benches behind the wood barrier.

It could have been evening outside, but there were no windows to mark the passage of time. The only light came from Leerings hidden by translucent glass. It was Cettie's turn at last. Whatever came next, she was comforted by the knowledge Mr. Sloan had done his best to defend her. She did not feel exempt from justice. She embraced it.

"Now hearing," said the ministry official standing at Lord Coy's elbow, "the verdict of the case of Celestina Pratt of the Fells."

Mr. Sloan nodded to the man and leaned back in his chair. He looked completely at ease. Cettie wished she felt equally confident in the outcome.

Lady Maren squeezed her hand again.

Lord Coy cleared his throat. He was a large man with a reddish-brown beard that clashed with the white wig. He had penetrating eyes and a solemn expression.

"Now to the next case at hand," he said, looking through the papers stacked before him. "This is a complex case, and as such, we saved it for the end of the session today. Lady Fitzroy, our apologies you've had to wait so long for a resolution to this matter."

"Her ladyship thanks you for your consideration," said Mr. Sloan, dipping his chin.

"In summary," said Lord Coy, "Celestina, known as Cettie Pratt, willingly joined the woman declaring herself as Lady Corinne Lawton of Pavenham Sky, who was, as the record now shows, an imposter by the legal name of Christina Towers . . ." The judge went on to describe, in brief, all that had occurred since, but Cettie found her thoughts wandering. The legal talk made her story feel like something that had happened to another person altogether. A tale completely bereft of emotion.

She snapped back to attention when Mr. Sloan gently tapped her arm. He glanced toward the judge, his message obvious. Her attention was once again required. The verdict was about to be announced. Lord Coy folded his hands together, leaning forward on his desk. "All charges against Miss Cettie have been withdrawn. As the natural daughter of Christina Towers, Miss Cettie is considered a full member of the empire, entitled to all its privileges and rules of adoption.

"Lord and Lady Fitzroy have pursued the rights of adoption for many years and were only barred because they lacked the consent of Mr. Pratt, who now holds no legal rights over her whatsoever. The motion to adopt her has now been granted, and the Ministry of Thought has given its permission for Miss Cettie to be bound to the Fitzroy family by irrevocare sigil. Once the ceremony has been performed at the abbey of their choice, her legal name will henceforth be Cettie Fitzroy."

The magistrate smiled at her as Cettie's eyes widened. She could hardly breathe and stifled a sob. She'd expected she might face punishment, imprisonment or exile or worse, for her part in the events of the last months. She hadn't expected this . . . But judging by the pleased expression of her mother and Mr. Sloan, they had been keeping this secret from her.

Lord Coy tilted his head. "It is my understanding, Lady Maren, that your son, Lord Stephen, has agreed to act as proxy for his father in the ceremony?"

"I have," said a voice from behind them.

Cettie hadn't known he would be there, and she twisted in her chair, gasping when she saw Stephen, Anna, Phinia, and Milk were all seated in the row of seats behind her. They had slipped in without her noticing. Her throat was so constricted she couldn't speak, but she smiled at them. Then she saw Adam, sitting farther in the back, as if he wasn't quite sure he belonged. A congratulatory smile lit up his face. She blinked quickly, struggling to contain the tears that had welled up in her eyes.

"This is by order of the Ministry of Law and the Ministry of Thought. The adoption decree has been approved. This court is now adjourned. Congratulations, young lady."

Cettie turned and embraced Mother, squeezing her. She felt wet tears on her cheek, not her own but Lady Maren's.

"How long have you known?" Cettie said, choking on her words.

"Sera wanted it all done legally. She could have ordered it so, but she felt that a trial would do more to appease your conscience than anything else we might do." She caressed Cettie's cheek.

The other family members came around the barrier, and Cettie hugged them one by one. Even Phinia seemed sincere in her congratulations.

"Do you know what abbey you would prefer?" Stephen asked her after embracing her. "You get to decide."

"Muirwood," Cettie said without hesitation.

Stephen's eyes crinkled. "I thought so. We'll make the arrangements. I'm glad you'll be my sister at last."

She felt a rush of warmth. Once again, she reflected on how proud she was of the man he'd become. Stephen had stepped into his role as the leader of the family, and he wore it well.

"I think someone else is waiting their turn," Stephen said, giving a subtle nod toward Adam Creigh, who waited at the barrier patiently, his palms resting on the wood.

Anna turned to look, and when she saw him, she walked over and put her hand on Adam's. She said something to him, and he nodded. Butterflies fluttered in Cettie's chest. Were they about to announce their engagement? If so, she would bear it. She would be happy for them, no matter how much her heart hurt for what could have been. Then Anna left him and joined their mother, pausing only to squeeze Cettie's hand, and Cettie knew the time had come for her to greet him.

"I'm happy for you," he said as she approached him at the barrier.

"Thank you," Cettie replied, feeling her cheeks growing warm. "And thank you for coming."

"If you have time in the coming days, I would like to show you the hospital," he said. "But I'll admit I have selfish motives. I've studied the cholera morbus for years and am no closer to discovering how to stop it. I hoped . . . if you're willing . . . to share the information I've collected with you. I haven't forgotten how you and Fitzroy discovered the storm glass together. Perhaps you might see something I haven't. I would be grateful if you'd come."

"Of course," Cettie said. "I doubt I'd be much help, but I'm willing to learn."

Lady Maren approached them. "She can borrow the zephyr tomorrow and come to you in the morning?"

"That would be ideal," Adam said. "I look forward to it. Come as early as you like."

Cettie visited Killingworth every day for the next week and soon was known throughout the hospital as Dr. Creigh's particular friend. The building had once been a manor house, though it had been refurbished to make it suitable as a hospital. She was impressed by the order, the rhythm of it, and especially Adam's insistence that whoever came there was treated, regardless of their ability to afford it. No one was turned away. With the empress as his patron, he did not lack for funds. Cettie learned that another hospital, similar to it, had been chartered in the City.

They spent hours together poring over his studies, especially the map he had made of the latest victims of the cholera morbus. Some days they traveled together to new neighborhoods where deaths had been reported. The danger she'd felt as a child in the Fells was slowly changing. Officers from the Ministry of War had been assigned to patrol the streets. The gangs feared the dragoons, and so the thievery and violence had diminished. There were also many construction projects underway, putting people to work and improving their living conditions.

Cettie had always shared Adam's passion for the work of the Ministry of Wind, and the days seemed to go by in a blur. At the end of each day, she'd return by zephyr to Fog Willows. Part of her didn't want to go back. She wanted to stay with him. He didn't speak of Anna, which made her wonder whether there was indeed something between the two of them. She dared not ask. To be near to him and discuss his work at the hospital was not a duty to her. It was a passion. Her mind kept racing to solve the mystery of the disease. Though Adam had come so far on his own, something was still missing.

A week after the trial ended, she was poring over his map yet again in his office, the two of them alone, considering the various houses and buildings. Why were so many of the deaths clustered in the same general area? Not all of them, of course, but so many.

"There is something they have in common," Cettie whispered. "We just can't see it."

"There were four more deaths yesterday," he said, joining her at the map. "Here and here. Three from one household. One from that house, there."

Cettie remembered walking down that street with Adam over the last week. She could imagine the houses perfectly in her mind. She remembered the cries of street vendors, the rush of children, the washerwomen gathered at one of the Leering wells washing clothes.

Cettie remembered how filthy the water was.

"The Water Leering," Cettie said, the image of the gouged face hidden from sight with stone panels sharp in her mind.

"I've examined the Leering," Adam said, shaking his head. "It's perfectly sound. The water is clear. It supplies the entire neighborhood."

Cettie scrunched up her nose. "But the water in the fountain . . . the water they wash with. That water is filthy."

"Of course. So is the water from all the fountains."

Cettie stared at the map. A thought niggled in her mind.

"What if the disease is in the filthy water? Some people are so thirsty they'll drink anything. What if . . . what if something is poisoning the water after it comes out of the Leerings?"

Adam gazed at her. "Why would anyone drink from it?"

"Let's go back to the Leering well we went to yesterday. The one here," Cettie said, pointing to the middle of the dark marks on the map.

"Very well."

He grabbed his coat and her cloak, and the two of them left Killingworth together, walking side by side down the busy street. In half an hour, they had arrived at the well and found, as they had before, the washerwomen scrubbing laundry in the fetid water.

"Let's sit for a while and just watch," Cettie suggested.

They picked a place away from the others and sat on the edge of the fountain. Just as they both remembered, the water was murky and full of filth.

"I appreciate that you keep coming every day," Adam said, folding his arms. He didn't look at her, just gazed at the crowd walking to and fro around the fountain.

"I like coming to the hospital," Cettie said, rubbing her palm on the smooth cool stone.

"Could you see yourself living in the Fells someday?" he asked her. "It's changed quite a bit already, and Sera says her work isn't done."

She felt a prickle of gooseflesh on her arms. "What do you mean?" she asked, looking the other way.

"If you had to choose between Fog Willows . . . and living here."

She swallowed, feeling heat rising up her neck. "Do you need more help at the hospital?" She glanced his way.

"Always." He chuckled softly. "But that's not what I had in mind."

She licked her lips. "What did you have in mind?"

He turned and met her gaze. "I still love you, Cettie. I've never stopped loving you."

Her heart lifted. She'd longed so dearly to hear those words from him again. Had she dared believe he might say them? "What about Anna?" she forced herself to ask.

Adam's eyes softened. "I tried loving her. I knew you'd expect me to. So did she. We went on walks together at Fog Willows. Sometimes she came here, but she was always so uncomfortable. Not like you." He looked down. "At the end of the trial, she told me that she wanted you and me to be happy. She knew she'd rather have me as a brother than

341

lose me to the family completely." He stared into Cettie's eyes. "I did try, Cettie. But my heart wouldn't have it."

Cettie folded her hands on her lap. "After all I've done?"

His hand snaked over and clasped hers. Then he met her eyes again. "It's you. Or it's no one. Take as long as you need to decide. I'll keep waiting. I didn't want to rush you."

She didn't need time to decide. Her greatest hope had been answered.

"I will," she whispered to him, smiling. She could imagine their future together at Killingworth. Husband and wife, they would work side by side to right wrongs and provide for their people. From time to time, Sera would need her as a protector, a guardian, and a hunter of evil people who sought to destroy the peace they were cultivating, but this would be her home. *He* would be her home.

And then she noticed the weeping woman washing soiled baby linens. Her mind opened up in a vision, and she saw the woman's baby dying of the cholera morbus—and the waters in the fountain spreading the disease to everyone else who washed clothes there.

The disease was being spread by the washerwomen. And they didn't even know it.

Her hands tightened on Adam's.

"You will?" he asked, his mouth turning to a smile.

"Yes. Yes, I will!" she said, growing more excited. "But I see how the disease is spreading. I see it, Adam, and I know how we can stop it!"

She flung her arms around his neck and hugged him tight. Her feelings were so overwhelming at that moment, she couldn't bear the ache of joy. With her hands clasped around his neck, she leaned forward and kissed Adam, grateful for the kindest of men who had rescued her heart.

EPILOGUE
BEYOND THE VEIL

It was a day that would be burned into Cettie's mind forever, fastened there by the power of the Dryad's kiss. The Aldermaston summoned her and Adam from the soft stuffed couched where they sat, side by side, wearing the same supplicant robes they'd donned as learners about to take the Maston Test. She remembered Adam being there that day.

They were not in the learning room, the place where they'd been instructed in the Mysteries of the abbey. This room was in the upper spire of the building. Two stained-glass windows, side by side, were mounted on the wall opposite the staircase. Three carved chairs sat beneath them. Cettie felt the Leerings hidden behind the glass panes. Though it was midmorning, they let in light that was as bright as a regular afternoon sun. The carpets had been painstakingly embroidered and designed. On opposite walls, two enormous gilt-framed mirrors were suspended, casting a mirrored image that made the room look as if it went on forever.

"Come forward," the Aldermaston said. He stood before the trio of chairs. In the middle of the room was a plush pedestal with kneeling cushions on each side. Along the wall, by the mirrors, family and friends had gathered to witness the special occasion. The Fitzroys and the Hardings, Sera and Trevon, Mr. Durrant, and a few officials from the privy council. Anna's smile was radiant and encouraging. There was no jealousy now—nothing but devoted affection. Adam, still holding her hand, squeezed it, as they both rose from their chairs.

Cettie felt anxious about being a spectacle, but her steps were sure. They reached the foot of the pedestal and remained standing along with the Aldermaston, who'd approached it from the other side. His robes were reminiscent of the ones he'd worn during the Test, and he had a slight limp, perhaps a remnant of the gunshot wound he'd sustained years before.

"My friends," the Aldermaston said. "We are gathered here for a special occasion. We come not only to unite these two young people in holy matrimony, joined together by irrevocare sigil, but also to perform a ceremony of adoption. Before she becomes Mrs. Cettie Creigh, she must first become Miss Cettie Fitzroy."

A tingling feeling went down Cettie's spine. The music of the Medium was louder than she'd ever heard it, almost drowning out the Aldermaston's words.

"Mr. Creigh, Mr. Harding—would you two stand at my side as witnesses of this solemn event?"

Adam gave her hand one final squeeze before releasing it, then joined the Aldermaston at the head of the pedestal. Cettie thought he looked particularly handsome that day. His eyes never left hers. She could almost drown in their color. He looked very pleased, but he was as dignified as ever. Oh, how she loved him.

"Lady Maren, if you would kneel at the pedestal. Lord Stephen, you may take the place of your father, Lord Brant Fitzroy."

Upon hearing her father's name, Cettie felt a strange shift in the magic's music. There was a prickling awareness at the back of her neck, a small shudder passing through her. She felt a presence join them in the room.

"If you would," the Aldermaston continued, "kneel before each other and take each other by the *dextrarum coniunctio*, the joining of the hands."

Lady Maren and Stephen positioned themselves accordingly.

"Very well. Now, if the other members of the family will stand around you, you will clasp each other with the left hand on the left wrist, standing as a circle within a circle. This is the *umbelica stella*, a sign of the cosmos."

Cettie felt the skin at her neck begin to quiver. Phinia and Anna had joined them, and the three of them stood next to one another at the base of the pedestal. She heard the Aldermaston's words, but her attention was drawn to someone approaching them.

Unable to resist, Cettie risked a glance and saw, to her astonishment, Lord Fitzroy.

Father! she silently thought.

She could see him as if he lived in the flesh, although he had a radiance that was positively dazzling. He smiled at her, giving her a look of tenderness and love.

They cannot see me, he thought in reply. *Only you can.*

Cettie felt a thrill go through her. Her heart leaped with the joy of seeing his face. There were no more wrinkles, though his hair was white as snow.

Will we see each other again, Father?

He smiled at her question.

Of course we will. This second life is not the end. Only a bridge to a far better world. I was allowed to come here to witness this event.

Cettie bit her lips, hearing the Aldermaston speaking the words of the ceremony. But she wanted to speak with her father instead.

Thank you for sending Owen to save me, she thought with gratitude swelling inside.

You have always been precious to me, Cettie. Look at the change that has come to our family . . . because of you. You brought us together in ways

Maren and I could not. Even Phinia has passed the Test now. Something I feared would never happen.

Cettie felt a jolt of love go through her. *I miss you, Father. Can you see us always? Do you know what we're feeling?*

He shook his head slowly. *You must understand, there is order in all things. I was granted a special dispensation to come here today, to be with you. Someday, we will be a family again, but in the meantime you must live your lives here.*

I long for the day when we will all be together again, she thought, tears falling down her cheeks.

When the ceremonies are over, after I am gone, tell the others that you saw me. It is a special gift you have, Cettie. I understand that now. I felt it in you when we first met in the Fells. It enables you not only to see the malevolent spirits of the Unborn, but to see the rest of us as well. I love you all. Tell them, for me.

I promise, Cettie agreed.

"By the Medium's will, make it thus so," concluded the Aldermaston.

"Make it thus so," murmured those assembled.

Her heart full to bursting, Cettie embraced her new family, holding each precious one as they clung to each other.

"I wish Father could have been here," Anna whispered, sniffling.

Cettie gazed at his beaming smile. Her own throat was too thick to speak, to say what she knew. What she could see and they could not.

Sera spoke up, her voice bright and cheerful. "We also came to see a wedding, Aldermaston." As she said it, she squeezed her husband's hand. Both of them had a bright-eyed look of love. "I think that young man has been patient enough waiting for his bride," Sera continued. "Please proceed."

"As you command, Your Majesty," the Aldermaston said, his eyes twinkling.

Cettie and Adam took up the position Stephen and Maren had vacated, standing across the pedestal from each other. Her knees sank into the plush cushions. They joined hands. She felt his strength, his firm grip. His eyes were narrowing, curious.

"Are you all right?" he whispered to her.

She wiped tears on the sleeve of her supplicant robe. "I am," she breathed, feeling Father come closer. He put his hand on top of theirs, as if joining them himself.

The Aldermaston smiled at them. "It is time to begin."

Cettie Fitzroy was a harbinger. The first in over a generation. She knew her life was far from over. Ereshkigal was free and would rally enemies to thwart them. She also knew that the Medium still had work for her to do. With Adam at her side, she could accomplish anything asked of her.

And they would start by ridding the world of a plague they at last understood.

I love you, Adam Creigh, Cettie thought to him.

Have you any doubts, my Cettie, of my love? She heard his thoughts as if they were whispers.

None at all, she thought in return, smiling.

And you never will.

AUTHOR'S NOTE

Some fans have already figured out that several aspects of this series were inspired by a favorite Dickens novel, *Bleak House*. But it's more than just a retelling of that story. It was also inspired by elements of *Sense and Sensibility* by Jane Austen, and *Can You Forgive Her?* by Anthony Trollope—the author, by the way, who was the inspiration for Aldermaston Thomas Abraham.

When I set out to write this story, I didn't have the ending solid in my mind. Planning it in advance was difficult, knowing it would take five books to tell this particular tale. The closer I got to the end, the more nervous I was about how to tie the loose ends together and deliver a resolution that would be both satisfying and memorable. I also didn't want the resolution of the major conflict to come from a fight scene as I've done in some of my other books.

Inspiration comes in different forms. The climax of the book, when Sera invokes the Medium to save Cruix Abbey and send it up to the stars, came during a concert I attended of Beethoven's Ninth Symphony, which was performed (and sung) in a concert hall near where I live. This is the famous "Ode to Joy" symphony, probably his most famous one and composed while he was totally deaf. Although the lyrics are sung in German, they had an English translation up on the screen. The majestic music kept building, louder and louder, with a refrain that Beethoven could not hear with his ears but that was repeated over and over, as if the composer was trying to help us, the audience, hear the music only he could hear. The refrain at the end of the symphony goes like this:

> *Thus, brothers, you should run your race,*
> *Like a hero going to victory!*
> *You millions, I embrace you.*
> *This kiss is for all the world!*
> *Brothers, above the starry canopy*
> *There must dwell a loving father.*
>
> *Do you fall in worship, you millions?*
> *World, do you know your creator?*
> *Seek Him in the heavens;*
> *Above the stars must he dwell.*

Over and over it was repeated, the words showing up on the screen as the performers sang. It was like Beethoven was giving us a message he'd learned through the experience of his own suffering, his trial of deafness. And still, hundreds of years later, that symphony is performed around the world. It was a deeply emotional experience for me, and the idea came of Cettie, injured and hurting, hearing a song that Sera could not hear, knowing that help was coming but not being able to explain how. I loved writing that scene.

It's true that I put my characters through many trials and miseries in my books. But isn't life that way? I've experienced some dark events while writing this series, but I have hope that the experiences have taught me lessons on being a better person. I deliberately made Cettie and Sera flawed—each made serious mistakes, each struggled with doubt and regret. I wanted to give you, my readers, hope. That good can still come when tragedy strikes. That tears can be later remembered for the good they ultimately do.

So I leave you with a final quote, from my hero C.S. Lewis, who put it this way:

"That is what mortals misunderstand. They say of some temporal suffering, 'No future bliss can make up for it,' not knowing that Heaven, once attained, will work backwards and turn even that agony into a glory. . . . The Blessed will say, 'We have never lived anywhere except in Heaven.'"

Until we meet again in another world, another story.

—Jeff Wheeler, Imperial City, Beijing China

ACKNOWLEDGMENTS

This has been a rewarding and thrilling series to write. I love period dramas, and it was so enjoyable to write one but with all the excitement and intrigue you've come to expect from my books. I've been blessed with an amazing team, without which my books would have floundered long ago.

To Jason, for his astute feedback and endless championing for my career. His ideas help improve each story, and he has kept up with a truly dizzying pace to get this entire series to you in about, more or less, a year. That would be daunting for any editor, but Jason is a superstar.

To Angela, my brilliant developmental editor, who adds so much to the romance and tension, and can spot an inconsistency miles away. She earns her nickname "Eagle Eyes" with every book.

I'm also grateful to my other editors Wanda and Dan who have been with me for a while too. There are so many mistakes that happen in a manuscript. No book is totally flawless, but they sure make me look good by finding the majority of them!

And to my dedicated first readers who endure the torture of keeping quiet about my latest works: Emily, Shannon, Robin, Travis, Sunil, and Sandi. Thank you all!

My daughter Isabelle left on a mission for our church and won't be able to read this final book until she gets home. Her influence and input on this entire series has been so helpful. I couldn't be prouder of her.

ABOUT THE AUTHOR

Jeff Wheeler is the *Wall Street Journal* bestselling author of the Harbinger and Kingfountain series, as well as the Muirwood and Mirrowen novels. He took an early retirement from his career at Intel in 2014 to write full time. He is a husband, father of five, and devout member of his church. He lives in the Rocky Mountains and is the founder of *Deep Magic: The E-Zine of Clean Fantasy and Science Fiction*. Find out more about *Deep Magic* at www.deepmagic.co, and visit Jeff's many worlds at www.jeff-wheeler.com.